ROSA

ROSA

Lyndon Haynes

ISBN, paperback: 978-1-80227-057-0
ISBN, ebook: 978-1-80227-058-7

This book is typeset in Archer

Dedication

My mother and my brothers Godfrey and Rodney, my sister Melanie and my son Marcel. To my nieces and nephew and my inner circle, Gladstone Redwood Sawyer, Richard Emberstone, Gareth Morris, Cabral Mercer, Durrant Morris, Stuart Lee, Kirsty Sandhu, Shelley Feroze and Michelle Smart – thank you all for your unwavering support.

Special mention to Luke 'Screechy' Egan and my godbrother, Marlon Chand. May you both rest in the arms of angels; your lights will forever keep shining.

I hope my passion inspires others to #Chasedemdreams.

Contents

Rosa

x

Prologue
Ten years earlier. Sinaloa, Mexico

Glass and furniture crashed to the floor. The desperate, pained screams for mercy rang through the ramshackle home that belonged to Hector and Pina Chavez.

Jesus, Rosa and Dani hid huddled together behind the basement door. Jesus, the eldest and feistiest sibling, barely sixteen, scrawny yet brave, pushed the door slightly ajar. He peeked out, fearing what he would see. Rosa, the middle child at eleven years old, four years older than Dani, sat holding her hands over her ears, terrified, while Dani held his hand over his mouth to stifle his cries.

'Please, take my life. Let Pina live, I beg you,' Hector cried on his knees, hands bound behind his back, his long, black, oily hair straggled over his bloodied face.

Next to him, a beaten and bloodied Pina lay on the floor half-naked, clothes torn, revealing her midriff. She was semi-conscious and groaning from her injuries.

Two men, bandits, continued to trash the house, searching through drawers and smashing cabinets. 'Where is it, Hector?' asked one of the men. He had a long, thick moustache and wore a tan leather jacket. He stooped

11

down so he was at eye level with Hector. His eyes bored into Hector's face, fierce yet brooding. 'No more games, Hector. Where's the bag?'

Hector stared back sleepy-eyed, swaying back and forth, wavering. 'Please, spare Pina. I will get it for you.'

The bandit grabbed Hector by the throat, each finger on his clasped hand decorated with silver skull-shaped rings. Hector choked. He began to froth at the mouth.

The other bandit, stouter, more muscular, his belly held in tightly by a large cow-horn buckled belt, walked heavily in black cowboy boots over to where Pina lay, still groaning in agony and barely moving. He, too, crouched down, a black cowboy hat obscuring his face, the glint of a long steel blade catching the light.

Hector's head turned towards the bandit crouched over his wife. He squinted from the corner of his eye. 'No, I beg you, Pina!'

At this point, Jesus attempted to break ranks and come out from the basement but was hauled back by a tearful, scared Dani.

'Jesus, noo!' Dani whispered, grabbing his brother by the arm and pulling him back.

One of the men let go of Hector's throat and stood up after hearing the noise from the basement. He pushed Hector to the floor and put his finger to his lips. He walked around slowly, trying to sniff out where the noise had come from. His shoes created a dull thud on the wooden floor.

Both Hector and Pina continued to whimper, battered from their ordeal. The other bandit stayed crouched over Pina. He held the blade to her throat.

'The bag, Hector, give me the bag!'

Hector slowly nodded, still holding his throat—coughing up blood. '*Sí*, OK, it's in the cupboard under the sink. Please leave my . . . '

Before Hector finished his speaking, the bandit pushed the blade into Pina's throat and slowly slashed across her neck. A huge gasp, an intake of breath, a silence, then an anguished cry. The bandit got up and wiped the bloodied blade across the leg of his jeans, leaving a crimson stain on the denim.

The bandit turned his attention to Hector, who was squirming on the floor, crying 'Pina, my darling, Pina . . . ' As he tried to crawl on his chest towards her dead body, he felt the full force of the bandit's boot against his back, pinning him to the floor.

'Crawl like a gutless snake,' he hissed, still holding his foot in the small of Hector's back.

The brawny bandit continued to search for the hidden bag, thrashing around until eventually he stopped and let out a deranged, wheezy smoker's laugh. 'It's here.' He dragged out a brown leather bag, knelt down and unzipped it. 'It's all here.' He zipped up the bag, got up and tossed it over his shoulder. 'Let's go.' He signalled to his accomplice whilst lighting up a cigarette and surveying all the carnage.

The other bandit stooped over Hector and pointed the tip of his knife at Hector's neck. 'Why did you make it hard, Hector?' He pressed the tip of the knife into the skin until a drop of blood appeared.

Hector continued to struggle and crawl towards Pina; he was visibly weak but still clawed his way inch by inch across the dirty wooden floor towards his wife. The bandit let out another husky laugh. 'I admire your efforts, Hector. It's a real shame.' He continued to laugh and plunged the blade further into the back of his neck.

Hector let out a squeal as the steel cut deeper. He wriggled uncontrollably, jerked a few times and lay still.

Rosa, Jesus and Dani clung tightly to each other, suppressing their cries and shivering with fear. The bandit's footsteps could still be heard traipsing through the debris of their kill like two hyenas scouting for more scraps, trashing the rest of the house.

Rosa began to have a fit of hysteria. Unable to control her sobbing, she drew sharp intakes of breath as she huddled into Dani's chest.

'Mama,' she cried, between her hiccups.

Dani looked at her, tears streaming from his own eyes, pain and fear etched into his young, chubby face.

Jesus turned to them, his emotions a stark contrast. Fury shot from his narrowed eyes, with barely a tear in sight and sweat dripping from his forehead.

'Ssh. Shut her up,' he whispered angrily so as not to draw any attention from the two marauders.

Rosa still hyperventilated, with Dani's hand clasped over her mouth trying to suppress her sobs.

Introduction
School run

The school playground was packed with hyper schoolkids running around on a crisp spring morning. A large and manic football match was taking place.

Rosa sat alone on the floor reading a book on English language, her dark hair dangling over her face, touching the pages. She had just turned fifteen. It had been four years since the horrific murder of her parents in Mexico, and after a difficult start, she had tried her best to settle into a new life at St Mary's Mixed Academy.

Her brothers, Jesus and Dani, apart from the language barrier, had submerged themselves into their new surroundings without a second thought.

Rosa looked up from her book. The game continued. She watched on as Jesus and Dani enjoyed themselves chasing a ball around the playground.

Look at them running around without a care in the world.

It's alright for them, boys are easier to make friends with.

The girls here are all bitchy; all they do is make fun of me, they're rough, smoke and swear a lot and look down their nose like they're any better.

I hate it here; the weather's crap all the time, the lessons are boring and the food is shit, too.

I just wish I was back in Sinaloa helping mum cook or dad on the farm.

I feel so lonely, no one understands or even asks me how I feel.

'Is it interesting?' A barely broken male voice interrupted Rosa's train of thought. She looked up and saw a tall figure looming over her.

Rosa shielded her eyes from the sun just enough to make out the teenage boy who stood next to her.

'What?' she answered. The boy crouched down in front of her and took the book out of her hand.

'English language? I could probably teach you more than this book.' His tone was confident as he flicked through the pages. 'Can I sit?' he asked.

Rosa shrugged, not fussed. The boy sat beside her still holding the book, his back against the wall. He looked over at Rosa. His eyes caught hers, green-tinted by the sunshine, carefully groomed hair, not bad-looking.

'Ryan, Mr Padbury's class. I've seen you around—the Mexican girl, innit?'

Rosa shuffled uncomfortably, inching away, shyly. She just nodded.

'You're Narcos's sister, innit?'

Narcos is what the other boys called Jesus and Dani—a really obvious nickname for Mexicans.

Rosa stared ahead, blanking him.

Hope them two don't look over here otherwise poor Ryan will get the worst of Jesus.

My brothers are dumb and dumber as I call them.

So over protective, sweet but annoying, especially when I try to make friends and I get a lot of attention from boys like Ryan.

Maybe my olive skin is better than the white girls with fake tans or the black girls with skin like chocolate.

Ryan watched the game of football for a few seconds then turned to her.

'Fancy getting out of here?' Once again, his cocksure tone and confidence enticed Rosa into thinking it was a good idea.

'And go where?' she asked, finally plucking up the courage to engage directly with him. He was fresh-faced with a cheeky smile.

'Could take you sightseeing—go to the city?' Again, his confidence lured her, but before Rosa could answer, the football bounced towards them.

Jesus, scrawny, slim and bedraggled from his exertions in his oversized uniform shirt, ran over to retrieve the ball, which had now bounced into Ryan's hands. Ryan threw the ball back to Jesus, who took it and kicked it back towards the game, then walked over to Rosa and Ryan.

'What you doing?' he rasped in his Anglo-Spanish accent. Rosa shook her head.

'I was reading.'

Ryan sensed Jesus's mood as he stared down at them. He got to his feet, still clutching the book.

'Was just helping her with ...' Ryan handed the book to Rosa then made to leave, but Jesus stepped in his way. His sharp, weasel-like face sniffed at Ryan, his eyes squinting as he gave him a cold stare. He was about to say something to Ryan when shouts from the boys in the football game distracted him.

Ryan sloped away quietly.

Rosa stood up, ready to make her way back into class. Jesus grabbed her arm.

'Watching you,' he warned, before turning back towards the game.

The sound of the final bell rang out and hordes of kids poured out of their classes and into the corridors. Rosa made her way slowly, getting jostled by eager pupils rushing towards the exits.

A bunch of girls approached, bumping into her deliberately. Shoving her into the wall, they surrounded her like a pack of wild dogs.

Vanessa, a tall, heavy-set black girl with candy-red lips, bolshy and sure of herself, pushed forwards as the others in her crew, all rough street girls, backed her up.

'So what, Miss Taco? Can't you walk straight?'

Rosa made an attempt to sidestep them but was forced back against the wall by the heavy palm of Vanessa. The other girls stepped forwards, sneering and gesticulating. Rosa took a deep breath.

'Why you only pick on me all of the time? You against me?'

Her blood boiled, but before she could utter another word she felt a stinging slap connect with her right cheek, forcing her to jolt back and bang her head against the wall.

'Whooa!' A loud roar in unison from the other girls, and Vanessa turned to her friends, who all acknowledged her by sharing high fives and pats on the back.

Rosa, stunned by the viciousness of the slap, struggled to hold back the tears of pain.

Vanessa, still milking the glory from her entourage, failed to notice Rosa's recovery. Filling up with rage, she pulled hard at the thick braids of Vanessa's hair.

'Arrgghh, you bitch,' Vanessa screamed, as Rosa used all her strength to try and wrestle her but was thwarted as the other girls all piled in.

A manic tussle ensued, and screams and shouts echoed through the school corridors as other pupils rushed to see what was going on. Ryan was amongst them.

Rosa was now in the thick of a full scrap. She was trying to give as good as she was getting but was overwhelmed by the sheer number of girls all lashing out wildly.

Ryan forced his way into the middle. He noticed it was Rosa getting hit on and dragged Vanessa off. Other pupils were going crazy, jumping up and down, filming on their phones, screaming and shouting, until a few teachers waded in after hearing all the commotion.

Ryan pulled Rosa away, shielding her.

Rosa managed to grab her school bag, which had fallen by her feet. She gripped Ryan's arm until they finally made it out into the playground. They kept running away from the school and the mob of pupils who chased after them.

'Come on! Stay with me,' Ryan shouted.

At this point, Rosa's mind became blank. She began blacking out and could barely remember running or being dragged by Ryan.

* * *

Rosa slowly opened her eyes. It took her a few minutes to gather herself. Her eyes focused on the room around her. It was unfamiliar, as was the soft bed she was lying on.

Groggy, her body aching, especially around her ribs and back, she noticed she had no clothes on. Naked under soft sheets, she began to panic, touching herself. Below, something didn't feel right—her vagina was sore and moist.

Ryan, now dressed in casual jogging pants and a tee shirt, sat on a chair staring at her.

'Sleepy head.'

He used a soft tone so as not to startle her, but Rosa jumped anyway and gathered herself.

'What have you done? Where's my clothes?' she asked urgently.

Ryan stood and walked towards her.

'I never did anything you didn't want.' He smirked. Rosa was aghast.

'What do you mean?' she asked, becoming slowly enraged.

Ryan, though, remained calm.

'Bloody nose.' He pointed to her face.

Rosa felt her face, touching the crusted blood around her nose. She got up, wrapping the sheet around her body.

'What did you do to me? You prick, you raped me! Where's my underwear?' Rosa screamed as the realisation hit her.

Ryan laughed pathetically, stepping back.

'I'll get you something to clean your face,' he said, quickly backing out of the room.

Rosa's head throbbed like a sledgehammer against her temple. It stopped her in her tracks, disorientating her for a few seconds, before she was able to walk over to a mirror hanging on the wall next to a poster of the Chelsea football team.

She studied her face. No damage apart from her bloodied nose. Her attention quickly turned to her clothes, which she could see strewn on the floor. She picked them up and slammed the door shut, locking it.

Shaking, Rosa could barely dress herself. As she pulled on her school skirt, tears ran from her eyes, and she vomited bile onto the floor.

Ryan banged on the door, jolting Rosa back into the present.

She tried her best to dress quickly, wiping away the residue of the vomit from her mouth.

Her school bag, which was on the floor beside the bed, began to vibrate aggressively. She picked it up, rummaging through it until she found her phone.

'Shit, it's Dani!'

She was rattled as Ryan continued to thump and kick the door.

'Open the fucking door, Rosa!'

Barely dressed and still feeling like she'd been hit by a train, Rosa opened the door and pushed past Ryan, who stumbled back, dropping a glass of water, which smashed onto the floor.

With her heart beating out of her chest, she stumbled down a flight of wooden stairs, losing her footing on the last step and falling to her knees.

She looked behind her and panicked as Ryan came down after her.

'You better not say anything. I'll tell everyone you was up for it,' he shouted.

Rosa managed to get up and ran straight for the large, almost church-like stained-glass wooden front door. She struggled with the lock for a few seconds as Ryan bounded down the stairs behind her.

'Rosa, wait! You better not say anything. I'll tell them you're a slag!' he shouted in frustration at Rosa.

Rosa managed to get the door unlocked. She opened it and dashed out into a suburban street, her sense of direction having completely deserted her.

Ryan came flying out after her, trying to grab her, but Rosa let out a pained scream and managed to escape, running at speed down the street. Ryan decided to give up the chase after he was spotted by a neighbour who was unloading some boxes into his car. The man watched as a frightened Rosa pelted away. Ryan could only observe as she disappeared into the distance.

Dani sat in the backyard, young, chubby-faced, scruffy and still in his school uniform. His face wore a mask of frustration as he checked his phone before opening the back door and going back inside the flat.

Jesus met him at the door.

'Did you get hold of her?'

His eyes drilled into Dani as he sucked on a cigarette, his skeletal frame tense, every vein visible through the pale skin on his arms.

Dani shrugged, shaking his head, subservient to his older brother, knowing the chaos about to ensue.

Jesus was an embittered soul. He had never recovered from the horror of his parents' murder, the violence witnessed as a youngster branded into his mind. He had settled into life in London, making the wrong type of friends at school, attracted by the hustlers involved in get-rich-quick schemes, all while throwing a long, bony, protective arm around Dani and Rosa.

His mood swings and aggressive nature showed that he had struggled to overcome his grief by channelling it outwards and ruling his siblings through fear.

Dani, being younger, followed Jesus around like a lost lamb detached from the main flock, in weird awe of his brother, but often showed some sensitivity towards Rosa—but only away from the evil eyes of Jesus, knowing he could stir up a hornet's nest of fury if Jesus believed he was treating her any differently than him.

Dani, though, was careful not to break his fragile bond with his sister.

'She'll be back soon.'

He offered a weak excuse to reassure an already very agitated Jesus.

Rosa rushed through the streets, panicked, with a face of worry. It was almost evening when she finally made her way back towards the tower blocks of the estate where she lived.

The streets were busy, the usual bustle of people making their way home from work, as well as the coffee shop moochers enjoying a late latte and a smoke at the outside tables during the never-ending heatwave.

What has happened to me?

I'm gonna get into more trouble now.

I can't tell them, either, they'll never believe me.
I just want to get home and wash myself.

No members of the public showed any concern for a young schoolgirl running through the streets with a bloodied nose and bedraggled uniform—not that Rosa cared. All she wanted was to get home, bathe away the dirty, sticky feeling she had between her legs and rest her aching body.

Rosa finally arrived and ran through the narrow, dirty corridors and stairwells that lead to the flat; the repeated sound of dogs barking from the various gardens as she went by echoed into the evening sky.

She crashed through the rickety wooden gate into the backyard, where she was greeted by Dani.

'Ooh shit, what happened to you?'

Dani approached her, holding her face and looking at the dried blood on her nose.

'Dani, please. I just want to go to my room.'

Dani instantly sensed how upset she was. He held her and could feel her body shaking. She winced as he touched her side.

'Was this from the fight at school?'

Rosa tried to bundle past him but didn't have the strength.

'Please, Dani.'

Again, she tried to move past him.

'Listen to me.' Dani stopped her. 'Jesus is seriously pissed. I don't care where you've been, just tell him you went to the hospital after the fight, no reception, OK?'

Rosa nodded her head in agreement, barely holding back the tears and sniffing up the snot streaming down her nostrils.

Rosa hesitantly stepped into the flat, a small ramshackle kitchen leading to a small flight of stairs just off the front room. She walked towards them, heading for the bathroom, but was stopped in her tracks by Jesus. His eyes pierced into her as his lanky frame acted as an intimidating buffer between her and the sanctuary of the bathroom.

Rosa yelped sharply at his presence; the stench of his tobacco breath wafted into her face as he leant down, staring at the dry, crusted blood that had clotted around her nose.

'Heard you got jumped by some girls at school.'

Jesus used one of his twig-like fingers to lift her chin to get a better look at her face. Shivers ran down Rosa's spine.

'Yeah, so what?' Defiantly she swiped away his finger and attempted to move past him. Jesus suppressed a smarmy snigger.

'Hope you got the better of them.'

His tone dry, deadpan.

Rosa had heard enough. Her emotions shredded, she bundled her way past and ran up to the bathroom.

She eased her body into the warm water of the bath, stiff and achy. She could barely move but managed to rest her back against the tub.

As she splashed the water onto her face, it stung at first, but she continued rubbing and the clear water beneath her turned a pinkish colour as her blood dissolved.

Rosa felt the soreness between her legs. She touched herself tenderly, a feeling she had never felt before.

He's touched me, that bastard Ryan.

I can't believe this.

He's done something, drugged me, raped me, I feel sick, my head is cloudy and I don't remember anything from the fight until the moment I woke up in his ... naked.

Why would he do that to me? I liked him, I really did.

He has taken away my innocence. I have to report him to the police.

Rosa scrubbed her skin roughly with a flannel, inflicting more pain to her already aching body. She splashed her hands down into the water, angry she had not been able to prevent her ordeal.

Eventually, she slid her body beneath the water until her head submerged, her face barely above the surface. Her eyes rolled around from side to side, looking around the dingy, steamy room, before she closed her eyes and her head sank beneath the water.

Two months later

Rosa ran from her bedroom to the bathroom, kicked open the door and just managed to make it to the toilet before spewing up her guts.

She spat, then sank to her knees hugging the toilet bowl.

I feel awful, my stomach constantly feels queasy and my mouth tastes like metal.

I'm late, as well, by a month, I need to see a doctor.

Not been to school since the fight but heard Ryan has told all the boys we had sex, bastard's covering his back.

Jesus and Dani fucked him up, though, once they heard.

Now they've been expelled, which don't help me as I never get any peace in this place.

Wish I was there, though, just to see his smug face get punched.

Those two are getting worse, though no school means they are outside doing crazy stuff.

I'll not go back, not after this.

Keep getting letters from the school and social services but Jesus burns them.

He's so angry and blames me for the stuff with Ryan, thinks I'm a whore.

I want to tell them about the rape but I'm scared and now this.

I can't be pregnant, not now, not to him.

Rosa managed to drag herself up from the floor. She flushed the loo, then rinsed her mouth out, bending over the sink and drinking water from the tap.

She lay curled up on her bed in the small, cramped bedroom. Not much luxury, just the single bed and a small wooden chest of drawers, which held a small mirror and a small, old tv.

One thing that was noticeable was a stack of magazines—mainly beauty and trash like *Heat* and *Hello*—piled on top of each other in the corner next to her bed.

When Rosa first came to London, she was drawn to these magazines, checking out the fashion and make-up pages and dreaming of having her own front cover one day. She'd always imagined herself stood in a glamourous designer dress on the red carpet next to a handsome actor or footballer.

I constantly feel sick like I wanna throw up all time.

I'm fifteen with a fucking child of a sicko growing inside of me, how did I get into this shit situation?

I can never go back to school, I need to see a doctor before it's too late but what do I tell them?

They'd surely ask me about the father and what happened.

I have to tell Jesus.

He's going to go mental and probably kill me but he needs to know otherwise he won't let me out to see the doctor.

Shit, this is scary but here goes.

Rosa hauled herself up. She looked worse for wear but bravely got to her feet and left the room.

Dani and Jesus sat around a small kitchen table eating a fry-up. The odour of fried bacon and eggs hit Rosa's nostrils as she entered the kitchen, still wearing her pyjamas.

She looked rough, her jet-black hair messy and her normally healthy olive skin pale.

'Stinks in here.'

Her brothers ignored her and continued stuffing their faces.

'It's alright, I'm not hungry,' said Rosa sarcastically, but it fell on deaf ears.

She continued over to the sink, which was full of dirty pots, pans and the food debris created by her brothers.

Rosa could barely hold it in as the nausea continued to render her lifeless.

Dani gave a slightly concerned glance towards her while Jesus carried on chewing down on a piece of toast.

'Come on, finish up. We got to collect that shit from Franky.'

Jesus pushed his plate to the side, wiping his mouth with his bare hand, then stood up. He pushed Dani in the head.

'Come on, *vamos!*'

Dani had hardly finished the rest of his plate before he was dragged up by Jesus. They were about to leave when Rosa blurted out her news.

'I think I'm pregnant.'

Her voice trailed off as she waited for the reactions of her brothers to kick in.

Jesus stopped dead in his tracks and turned to face her.

'What?' His normal rasp rose an octave.

Dani stared in amazement at Rosa, whose tiny frame stood alone. She chewed on a fingernail, nervously anticipating their response.

Jesus ran his fingers through his long greasy hair, moving ominously towards her.

'I said what?' he repeated, moving closer.

Rosa's body shook with fear. She knew what was coming and braced herself.

'I'm late and being sick, so I need to see a doctor.'

Her brave words were met with a sharp stinging slap to the face, which knocked her back against the counter. Dani rushed to intervene but was held off by an incensed Jesus.

'You dirty whore!' he screamed. 'Fifteen years old and letting gringos get you pregnant.'

Jesus laid into her, punching her in the stomach. Dani struggled to pull him away.

'Jesus, no, please don't do this.'

He managed to get Jesus partially off Rosa, who was now crumpled in a heap. She screamed as the pain inflicted took hold.

'He raped me!' Rosa squealed, but instead of stopping, Jesus launched a long leg forwards, kicking out, whilst a terrified Dani tried to pull him away. His boot connected to her stomach before he fell back onto Dani.

All three of them were on the floor. The only sound was Rosa's whimpering. Jesus and Dani scrambled to their feet.

'Jesus, no! She needs a doctor,' pleaded Dani as Jesus stood over Rosa before crouching down beside her.

Dani was struck frozen with fear.

'Jesus, please.'

He made a faint attempt to distract his brother from his frenzy.

Jesus noticed a patch of blood seeping through the crotch area of her pyjamas. He turned to Dani, giving him a cold stare.

'Call an ambulance,' he ordered, as Rosa lay nursing her stomach on the dirty kitchen floor.

Rosa

Chapter 1
How is life in London?
Seven years later

Sweat beads ran down Rosa's tanned forehead. She perspired profusely as the summer afternoon heat began to take its toll.

She had just finished cleaning, chores, washing the back windows and sweeping out the small backyard afforded by the council dwelling, and she sat down on the doorstep to take a well-earned break.

The sun continued to beat down unmercifully. Rosa looked down at the grey, uneven concrete, inspecting her work. She wiped her brow and reached around with her arm, rubbing her back which had been sore for a while now due to all the bending and lifting.

Rosa found it tough being the only girl sandwiched between two brothers. She was a few years younger than Jesus but felt like the surrogate mother—taking care of all the household chores and constantly cooking for her brothers since the fallout over the whole 'Ryan rape and pregnancy' debacle.

Because of that, Jesus had taken it upon himself—as he always did—to impose some sort of house arrest rule on her.

She had never returned to school and became the shamed burden of their little family.

Jesus was responsible for her untimely miscarriage, something that he had never apologised for, and even years later he could not cast his eyes directly at her.

The present pain she felt in her back was only a pin prick compared to the emotional trauma she'd been living with since then.

Her miscarriage was followed by Jesus almost killing Ryan, dealing out a severe beating. They were both arrested, Ryan for the rape and drugging of Rosa and two other girls from school, who bravely came forward with their own allegations, and Jesus for assault.

'Ryan Rohypnol' the local papers labelled him. Apparently, he was ahead of the curve in knowing how to use the drug way before anybody realised. His smarmy veneer was just a guise to lure his female classmates into his lair.

Rosa felt vindicated. At least she now knew why her head had been so fuzzy that day, but what Jesus did only resulted in the way her life was now.

He no longer trusted her. He never spoke to her—just shouted random orders—and the irony was that even though Ryan had been sent to a detention centre for his crimes, it was Rosa who was now a prisoner in their derelict council home.

Jesus imposed this; it was his way of keeping her on a tight leash. No leaving the house without his permission except to get food and groceries, when she was usually escorted by Jesus or Dani.

Bless him, Dani could see how much this affected his sister, but with Jesus's paranoia, he dare not disobey.

It had been years since the family tragedy—the reason for their move to London where they now lived in the concrete jungle of the inner city following at stint in social care under a so-called crime protection program, which had promised so much yet delivered nothing but being dumped unaided in the belly of the beast on a drug- and crime-riddled council estate.

Rosa felt embittered, left at home paying for a misdemeanour where she was the victim, while her two brothers were walking contradictions. Constantly out, loving their freedom amid the intricate underground labyrinth of the big city, waist-deep in shady deals and petty crime.

It was just after two o'clock, and with the afternoon temperature rising, Rosa went back inside and up to her room.

Most of the time Rosa would sit alone, listening to the radio or reading her tabloid magazines, trying to improve her English.

Every day is the same.

I'm a young woman now nearly twenty-two.

I have no life except for cleaning and cooking for them two and that's whenever they have the decency to come home.

In fact, I prefer when I'm alone, at least I get peace and quiet.

Those two get on my nerves.

Sometimes I don't see them for days then they come back and expect the place to be clean and food to be cooked.

Only Dani, bless him, tries to help or talk to me but he's under Jesus's spell and when he's around he can't think or speak for himself.

Spending so much time alone gave Rosa plenty of time to think. She had become a bit of a fantasist, creating a world for herself—imagining she was a rich princess or a beautiful model. Most of the ideas were born from reading the gossip magazines and seeing all the famous actresses and models on the red carpet.

She, herself, had grown into her features and body and was an undiscovered beauty. Her flawless dusky skin, bold brown eyes and jet-black hair were wasted cooped up in the house.

As she sat on her bed listening to her favourite presenter, Maya Jama, play the latest songs on the radio, she flicked through a magazine.

She gazed at a picture of a well-known actress draped in a beautiful designer dress holding onto the arm of her boyfriend, an American basketball player. She studied the photograph, looking at the broad smile across the actress's face.

One day I'll be the one strutting on the red carpet on the arm of a handsome Prince Charming who looks like Channing Tatum, having a crowd of paparazzi take pictures of me.

I believe there is more to life than just being trapped in a small flat with no friends.

I've often thought of running away and leaving them to it but where would I go?

Probably be worse on the streets and I know Jesus, he would find me, hunt me down somehow.

With her mind wandering, dreaming of escape, she was interrupted by the brash sounds of her two brothers hurtling through the back gate.

Jesus, now a young adult and the taller of the two, entered hastily followed by his ever-present shadow, Dani.

Jesus was still scrawny, with a greasy ponytail and tattoos all over his body, which were accentuated by his dirty, grey vest.

'We should have taken him out like I said,' he snarled, his Latin accent still apparent, mixed with a slight cockney twist.

They crashed into the house unceremoniously, disturbing Rosa's peace.

'Forget him,' Dani shouted back, his face etched with anger, attempting to impose his shorter and more filled-out frame on his brother.

Rosa flinched on hearing their return as the two continued to shout, not even acknowledging her when she entered the room.

'I'll make some food,' she dutifully mentioned, but she was brushed aside without a response as the two brothers went into the other room to continue their argument.

Deep inside, Rosa hated them. She despised what they stood for, all their petty squabbles, dodgy dealings and disrespectful acts born out of their grieving. She couldn't wait to escape. If only she had the strength to walk away, she would have gone a long time ago, but in her heart she knew she dare not take that first step.

She still felt a crumb of family loyalty, only because she knew her parents would expect nothing less. Without her, they were nothing but two big babies who could not fend for themselves.

Over an hour had passed since her brothers had returned, and even now, neither had even come into the kitchen to speak to her. She had finished cooking meat stew and potatoes, nothing fancy. She served up a small plate for herself, then went to check whether either of them wanted her to serve them.

Apprehensively, she slowly pushed open the door, poking her head around to see both crouched on the floor, picking through some pieces of jewellery which were lying on a sheet of crumpled newspaper alongside some battered-looking twenty-pound notes.

'Fuck do you want?' Jesus scowled.

'Dinner's ready,' she replied meekly before exiting the room.

Rosa sometimes wondered why she bothered making the effort; they were probably going to go out again without even touching their food, but if she didn't make anything, sure as hell Jesus would make a big deal about it.

Rosa left them to it and took her food up to her room. This was her only sanctuary, somewhere she could sit and eat in peace.

She had a small TV which she fondly called a 'fuzz box', referring to the scrambled picture she always received, even after tussling with the makeshift wired hanger that acted as an aerial.

After she had eaten, Rosa lay perusing the gossip pages. She looked at all the pictures and continued to daydream.

She spent most of her time in her own head. It was as if she were mute—she had no voice in the house and no personality as nobody knew her. Now all she had was the tag of the girl who got drug raped.

She longed for the day she could go out and dance, listen to music, laugh and wear a beautiful dress like her idol, Jennifer Lopez.

A pained smile crept across her face. She imagined herself free and happy, but any realistic hope was quickly interrupted by the heavy stomp of feet bounding up the stairs.

Rosa quickly shoved the magazine under her pillow before the tall, scrawny figure of her brother burst into her room.

'Hey, where the fuck are my clean tee shirts?' he screamed.

'Sorry, but the machine is broken. I told you last week,' she replied, as his lanky body became tense with anger.

'Well I need a clean shirt!' he shouted back aggressively. 'Take the washing to the launderette or do it with your fucking hands or something!'

Saliva sprayed from his mouth. He dug around in his pockets and threw some coins to the floor.

'Get it done, *rapido!*' he yelled, before storming out of the room.

Rosa's heart pounded.

Fuck you, Jesus!

Bastard talks to me like a dog.

Frustrated rather than hurt, her hands shook with fear. She could hear another set of footsteps coming towards her room, and she quickly composed herself before Dani pushed his head around the door.

'You OK?' He spoke quietly, aware that Jesus was still in his foulest of moods.

Rosa shrugged.

'I'll help you with the clothes,' he offered.

'No, it's fine,' she answered, not even making eye contact with Dani. 'You can go.' Rosa ordered him away, and Dani looked on, helpless, before leaving without a word.

Rosa looked down at the scattered shrapnel of coins. Again she felt demeaned, belittled and worthless—the normal emotions she felt when her siblings were around. Her esteem was at rock bottom, but as usual, she just carried on. This was life.

Rosa got on her knees and picked up every single coin. She knew she had to do what she was told, otherwise it would just evoke another merciless tongue-lashing or worse from Jesus.

While Rosa collected the dirty clothes from the overflowing laundry basket, she overheard a conversation. Her brothers were talking loudly and aggressively.

'We go back to Franky and tell him we can shift it all.'

A testosterone-fueled Jesus was again calling the shots, probably thinking up another hair-brained money-making scheme. He was not the brightest, but his personality made him seem like he was in charge, whilst Dani seemed to be in awe and just happy to follow.

Rosa went and stood by the door, trying to eavesdrop, but within seconds she heard them both leaving and the scrape of the garden gate signalled their hurried exit.

Rosa pawed her way through the bundles of dirty clothes which lay strewn in the boys' bedroom.

I hate coming in here, it's dingy and stinks like the boys' locker room at school.

It's musty and they always keep the curtains closed, never open the windows.

Look, there's even dirty dishes with mould on them.

I have to cover my mouth it makes me gag, they live like animals.

Rosa shuddered, pulling off the dirty sheets and pillowcases from the bed, but as usual, she soldiered on, gathering other loose items of clothing.

It was now early evening; the bright sunshine began to subside, although the temperature was still high, making it very humid.

Rosa sat in the kitchen counting the coins that had been rudely dispatched by Jesus. She had just enough to wash the clothes but would have to carry them back without drying them, which meant she would have the long journey back having to carry a heavier load.

Rosa checked the pots and, as predicted, they were still full of the stew and potatoes she had made earlier. She shook her head, fed up that yet again, her efforts had gone to waste. This was a regular occurrence, but undeterred, she knew it was just another day and she would repeat the feat tomorrow.

Rosa locked herself into the tiny bathroom and sat on the toilet, fed up. Finally, her guarded resistance weakened; she allowed herself a couple of minutes before standing up and dusting herself down again.

Looking in the mirror, she swept her hair up and away from her smooth, olive-skinned face and viewed her reflection. Rosa's brown eyes reflected a depth of sorrow embedded within her, but again, for her, there was no time to stop.

She splashed her face with water and continued to get ready to leave. At least she was getting out of the house for once—a small crumb of comfort salvaged from her troubles.

Rosa gathered her things and lifted the heavy bag. She stuffed some washing powder into the side compartment and began to make her journey in the warm evening sun.

Dressed in a short jean skirt, flip-flops and a white tee shirt, she wore her hair in a ponytail and hugged the big bag of clothes.

Squeezing out the gate of her backyard, she squinted as the bright orange tinge of the dipping sun blinded her.

It was at least a fifteen-minute walk to the launderette through the busy maze of the estate, which was overrun with juveniles hanging out. Kids raced around on their bikes, heavy bass music pumped out of cars and flats, dogs barked and ran around freely and gangs of youths stood menacingly on the corners of the entrances, smoking weed.

Rosa walked straight ahead. She dared not look at anyone. Even hearing a few catcalls, she continued walking. She was not intimidated as she knew her brother's reputation would protect her if anything happened, but running this gauntlet was not something she enjoyed.

Rosa strolled on, struggling with the awkward, heavy bag. She had only gone a few yards before she was approached by a stocky teenager who had separated from his gang.

"Allo, darling. Want some help with that?'

He was jogging to catch up to her. Short, red-eyed and with a spliff hanging from his blackened lips.

'Come, man, let me help you.'

He sidled up close, gesturing towards the bag.

Flip sake just fuck off.

Hate these little boys, why would he think I want anything to do with him?

Look at him, urrgh.

Rosa sped up.

'Go on then, piss off, you little slag.'

The youth suddenly turned aggressive, spitting on the floor towards her.

Rosa, now sweating, kept on walking swiftly, hearing laughter from the other kids echoing behind her. She was not scared, just angry at the taunts she had to endure. They reminded her of her schooldays.

Finally, Rosa made it to the launderette. It was hot inside, the heat from the dryers adding to the already sauna-like feel, but at least there was only one other person plus the attendant inside. She dumped the bag down on the floor, took a breath, her mouth dry, and proceeded to find an empty washing machine.

After emptying in the clothes and putting in the detergent, she gathered the coins that her brother had thrown at her.

The elderly attendant, who was dressed in a light blue overall with her grey hair tied in a bun, mopped the floor in front of Rosa.

'You alright, darling?' she asked slowly, moving the soggy mop back and forth.

Rosa nodded politely, trying not to engage in any conversation.

'Nice girl like you should be out there having fun,' the old attendant continued, leaning unsteadily on the mop handle. Her wrinkled face and bloodshot eyes showed the strain of a long day as she regarded Rosa, who smiled back politely whilst pushing the coins into the machine.

'Dunno what's wrong with you young girls nowadays,' the attendant continued to witter, still leaning unsteadily on the mop handle.

Rosa turned around and sat on the wooden bench as the large machine whirred into action.

Again she afforded a smile at the old attendant, who, in turn, smiled back, dragging on the cigarette before carrying on with her mopping, still mumbling to herself.

'We'd be at the ballroom dancing . . . '

Rosa sat with her arms folded. She was bored and now alone as the other customer had left; the old lady attendant was now sat on a stool outside, puffing on another rolled-up cigarette. Rosa wondered why someone so old and frail would still smoke.

She looked back at the large drum of the machine, watching the clothes being rotated. Her calm was soon interrupted by a loud, commanding voice.

Rosa turned to see a tall, smart business type dressed in an open-necked pink shirt and blue pin-striped trousers, finished with polished black shoes. He was carrying a large sports bag in one hand and continued to shout down his mobile phone.

Rosa looked towards him, his tall frame silhouetted against the evening sunlight coming through the door.

Oh boy who's this now?

'Get it done today!' he shouted assertively before clicking off the device. 'Bloody hell,' he said, not directly to Rosa but in exasperation, tossing the bag down just in front of her. 'So sorry,' he continued, staring in her direction and pointing to the bag.

Rosa acknowledged him by nodding her head. She did not look directly at him but could see he was athletic in build and could hear he was English. He sat down beside her.

'I don't have a scooby how to use all of this stuff.'

He raised his arms in despair. Rosa maintained her wooden stance, barely looking to even engage in conversation.

The old attendant toddled back in, the smell of tobacco smoke following her as she shuffled into the back office.

'Do you know? Can you help me?'

The man shot his question at Rosa, who tried her best to remain poised. She wasn't used to talking to anyone and was trying her hardest to remain passive.

'I'm Daniel, Daniel Rosewood.' He stretched out his hand, offering a handshake.

Rosa's heart pumped fast. She was unsure whether to respond.

Oh my gosh he's talking to me, I don't know what to say.

She turned belatedly and looked directly at him.

'Hi,' she whispered shyly, offering a limp shake of the hand.

Fleetingly she glanced up at his face. He was clean-cut, handsome, with short dark hair. His eyes were dark but welcoming.

'And you are?' he asked calmly.

Rosa felt butterflies in the pit of her stomach. She shifted nervously on the hard bench. She looked down towards the floor before responding.

'I am Rosa.'

Her broken English accent quietly emerged as she raised her head and looked at him. Her eyes connected with his. They held their gaze for a few seconds before Daniel suddenly sprang into action, jumping up and rubbing his hands together.

'OK, what do I do here then?' he joked.

Rosa could not take her eyes off him.

He's confident, funny, energetic and good-looking.

Not the type of person I thought would be in a poky launderette doing his dirty washing.

She continued to watch him as he fussed around trying to figure out how to wash his clothes.

Daniel took out his clothes and placed them in one of the light-blue plastic woven baskets which were placed on top of the machines. Rosa sat watching as he continued to look clueless. He seemed frustrated, huffing and puffing as he went about counting the change in his pocket.

'Cor, they don't make these things easy, do they?' He aimed the rhetorical question towards Rosa, who could not help but be amused by his Neanderthal antics.

'OK, let me show you,' she conceded, her motherly default kicking into gear.

'Ahh thanks, you're a diamond.' Daniel stepped back, allowing her to step in and take control.

She collected his clothes—not many, just a few shirts and some sports gear—and put them into the machine. She did this for her brothers, anyway, so her natural inclination was always to help.

'Do you have powder?' Rosa asked coyly.

Daniel looked at her with a confused expression on his face. It took a few seconds before the penny dropped.

'Oh my God,' washing powder? What a lemon!' he exclaimed.

Rosa stood looking at him with a bemused smile on her face.

'Lemon?' she quizzed, not quite understanding Daniel's terminology.

But for some reason, she found his lack of domestic nous funny.

'It's OK,' she replied, turning to grab the remaining detergent from her bag.

Daniel watched as she placed the powder into the machine.

'OK, now you put the money in here.' She pointed out the slot where the coins were to be inserted.

Both now sat on the bench watching the machines tossing their clothes in the big drums. Daniel seemed very jittery, as if he had a lot on his mind. He kept fiddling with his phone, tapping its screen randomly. Rosa, by contrast, sat serenely. She was hot and her face was flushed. Despite his fidgetting, for some reason, she felt strangely intrigued by him.

Rosa was conditioned not to speak or socialise with anyone and knew her brothers would go crazy if they saw her talking to any man, but just the change of scenery was welcome.

'So, Rosa—lovely name that. What do you do for a living?' Daniel asked, continuing to play with his phone. He seemed consumed with thoughts but not distracted enough not to ask a question.

Rosa bowed her head shyly.

Man, I don't even know what to say, maybe just ignore him and he will stop talking to me.

She felt uncomfortable even with normal conversation. This was not something she was used to.

'Don't be shy,' he continued, offering a smile showcasing his set of perfect, pearly-white teeth. 'Model?' he quipped. 'Don't tell me you're an undercover princess doing your own laundry?'

Again he cracked a joke that actually made Rosa's face transform into a smile. She looked up towards him.

'You really think?' Her accent again, profound in her response. This time she looked serious, staring at him, waiting for an answer.

Daniel paused. He looked back at her, and for once his expression reflected his true emotion—no jokes or arrogance—and he just gazed deeply into her eyes.

Rosa turned her face away again shyly.

'You actually could be.'

This time Daniel whispered his words tenderly. 'I mean that,' he said, still staring at her. He seemed captivated, and for once his energetic jitters had been replaced by a calmer demeanour.

'Yeah, right,' Rosa quietly answered back flippantly, trying not to take anything he said seriously. 'Thank you,' she politely replied, again not confident enough to look back at him, knowing he was still staring at her.

'I don't work,' she commented, fixing her hair.

'Well, you look lovely.' Daniel continued his charming patter. He was confident, as his entrance had displayed, yet showed he could also be calm and sounded caring.

Rosa, though, was not receptive to such compliments; it wasn't something she was used to or could afford to entertain. She didn't respond to his last comment and instead just looked up at him and smiled.

'I own a luxury car company,' he spouted. 'Mainly sports cars.'

He carried on talking, and again Rosa was unmoved, trying not to engage in conversation. Not because she did not want to—she craved conversation and a different type of attention; anything was better than her two brothers shouting instructions and expletives at her—but she knew that it would never lead to anything. She was so insular and limited in her interactions with people.

Rosa's washing spun vigorously as it neared the end of the cycle. Daniel had gone quiet and just sat staring ahead, watching the machines. He had thought better than to continue to pursue a conversation, although he still sneaked in the odd cheeky glance towards her.

The old attendant came out of the back room with a bunch of keys in her hand; the jangling sound could just be heard above the noise of the machines.

'I'm closing in ten minutes,' she grumpily declared, shuffling her way around, wiping down the empty machines and casting her eyes towards the two of them.

Daniel looked at his watch, yawning.

'How long has this got left?'

He threw the question out there, standing up to view the small dial on the machine, trying to make head or tail of the timing.

Rosa's washing had finished and she got up to empty the clothes into her large bag.

'Yours should be done soon.'

'Cool, thanks,' Daniel responded.

He again began to look agitated, walking towards the door and looking out to the main street before turning around and marching back. His behaviour was erratic. He seemed impatient and out of his comfort zone, sweating and tapping his fingers on the machine.

Rosa looked at him, still unloading her clothes.

'Are you OK?' she asked.

He stopped in his tracks.

'Yeah, thanks. Just want to get these done!'

Again, they stood and looked at each other for a few seconds.

Rosa felt an empathy for him. He was just like the men in her life—not able to do anything for himself. She thought he looked helpless and forlorn, although his dress code and style denoted a confident person.

'Not drying them, then?' He fired another question as he walked towards her. She felt a little afraid as he approached. Her heart pumped fast again, her eyes widening.

'It's fine, I just came to help.' He spoke softly again, grabbing the bag and holding it while she continued to pull the clothes out of the machine. 'I don't bite.' He smiled that dazzling show of white teeth, sensing that she was uncomfortable.

Rosa, in turn, grinned nervously.

'Thank you, and we have sunshine,' she quietly responded, continuing to pack the clothes into the bag.

Her eyes expanded, fixed on this strange man, and for a moment she really wanted to stay and talk with him. Such was her yearning for a different type of attention that outweighed any form of sense or constraint, but the reality of getting home before her brothers came looking for her halted any wayward thoughts.

Rosa hurriedly stuffed the rest of her clothes into the bag as Daniel came alarmingly close. His tall figure loomed, he looked warmly into her eyes and she could smell his heady, sweet musk.

'Any chance I could see you again, Rosa?' he asked respectfully with sincerity.

She shook her head, flustered, before darting away.

'Bye,' she added hastily before making her way out into the balmy evening.

Daniel stood hands on hips, shaking his head in disbelief, sunk by her rejection.

'Wow,' he mumbled under his breath, looking down at the floor.

He bent down quickly, noticing she had dropped a black sock. Quickly sensing another meeting, he grabbed the sock and ran out of the launderette.

'Oi, Rosa!' he shouted, his shoes skidding out onto the pavement.

'Hey, I'm closing!' the old attendant shouted as she saw him bolt out of the door.

The streets were still busy, with lots of people milling around, strolling in the warm evening air. Daniel looked ahead, trying to train his eyes between the crowds of people. He skipped between couples and kids on their bikes but Rosa seemed to have disappeared into the distance.

Daniel continued scanning the crowd until he caught a glimpse of her carrying the heavy bag.

'Rosa!' he shouted, as he dodged past people, gripping the sock firmly in one hand and his phone in the other.

'Rosa!' he shouted again, bumping into a couple who

sent him stumbling into the road, narrowly avoiding an oncoming car, but this did not put him off his stride.

'Rosa!' he called as he skipped through the urban obstacle course.

Finally, Rosa stopped on hearing her name and put the bag down. She looked behind her and at first could not see anyone, but then the image of a tall man in a pink shirt running in the darkening evening light was a vivid sight. Her heart pumped, although she was confused as to why he was hurtling down the street calling her name.

Oh my gosh what is he doing?

I can't be seen out here talking to him.

Eventually, a flushed and out-of-breath Daniel caught up with her. He stood forcing a smile through a grimace.

'Wow, am I going to have to do that all the time?' he said, trying to catch his breath.

Rosa looked back at him, confused.

'Huh?'

She was impatient, knowing she had to get home.

'What is it?' she questioned, bending slightly to pick up the heavy bag.

Daniel tossed the sock into the air.

'You dropped this,' he said, with a satisfied look on his face.

Rosa did not know what to say. Flustered and embarrassed, she grabbed the sock quickly.

'Oh, thank you, I must go,' she said, frantically stuffing the sock into the bag.

She turned to walk away, but Daniel walked beside her.

'Rosa, what's wrong? I just wanted to ask you if I could see you again.'

Rosa continued to walk with purpose, clearly struggling with the heavy bag of damp garments.

'Let me help you.' Daniel tried to take the heavy bag from her.

'Please, I must go,' she reiterated, giving him a worried look.

'Cool, but wait, give me a second.'

He dug in his pockets and presented his business card.

'Wait, Rosa. Please, just take this.'

She stopped again, slightly frustrated now.

'OK.'

She grabbed the card from his hand, and a panicked smile appeared on her face before she walked away.

Daniel was exhausted. He got down on his haunches, still watching as she went off into the estate. He laughed to himself.

'She's a diamond,' he panted, still out of breath.

He shook his head and walked slowly back towards the launderette, completely lost in thought, until he was aggressively knocked into by two squabbling men.

Daniel turned around.

'Oi, how about a sorry then?'

Daniel was looking for an apology, but the men walked on, too deep in their argument.

It was Dani and Jesus on their way back home in the same direction as Rosa.

Dani spun around and trained his eyes on Daniel. Jesus paid no attention and kept on walking.

Daniel stopped for a second, looking back in their direction.

'Yeah, sorry, mate,' he gestured, holding out his hand

in a plea-like stance. 'Clowns,' he muttered, strolling back to the launderette shaking his head.

Rosa returned home exhausted. As she pushed the old wooden gate open, her back ached from carrying the weighty bag of damp clothes, which she dumped on the concrete in the yard. She stretched upwards, arching her back and rubbing it at the base. She then pushed her hair back and bent down to take the washed clothes out to hang on the line to dry.

Rosa never rested. She was always working, but this time she was working with different thoughts in her head.

That crazy, handsome man, she reflected.

A weary smile crept onto her face. She patted the back pocket of her jean skirt where she had placed his card. Maybe it was a crumb of hope.

Rosa's happy daydream was soon rudely interrupted when the scathing whirlwind that was Jesus crashed through the gate like a force-ten gale, almost knocking Rosa over in his wake.

'Get the fuck out of my way, stupid!' he growled, gnashing his teeth, shooting a cutting look back in her direction before bundling his way into the flat, nearly breaking the door off the hinges as he slammed it shut.

'Jesus!' a startled Rosa screamed, her frustrations boiling over for once.

A couple of seconds later, Dani also came through the gate. He was more broody and mysterious, not really affording anyone a window to his mood.

He looked at Rosa, sensing, by her furrowed brow, the pent-up anxiety she was trying to subdue.

'Fuck sake, Dani, can't you see I'm trying to ... '

Dani moved towards her.

'Shut up,' Dani whispered in a deep, low tone.

Rosa sucked in her breath. Her eyes began to fill with tears which teetered on her lower lids before she blinked, making them trickle down her face.

Dani put his finger to his mouth, motioning for her to keep her emotions suppressed. Rosa's lip curled and trembled as she fought to hold back her tears.

Dani was not as extrovert and as outwardly emotional as his brother, but his mood was just as forceful. Although he did show slight compassion when it came to his sister, he never said much due to the firebrand Jesus, who was always lurking somewhere.

'Finish the clothes, then come inside,' he ordered before disappearing into the house and leaving her alone.

Rosa sniveled as she hung up the remainder of the clothes. She took her time, not wanting to enter the house whilst the tension was high. She was treading on eggshells. She knew that whatever had set Jesus off would be taken out on anyone who did or said the wrong thing.

Sat in the clustered living room, an evil-faced Jesus seethed silently, his weasel-like features pinched, his tight lips pursed. A large vein protruded from his forehead, indicating the level of anger he was feeling inside. He kept muttering to himself sporadically and shaking his head as if he were having a conversation, but he was sat alone.

Rosa bravely poked her head into the room.

'Jesus, do you want anything before I go to bed?' she asked in a hushed tone.

Jesus looked wide-eyed in her direction for a few seconds. His eyes displayed no emotion before he diverted his gaze without a word, continuing to stare ahead, face screwed up tight. Rosa knew it was time to exit, which she did, silently tiptoeing away from the room.

Rosa went to her room and closed the door. She was tired and her back was aching, so she lay down on her bed.

Man, what a day, just wanna sleep.

I wonder what those two are pissed off about.

It must be something stupid again.

I'm fed up with having to hide away every time they get into some sort of argument.

My bloody back is so sore.

She reached towards her small chest of drawers and pulled out a packet of painkillers.

Rosa's life was one big, dark well of despair. There was nothing she could do; she had no one to turn to. She'd felt like ending her life on several occasions but never had the courage. She always thought how strong a woman her mother was and knew that she could never disappoint her by taking an easy way out, but for all her best intentions, the numbness of life still ate away inside. She missed her family as they had been before the tragic circumstances diverted her path. She often got flashbacks of being a carefree young girl learning to cook, helping her father on the farm and shopping with her mother. It did not seem that long ago, yet now her life was such a complete turnaround.

Rosa sat up slowly on the edge of her bed and took out the elastic band which held her hair in a ponytail. Her long locks fell onto her shoulders.

She stood up, walked over to her table and looked into the tiny, cracked mirror which barely allowed her to see her whole face. The reflection showed her tired eyes and flushed cheeks.

Rosa viewed her reflection intently for a few seconds, hating that this was her life in this big, unforgiving city.

Rosa

Chapter 2
Meet me at the crossroads

'Rosa! Rosa!' The sound of the door being hammered woke a startled Rosa.

'OK!' she yelled back, grumpy at being woken up so urgently.

She stumbled out of her bed feeling ragged and tired, trying to wake properly before finding out what all the noise was about.

'What!'

Moodily, she pulled open her door to see an agitated Jesus standing in his grimy, stained, white vest, his bony frame leaning in towards her. She could smell his bad tobacco breath, and his twisted facial expression indicated the seriousness of the intrusive wake-up call.

'Where is Dani?' he snarled.

'I don't know,' she answered back, confused at the sudden news of her brother's disappearance.

A stinging slap lashed across her face, causing her to yelp and stumble backwards.

'You spoke to him—where is he?' Jesus shouted, waving his hands around and invading her room space.

'I don't know!' Rosa screamed back, holding her arms up to shield her face from another strike from her hysterical and frenzied brother.

She recoiled with fear as Jesus looked around deliriously before storming out of her room. His heavy footsteps could be heard stomping down the stairs.

Rosa, shocked and shaken, held the side of her face, her hair dangling messily over her reddened cheek. The shock and intrusion were just other examples of what she had to deal with. She sat on her bed, back against the wall, drawing her knees up to her chest.

How long do I have to put up with their shit?

I just wish they would disappear and leave me alone in peace.

Every day something different, I don't know where Dani is, why'd he come and bother me?

Slap me, why?

I ain't done anything, why should I keep taking their shit just because I messed up once?

Which wasn't even my fault, I was the one who was raped, drugged, beaten up, made to look like a slut.

It's not fair.

An hour later, Rosa eventually found enough energy to rise from her bed.

She looked into her little mirror, her once fresh face now looking drained and sore. A deep red mark appeared across her cheek where Jesus's bony hand had viciously connected.

Rosa's eyes were sunk deep into her face, which she tenderly touched. She knew she had to pull herself together to face another day of chores.

Her back pain reminded her of the night before. Looking around, she felt an overwhelming wave of frustration. She picked up her pile of clothes and magazines and flung them down in anger. She picked up one of the magazines and started ripping the pages, frantically throwing the pieces around the room like confetti.

Normally she did well at suppressing her angst and putting on a brave face, but for once she gave in to her emotions. Eventually, she ran out of gas. Crumpling to the floor, she glanced around at the torn pieces of magazine and caught sight of a famous actress looking happy in an expensive gown. She picked up the piece, staring at it, before breaking into forced laughter, a poor attempt to veil her inner turmoil.

Rosa rummaged through her scattered clothes.

Come on, where is it?

I know it's here somewhere.

She found the jean skirt she'd worn the day before, dug into the pockets and found the business card that Daniel had given her. She stared at it, almost memorising its text, and a small smile appeared as she remembered their chance meeting.

Daniel Rosewood.

He seemed nice, kind eyes, funny and those teeth!

He was handsome, probably the only man who seemed to be genuinely interested in me.

He was just different.

She sat in the middle of her room amongst the mess of clothes and magazines. Her cheek continued to tingle sharply, a reminder of what might come again.

Raised voices could be heard downstairs, predominantly from Jesus. Dani had returned.

Rosa walked over to her door and opened it slightly, just enough to hear the argument raging below. This was a common pattern, but today the tension felt more serious, especially as Jesus liked to be in control of everything.

They were like animals at each other's throats as all she could hear was a string of expletives being shouted back and forth, the slamming of doors and the stamp of heavy feet.

Rosa got up and closed her door, then tiptoed back to her bed where she sat and waited until this particular storm had blown over.

Jesus paced around the room, fuming at Dani, who was sat slumped in a chair.

'Are you fucking crazy?' Jesus continued, slicking back his greasy hair in frustration.

'I wanted to prove to you I could do something good,' Dani responded, solemn-faced. He leant back in the chair, his eyes on the floor, not confident when trying to be the assertive sibling.

'Fuck, Dani, man! Now we are in deeper than before,' Jesus remonstrated, kicking a box of old electronic devices.

'We already owe Franky; now you make a deal that puts us in the shit.'

Jesus moved forward, grabbing Dani by his arm, dragging him up from his seated position and shaking him violently.

'Goddamn, man!' Jesus pulled him aggressively, spitting saliva into Dani's face.

'I'll fix it.'

Dani attempted to cool down his overheated brother. He pulled away his arm and placed his hands on his brother's bony shoulders reassuringly with a nervous smile. Jesus wiped his sweaty face, his eyes locked into his brother, his breathing still erratic.

'OK, you're right, we'll fix it.' Dani breathed a sigh of relief, stepping back nodding, retreating to his seat.

Jesus sprang like a cat, launching himself at Dani, cuffing him on the side of the head. Dani stumbled back, just about regaining his balance, and turned towards Jesus, shocked.

'What, man?' he said, holding his hand on the spot of impact.

'Think you're in charge?' Jesus snarled, venom in his voice. 'Now pick this shit up—we need to flog it today.'

He pointed to the tipped-over box of assorted electronic goods before stomping out of the room.

After an hour of tension, Rosa cautiously emerged from her room, dressed and tidied. She wore a black tee shirt and jeans with flip-flops, with her hair tied into a ponytail. She took a deep breath before venturing downstairs into the kitchen.

At the bottom of the stairs stood Dani. He was very distracted, scratching his chin repeatedly as he watched Rosa's descent.

'You better go get some food; we have no food,' he said. His voice quivered with emotion and his frown told Rosa that he was still shaken from his last bout with his brother.

Rosa approached him at the bottom of the stairs and tried to squeeze her way past.

'Dani, what happened?' she asked quietly, trying to sound sympathetic.

Dani's hollow gaze spoke volumes to Rosa, who patted him on his shoulder and shuffled into the kitchen. Dani followed her.

'Here, take this, get some stuff for us to eat.'

Again his voice was not strong. He held out a shaking hand with a crisp fifty-pound note in front of her. Rosa gently took the money, then went to assess the bare cupboards and make a list of things she had to buy.

She left through the backyard and closed the gate, appreciating another opportunity to be away from the tension in the house.

As the warm air and sunshine hit her face, she felt free from all the craziness in the house. She knew she could not go on living like this. Being caught in the middle of two warring brothers was like living on a ticking time bomb.

Rosa walked through the estate, looking around at the concrete towers which were the backdrop to her life.

I may as well be back in Sinaloa, hiding from the murderers.

What's the difference from here?

Nothing.

I feel cooped up, hate this stinking, pissy-smelling, rat-infested shit.

No nature or fields and stupid boys smoking their drugs, trying to hassle me.

She felt totally isolated strolling through the maze of blocks, which for once were quiet.

As Rosa hit the main parade of shops, she dug deep into her jeans pocket and pulled out the card that Daniel had given her. She glanced at it again, then put it back into her pocket, only to reach back in and take it out again.

She ran towards one of the local shops, burst in and grabbed a hand basket. She walked through the aisle, selecting tins and packets of food, then she picked up some vegetables, potatoes, eggs and bread.

When Rosa took her groceries to the counter, the man at the till smiled at her. He was an old Eastern-European man with a thick grey beard.

'Anything else?' he asked.

Rosa grabbed some packets of sweets and chocolate. She turned to the tall fridge which stood beside the counter and took out a can of Sprite and put it all on the counter.

'That's it.' She handed him the fifty-pound note.

The man counted out the change and handed it to Rosa, who was already ripping open a packet of Haribo assorted soft sweets. She took the bag then looked back at the man.

'Can I use your phone?'

The man returned a look of confusion.

'Use the phone? You don't have a mobile?' he replied, surprised at her request.

'No, I don't. Please, I need to make a call.'

She took some of the change he'd just handed to her and stretched out an open palm full of coins.

'Just one call.'

The man pushed her hand away and handed his phone to Rosa.

'No international, please.'

65

Rosa took the phone.

'No. Thank you.'

Rosa took out the business card and dialled. She smiled back at the man; her heart raced, thumping harder as she waited for the connection. She twisted around, checking that Dani or Jesus had not followed her, before the sound of the ringing kicked in.

In her mind, she should have just done as ordered and gone about her business, but, for some reason, as much as she shook and was nervous, she continued to hold the receiver to her ear until a bright, chirpy voice answered.

'Daniel Rosewood.'

Rosa took a deep breath but no words came. She froze.

'Hello, is anyone there?'

Rosa could barely breathe.

'Look, is this a wind-up or what?'

She could hear Daniel getting agitated.

Rosa looked at the man who was watching her, intrigued. She was in two minds and about to cut the call. Eventually, her voice took over.

'Daniel . . . it's Rosa.' She spoke with a quiet urgency, her voice cracked with emotion.

'Rosa?' Daniel answered back, sounding slightly confused before the penny dropped. 'From the launderette! Yes, how are ya?'

'Fine.' Her voice trembled as she smiled with relief. She did not know what to say but knew he was the only person she could reach out to.

'Everything OK?' a surprised sounding Daniel asked, his voice now quite sincere but curious, completely opposite to his salesman patter.

Rosa was silent. Daniel could hear her obvious hesitancy.

'Can I see you?' Daniel asked boldly, sensing something was off.

Be brave, Rosa, come on be brave.

Just speak.

Come on, you might not get another chance.

Rosa knew what she was doing was completely crazy, but in her mind, Daniel was the one small chink of light at the end of a very dark tunnel.

'Please come to the launderette quickly.'

She just about got out a jumbled sentence. She was sweating. The adrenaline kicked in and her head exploded with a million different thoughts until Daniel answered back calmly, 'Course. Be there, ASAP.'

She disconnected the call, barely realising that she had committed a cardinal sin by contacting him.

'Thank you.'

She handed the phone back to the man, who observed her with concern.

'Everything OK? You in trouble?'

Rosa wiped the sweat from her face, took her bags and left the shop.

She started to make her way to the launderette, her body shaking with fear, scared by her own act of desperation.

Oh my days, I did it!

Shit, hope he hurries up.

I ain't got much time before them two come looking for me.

In a strange way, she felt relieved, but at the same time, she was frightened that her actions could have big repercussions.

Rosa hurried back to the shopping parade and tried to focus herself, but she did not know what to do.

She rushed towards the launderette The afternoon sun was now high in the sky and heating up the streets.

As she approached, she saw a bright-yellow Lamborghini parked outside. It was so vivid—the sunshine glinted sharply off every reflective surface of the sleek chassis.

At first, she only glanced at it because it was so startling against the usual dull and unspectacular backdrop of the urban canvas, but as she came closer, she noticed a tall, smartly dressed man awkwardly elevating his frame out of the low vehicle. She knew instantly it was Daniel, who looked as if he had just stepped off the cover of GQ magazine.

Daniel, wearing black, fitted trousers and a crisp, white shirt, with mirrored sunglasses dangling from his neck.

'Rosa!' he shouted as he caught sight of her with the two heavy plastic shopping bags in her hands.

She stopped dead in her tracks and looked around to check that the coast was clear. She looked worried as she saw Daniel rushing towards her.

'We must go into the launderette, quick,' she motioned.

Daniel looked confused, but her concern outweighed his confusion. He put his hands out to take the bags from her.

'What's going on?' he asked her, with an expression of concern.

They bundled their way into the launderette where they startled a couple of people who were washing their clothes.

'Rosa, stop. Please, tell me what's going on?' he again pleaded, as the other people in the launderette looked on. The old attendant came shuffling out of the tiny backroom to see what all the fuss was about.

'Oh, not you two again! Behave yourselves or I'll call the police,' she grumbled, wagging a crinkled finger in their direction.

Daniel nodded in agreement, holding the bags as Rosa plonked herself down onto the bench. The other two patrons pretended to ignore the commotion and looked away.

Rosa sat with her hands on her face and began to cry uncontrollably. Daniel did not quite know what had hit him.

He placed the bags down and stood in front of her with his hands on his hips before crouching down and whispering gently, 'Rosa, come on, you called me. What's wrong?'

His patience and compassion now outshone the cheeky persona he'd displayed on their first meeting.

Rosa composed herself. She was overcome by a flood of emotions, which Daniel was not expecting.

'I'm sorry I called you,' she finally said, her voice cracked and hushed.

She looked into Daniel's face, her big brown eyes reddened and her skin flushed. The trickle of tears had left transparent traces on her cheeks. She took a deep breath, trying to pull herself together.

'I don't have long, but I should not have called you here. I don't know . . . '

Daniel interjected. He still looked confused and

concerned at the same time. He sat beside her, moving the shopping to the side.

'I did not expect all this. I thought this part only came if I broke your heart,' he said cheekily, trying to inject a bit of his usual confident banter.

Rosa forced a smile as she continued to sniff. Daniel pulled out a clean, white handkerchief and tenderly dabbed the remaining tears from her face. She flinched and backed away.

'It's cool, tell me what happened,' Daniel said, as the machines whirred in the background.

Rosa turned and looked deeply into his eyes. She seemed very hesitant and was still shaking.

'I'm sorry for calling you. I don't know why I did.'

Daniel rolled his eyes. He was still baffled by the sudden urgency. He thought she was calling to see him but was not sure what was going on. He sat back, resting his head on the wall. The attendant and two customers were engrossed.

Rosa suddenly got up, grabbing the two bags from the floor.

'I must go now,' she said.

'Wait . . . I mean, what's this all about?'

Again he was at a loss and none the wiser.

'Look, Rosa, I don't know what this is all about. I don't have the time . . . ' He stood up, put on his shades and walked towards the door, leaving her standing with the two bags of shopping in her hands.

'Please,' she begged. 'I'm sorry, but you don't understand.'

Daniel turned around.

'Too right I don't,' he fired back, his anger now beginning to surface.

Daniel walked towards her, taking off his shades so he could look her in the eye.

'Just tell me what's going on,' he again pleaded.

'Yes, what's going on, love?' came the old, croaky voice from the attendant in the background, followed by nods from the other two customers who were now sat on the edge of the bench, fully tuned in to what was happening.

'Can we meet again tomorrow? I promise I will explain.'

Daniel stood with his hands on his hips. He was about to speak, then just shrugged, turned away and marched towards the door.

'Daniel, please,' Rosa shouted. She was desperate. She knew that her actions had already spiralled everything out of control, but she also knew that he was her only hope.

Daniel turned around and looked back.

The image of Rosa standing there alone, disconsolate, jarred his senses. He scratched his head and clenched his jaw, agonising for a few seconds. He saw something alluring in her eyes—she was a diamond in the rough—and Daniel, as cocksure and confident as he was, felt empathy towards whatever her plight was.

He strode back towards her purposefully, and she caught a shiver as he approached.

'Hey, come on. It's OK.' He now spoke softly, swallowing any doubts, and touched her face with his hand.

He was tender.

'Just call me tomorrow . . . OK?' he asked quietly.

The prying eyes of the attendant and other customers continued to peer. Only the sound of the drying machines humming distracted from the lingering tension.

'*Sí*, I mean yes.'

Rosa could barely speak; her heart thumped harder from his touch.

'I must go.'

She scuttled towards the door, stopping fleetingly to glance back to a bemused Daniel. The rays from the sun cut in, sharply illuminating the launderette before the door closed on Rosa's exit.

She walked back quickly, trying to control her breathing, which became more erratic as she neared her home. She could barely carry the bags, such was the weakness in her whole body, her legs like jelly.

Oh my God, what have I done?

Jesus will kill me.

Let me just get home and start cooking, act like nothing and if they ask, I'll tell them I just wanted to walk slowly, enjoy the sun or something like that.

She felt nervous but elated at the same time. As she made her way back through the streets, she saw the flash of yellow speed past her. Watching the car disappear in the distance, she could only hope that she would see him again and not feel regret for her high-risk maneuver.

Closer to her home, Rosa stopped to catch her breath and control herself.

OK, just be cool, go in and get on with it.

She placed the bags down and quickly wiped her face to clear the stains of the tears. Her back was aching, but she knew she had to compose herself and make the final few yards to her home.

As she got closer to the gate, she saw a plume of cigarette smoke being blown from inside the yard. Her heart was in her mouth. She knew Jesus was waiting.

Rosa pushed the gate open slowly and sure enough was confronted by the skinny but fearsome figure of Jesus, who stood in front of her, just staring coldly into her face. His eyes, as usual, squinted. The smell of nicotine smacked her in the face, and she froze in front of him. His silence was unnerving.

Jesus stretched out his hands, and Rosa stepped back, turning her head, thinking he was about to aim another shot at her. She was exhausted, sweating and her eyes bulged with fear.

'Give me the bags,' Jesus hissed, as his long, inked arms jutted forward to take the shopping from Rosa.

'Took your time,' he continued, spitting the dangling cigarette from his mouth onto the ground.

He sneered in Rosa's face, curling his lip and showing his yellow teeth, before turning away and heading back into the house without a word.

Rosa gulped. Her mouth was dry; she could barely swallow or breathe. Chest tight and thumping from heart palpitations, she wiped away the perspiration from her top lip and reached behind to rub her back, which ached. She knew that once she had entered the house, the ticking time bomb of Jesus's temper would explode at some point. It was just a matter of time.

Rosa

Chapter 3
Just a taste

All three sat in the living room eating a late lunch of burgers, scrambled eggs and chips prepared, of course, by Rosa. There was a silence interrupted only by the scraping of forks on plates and the opened-mouthed chewing of Dani.

Rosa picked at her food. She was still nervous, trying to sense her brother's mood.

Jesus, meanwhile, chomped down hard on his burger, his jaw working the food vigorously. He stared straight ahead in the direction of his little sister. He did not even look down at the food, just stabbing recklessly at the plate.

Dani could feel the tension rising in his brother and tried to break the icy atmosphere by coughing violently as if he were choking. This distracted Jesus, who scoffed at him, grunting at the interruption.

Rosa stood up and ran to the kitchen, throwing down her plate before running up the stairs into the bathroom and slamming the door shut.

The two brothers looked at each other. Dani shrugged and continued eating. He showed no care or concern, which was normally how things were.

Jesus threw down his plate and spoke with a full mouth. 'She's so fucking stupid!'

His vexed growl continued. 'Hurry up and finish, we got to sort out this shit you got us into with Franky.'

He wiped his mouth while still chewing savagely and stood up.

'Let's go,' he mumbled, slicking back his greasy hair.

Dani, on command, followed his brother's instructions, copying him and slamming his plate down, also.

'I'm ready,' he announced, wiping his hands on his chest.

He grabbed a bottle of Coke from the fridge as he stomped through the kitchen, belching loudly as he exited. For a few seconds, a silence ensued; the tension had left at the same time as Dani and Jesus.

Rosa stayed in the safe solace of the bathroom, sitting with her back up against the door. She clutched the base of her back, her head tilted backwards, shaking erratically while trying to control the rhythm of her breathing.

Eventually she managed to stand again. She opened the door slowly, poking her head out to listen for any voices or movement before stepping out.

In agony, she made her way to her bedroom and fell onto her bed, exhausted, staring up at the stained, magnolia-coloured ceiling.

She cursed under her breath.

'What am I thinking?' she muttered, covering her eyes with her hands. 'Arrrrgghhh!' she screamed, her frustration finally boiling over.

Rosa knew her anguish was confined to the small space of her room. No one could hear her or share her feeling of entrapment. Her desperate actions with Daniel were a scream for help, let alone a cry.

Irrational? Maybe.

But what other choices did she have?

She curled up gingerly into the corner of her bed, her body numb with pain, her mind blown to pieces. Fragments of fear, relief, pain and confusion were scattered through her mind like the aftermath of a minefield.

The only shred of hope was that she could talk to Daniel—that's if he had not run a mile yet.

Her eyes became heavy, her spirit was drained. She closed her eyes and drifted into sleep.

Jesus paced up and down a narrow back alley behind a backstreet nightclub. He pulled fiercely on a rolled-up cigarette, looking shifty and nervous.

Dani, hands in his pockets, leant against a brick wall, looking down. He knew he had taken them into deep waters and was unsure whether it could be fixed.

A rusty steel door scraped open to reveal a tall sturdy unit of a security man, Afro-Caribbean, short dreadlocks, dressed in all black. He stood for a second, looking menacingly at the two of them.

Dani lifted himself from the wall, taking his hands out of his pockets. Jesus threw down his cigarette and approached the man.

'Is Franky ready for us or what?'

His no-fear tactics did not impress the robotic gatekeeper.

'Lickle man, calm down,' he responded, with a deep baritone street accent, a glint of gold in a tooth prominent as he spoke.

'Come thru, innit.' He ushered them through the door into a dimly lit corridor.

'Wait,' he ordered, then dragged the rusty door shut.

His tall, imposing frame loomed in the narrow space.

He took out a small torch and shone the bright light into the faces of Dani and Jesus, who frowned at the blinding intrusion.

'Follow me.' His voice reverberated off the walls.

The security man led them down a metal spiral staircase deep into the bowels of the club. Jesus groaned the further down he took them, disgruntled and moody. Dani just followed silently.

Eventually, they reached the basement. A rusting belly of dripping pipes, cobwebs, wet brick walls and uneven concrete flooring. A black metal door with a rusted bolt lock stood before them.

The security man banged three times against the door. After a couple of minutes, it slowly opened, revealing a darkened room.

'Get in here, now,' a voice thrown from inside the room instructed them.

'You heard,' the burly security man said, shoving Jesus in his back, much to his annoyance.

Dani shuffled in behind his brother.

On entry, they saw Franky seated at a large desk. White vest, laden with gold chains, oak tree arms covered in tattooed sleeves, shorn blonde hair. He crunched on a large bowl of Rice Krispies, slurping with each spoonful.

'Come in.' He spoke between mouthfuls, not even looking up at Dani and Jesus.

Franky's two henchmen, both Afro-Caribbean, looking like bodybuilding gym buddies, stood steadfastly on guard behind their leader, unmoved and focused.

'Dani, lad, I thought we had a deal. Why the fuck are you here?'

At this point, Jesus stepped forward, his skinny frame dwarfed by the huge, muscular accomplices.

'Franky, my friend. Please excuse my brother; he made a mistake.'

Jesus's opening plea laid the blame firmly at Dani's feet. Franky continued to munch on his strange but obviously tasty choice of dinner.

'So what are you saying, Jeezos?'

Jesus took another step closer to the desk, only to be pulled back by the security man behind him.

'Franky, come on, you know it's only me . . . '

Franky splashed his spoon down into the deep bowl.

'Come in here acting like the big "I am". Who the fuck do you think you are?'

For once Jesus was in submissive mode.

'No disrespect intended, but—'

Again, Jesus's speech was interrupted by an increasingly frustrated Franky.

'Look, mate. Your bro here came in giving it the big 'un.'

Franky rose from his seat, his figure matching those of his security team—tall, chiselled, squashed boxers, a nose-bruiser of a man.

'The deal's done, Dani. Lad agreed to move a load of merchandise. Man of his word, that's what you said, didn't ya?'

At this point, Dani mumbled something under his breath.

'What, mate?'

Franky stepped from around the table towards the two brothers, his chunky legs revealed by his grey lycra gym shorts.

Dani began to fret. He looked around, knowing he was in deep, way over his head, and taking his brother with him to the depths of a murky ocean of trouble.

'Sorry, I wasn't thinking,' Dani blurted out, backtracking until he bumped into the solid frame of one of the security men, who sneered and choked out a wheezy laugh.

'Problem is . . . ' Franky now towered over Jesus, making him look like a scrawny, underfed ferret. ' . . . I'm a man of honour, so when I make a deal, it's gold. Understand?'

Jesus looked back at Dani, giving him daggers.

'You really fucked up,' he rasped.

He turned back towards Franky, who still violated his space by standing toe to toe.

'Come on, Franky, we can try to make another deal.'

Jesus attempted to assert some leverage, much to Franky's amusement.

'Gold. I said that deal is gold.'

He peered down at Jesus's greasy head. A loud banging on the metal door interrupted the tense standoff.

'Find out who that is,' Franky ordered his cohorts, who sprang into action like two faithful Doberman pinchers and ran towards the door.

Jesus and Dani looked at each other, confused at the timely yet sudden fracas. The banging on the door continued, causing panic amongst Franky's crew.

'Fuck sake, open the door!' Franky shouted, clearly agitated.

One of the muscular men slid back the rusty bolt and unlocked the door. A frightened young man dressed in what resembled a waiter's outfit—black waistcoat and white shirt—burst through the door.

'Franky, man! The feds are raiding us, man. It's carnage upstairs.'

A state of panic set in. Everyone looked at each other then back to Franky.

'You cheeky bastards, you set me up,' Franky growled, pointing at Jesus and Dani, who seemed just as bemused at all the commotion.

'No, not us,' Jesus snapped back. 'Never will I do that,' he pleaded.

'Mugging me off, you cunt.' Franky stepped forward with menace a few feet from Jesus, strong, pumped up and intimidating.

'No! We had nothing to do with it.'

Dani bravely stepped in front of his brother. Franky boiled with anger, his face now bright red. He took a forceful swipe at Dani, catching him on the head with his blunt fist.

Dani reeled back from the blow, staggering into Jesus.

'Little snitch, shut the fuck up.' Franky continued to rage. 'We have a deal. You honour it or I'll kill the both of ya.'

Jesus helped Dani to maintain his balance.

'Franky, my friend, believe me. We would never . . . '

As Jesus spoke, the sound of raised voices and heavy footsteps echoed through the bowels of the club.

'Franky, let's go man!' the young chargehand reiterated, panicked and jittery.

'Grab them and let's cut,' Franky ordered.

His security team responded forcefully, dragging Dani—who was still dazed from his blow to the head—and Jesus towards the door.

The footsteps pounded against the concrete in unison like an army squadron. A posse of men charged through the narrow underground maze in a bid to escape the bloodhound-like police unit.

'Come, boss, let's use the fire exit,' one of the musclebound henchmen urged.

But as they burst through the door seeking an easy escape route, they were met with a wall of burly men dressed in black, looking like an American SWAT team.

Panic broke out as the men clashed. Grunts, groans and screams could be heard. Jesus and Dani tried to avoid the commotion and slip out through the side, but their plan was floored as Dani received another blow to the head, which this time sent him sprawling.

Jesus turned to rescue his stricken brother.

'Dani, get up. Come on, we have to go.'

He attempted to drag him to his feet but felt a heavy hand grab his arm and drag him back.

'Little bastard,' said a deep, gruff voice.

Dani was out cold on the floor but was still getting kicked and stamped on like a rag doll under the feet of a thousand bulls.

'Dani. Get up, man. Get up!'

Jesus continued to shout and struggle, but his waif-like frame was no match for the adrenalin-pumped police crack team. He was dragged away into the street. He could see Franky putting up a hell of a fight against a crew of policemen.

'You're dead, Jesus. Dead, you hear me!' he managed to scream at the top of his voice before succumbing to a rain of blows that forced him to his knees.

'Believe me, Franky, it wasn't us.'

Jesus made a final plea before a jolting blow to his side winded him into submission.

A sharp pain in her back caused Rosa to wake up alert. She rolled onto her side, but the pain intensified. She rubbed where it hurt, groaning as she tried to get up from her horizontal position.

Ow shit, man.

This is getting worse.

I need to see a doctor; this don't feel normal.

But she knew she would have to suck up the pain.

Eventually, she arose and shuffled towards her door. She was overtired and barely had the energy for anything, but, as usual, she had to grin and bear it, otherwise that would give Jesus another reason to start, not that he needed it.

Rosa entered the front room. She glanced around, staring at the dirty plates which were still there from yesterday's dinner. She hated this place; it depressed her.

There was nothing to look forward to, just the stench of her two dirty brothers and their cigarette smoke.

Rosa began to clear away the dirty dishes, bending gingerly to pick things up. Her thoughts turned to Daniel.

I wonder what type of life he lives?

What would he think if he knew I lived in a rundown council estate?

What would he think of my two neurotic brothers?

I have no money, nothing to offer except hard work.

Why would he even want to talk to me?

Rosa stood over the hot stove peeling potatoes in preparation for her two hungry brothers to come crashing through the door.

As she cooked, her mind was consumed with the thought of how she could get away to contact Daniel again. She could not do it without Jesus and Dani becoming suspicious, except by using the excuse of having to wash clothes.

Rosa kept telling herself that she would seize the first chance she got and run away.

Escape, but to where? She did not know.

She thought of going to the police and telling them she had been raped or abused. Maybe they would give her a shelter, a safer place to stay, but she knew that her brothers would always come looking for her and most likely find her. She was a prisoner, not only in her own home but also in this city.

The one thing that kept her alive inside was the hope and dream of having that red-carpet moment she'd dreamt of since she was a little girl. It was more than a pining, it was an obsession.

She was fed up with her brothers running and ruining her life. It was slowly killing her inside and made her feel aged. She was young and wanted to do and see more of life than cooking and cleaning.

Maybe Daniel was that small crack of light in the darkness that could help her.

After nearly two hours of chores, a weary Rosa went back up to her room. She went to her little table and stared into her tiny cracked mirror. Her reflection presented a tired face, but she still fixed her hair, brushing it back into her signature pony tail.

Rosa's back still ached, although the pain had dulled. She threw on a fitted, grey tee shirt and a baseball cap, then searched for her purse, which was on her bed.

She emptied the contents onto the bed. A few coins fell out. Not much. But maybe enough to pay the man in the shop to allow her another phone call.

Rosa had one intention and that was to sneak out and meet Daniel.

The fear factor had now become a less significant hurdle. As far as she was concerned, she was not letting this glimmer of hope fade away—she was willing to throw a little caution to the wind. It was not as if her brothers would be back for a while, so it was a perfect opportunity, although time was limited. Rosa knew she would dice with death if caught. A small part of her cared but was outweighed as her defiance grew.

Rosa put on her worn flip-flops and stepped wearily down the stairs. She patted her back pocket, making sure she had Daniel's business card.

She stopped on hearing voices at the back of the yard.

Quickly, she turned and sat on the stairs, holding her breath, and waited until the voices had passed.

Rosa then moved to the back door and opened it slowly, peeking out into the yard. It was quiet; the air was still warm; it was a perfect summer's evening. She took a few deep breaths before stepping out and gently closing the door behind her.

It was now or never.

She pulled the cap down over her face and walked towards the back gate. She opened it carefully and looked left and right. She could see some of the local youths hanging out in the distance, but there was no sign of her brothers.

Bravely, she walked briskly towards the main parade where the shops were, just beyond the group of vocal youths.

Her heart pounded. It felt as if she had escaped prison and had no sense of direction.

Just keep walking.

Ignore those boys.

Rosa approached the gang of youths, most of whom were no older than eighteen.

One of them shouted at her, 'Wha gwan peng tings. Ain't I seen you before?'

Rosa kept on walking until she felt the presence of the same youth walking beside her.

'Trying to air me, bitch?' he questioned in a cocky tone, just loud enough so his friends could hear, too.

'Leave me alone,' Rosa replied.

'Sket's got a gob on her,' the youth continued.

Rosa walked faster.

'Piss off,' she retorted, looking back.

Surprisingly, the youth stopped and left her to walk, but not without first spitting in her direction.

'Stupid freak!' he shouted, to the amusement of his friends, who all cackled with laughter at his juvenile actions.

Finally, Rosa made it to the main road, panting. She looked around. There was still a steady flow of people on the streets, but she saw no trace of Jesus and Dani. She continued, quickly making her way to the shop.

When she entered, she was greeted by the shopkeeper, who was happy to see her.

'Back again,' he smiled.

'Yes. I was wondering if I could use your phone again.'

She spilled the coins onto the counter.

'Please,' she asked.

The shopkeeper gathered up the coins and gave them back to her, then slid his phone across the counter. The phone barely connected before a relaxed voice answered.

'Hi, who's that?' his deep tone responded.

'Daniel, it's Rosa,' she answered back hopefully.

'Allo?' Daniel's voice rose an octave; he now sounded awake.

'Can you come now?' Rosa asked quickly, with no hesitation, although she was trying to control her breathing.

A long pause ensued.

She could hear Daniel moving around.

'Now? Where?' he asked, sounding a bit surprised at her request.

Rosa was unprepared—she had no idea of a location.

'Please, just come to where I met you before. Quick, I don't have long.'

She sounded nervy under the watchful eye of the shopkeeper.

'Alright, on my way,' Daniel answered.

'Thanks.'

Rosa cut the call and handed the phone back to the shopkeeper. He picked up the phone.

'Why you don't have a phone?' he quizzed Rosa.

She peeked up at him from below her cap.

'It's a long story,' she countered, before exiting onto the street.

Rosa approached the launderette, but the doors were closed, lights off. She turned and looked both ways but could not see anyone or any car that resembled Daniel's.

She sank onto her haunches, her back against the glass door. She heaved a big sigh and took off the baseball cap, wiping away the perspiration from her forehead. She put her flip-flopped feet onto the pavement and waited.

An old homeless man, dishevelled and inconspicuous in his thick overcoat, with straggled hair and beard, stopped and peered at her.

'Got any change? Anything . . . '

His bloodshot eyes bore down at Rosa, who quickly put her cap back on and looked away.

'Fuck ya then,' he growled and continued to walk on by, leaving a stench of alcohol and BO behind.

It seemed like an eternity that Rosa sat in front of the launderette. Her back was becoming stiffer by the second, so she slowly eased herself up into a standing position.

The air was still warm, although the orange glow from the street lights signified the imminent nightfall.

Rosa now doubted that Daniel was coming. It crossed her mind to go back home as the reality of her actions began to dawn. She stepped out into the street, feeling hot and bothered, and her fear increased as the seconds ticked by, but strangely, her will to see Daniel gave her a strong pull across the line of danger, more in hope than logic.

Finally, from the corner of her eye, she saw the bright yellow flash of Daniel's Lamborghini whizz past and park just a few yards from the launderette.

She walked quickly, feeling a surge of relief that Daniel had arrived—this was the first time in her life that any male had kept his word.

She ran over to meet him, and as she reached the shiny vehicle, she pulled down her cap and bent down to the passenger window. She tapped lightly and put her head parallel with the driver.

Daniel looked and saw a figure staring through the window. He lowered the glass.

'Rosa?' Daniel quizzed, shocked to see a boyish-looking Rosa peering into the car.

'Thank you for coming.'

Her eyes told a story of happiness and relief.

'Get in.'

Daniel was dressed very casually in a pink Polo shirt and shorts.

Rosa lowered herself carefully into the leather-contoured bucket seat of the luxury car. It was clean, cool and smelt like fresh pine.

'What's all this? What's happened?' he asked, with the same look of confusion that he'd expressed when last in her company.

'Just drive away from here, please,' she pleaded.

Daniel looked at her for a moment before thrusting the chrome gearstick into position and pulling away at speed.

This was the first time Rosa had experienced a smidgen of freedom, although her heart was racing as fast as the engine horsepower which accelerated Daniel's car through the city streets.

They had driven for about twenty minutes. Rosa sat staring out through the window at the bustling streets.

'It's my first time away from there,' she said softly.

She felt safe enough to take off the baseball cap, revealing her dark hair. Daniel continued to drive, staring straight ahead, focused on the road. He was listening but seemed consumed in his own thoughts.

Rosa continued to stare through the window, marvelling at the unfamiliar landscape that raced past her.

'My brothers . . . '

She paused in mid-sentence, choosing her words carefully. Daniel finally summoned a glance in her direction; he was still confused.

'It's ok, take your time.' He spoke quietly, his cockney patter a soft undercurrent laden with concern.

'I'll take you somewhere special, then we can talk properly,' he continued, increasing the speed of his car as he recognised the urgency of the situation.

They reached the destination: a high rocky perch above the city, remote and quiet. They got out of the car and stood looking awkwardly at each other over the vehicle.

Daniel was striking in his fluorescent pink top, white shorts and trainers. His face still wore a concerned and curious mask as he looked at Rosa, who was quite the opposite—weary, withdrawn and worried.

'Come and sit.' Daniel cajoled her to come to the front of the car and sat on the bonnet, looking out to the dotted red and tangerine lights in the distance, which framed the frenzied city beneath.

'Look at that,' he beckoned, pointing down at the city. 'Don't seem real when you look at it from here.'

He continued to muse, taking in the view. Slowly, Rosa made her way to Daniel. She was very shy, not sure how to act in his presence.

'Thank you,' Rosa mumbled feebly.

She sat beside him and looked into the distance, shivering, unable to control her body as the nerves took hold.

'You mentioned something about your brothers?' Daniel asked.

Rosa shuddered at the mere mention of them, which Daniel picked up on.

'Tell me about them.'

Daniel moved closer and stretched his arm out to offer a hug. Rosa at first flinched then cowered away from him.

'Hey, it's OK, I'm not going to hurt you,' he reassured gently, aware of the delicacy of the situation, holding his hands up in surrender so as not to incite a reaction.

'I hate my life because of them.'

A stark, emotional statement that came from Rosa's gut, her accent coming to the fore as the rawness took control. She shuddered again, looking out to the night skies. Daniel stayed silent and listened as a visibly perplexed Rosa continued.

'They treat me like a dog, a slave.'

She paused again, trying to control her emotions.

'Ever since my parents were killed . . . I miss my mama . . .'

Her voice strained with emotion as the mere mention took her back to the terrible childhood experience.

She turned to Daniel, staring at him.

'It's not your burden, but I have no one else to talk to.'

Rosa walked over to the edge of the ridge, letting out an anguished scream born more out of frustration than anything else. Daniel could only watch on.

Rosa continued to walk along the edge, visibly upset.

'I cry inside every day.'

She was about to break, summoning all her will to contain years of pent up emotion, stepping closer to the edge of the ridge.

Daniel felt sick in his stomach. He wrung his hands, nervously watching Rosa.

'Rosa, stop. Don't go any—'

He had to act on impulse and ran towards her.

'No, Daniel. Stay back!' she warned, her reaction causing her to stumble on the rocky edge, and she fell a few yards down onto a bushy verge.

'Rosa, please...Take it easy. I'm here, look at me.'

He shuffled closer, trying not to startle her further.

Rosa managed to regain her footing and attempted to scramble to safety. Daniel held his head in shock, paralysed by the events unfolding.

'OK, just stay there, don't move,' he reassured her, stooping down and creeping towards Rosa. 'I'm coming, stay put.'

But Rosa slipped and landed on her back. Daniel inched closer until he was just behind her.

'Right, I'm gonna place my hands around your waist.' He spoke calmly, although he himself was shaking with fear.

He placed his hands carefully around her.

'Got you, babe. I got you.'

His voice quivered with relief as he pulled her to safety.

After a long silence, Rosa moved closer to Daniel. She shuffled up next to him and placed her hand on his shoulder.

'I'm sorry. Didn't mean to freak you out.'

She reverted to a childlike persona.

'Can I have a hug?' she asked.

Daniel turned and looked at her. He pushed his fingers through his hair and breathed out heavily, acknowledging the weight of the situation.

'Look, whatever you got going on ...'

He took a deep breath. For some reason, Rosa had touched his heart. There was something about her— she had a strong pull.

Daniel moved closer and slowly put his arm around her. He could feel her still shaking like a leaf as she buried her head into him.

'Hey, come on, I'm here for you now,' he whispered.

A few minutes of silence passed before Rosa detached herself from Daniel, wiping her face with her hands.

'I must go now, please,' she said, composing herself.

'Right, OK.'

Daniel stood up, his pink tee shirt and white shorts now covered with dried dirt, and walked a couple of paces in front, gathering himself. He was trying to get his head around everything. His swanky, wide boy exterior was shorn, leaving his sensitive side exposed; the flashy car and clothes seemed detached from the person who had chosen to rescue Rosa from despair.

'Let's go. I'll take you back.'

He turned and walked towards the car. Rosa looked up at him.

'OK, let's go.'

* * *

They drove back in silence, both lost in a sea of thoughts as they cruised through the busy streets.

Daniel glanced over at Rosa, whose head was leant against the window. He could tell she was far away. It was hard to read her thoughts, but she had taken a giant step in her tortured life.

Daniel pulled the car over to the side of the street just around the corner from the launderette. It was late now, and the headlights from other cars flashed by.

Rosa did not budge; she just sat still in silence.

'You OK?' Daniel asked.

Rosa turned slowly to face him.

'I'm as good as dead . . . maybe this is the last time you see me,' she replied, with a solemn look.

The sadness in her eyes touched Daniel. He could feel his heart leap as she spoke those words.

'Nah, don't say that,' he interjected. 'Just go home. I will see you soon . . . Call me, OK?'

His voice was strained. He reached out and placed his

hand on her shoulder. She pulled the baseball cap onto her head.

'I must go...thanks again,' she said before she removed herself from the car and began the walk back towards her place.

Daniel sat for a few minutes. He watched her walk into the night. Part of him wanted to get out and chase her, but he felt it would serve no purpose.

'Fuck, man!'

He banged the steering wheel and banged his head against the leather headrest in frustration before peeling off at high speed.

Rosa walked slowly through her estate. It was quiet now—no raucous youths or crazy barking dogs. She neared the gate to her backyard.

Oh well, I've done it.

Crossed the line.

Just have to take whatever's coming my way.

Her heart thudded against her chest as she prepared for the inevitable.

Rosa stopped short before entering, pausing to collect herself.

Fuck it, here goes.

She took a deep breath. Still shaking uncontrollably, she pushed open the gate, peering round before walking in on tiptoe.

Everything was silent. There were no lights on in the flat. She was terrified. It was a struggle to even put one foot in front of another, knowing a bony slap or punch from Jesus was imminent. Again, she drew a breath and moved towards the door, taking off the baseball cap.

Rosa quietly opened the door and stepped into the kitchen, bracing herself for the barrage of abuse, but nothing came.

It seemed that there was no one home. She switched on the lights and found everything as she had left it—no signs of her brothers' mess or intrusion.

Emotionally drained, Rosa flopped onto her bed. She was exhausted but happy she had finally broken the chains of confinement. Daniel had done something for her that no one had before, and she could not get him out of her head. For once, a small smile crept across her face, albeit a tired one. Her eyes, heavy, began to close and she drifted into slumber.

The sound of a door slamming downstairs jolted Rosa out of her sleep. She was still in her clothes and rubbed her eyes harshly before sitting up and listening intently. She could hear someone thrashing around, probably the return of her brothers.

She crept to the door and opened it slightly. It was dark so she switched on her bedroom light before poking her head out. The noise had subsided and all seemed quiet.

Rosa stepped lightly as she made her way down to the front room.

'Who's there?' she called out. 'Jesus, is that you?'

Rosa paused to listen but could hear nothing. Now alert, she pushed the door open.

'Who's there?' she repeated hesitantly, before switching the light on.

'Oh my God!' she shrieked, seeing Dani slumped in a chair, covered in blood. 'Dani, what happened?'

Dani sat back in the chair. He was beaten and weary, his face twisted in anger and his features stained by the dried blood which had oozed from a cut on his forehead. He looked demonic as he eventually looked up at his sister.

'Bastards!' he shouted, wincing at the same time.

'They got Jesus at Franky's. Pigs took him,' Dani vented.

'Who . . . what?'

Dani attempted to stand, grimacing again and holding his arm. He appeared to be in a cold sweat, pasty and shaking with fury.

'Those fucking pigs, cunts, took Jesus, man! They beat us and took him in . . . I ran.'

He stopped in mid-flow.

The anger grew as he tried to reenact the scene.

'I ran . . . '

Again, he stopped short and clenched his teeth as pain jolted through his body.

'I ran . . . Franky and his gang . . . they beat Jesus and took him away.'

He limped towards Rosa and barged his way past, leaving her to digest the craziness.

In a selfishly weird way, a wave of relief washed over her; she knew that without Jesus, Dani was weak, which meant, for her, a break from the terror.

Dani retreated to the bathroom. He splashed water over his face, flinching with pain. Rosa followed.

'Dani, let me check out that cut.'

She soaked a flannel with warm water and dabbed it gently over his wound. Dani stiffened up and scowled at Rosa, trying to be stoic. Even without Jesus, he still showed no gratitude towards his sister, pushing her hand away and growling at her.

'Enough!'

He stomped away, leaving Rosa annoyed and frustrated. She threw the wet flannel into the sink and made her way back to her room, once again cast off and rejected.

For most of the night, she lay in her bed unable to sleep. Millions of random thoughts flowed through her brain, and as much as she tried to close her eyes, it just was not happening.

She kept playing back her night with Daniel, the freedom, the bond. She could still smell his sharp aftershave on her. She felt being with him was better than anything she had experienced.

It reinforced the fact that she needed to take drastic action and escape her life of confinement; her brothers were only going down one road, and although family loyalty was high on her list, she was at the tipping point.

Time ebbed away. Rosa barely slept, unsettled by her overactive brain.

At one point, she contemplated leaving right there and then, but she knew she had to be sure that everything was in place, especially with Daniel.

Questions sporadically popped into her mind: where would she go? How would she survive? And what would happen to her brothers? So much conflict, too much for a young girl to have to entertain.

Before dawn broke, Rosa was up and cleaning the kitchen. She had given up her right to a good night's sleep and decided to plough ahead with her daily chores. She swept whimsically, still lost in thought.

There was no sign of Dani, much to her relief. For some reason, Jesus's arrest felt like a new dawn. It was as if a giant, dark cloud had been lifted from her world.

Rosa knew that Dani was not much of a threat without his brother's presence, although she could not get too carried away. But the feeling she had today was different from any other day—she had hope and excitement about seeing Daniel again.

The shock of her brother sitting in blood-soaked clothes still did not deter her from wanting to escape. Daniel had given her a glimpse of another side to life.

I wonder how his day has been, what he would be doing after work.

What type of home did he have?

And does he even have a family or a girlfriend?

The fact that he took an interest and was there whenever she needed him gave her hope that there could be a real chance of something new on the horizon.

Rosa

Chapter 4
Love's gonna get ya

It was mid-morning. The long summer heatwave showed no signs of abating as the sun blazed against the backdrop of a clear blue sheet of sky.

Rosa sat on the doorstep in the backyard, head tilted up, eyes closed, enjoying the warmth of the rays on her face.

This feels so nice.

I could sit here all day, chilling.

She had, for once, done all her morning chores under no duress. It seemed strange that the flat was silent, although she knew it was just a matter of time before Dani emerged like a bear with a very sore head. But for now, she took the time to relax and soak up the sun.

Rosa's mind was still a see-saw of thoughts. She had flashbacks of speeding through the city streets, she could picture the bright yellow Lamborghini vividly, but what was most important was the feeling she'd had when Daniel rescued her from that moment of madness and placed that protective arm around her.

Could never imagine I would meet a man like Daniel.
He is different.
What he did for me was something I'll never forget.
He is a man of honour.
That car is amazing, too, so sick.
I felt like the most important person in his world.
He came for me when I needed him most.
I wish I could be with him all the time, away from this dump.
Just us.
Just me and Daniel.

A smile broke across her face. She shook her head even contemplating the possibility. Daniel giving her that hug just when she needed it. Her mind was made up: she was going to escape, and she only wanted to be with Daniel. He was that sliver of opportunity that she was going to grab with both hands.

Rosa's relaxed morning thoughts were rudely interrupted by a grumpy Dani who, for some reason, had morphed into Jesus. He kicked her spitefully in the back, right in the spot where it pained her the most, and yelled at her.

'What the fuck are you doing?'

Rosa felt the full impact, moving away in pain.

'Oww, Dani!' she screamed, turning to see her scowling, moody brother stood in the doorway. His bare chest showcased the extent of his battering, the bruises like a patchwork blanket covering his chest.

'Get inside . . . I'm hungry.'

He pulled her by the hair, dragging her forcefully back into the kitchen. Rosa screamed.

She turned to look at him, shocked and confused—this was not the normal Dani. He assumed the role of his brother and showed Rosa no mercy, slamming the door once he'd pushed her aggressively in her back.

'Don't piss me off today,' he shouted.

Rosa winced, curling up in pain.

'I'm in charge now,' he continued, clearly enjoying his new position of head of the house.

Rosa managed to haul herself up from the floor and leant on the stove, trying to suck up the pain, which intensified every second.

'Make me some food, then go to your room,' he ordered. His tone was deep and threatening. He was obviously on a power trip, unrecognisable from the usually submissive Dani who walked in Jesus's shadow.

Rosa kept her head straight, concentrating on the pots on the stove. She took a minute to regain her breath, then she gingerly took some plates out from the cupboard.

Dani finally left her to it, walking away into the living room.

Rosa fought back tears. This time her anger bubbled to the fore.

Bastards.

Both of them.

No better than the other.

They treat me like a dog.

Well, that's it now.

Fuck loyalty.

They can both suffer like the pigs they are.

Dani had jolted her from a euphoric dreamland back into the raw reality that she detested.

For the next few hours, Rosa and Dani sat in their respective rooms, mulling things over. It was ironic because although their moods were for different reasons, both were scared and unhappy.

Dani sat on his ramshackle bed, mind racing. He was lost about what to do without his brother. He was like a rudderless ship alone in an uncompromising ocean. He could not go to the police or even check with the hospital about Jesus's health. If anything, he had to lie low for a long while.

In contrast, Rosa lay on her bed, staring up at the ceiling, her back throbbing with pain, her body rigid, still fuming and unable to hide her disappointment with Dani. The crippling effects of her injury meant she could not chance sneaking out to contact Daniel. She could not tell him what she was thinking or how her feelings for him were growing stronger. She did not give even a second thought to Jesus.

Rosa was focused on her next move. She hoped that whatever had happened with Jesus, he would never return. Family loyalty meant nothing to her now. She knew her father and mother would be turning simultaneously in their graves at her treatment by her so-called brothers. She now had to be more single-minded for her own sanity and cast out any lingering emotions towards family.

Rosa lay static; she could feel her mother's presence in the room.

Mama, I know you are with me.

You can see what's happening in my life, what should I do?

I miss you and Papa so much.

She drifted in and out of sleep. She could hear her mother's voice telling her only to be happy. Rosa could see her mother's smile—a beautiful, caring one—which then turned into a frown and an expression of disappointment. Her mother's voice became angry. She spoke of her brothers, how they had become something born of the devil, not fit to carry their family name.

Rosa attempted to turn onto her side. She grimaced, the pain continuing to drill into her back. She curled up into a ball, pulling her knees in tightly towards her chest.

I really need to see a doctor and get my back sorted. These bloody painkillers don't do anything.

The pain was crippling, but the remote chance that her now reinvented tyrant brother Dani would show sympathy to her plight was just that, remote. All she could do was try to sleep the pain away and hope that sooner or later, a chink of opportunity would appear for her to execute her next move.

The warm evening breeze rippled the stained net curtains which hung loosely at the small window. Everything was silent—no movement, loud voices or thrashing about from her rogue brothers. She eventually dozed off.

Rosa opened her eyes and tentatively unfurled her body until a twinge brought her back to reality. She sat up and lit a candle on her bedside table, her face partially illuminated by the small yellow flame.

Although she had just woken, shades of her beauty could still be detected as the flame flickered in the dark room, catching her big brown eyes.

Rosa yawned then began to pray quietly.

Dear Lord, please make this day better than yesterday.
Bless me, heal me and show me the right way.
Give some light in my life.

She made her way out of her room, listening for any movement from Dani.

She tip-toed down the stairs, trying not to make the floorboards creak.

She nudged the door open. Still nothing. She put her head in, her eyes trained towards the sofa. In the dim light, she could barely make out the shape of her brother.

'Dani?' she said quietly, switching on the light to reveal her brother sat stiffly on a chair.

He was holding his bare torso tightly. His plate of food was in front of him, hardly touched, just a few bites taken out of the stodgy potatoes. The only movement came from his eyes as he looked up and glared at her.

'Dani, what the fuck?' she screamed, shocked at seeing her brother paralysed and doubled up in pain.

She knelt in front of him. Dani shivered uncontrollably and sucked in his breath.

'You need a doctor. Get checked at a hospital—you're in a lot of pain.'

Dani shook his head defiantly, responding through gritted teeth.

'Can't.'

A cold sweat had formed on his clammy forehead.

'You have bad injuries,' she pleaded.

Dani remained stoic, shaking his head, his eyes bulging with both fear and menace as if to warn his sister who was in charge.

'I'll go and get some medication,' Rosa decided.

Dani rolled his eyes; he was in no position to argue, but he grabbed her wrist tightly.

'Let me help, Dani. I must go.'

She snatched her arm back, knowing for once she had the upper hand.

Rosa went back to her room and scrambled around for her clothes. She was surprisingly calm as she dressed. She shrugged off her own pain and anxiety, switching back into her usual selfless sister mode.

She threw on a pair of jeans and a red vest top. She rubbed her face. Her tiny mirror reflected a tired face with dark circles under her eyes from the lack of sleep.

Rosa was about to leave the room in haste, then suddenly stopped.

Wait!

Hang on, what am I doing?

Rosa, this is it, this is your chance, this really is!

I must call Daniel.

She turned back and searched frantically for Daniel's card. This was an ideal opportunity to contact him again. She picked up her tatty jean skirt and the card fell to the floor. She picked it up, stuffed it into her pocket and went back downstairs.

'Dani, I need money,' she said, poking her head back into the front room where Dani was attempting to rise from his seated position.

He struggled and motioned for his sister to give him assistance, but Rosa just stood and watched.

Look at him the big baby, he can't do nothing without Jesus or me.

I'm sorry but it's my time now.
Time for me to have a life.

Dani groaned loudly, frustrated by his pain and restriction. He pushed his hand into his pocket and took out a crumpled, bloodied twenty-pound note, which he dropped feebly onto the floor.

'Hurry . . . the . . . fuck . . . up,' he spoke through gritted teeth, slowly levering himself back onto his chair.

Rosa picked up the money and turned to leave. As she reached the door, she looked back at Dani.

Adrenaline flowed through her. She felt for her brother, leaving him under such conditions.

Hate what I'm doing but it has to be done, now or never.
If Jesus comes back then I'm trapped forever.

I feel sorry for Dani even though he's been a complete bastard.

Rosa took a deep breath. Her heart ached, but she knew the time was opportune. She closed the door, leaving him alone in the room.

She charged out through the back door into the yard. At the gate, she stopped to vomit, puking nothing but liquid and spit. Her heart pumping harder than ever, the weight of leaving overwhelmed her.

Rosa took a few seconds to compose herself. Holding her chest, she wheezed and spat until her breathing was under control.

Once she'd closed the gate, she did not look back but marched purposefully towards the parade of shops.

Ahead of her was clear. Again, no youths or barking dogs to annoy and intimidate her, although she could hear boisterous laughter and shouting from the inner sanctums of the estate.

Rosa walked as quickly as her feet would take her, the pain in her back throbbing with every step she took. The world was spinning around her. She could not focus. Everything seemed to blur into a collage of colours—bright white beams from the oncoming cars which raced along the roads, the orange street lights and splashes of light from shop windows.

Oh, fuck, I've done it, can't breathe.

Just keep walking.

Keep going.

Rosa managed to reach the mini supermarket. Her mouth dry, out of breath and sweating, she paused before entry to consider her options. Staring vacantly, she dug his card out of her pocket, clutching it tightly in her hand.

Rosa took a deep breath before stepping into the store.

'I need the phone?'

She barely kept her cool. When she stretched out her hand offering the bloodied note, the shop assistant behind the counter gave her a weird look.

'You again?'

He looked down at her.

'Problem?'

Rosa leant onto the counter, the crumpled note in her hand.

'I just need to make one more call. Here, you can take the money.'

The shopkeeper looked down at the bloody money, pushed the note back into her hand and took out his phone. A relieved Rosa took the phone.

'Don't worry, the number is already on here—' the shopkeeper scrolled through his phone screen '—from last time.'

'Come on, pick up.'

Rosa was impatient. Daniel's phone just rang.

'Daniel, pick up, please.'

After a few more seconds, Daniel picked up, sounding half asleep.

'Hello.' His voice was a deep croak.

'Daniel, it's Rosa. Come and get me now! Please, come now, come now!'

She became hysterical, raw emotions flooding her system. The shopkeeper watched on with concern on his face.

Daniel sensed the urgency in her voice and suddenly sounded wide awake.

'Come where? What's happened?'

'I am here. I've escaped. Come now, please!'

All control was lost. Her hand shook as she held the phone to her ear.

'I am here, please!'

'OK, stay calm, on my way,' Daniel shouted back.

She could hear him shuffling around in the background before the phone cut off.

Rosa collapsed into a heap on the counter. The shopkeeper ran to the fridge and took out a bottle of water.

'Here, take this.'

He handed the water to Rosa, who managed to lift her head. Her face was drained of energy but filled with fear. Her eyes welled up with tears. She took the bottle, opened it and took a large gulp.

'You want me call the police?' the shopkeeper asked.

Rosa shook her head.

'No! Please, I'm OK, everything is fine.'

She handed him back his phone.

It seemed like forever. Rosa was sat on the steps of the launderette, sweat dripping from her face and drizzling down her neck. She was weak and hot, and her mind was all over the place. She questioned her sanity, and her eyes could barely stay open. She felt dizzy and blacked out, flopping down onto the pavement.

A few minutes later, the smoothly-contoured super car screeched to a halt outside the launderette. Daniel stepped out to see Rosa's limp body in a heap on the floor.

'Rosa? Shit, babe!'

Daniel bent down and lifted her head; her eyes had rolled back.

'Hey, Rosa, wake up.'

He was dressed in a Nike tee shirt and tracksuit bottoms, and for once his immaculately slicked hair flopped down over his face.

'Come on, let's get you up.'

He carefully placed his hands under her arms and pulled her up into a standing position.

They were about to leave when Rosa regained partial consciousness.

'Daniel, wait.'

She could hardly speak.

'Call an ambulance,' she whispered.

'Why, what's wrong? Are you OK?' He checked her over for damage.

'It's for my brother. I will explain later,' she replied in a tired, breathless tone.

Daniel swept his hair back, looking as confused as ever.

He put Rosa into the car then took out his phone and dialled the emergency services number. He passed the phone to Rosa, who answered with what seemed like her last bit of breath and energy.

'Ambulance to 23 Crofton Court, urgently,' she wheezed before cutting off the phone and handing it back to Daniel.

Daniel looked at her.

'Let's go!' Rosa pleaded.

Then she passed out again in the seat of the car.

Chapter 5
Bleeding love

Something felt different. When she finally opened her eyes, there was an unaccustomed feeling of comfort. The bed she lay in felt unfamiliar yet nice, warm and very snug. She did not want to move.

Rosa's eyes began to focus. Everything was bright; she could make out sharp shards of sunlight slicing through blinds. Her head felt heavy. All she could see was bright, clean, heavenly light as if she were in a beautiful dream.

A familiar voice soothed her out of her slumber.

'Good morning, sleepyhead.'

Rosa turned her head to see a clean-cut, smartly dressed Daniel sitting on the edge of the bed like a godly figure shrouded in the glow of morning sunbeams. Rosa was startled, moving away as the realisation kicked in.

'It's alright, sweetheart, you're safe now,' Daniel continued, his voice caring and chirpy.

Rosa looked around, feeling the bed and the duvet. She tried to sit up until the pain in her back reminded her of the long ordeal she had endured.

'Daniel, what's going on?' she asked. 'Where am I?'

Her voice trailed off.

Oh my days, I have to go!

She tried to get out of bed, but the piercing pain shot through her back.

'Relax,' Daniel reassured her. 'You're with me now.'

He moved forward to stroke her hair. Rosa flinched, her eyes unsure, connecting with Daniel's ice-blue eyes.

Rosa recoiled, dragging her knees up to her chest.

'What have I done?'

She buried her head into her quilt-covered knees.

'Look, you told me to come remember?'

Daniel was trying his best to be the reassuring, compassionate man she knew, and his tone was sincere.

'Stay here for as long as you want.'

Again, he was very affable and caring.

'I've made you a cuppa.' Daniel smiled, raising a white mug towards her.

Rosa looked up and around the room; she could not fathom what was happening.

This can't be real, I'm here?

Shit feels weird.

His place was like something out of a lifestyle magazine—big, clean, warm and contemporary. His taste was obvious. Her eyes were now wide open, looking at every detail.

This is amazing.

It's like a show home, so much better than our crappy place.

It smelt nice, fresh and welcoming.

She moved to the edge of the bed and tried to get up, but the pain in her back kicked in again.

'You OK?' Daniel asked.

Rosa looked at him.

'Yes, just have a bad back,' she replied, giving it a rub. The enormity of her actions began to set in.

'Wait,' she said. 'I called you . . . you came?'

'That's right,' Daniel replied, excited that her memory was beginning to surface.

He took her hand and looked into her eyes.

'Everything's OK now, you lemon.'

He injected his usual chirpy charm into the taut situation, giving her that bright all-star smile.

'Drink your tea,' he whispered, stroking her hand.

The whole thing felt surreal. She squeezed Daniel's hand. She could not understand how she was feeling—a mixture of guilt, confusion and surprise.

Rosa looked around the room again, viewing the nice arty pictures hung on the wall. Tall green plants stood in black onyx pots; a large flat-screen television was mounted on a wall at the end of the bed. She was like a child in a fairground, totally enchanted by her new surroundings.

'Nice place,' she muttered, laying her head on Daniel's hand. 'Could do with a woman's touch, though.'

She'd redeemed her long-lost sense of humour. Daniel chuckled.

'Rosa, I have to go to work for a bit. My sister, Leah, is here downstairs. She'll look after you until I get back. I'll just get her.'

Rosa looked up at him.

Sister?

He never mentioned any sister before.

Her face cringed in trepidation.

'Trust me,' Daniel again reassured her. 'It's all good—she won't bite.'

A few minutes later, Daniel returned with Leah. She was a female version of Daniel, slightly younger, a year or two older than Rosa, tall, fit, toned body, well dressed, flowing dark hair; her face was fresh, make-up flawless, and she seemed happy to see her.

Wow, she's gorgeous.

Rosa attempted to fix herself by sweeping her hair back from her face.

'Alright, babe, I'm Leah. Heard loads about ya.'

She breezed in, totally unperturbed. She came across as genuine, bearing all the signs of someone who looked after themselves.

Stretching her manicured hands towards Rosa, she pulled her into a warm embrace. Rosa was hesitant but welcomed the hug, something that was alien to her, and awkward, too.

Leah's fresh, sweet fragrance caught Rosa's nostrils.

'Hi,' she muttered shyly, her head bowed slightly. She felt out of her comfort zone, but seeing Daniel smiling at her, she knew that she was safe.

Rosa looked up at Daniel and smiled.

'Thank you.'

'I'll be back in a few. Leah will get you anything you need.'

Daniel came towards her and hugged her. Rosa at first resisted. She was still shy, but Leah reassured her.

'It's alright, babe.'

Her cockney accent was like her brother's but with a smokey husk.

'Hungry? I'll fix you some breakfast.'

It was overwhelming for Rosa. She was not used to this sudden role reversal.

Whilst Leah was in the kitchen making some food, Rosa took the liberty to have a snoop around. She was amazed at the size of his apartment. Everything looked new. It was also exceptionally clean, especially for a man— the total opposite of her brothers.

Rosa gazed through the large windows. The view was of beautiful green leaves from large trees, a small stream that twinkled as the sun reflected on it and perfect, lush, mown lawns.

It was peaceful and in complete contrast to her world. She gazed around for what seemed like an age, motionless and numb.

Did I really do it?

Don't even know what to think it's crazy.

Hope Dani is OK, he was really in a bad way but I had to leave, couldn't take anymore.

Things had not quite sunk in yet. She was free. Finally breaking the chains from her cruel brothers. Rosa expected to feel a wave of exuberance and liberation, but all she felt was guilt. She knew that Dani would suffer the same fate as Jesus, and even if he did deserve it, she could not help but feel responsible.

Rosa's thoughts were interrupted by a breezy Leah.

'Hey, Rosa, I've got some fresh towels and clothes. You can take a shower, then we'll eat,' she said with a broad smile, handing her the items.

It was such a difference from having Jesus screaming at her and abusing her. Leah seemed so different, kind, confident and self-assured.

Rosa stood under the large chrome shower head. Hot water sprayed over her body, invigorating her. It really felt as if she were washing away the stains of her past as the soapy suds drained through her toes into the plughole.

This feels so nice, it's like the best shower in the world!

Fruity scents wafted from the expensive-feeling toiletries assembled on the clear glass shelves in front of her.

Rosa massaged the base of her back, allowing the hot water to work on the sore spot. She felt a strange kind of peace, but although she had finally escaped the misery she called life, she was burdened by a nagging feeling that she was still not completely safe.

She let the water run through her hair and onto her face, knowing that she was free. She never thought a day like this would come and was still trying to come to terms with how freedom felt.

'Rosa, I'm back.'

The voice of a chirpy-sounding Daniel came bellowing through the apartment. Rosa afforded herself a chuckle as she sat on the bed, wearing a white, fluffy towel robe, with her hair wrapped turban-style in a towel. It was so comfortable and a nice change for her to be treated. She felt like a queen.

There was a gentle knocking and Daniel pushed the door slightly ajar.

'My little diamond, you decent?'

Rosa's heart leapt every time she heard his voice and knew that he was near. All the time she'd spent dreaming about this situation had now manifested into reality.

Daniel poked his head around the door.

'Are you in here?' he asked playfully.

Rosa shyly recoiled back onto the bed. She was a bit embarrassed that he would see her in a bathrobe, but at the same time, she was happy that he was back.

'Hello,' she responded, quietly grabbing the collars of the robe, holding them together.

'How's my little diamond?' he asked, letting himself in before putting one hand over his eyes playfully. In the other was a massive bouquet of flowers.

'I'm OK,' Rosa responded quietly.

Rosa remained numb to all that was happening. She felt as though any minute she would forfeit this dream for a nightmare and again be in her tiny room hearing her brothers causing mayhem downstairs.

Daniel came towards her smiling, that clean set of white teeth shining as brightly as the sun which beamed through the slits in the blind.

'Can I sit?' he asked politely, pointing beside her on the bed.

Rosa nodded in agreement. Her face lit up looking at the beautiful flowers.

Daniel placed his tall frame next to her. She giggled, touching the tightly wrapped towel on her head.

'I look silly.' She laughed, putting her hands over her face in embarrassment.

Daniel took her hands and slowly peeled them from her face.

'You look beautiful, like these,' he said softly, pointing to the flowers.

'I'm gonna make you the happiest girl in the world,' he continued, his cockney charm blossoming.

Rosa stared dreamily back into his blue eyes.

He is so handsome, such a sweet man, nobody has ever bought me flowers before.

She knew he was serious. The gentle way he touched her hands and the sincerity in his voice. She knew he was a different type of man to her brothers.

'I feel . . . lucky,' she said, her voice was barely audible.

Daniel squeezed her hand tighter.

'No, ya lemon, I'm the lucky one.'

He laughed, then delicately touched her face.

'I knew that the moment I saw you,' he continued, sounding as soppy as a lovesick pup.

'You came for me,' she muttered, still in disbelief.

Daniel leant forwards to embrace her. The two hugged, his sharp, clean scent and her fresh, fruity showered aroma fusing.

A cherished moment for both before Rosa felt a twinge. 'Ouch.'

Daniel let go quickly.

'Am I squeezing too tight?' he asked with concern.

'No.'

She smiled reaching round to her back.

'My back is sore.'

She laughed, seeing Daniel's frightened expression.

'We'll get that seen to.'

His tone became serious before he saw the funny side, too, and placed his hand on her back, rubbing gently.

'Did you eat?' he asked.

'No, but Leah made some food.'

Daniel stopped rubbing and stood up in front of her.

'You get dressed and eat and I'll put these in a vase.'

Again, Daniel took control. He was confident and more than hospitable, which left Rosa in awe.

Later that evening, Rosa got dressed in some of Leah's clothes, which she adored. She thought Leah had good taste and could not stop staring into the mirror and stroking the nice texture of the materials.

Rosa was still uncomfortable with her surroundings; it was a new world for her.

So this is it.

A new life away from those two.

I have to make this work with Daniel, no way will I ever see them again.

Hope Dani is OK.

Feel bad leaving him like that, but he was becoming like his bastard brother.

She knew there could be no going back.

Rosa's moment was interrupted by Leah's slightly cockney accent.

'I admire you; you're a brave and beautiful girl.'

Leah stood in the doorway armed with a compact, silver make-up case and a bottle of white wine. Rosa turned to her shyly.

'You think so?' She humbly bowed her head and clasped her hands behind her back.

Leah strode forwards.

'Yes, my darling, and tonight you're getting a makeover.'

She walked over to Rosa, taking her hand and gently leading her away from the mirror to the bathroom.

'Makeover?'

Rosa looked confused but smiled and followed Leah.

'Yes, babes, we are having a girly night in and this is what I do. Beauty.'

A series of giggles and Leah's overexcited chatter could be heard coming from the room. It sounded as though a small party was happening, but only two people were in attendance. For once, Rosa was crying with joy rather than pain, unable to laugh anymore due to the ache in her cheeks. The strong smell of nail polish and perfume punctured the air with an acute fusion of alcohol.

Daniel poked his head around the door to view the shenanigans.

'Oi, oi, what's going on in here then?'

He was smacked in the face by the stunning beauty of Rosa.

'Oh my days,' he stuttered, spacing out his words. The shock hit him square in the jowls.

Daniel stood mouth ajar, looking on in awe.

'Well, bruv, what do you think?' Leah quizzed, standing back to admire her work and raising her glass of wine to her mouth.

Rosa giggled, tipsy from the wine. She had never been big on alcohol but was also giddy on happiness. She looked stunning even in her state of flux; her jet-black hair flowed down to her shoulders. There were kinks, curls and an added sheen that glistened under the bright spotlights from Daniel's bathroom ceiling.

Rosa's face was perfection. Her olive skin was smooth and clear, her brown eyes finally sparkled, with a hint of innocence that lured Daniel, and her lips were plumped and glossed.

'Speechless,' he uttered.

Rosa smiled coyly, again looking to Daniel for some form of approval. For the first time, Daniel was stumped, rubbing his eyes.

'Stunning—what can I say? Hat's off to the beautician, too,' he said, still reeling from shock.

'She scrubs up well,' Leah confirmed, squeezing past Daniel and out of the room. 'Guess that's my cue. I'll leave you two lovebirds to it,' she remarked and made her exit.

Daniel walked towards Rosa with his hands outstretched. He was totally enchanted.

'Stand up for me, princess.' He motioned Rosa towards him.

She stood up, tilting back slightly, attempting to catch her balance after the effects of her wine. Again, she giggled but this time more out of nerves than humour.

In admiration, Daniel stood to attention like a proud soldier on parade.

'May I?'

He pulled her in close to him, and Rosa's heartbeat intensified. She was sucked in by the emotional vortex of this heady moment.

Whoa!

My head feels light, did he just call me princess?

Oh my God.

Be calm, be calm, my heart's gonna explode.

Daniel leaned in and placed a soft, tender kiss on her freshly moistened lips. This sent a tingle of electricity which ignited an explosion of emotions through her body. She could not even respond except to smile sweetly once she had reopened her eyes.

'I'm gonna take care of you,' Daniel whispered.

Rosa mouthed the words, 'I know,' before they kissed again and embraced tightly.

Rosa gasped as she buried her head into Daniel's chest.

Chapter 6
Lock diddy

A damp, musty stench hung in the air. Loud voices could be heard hollering in the background before the jangling of keys and the sharp piercing of a whistle cut sharply across the moans and raised voices.

'Lights out, you horrible bastards,' a prison officer bellowed through the cavernous wing of Didcourt Remand Prison.

Loud bangs could be heard as the inmates, like captive apes, hammered on the metal doors of their cells.

Jesus sat motionless on the cold concrete floor of his single cell, next to a blue sliver of a mattress and a tiny silver toilet bowl. His bony frame bore deep purple and black bruising to his arms. His greasy hair dangled messily over his face, partially covering his hollow, sunken eyes.

The back-and-forth shouting between inmates continued until he was plunged into darkness. Jesus remained in the same position, eyes focused on a slit of light from underneath the door to his cell. He inhaled deeply, growling as the tension built within him.

These bastards treat me like an animal.

What happened to my immunity?

My crime protection program?

I'm going to kill Dani.

It's his stupid shit why I'm here.

Those fuckers set us up ... Franky and his bastard gang.

The sound of a loud bell clanging repeatedly signalled daybreak in the old, characterless building. Again, raised voices of other inmates rising echoed through the corridors. Jesus was still sat coiled up, knees to his chest, head bowed to the floor. He shivered uncontrollably in the drafty cell, sniffing like a hound on the hunt.

The letterbox-sized metal flap slid back harshly.

'Up, you piece of shit. Shower then breakfast in thirty minutes!'

The frothy mouth of an overexcited screw barked through the small partition like an army drill officer, shaking Jesus into action as the bolt was pulled back on the door.

He extended his long body into a standing position. He looked tired and drawn, yet still angry. His reddened eyes peered like a wolf through the strands of his straggled hair.

A queue of male inmates stood in line waiting to enter the clinical, white-tiled showers. Jesus waited—towel slung over his shoulder and holding a plastic pack of toiletries—surrounded by brawny, hardened men. He felt a forceful push in his back, hard enough to make him stagger forward into another inmate.

'Come out the way, skinny fucker,' boomed a deep, gravelled voice in his ear.

Jesus spun around to see a huge, imposing figure.

Shit, man.

Chocolate brown, large afro hair, scars embedded in his skin, the tracks of inked tattoos like ivy around his arms.

'Da fuck you looking at, fam?' he snorted back at Jesus, who, for a second, was about to answer but instead chose to screw up his face then turn back to face the queue.

Fucking crazy, man, I don't need this.

Once again, but this time with excessive force, he felt another blow to the base of his back, sending him flying against the man in front of him, causing the rest of the inmates to cheer and roar as Jesus, along with his towel and toiletries, landed sprawled out on the floor.

A posse of inmates darted in like a hungry pack of hyenas, picking up items of Jesus's toiletries, then turning to kick him violently on their way back to the queue. There was a chorus of cheers while Jesus curled his body up, trying to protect himself from the blows.

'Enough now, screws are coming.'

The order came from the intimidating ringleader.

'Get up, pussy.'

Again, the deep, dark, gravelled tone boomed in his ear. Jesus looked up to see the wild afro hair and scarred face with large, bulging, brown eyes glaring down at him.

Jesus got to his feet, nursing the pain in his back. His white vest was now covered with dirty marks from the kicks he'd received.

'Get in line behind me, dickhead,' the inmate snarled, before a couple of hardened, robotically moving prison guards arrived on the scene.

'Get in order, get showered and get to the mess hall or you'll all miss breakfast!' one of the guards barked viciously in the direction of Jesus, who, by now, was cowering in line before shuffling behind the rest of the inmates into the shower room.

Time crept by. It seemed like an age had passed, yet the large old silver clock which hung above the tables in the dining mess hall showed it was still early in the day.

Jesus sat alone at the end of a long table, picking at his lumpy excuse for a bowl of porridge and raisins which looked like dead cockroaches. For once, he felt intimidated and confused, his ego and body bruised.

The turn of events over the last twenty-four hours still spun around in his head. He was in such a strange position for someone who was usually the dominant force in his arena. Jesus's mind tried to piece together the sequence of events from the meeting at Franky's club.

How did I end up here?

Dani trying to be the big man, where did the pigs come from?

Franky's always been cool, don't understand, it doesn't make sense.

He wrestled internally, pushing away the bowl of mushy oats.

Jesus rested back in his chair as the throbbing pain in his rib area reminded him of the ongoing ordeal he faced. He stared around at the other inmates—grown men, hardened, bitter, hollowed—troubled, maybe, by the indicative reflection of his own crooked journey.

Jesus's train of thought was interrupted by a scrawny, nerdy-looking inmate, his face covered in red, blotchy patches, hair thinning and wearing large-rimmed circular spectacles.

'Best to stick together,' he whispered, picking at his lip nervously.

Jesus scrutinised him.

'They're out to get us,' he said, flicking a piece of skin into the bowl of porridge, much to Jesus's disgust. 'They told me to warn you,' he giggled nervously, looking around and scratching his flaky arms.

Jesus leant forward to confront him.

'First of all, who the fuck is you?' he hissed, squinting his eyes.

'Nozza,' he responded, repeating his quirky giggle and picking at his arms. 'Stormtroopers are coming, told me to warn you,' he repeated, his pitch increasing as he carried on twitching, scratching at his arm viciously until beads of blood appeared.

Again, he turned around to look at the other inmates.

'Do you like Star Wars?'

'I don't.'

His blunt response did nothing to dampen the enthusiastic Nozza.

'Chewbacca wants me to warn you.'

Nozza continued to babble, followed by an itch and a twitch. He was jittery, fidgety and frankly annoying. 'Want that?' Nozza pointed to the uneaten, stodgy bowl of porridge.

'Nah,' Jesus responded coldly, inviting Nozza, who slid the bowl in front of him.

This dude is fucking loco and he's making me feel sick.

Nozza began eating it with his hands, smudging the porridge over his face, licking his hands and stuffing the lumpy gruel into his mouth.

Jesus sat back. He could only watch until Nozza began laughing hysterically, leaning forwards looking like a baby who had just eaten a pureed dessert.

'Obi-Wan said Chewbacca tells you this.'

Nozza spat the contents of his mouth at Jesus, splattering it all over Jesus's chest.

Nozza ran away, stumbling through the mess hall's obstacles of tables and chairs, screaming, 'Stormtroopers are coming, haha.'

The claps, cheers and whistles of the other inmates left Jesus steaming and stewing.

Fuck this prick!

I need to get out of this fucking madhouse.

Jesus stood up, wiping the spewed porridge from his dirty vest. He was incredulous and embarrassed, kicking the chair over as he moved away from the table.

He took the vest off, revealing his skeletal torso. He looked a state—flushed and full of bruises.

As Jesus slinked off towards the exit, he was approached by a screw—a short, stocky, rugby player type with the sleeves of his shirt rolled up around his chunky arms.

'Go get yourself cleaned up, lad, then hit the yard for some exercise,' he instructed in a broad Northern accent.

The exercise yard was a bleak landscape of grey asphalt, concrete, high walls and barbed wire. Even the sultry summer weather could not lift the harshness of the surroundings. It was no holiday camp, perhaps more of a draconian concentration camp. Around thirty men milled around in the yard, while some sat around in huddles, smoking.

Jesus emerged wearing grey tracksuit bottoms and a white tee shirt two sizes too big. Alone, he skirted around the periphery, kicking the small gravel pebbles under his feet. He tried not to make eye contact with any other inmate. He stopped and stooped down onto his haunches, resting his back against a wall.

Jesus stared ahead, reflecting, still upset with his brother, whom he blamed for getting him into this situation. He crossed his arms, holding in the pain from his sore ribs.

His mind went back to the night at Franky's, the madness that ensued.

Set up, man. I know we was set up.

Why would the pigs know where we were?

Fuck Dani and his stupid deal.

How we gonna get rid of all that coke?

Franky's a snitch I swear.

He shuddered as the flashbacks played out in his mind. His peace was disturbed by the crunch of steps on the gravel coming towards him.

A dark shadow appeared over him, blocking out the sun's rays. Jesus looked up to see a looming figure outlined by afro hair. The bully from his earlier altercation.

'Nozza told you I was coming ... Chewbacca.'

He stooped down next to Jesus, chuckling. 'That's what they call me—must be the hair.'

He ruffled his afro whilst spitting a large ball of phlegm onto the floor.

'Franky. Dat's my guy, he gave me work.'

Jesus observed him. Suddenly it dawned on him that he was not safe. Even inside, Franky was stalking him.

'Look, my brother—he's young, he made a mistake—'

Jesus began to reason before a blow to his eye socket caused his head to crash against the wall like a squash ball against the backboard of the court. Jesus's frail figure slumped to the ground, and everything went black and silent.

Rusty metal creaked as the letterbox-sized flap was opened. A loud voice could be heard shouting above all the other din.

'Jesus Chavez! Get your arse up, boy!'

The voice sounded like a sergeant's command. Jesus was curled up on the small, thin mattress, covered by a grey blanket. He sported the biggest, blackest, swollen eye, which protruded from his thin, weasel-like features. He squinted as he looked towards the small gap in the metal door.

'Come on, boy, not got all day,' the chargehand squawked.

Jesus groggily picked himself up from his seated position, spat blood out onto the floor and wiped his mouth as if he was wiping away the disdain he felt for the orders barked at him.

Jesus looked skinnier than usual, while the bruise on

his face, a memento of his rugged journey, had weathered in the last few days.

As the door swung open, Jesus was manhandled by the burly officer and handcuffed.

'Come on, ya bag of bones, time to go home,' he growled, dragging Jesus along the dimly lit corridor.

Jesus remained silent. Only a wry smile gave an insight into his mood. His eyes were cold as he was escorted out of the cells and into the processing room where another intimidating chisel-jawed guard was waiting with an uncompromising scowl.

Jesus was calm and stepped towards the desk.

'You've been released, Chavez.' His voice was husky and cracked. 'Here are your things. One gold chain and two beaded bracelets.'

He held up a clear plastic bag.

'Sign here.'

Jesus looked directly at him, screwing up his face with discontent.

'Sure,' he rasped sarcastically, holding up his wrists for the guard to unlock the handcuffs before taking the pen and scribbling on the form.

'Get him out. Dirty piece of filth,' the guard barked, shaking his head.

'Have a nice day, fuckers,' Jesus retorted, before making his exit.

The hot, sticky air was a welcome change from the musty atmosphere of a prison cell. It was bright and sunny, causing Jesus to cover his eyes as he took his first steps of freedom.

'See you soon, Jeeesus.'

The burly guard could not resist a cheap verbal shot as Jesus strode away from the prison. He did not respond or acknowledge the guard's parting words but just smirked.

Not in this lifetime, pricks.

Jesus's face was hardened and battered from his recent battles.

He looked back at the dark, Gothic building in the distance before continuing with his long walk back home. He was still fuming, ready to seek retribution on Dani and Franky.

Chapter 7
Blossoms

This was the first time Rosa had been away from her hovel of a home. It was so peaceful and different to what she was accustomed to. She sat up, her eyes wide and bright, staring at the large flat-screen television which was mounted on the wall.

This is so much better than that crappy fuzz box—everything is so vivid.

She excitedly flicked through the infinite channels. She was like a child—her eyes glued to the screen—giggling as she watched the cartoon characters while Daniel took a shower.

She was comfortable now, relaxing on a large cushion. She felt as if she were in a different world, lounging in bliss. Her back was finally feeling a lot better after a visit to a specialist and some medication. It had now been a few weeks since her escape and she was beginning to feel at home.

Daniel emerged, whistling happily, wrapped waist-down in a white towel. His hair was wet and slicked back. Rosa looked up to see his half-naked body glistening, stood almost over her.

Holy shit, can he get any sexier?

She averted her eyes quickly back to the screen, trying to hide her obvious fascination.

'Hungry, babe?' he asked casually, wiping the excess water from his forehead. 'Was thinking of going out for a bite to eat.' Rosa shifted nervously before looking up at him.

'OK, yes,' she answered, her excitement suppressed into a nervous smile.

'Well, I'm glad you said that. Hope you don't mind, but I've bought you some stuff.' Daniel reached out his hands to help her up.

Rosa gulped, her heart beating fast.

Stuff?

She got up from her relaxed position, not sure how many more surprises she could take.

'What did you get?' she asked playfully, following close behind him. The scent of his fresh deodorant wafted into her face as she checked out his lean yet defined physique.

They entered the walk-in closet together. Daniel stopped and turned around to face Rosa, his chest still glistening with water.

'Hold up, close your eyes.' Daniel reverted to his cheeky playfulness.

Rosa giggled, like a little girl giddy with happiness. She closed her eyes and placed her hands over her face, then Daniel took her hand and led her.

A large cream box tied with a red silk ribbon and a gold shoebox also tied with a silk ribbon were sat on a chair.

'Open up!' Daniel shouted excitedly, ushering her over to the items.

'Daniel, what is this?' She looked at him with disbelief in her eyes.

'All for you, babe,' he said, pulling her gently.

Rosa screamed with excitement. 'Daniel, no.' She peeled the silk ribbon off the box.

I love surprises, I can get used to this.

Daniel stood back, folding his arms and watching proudly. Rosa lifted the top from the box, revealing a beautiful red dress nestled amongst soft white tissue paper.

'Oh,' she gasped, setting her eyes upon the expensive-looking garment. 'Daniel, no way! Why?' She hugged him tightly, her arms wrapping around his bare torso.

'Hey, it's OK.' He managed to get out his words before being engulfed in a hearty hug. Rosa stepped back.

OK, calm down, girl, on the realisation of her tight clasp around Daniel.

'Take it out. And the shoes,' he continued, quite excited himself, before Rosa turned around again, grabbing the shoebox, this time ripping the ribbon off then lifting the top off the box.

'These are beautiful.' She feasted her eyes on the shimmering crimson-red high-heeled shoes which were packed neatly.

These are so cool, he has taste.

It was the nicest gesture anyone had ever made for her. She turned to Daniel, who stood back looking chuffed with himself, watching an ecstatic Rosa. She already looked gorgeous, her dark tresses flowing down onto her shoulders, her face a picture of joy.

'I don't know what to say . . . thank you,' she gushed.

'Well, try them on and get dressed coz I'm hungry,' he said, walking out of the room to give her privacy. 'See you in twenty minutes.'

Rosa sat on the chair, running her hands over the soft, silky material. She picked up the dress and walked towards a large mirror. She held it against her body, gasping when she saw her reflection.

This is so gorgeous, oh my Lord!

She spun around in a dizzy, exuberant twirl before getting dressed. Once again, she stood in front of the mirror, transformed. She placed her hand over her mouth in awe of seeing her beautiful figure snugly fitted in the dress. She let out a nervy laugh.

Looking good if I say so myself.

Mama, can you see this?

She noticed her perfectly formed Latina curves accentuated in the right places.

The shoes fitted perfectly and made her feet feel as if they were standing in the softest feathers. Rosa toddled up and down, trying to get her balance in the high heels and continued checking herself out.

Wow.

Well look at you, Miss Rosa.

I can't believe how good I look.

Daniel knows how to make a woman feel good and sexy.

I'm impressed by his choices it's like he knows me so well already.

A knock on the door interrupted her one-woman fashion show.

'Rosa, are you ready?' Daniel's voice was playful. Rosa froze as she stood fixing herself, becoming hot and taking deep breaths.

OK, breathe, relax.

'Yes, come in.' Her voice cracked anticipating Daniel's entrance.

Daniel pushed the door open and put his head in, with his eyes closed. 'I'm not looking yet,' he mocked. He entered wearing fitted grey jeans and black Gucci loafers complemented with a white open-necked shirt.

Rosa held her breath, standing confident and regal. 'Open your eyes, Daniel,' she ordered, exhaling calmly.

Daniel slowly opened his eyes. 'Oh . . . my . . . God!'

Rosa shyly looked up at him. 'Like it?' She felt fidgety and awkward.

Daniel took a step towards her, shaking his head, admiring the smoking beauty. 'Have to take a picture for my Instagram.' Daniel took out his phone and swiped on the camera. 'Stay just like that. You look amazeballs,' he joked.

Rosa chuckled—she loved his cheeky language—before composing herself as Daniel snapped away.

'Let me get a selfie for Leah.' He stepped beside her and posed, holding the phone in the air. Daniel stepped back, casting his eyes at Rosa. 'Come here, let's have a proper look at you,' he said, continuing to admire. 'Gorgeous.'

'I know I have said this before, but thank you, it's too much,' Rosa said in a hushed tone. She smiled and her perfect set of white teeth was revealed for the first time in a long while.

'Let me get another pic of you.' Daniel, still excited, pulled out his large-screened smartphone.

Rosa giggled, shyly blushing, whilst at the same time fixing her hair to make sure she looked good for the shot.

'Oh, just one more small surprise.' Daniel was loving his moment, lavishing gifts on his beautiful diamond.

'More?' Rosa looked confused.

'Yep, just one more, I promise.' Daniel moved towards Rosa. 'Close your eyes, babe.' His voice softened as he stepped around her. He stood close behind her and lifted her hair gently.

Rosa felt his hot breath dance on the back of her neck.

What else has he got?

She felt the coldness of jewellery around her neck. 'What's that?' she asked.

'Just a sec,' Daniel answered, stepping away. 'Now open.'

Rosa opened her eyes and stared into the mirror. 'No, Daniel, no!' Her breath was taken away by a dazzling diamond necklace. Rosa touched the sparkling accessory. 'Too much. No, I can't,' she protested, before being interrupted by his hands around her waist.

'Got the earrings to match as well.' He pulled out a small black velvet box from his inside pocket. 'Put them on.'

Rosa was taken aback but she loved the fact he spoiled her and did as she was told, placing the beautiful diamond earrings into her earlobes. 'Daniel, no.'

Daniel put his finger gently to her lips, hushing her. 'What's the point of having all this if I can't treat you as well? . . . Selfie time!' He broke into laughter, placing his arm around her. 'Yeah, babe, one more of us both.' He hugged her tighter. 'Right, ready to eat? Let's hit the road.'

'Wait.' Rosa looked deep into Daniel's blue eyes, which sparkled back at her. 'This is amazing.' She leaned in and planted a soft kiss on his lips 'This is loco, crazy!' She stepped back, rubbing the lip gloss from his lips.

Daniel smiled back then took hold of Rosa's hand, leading her out of the room.

Outside the flat stood a gleaming, bright-red Mercedes with shiny chrome alloy wheels.

'Your chariot awaits.' Daniel ushered her towards the beautifully crafted vehicle.

'What! Where's the other one?'

'I own a luxury car showroom, duh!' he joked, unlocking the door with a remote key which made a high-pitched beep.

Daniel walked around to the passenger side and opened the door for Rosa like a true gentleman. She smiled at him adoringly. Her facial expression finally exuded happiness as she slid into the comfortable leather seat.

'*Gracias,*' she politely replied, looking up at her tall knight of a man.

Daniel looked smart, but she was attracted to him for more than his obvious riches—it was more for his kind, caring aura. Daniel sat in the driver's seat.

'Hope you like Mexican food,' he quipped, his pearly-white smile spread across his handsome face.

Rosa laughed as she tried to stay cool and enjoy the comfort of the car.

They cruised along the River Thames towards the London Bridge area. It was a sight to behold under the clear evening skies with the lights from the various iconic London landmarks shimmering in the distance, a blanket covering the calm ripples of the famous old river. Rosa sat quietly taking in the view.

This is the London I dreamt about, it's beautiful.

The sound of Dua Lipa played through the speakers. Daniel was focused on steering through the busy streets until he took them to a quiet backstreet courtyard.

'Here we are,' he said calmly as they pulled into a vacant parking space.

Rosa looked around inquisitively. All she could see was an old brown-bricked building with large arched windows. She fixed her dress, ready to step out, while Daniel the gentleman ran around the car to open her door. 'Are we here?' She smiled, no signs of her back pain, as she rose elegantly to her feet, looking as beautiful as ever.

'Trust me, you will not be disappointed.' Daniel held her hand, tenderly pulling her towards him.

Rosa's brown eyes looked deep into Daniel's. She was nervous but excited. She knew Daniel would have something special up his sleeve. Inside, she felt like a kid at the sweet shop. All this treatment was so far removed from anything she had experienced and it felt as if she had won the lottery.

If Jesus and Dani could see me now. I am a woman not a maid.

They walked side by side around the back of the building then up a black cast iron spiral staircase which led to a converted rooftop terrace. It was spectacular—polished wooden flooring and pastel pink, blue and orange hanging lanterns which swayed slightly in the warm evening breeze. The smell of seasoned food drifted past their nostrils, a panoramic view of London surrounded them.

Rosa's breath was taken away, especially when she saw that there was only one table set up in the middle of the floor, surrounded by plush cream sofas. The table was decorated with a crisp white tablecloth, white candles and silver cutlery.

A smartly dressed waiter stood by in a white shirt with a black waistcoat and matching trousers. Rosa stopped in her tracks and covered her mouth when she realised that this was all set up for her. She looked at Daniel, who simply held her hand tighter, squeezing it with calm reassurance.

'Mr Daniel.'

A loud, booming voice interrupted their developing intimacy. A short, stout, Mediterranean man with a thinning, swept-over hairstyle, in a black open-necked shirt showing his thick gold chain and medallion, came rushing towards them.

'Geraldo.' Daniel stepped forwards to greet him.

'Welcome, Daniel. And this must be the beautiful Rosa.' He grabbed Daniel's hand and shook it vigorously before stepping back to admire Rosa. 'Such a delightful pleasure to meet you,' he said, bowing in front of her.

Rosa smiled, watching the little bundle of energy bowing down in front of her.

'Come in, please.' He clapped his hands and scuttled towards the table.

'Daniel, all this?' Rosa gushed, genuinely shocked at the thought Daniel had put into the evening.

'I told you this is it now, you're my little diamond who

deserves it all.' Daniel winked at her. He was obviously chuffed with his efforts.

Rosa nudged him playfully, smiling back and feeling like a princess. This was something straight from the pages of her tatty gossip magazines she would read at home.

'How do you know these people?'

'I know a few people through my job.' He smiled as he poured some prosecco for Rosa and himself. 'Let's toast to a beautiful evening, me darling.' His voice was calm with a hint of his cockney lingo. They clinked glasses then took a sip. 'Hmm, that's bang on. Do you like it?' he asked, watching Rosa's face contort at the taste.

'I'll have to get used to the taste of alcohol—' she stuck her tongue out, 'and the bubbles.' She laughed, shaking her head.

'Are you ready for starters?' The ever-accommodating Geraldo ushered the waiter over.

'Hungry?' Daniel asked.

Rosa, still too overwhelmed to answer, nodded.

'We'll start,' Daniel assured the waiter, who bowed politely before retreating to the kitchen.

Rosa instinctively got up from the table and walked over to the balcony to check the view, the light wind fluttering her dress as she held onto the metal rail. She took a second to inhale the warm air and survey the night skies, her diamond necklace and earrings sparkling as they caught the light from the lanterns.

Unbelievable, everything is just amazing.

He has done all of this for me, what a special man.

I could never go back to them two, this is what I have prayed for.

Mama and Papa would want this for me wouldn't they?
Am I disloyal?
No!
I deserve this, yes, I deserve all of this.

Rosa returned to the table and took her seat, a little emotional as she took Daniel's hand.

'Ahh, don't get upset, my little diamond.' Daniel winked at her and rubbed her hand as Rosa choked up. 'It's OK.'

She composed herself. 'This is the best feeling I have ever...'

Daniel shook his head. 'Don't be silly. I've wanted to do this for ages. Now I have you, I can do it,' he responded with a big smile.

The evening progressed smoothly. Rosa became more comfortable in her surroundings, and the fine Mexican food was accompanied by good conversation. Rosa was educating Daniel on how she used to cook burritos with her mother as a child. She found it refreshing that she and Daniel could talk so open and intimately. This type of conversation was so alien to her, but there was not one ounce of hesitation on her part.

Rosa spoke freely, telling Daniel about her father's involvement with the drug cartel which led to the slaughter of her parents and how she came to London under the crime protection program. She felt ready to finally open up to someone as chilled as him, although she did hold back from telling him about the rape and pregnancy. As the evening drew on, she found herself falling more and more for Daniel's charm.

Daniel was also chatty, telling Rosa that he'd taken over the business from his father, who'd retired early and moved to Spain with his mother. 'I was always a young entrepreneur,' he continued, swishing round the last mouthful of his prosecco. 'Leah was always the creative one.'

Geraldo, as usual, was all smiles as they prepared to leave. 'Wonderful evening?' he asked, looking towards Rosa.

'*Sí, gracias,*' she replied as he kissed her hand.

'Beautiful princess. Take care of her, Daniel,' he boomed whilst giving Daniel a strong handshake.

Daniel embraced Geraldo. 'I owe you one, mate,' he replied, patting Geraldo on the back.

'Yes, a Bugatti!' Geraldo responded with a hearty laugh. 'My pleasure. Hope to see you again, Rosa.' He blew a kiss towards her as they disappeared down the spiral steps.

A tipsy Rosa, arm in arm with Daniel, toddled towards the car. It was still a lovely, balmy evening, the moon shining brightly in the clear sky.

'Daniel Rosewood,' Rosa slurred, with a short hiccup. She made it to the passenger door and turned to face Daniel. 'All of this for me?' she touched her dress and ran her fingers along her new necklace, which glinted every time she moved.

Daniel stood listening to her. He wore a satisfied smile, knowing his plan had been executed without a hitch. 'Yes, babe, for you,' he whispered.

Rosa gazed deeply into his eyes before dragging him forwards and burying her lips into his face. Daniel responded to the full-on kiss. As cool as he was, his heart pounded as the rush of passion rose through his being. Daniel placed his hands around Rosa's waist, gripping her tightly, pulling her into his body, their tongues intertwined.

Rosa pulled away, swooning, dizzy, catching her breath. 'Very nice,' she responded, resting her forehead against his.

Oh my gosh, what is happening here?

This is so crazy.

Daniel put his arms around her and they stood together in silence for a few seconds, letting the moment sink in.

The only good thing Jesus ever did was send me to that launderette.

Daniel tilted Rosa's head, kissing her tenderly again. After a few seconds, she pulled away.

'How come you were there?' she asked, leaning back onto the car.

'Where?' Daniel asked.

'The bloody launderette,' she slurred.

'Was looking for a new premises plus machine broke,' he replied.

'Me too.' Rosa laughed. 'Crazy coincidence—I'm glad,' she said, attempting to subdue her giddiness, her head still woozy.

'Time to get you home.' Daniel took charge, as he always did, by opening the door and helping Rosa into her seat.

When they arrived at his apartment, they bundled their way through the door, still inseparable, kissing, fumbling and giggling their way into the bedroom. Rosa kicked off her shoes, losing her balance and falling onto the bed, only to be caught by Daniel who laid her down gently on the quilted mattress.

Rosa clung on tightly, placing her arms around his neck and pulling him down on top of her. They devoured each other, kissing deeply. Rosa panted, taking a breather as Daniel began to move down to her neck. He was caring and tender, taking his time to dot his lips towards her chest calmly and seductively. Rosa writhed with pleasure—this was the first time she'd felt her body tingle with excitement. It tickled but sent waves of intense feelings dancing through her.

'Wait a sec.' Daniel paused, struggling to take his shirt off without having to interrupt the flow.

They continued their deep-kissing marathon in between polite whispers and compliments. Rosa's head spun—she was dizzy from the tonic of love and not just the prosecco. She could feel Daniel's excitement growing down below as he pressed harder on top of her. She closed her eyes.

Is it wrong for me to be enjoying this?

I want him so badly.

His hands wandered all over her body, squeezing her bum then stroking her thighs, rolling her on top of him. He knew what he was doing, giving her no time to compute the last touch to the next.

Rosa opened her eyes. Now on top, she looked down at Daniel, who was sweating, flushed, shirt open, revealing his waxed chest.

'Why'd you stop?' He looked up at Rosa, breathless, wiping the sweat from his forehead. Rosa, still radiant in her red dress, looked down at him.

Her eyes sparkled with passion as she confidently finished unbuttoning Daniel's shirt, popping the last few buttons slowly. There was a calm silence, interrupted only by their heavy breathing.

I am in control now, Mr Daniel.

She smiled down at him; he reciprocated in satisfaction and surrender. Rosa pulled his shirt apart, revealing his sculpted torso. She stroked his pecs, running her fingers through the wispy black hair around his nipples. Daniel closed his eyes as Rosa continued to rub softly, her confidence growing.

She stopped again. Daniel opened his eyes, watching as she unzipped her dress from behind. He lay quietly in voyeur mode, his eyes fixed on his subject. Rosa stood up on the bed, slipping out of her dress and revealing her white lace underwear. Her sexy figure, which until now had been understated, revealed full, pert breasts, accentuated by the gleaming jewellery, and delicious legs.

'Come here, you little stunner,' Daniel ordered, eager to savour some more, stretching his hands out towards her.

Rosa now lay beside him. Daniel was naked except for his boxer shorts. He smothered her body with kisses while reaching out and cupping her breasts. Rosa gasped at his touch, surrendering herself, her shyness evaporating at each touch. Rosa felt wanted, desired and emancipated all at the same time. Led by his hunger to please, he continued to lick and kiss her inner thighs, pulling on her knickers and moving his lips between her legs.

Rosa's body trembled and her mind exploded.

Oh, shit, this feels so good.

What's he doing to me?

Daniel boldly foraged towards her vagina, pulling her underwear to the side, slipping his tongue inside her.

'Ohh, huh.' Rosa let out a surprised groan as she felt his tongue begin to stroke her moistened pussy lips.

She gripped his head, grinding her hips as a million scintillating sensations rushed through her body.

Holy fuck, wow, oh my God.

Breathe, Rosa, breathe.

Daniel became more aggressive, thrusting his tongue up and down her clit, forcing Rosa to clamp her legs tightly around his back.

'Ohh . . . shit, Daniel!' Rosa shrieked, gripping harder and pulling his hair as he continued to work his mouth and tongue deeper into her without pausing. He had momentum and rhythm, working her up to the point where she began to shake uncontrollably, her lips curling. 'Yes, ah, ha,' she panted, twisting her body.

Oh, shit.

I'm gonna explode. I'm really gonna . . .

Jerking, spasming, until she finally came for the first time, much to her and Daniel's delight.

Holy shit.

Oh my God that was amazing.

Oh, wow.

Rosa flopped from exhaustion.

Daniel pulled himself up, taking a deep breath and wiping his mouth. 'Enjoy that?' he asked, feeling pleased with himself.

Rosa was still trying to compose herself. 'Yes,' she answered, pulling him towards her, kissing him passionately.

Daniel maneuvered his body into her, nestling his manhood between her legs. His lean body felt strong up against her.

'Daniel,' she uttered. 'I want you.' Nibbling on his ear, she stroked his face, looking up at him with glassy doe eyes, her cheeks flushed with the blood rush of her exertions.

'Are you sure?' Daniel questioned. 'Just that I don't wanna rush ...'

His response was cut short by the feel of Rosa's hand rubbing his bulge as she forced her hand into his boxers.

'Yes, silly.' Rosa broke into a giggle watching Daniel's surprised face. She could feel him becoming even more aroused.

'OK, well...' He gulped. 'Give me a sec.' Daniel hopped off the bed, disappearing into the en-suite bathroom.

Rosa removed her bra, throwing it onto the floor, leaving her topless except for her new piece of bling which nestled neatly on her chest. Rosa took a deep breath and closed her eyes, awaiting Daniel's return. She could hear him shuffling around and opening cabinets.

Why's he taking so long?

Her body was still tingling with excitement from the last bout.

Daniel reappeared, his frame silhouetted as he walked towards the bed. 'Hey,' he whispered.

Rosa turned towards him, stretching out her hand. 'Hey,' she replied. 'What's up?'

Daniel sat on the side of the bed, stroking Rosa. He slid himself next to her, causing her to budge up to make room for him. 'Thing is, babe, I can't find my Johnny's.' He kissed her tenderly, cuddling up to her.

'Johnny's?' she replied. 'What's that?'

'Protection, babe. We don't want babies yet, do we?'

Rosa began to laugh once she'd figured out what he was talking about. 'No! It's OK, we have time for that,' she replied, before smothering him with more kisses. 'Just hold me until I fall asleep.' Daniel did as instructed, spooning her until they both drifted off.

Chapter 8
Cruel summer

Jesus sat on the step in his backyard. The summer heatwave showed no signs of abating as the temperature reached oven-like proportions. His face still wore the remnants of his recent tribulations—patchwork bruising down half of his reddened cheek. He puffed hard on a cigarette.

This is a mess, man.

Whole shit is a mess.

His expression was stuck in serious mode. After his time in prison, Jesus's mood was one of complete fury, his mind ticking and mulling over his next move—although you could never tell from his stone-faced veneer. He continued to draw hard before flicking the butt of the cigarette to the side.

Can't sit around doing nothing, this is bullshit.

He wiped his sweat-coated face with a red bandana whilst blowing smoke through his nostrils, then got up and dragged open the gate, exiting into the road. Wearing baggy jeans and a crumpled tee shirt, he wandered through the narrow alleys of the estate. His skeletal frame was hardly intimidating, yet his menace was apparent.

He arrived at a set of concrete steps which led down to the garages where most of the gangs of youths congregated. He could hear music and laughter, and the pungent smell of weed mingled with the humidity. Fearlessly he stepped towards the group of ten or so youths who were hanging out in the shaded bowels.

'Oi!' Jesus bravely walked towards the huddle. 'Any of you lot seen my sister or brother?'

The youths turned towards Jesus and all stared him down.

'Nah, fam, not seen dem,' one of them with tall, twisted locks and sleepy eyes replied.

Jesus approached the group, sneering as usual. 'You sure?' he asked again, confrontational in his stance, rubbing his nose vigorously. 'Dani, you know him . . .'

The tall youth interrupted him. 'Fam, we know him *and her*. The peng ting. Cute, still.'

Jesus shuffled closer as a raw nerve was struck. 'Fucking have some respect.' He edged closer, his height dwarfed by the tall youth, yet no was fear shown. They eyeballed each other for a few seconds before the tall youth broke into laughter.

'Come on, fam, we from the same ends; ain't no beef here.' He placed his hand on Jesus's shoulder, only for Jesus to shrug it off aggressively. 'No beef, man,' he repeated, backing away.

'Dickhead, I'm from Sinaloa.' Jesus threw up a gang sign with his hand before slinking away towards the stairs.

He stopped, turning back towards the group. 'I've got iPads, phones, new lappies and coke if anyone's interested.'

The youths all looked back at him, shaking their heads and laughing him off.

Bunch of pricks.

He gave them the middle finger then skipped up the steps.

Jesus continued his quest, walking through the concrete maze in the heat. Sharp shards of light cut through the pillared blocks of flats. Jesus's long shadow projected onto the pavement.

He walked out onto the main high street and along the parade of shops, eyes still squinting from the direct rays of the sun. He wandered without a plan, just searching for anything—a sighting, a clue, a glimpse of either of his siblings through the smatter of people around him.

He randomly brushed and bumped into anyone, scowling—*out my way motherfuckers*—his inner frustration boiling over each step he took.

An Olympic-sized swimming pool shimmered under the bright sun. The aqua-blue water reflecting the sky above was interrupted by the heavy splashes and chops from a hulking swimmer thrashing his way to the end. A modern, white detached house surrounded by tall, leafy trees overlooked a large garden where a couple of sun loungers were parked close to the edge of the pool.

Franky emerged from the depths. His shorn, peroxided head thrust out of the water and his sculpted, tattooed body leant onto the concrete edge. He drew himself out of the pool and sat on the side.

Lying on a sun lounger was a slim, tanned young man wearing tight red swimming trunks and shades, cooking in the heat like a sausage on the barbecue. He looked like a teenager—no more than twenty.

'Oi, soppy chops, you should get in. Fucking mustard, that.' Franky scooped some water from the pool and threw it at the young man, wetting him.

'Fuck sake, Franky, it's gonna streak my tanning lotion.' The young man sat up in shock as the cold water hit its target.

Franky elevated himself from the pool, laughing and walking towards the loungers. 'Budge up, you little tart.' He bumped the young man to the side, pushing his wet body up against him.

'Such a cunt, Franky, seriously.' The young man straddled his legs over Franky's muscular torso, pulling him close until he was fully covering him. His lean, sweating body slithered over Franky, who responded by clutching him tightly before kissing him passionately.

They began to writhe aggressively, enjoying the clinch for a few minutes. Franky's big arms squeezed the young man's body into him before grabbing his hair and pushing his head down towards his crotch.

'Get down there and suck me off,' Franky ordered.

The young man pulled down Franky's wet shorts exposing his groomed crutch and penis then plunged his mouth onto it. Franky let out a groan, still gripping his head and forcing him to bob up and down.

'That's it, boy, nice and slow.' He steadied his head, lying back and twisting his face while the young man worked his mouth.

A mobile phone rang loudly, interrupting Franky. He sat up, still keeping his hand on the young man's head as he continued to be pleasured. He stretched over to the other sun lounger, picking up the phone and answering the call.

'What?' Franky's voice was strained, wavering as he struggled to contain his obviously aroused state. 'The slimy bastard! Keep eyes on him and get Jasper to pick me up in an hour.' He dropped the phone onto the lounger. 'Go on, boy, just like that.' He let out a deep growl, jerking and gyrating his body as he climaxed, holding the young man's head in place until he finished, his toes curling tightly. 'Fucking 'ell.' Franky contorted and twisted, his reddened face sweating bullets before relaxing back onto the lounger.

The young man raised his head, wiping his mouth with a smirk. 'Enjoy that?' he asked, fixing his shades back onto his face.

Franky offered no response and just sat up, his face barely relaxing from the contorted expression. 'Was alright,' he responded, standing up stark naked. 'Wait here till I get back.' He grabbed the man's face, kissing him sloppily before pushing him aside and retreating to the house.

'Such a prick,' the young man whispered under his breath before diving into the pool.

Jesus sat alone at a table in the chicken shop. He devoured the last of his meal, gnawing on the remains of a drumstick.

Wait till I find that little fucker.

He spat the remains of the bone back into the cardboard box, then slurped down a can of Coke. The street was busy with people strolling lazily in the heat. From the corner of his eye, he glimpsed Dani amongst the assortment of pedestrians out enjoying the sun.

Look at that, there he is.

Dani's appearance was different—his head was shaved, revealing a stitched gash. He was slimmer than before. He was clutching his ribs and limping, trying to navigate his way through the crowds of people.

Jesus jumped up, slamming the can onto the table and darting out of the shop in pursuit of his brother. He broke into a short sprint, dodging any oncoming human obstacles as he homed in on Dani. 'Where the fuck you been?' Jesus pulled hard on Dani's shoulder, spinning him around.

Dani turned towards his brother, ashen-faced even in the heat. 'Ugh, ow! Fuck, be careful, man!' he exclaimed, toppling off balance.

'Da fuck happened to you, man?' Jesus looked at Dani, seeing that he, too, was battle-weary and bruised.

'Rosa. She snitched and left, Bro,' Dani spluttered.

Jesus grabbed him unmercifully by the throat, Dani's eyes nearly popping out of their sockets as the pain riddled through him. Jesus stepped in nose to nose. 'Left where?' he shouted into Dani's face, tightening his grip, fury coursing through his body.

Dani summoned enough strength to escape Jesus's clutches. 'I don't know. Swear down. Jeez, man. I've been in hospital, questioned by the pigs.' He stepped back, crouching and holding his side. Bystanders watched on as the two continued to squabble.

'I've been in prison! Beaten by Franky's gang,' Jesus shouted back frustratedly, raking his fingers across his scalp.

A black BMW X5 was parked across the road. Three men sat inside watching the two continue their public display of disaffection.

One of them, who was sporting dark shades, placed a phone to his ear. 'Guess what, boss? Got 'em both in sight.' He grinned and a golden tooth glinted in the sunshine. 'Cool, say nuttin.' The man cut the phone call, continuing to watch the two bickering brothers. 'Follow them. Franky wants his coke back. Do what you have to.'

Jesus and Dani continued with their very public squabble, unaware that they were being watched.

'Let's go home; we need to sort this shit out,' Jesus commanded, storming off and leaving Dani stood in a painful, sweaty stew, once again under the tyranny of his brother.

They continued with their petty back-and-forth bickering as they entered the estate, completely oblivious of Franky's knuckle-dragging henchmen, who were hardly camouflaged against the background of the harsh brickwork.

Jesus smashed through the backyard gate and into the house, spitting incoherent verbal fire. Dani stopped short of entering, allowing himself a few seconds of reprieve—

sucking up some air and bracing himself for the imminent onslaught.

Jesus paced up and down amongst the entangled electrical wires and devices which were strewn on the floor of the front room. Dani watched on. He looked pasty, literally wilting under Jesus's wrath.

'You've put us in the shit trying to play the big man. Fucking Tony Montana, huh!' Jesus remained rampant, thrashing around, arms flailing, kicking a box containing tablets and phones. 'This is us, fucking jewellery and devices. Not drugs!'

'It was a mistake!' Dani replied, scrambling around picking up the devices off the floor.

Jesus lashed a kick towards Dani, just missing his face, stumbling onto his knees in eyeline with Dani. 'Crazy! This is crazy, and where is Rosa?' He grabbed Dani, his face contorted with anguish, unaware of both Franky's men lurking in the kitchen, watching.

'OK, enough of this pantomime.' One of the men clapped his big paws sarcastically—tall, dark-skinned, broad, a pirate's earring hanging from his lobe. The other man, shorter but no less stocky, munched loudly on a packet of Doritos crisps.

Dani and Jesus both jumped back with fright, shocked by the intrusion.

'Surprise! Guess what we want?' the tall one said, smiling in their direction. There was another loud crunch from his crisp-eating accomplice.

'Wait a second.' Jesus sprang to his feet, his bony arms held up in surrender. He stepped forwards again, stumbling over the debris. 'We're gonna give it back. It's cool, ain't it, bro?'

Dani remained on his hands and knees, his eyes towards the floor.

'Dani, tell them it's cool. We'll give back the coke.' Dani began to cough, hunched over.

'Ain't got all fucking day, mate,' the shorter man blurted whilst throwing his empty crisp packet to the floor and licking his fingers clean.

'It's gone,' Dani whimpered, much to the shock of Jesus, who began to laugh nervously, staring back at the two strangers.

'He's playing. Bro, just get the shit.' He turned to his brother.

Dani remained static, barely raising his head. 'Flushed it when the ambulance came—thought it was the pigs.' His voice was hushed.

'Nah, he's just joking.' Jesus tried his best to inject a sliver of humour whilst dragging Dani up from his crouched position. 'Come on, Bro, get the coke, man.' His voice quivered with hesitancy, looking back at a dejected, jabbering Dani.

'I panicked . . . thought Rosa . . . my sister called the pigs. She left me alone . . . I was scared,' a sorrowful Dani continued.

Jesus took a deep breath, shooting Dani a look of hatred. Dani stared back, his eyes welling with tears.

'Enough of this fuckery.' The tall henchman's voice cut through the already taut atmosphere. He moved towards them. 'Either he's lying and trying to bump us or telling the truth—which is it?'

Dani shuddered; he had disintegrated into a nervous wreck. 'Please, man, we'll pay him back, I swear, I'll . . .'

Before he could finish his sentence he received a sharp, powerful jab to his jaw, which sent him tumbling back over the jumble of boxes.

'Right, mate, you've got ten seconds to find the shit,' he snarled in Jesus's direction. Jesus gulped. He looked back at Dani, who was lying in a heap groaning.

'I dunno, man. I mean come on, I knew nothing,' Jesus pleaded, as the shorter cohort began to go through a series of stretching exercises, flexing his sizeable muscles and grinning ominously as he stepped in his direction.

An hour later, a groggy Jesus came back to consciousness. His eyes could barely open; everything around him was a fuzzy haze. 'Dani, urrgh . . . Dani.' He crawled around, barely navigating his way through the debris of plugs, devices and cables. He was finally able to focus. The room had been ransacked, furniture and boxes strewn everywhere.

Jesus started to panic, breathing heavily. His mouth tasted of blood. He attempted to drag himself into a standing position, but the pain in his ribs and torso paralysed him to the point where he could only raise his head. 'Dani!' he screamed, before collapsing, too weak and fragile for any further effort.

Chapter 9
Beautiful nightmare

Four streaks of bacon sizzled in a frying pan next to another saucepan which contained a couple of eggs in boiling water.

Rosa was in her element, loving the large, clean, spacious kitchen while she cooked breakfast for Daniel. She was beginning to find her feet, enjoying her role as a girlfriend and getting used to her new home. Rosa sang along happily to the Latino pop music which played through the radio. She loved playing house—it was in her nature to look after others. She knew that Daniel would be out of the shower soon and wanted to make sure he had a good breakfast before his day at work.

It had been a couple of months now since she had started living with Daniel. It was a totally different life from anything she had ever experienced. Daniel was caring, funny and hardworking, and she understood how he had reaped his material rewards. She loved his home and enjoyed keeping it clean for him. She also loved his athletic body, especially in bed. She afforded herself a smile as she recalled some of their most intimate moments. It was a major adjustment, and she still spent a lot of time alone, although Leah had been to see her a few times to help her settle in.

Daniel finally emerged, fixing a blue tie around his collar. 'Something smells good.' He looked fresh and smart as usual.

'Morning.' Rosa smiled, her face exuding happiness and energy. 'Sit down, I'll get you some tea. How many slices of toast?' She busied herself serving his food and pouring some hot water into a teapot.

'Was thinking, babe. There's an annual automobile award thing coming up,' Daniel said, still adjusting his tie as Rosa brought over his plate. 'Let's go together,' he continued. 'You up for it?'

Rosa brought the teapot and sat down.

I love how normal we are.

This is what I imagined my life would eventually be like when I came to London—having breakfast with a handsome Englishman, very civilized.

Daniel tucked into his food whilst Rosa poured the tea.

'Yes, I am up for it,' she responded, attempting to mimic his cockney twang.

'Cool, I'll take you shopping, get you a lovely new dress. My diamond has to shine.' He smiled, winking at her as he crunched on a piece of toast.

He really is too much, always thinking of me.

Rosa smiled back, taking a bite from her toast.

'What are you thinking?' Daniel asked, reaching over to touch her hand.

'Nothing.' She giggled. 'Just happy, that's all.' She squeezed his hand back. Daniel smiled at her and continued to eat.

Most days, Rosa filled her time watching cheesy lifestyle programs on the giant TV. She also loved sitting in the garden. It was so peaceful. She used this time to scroll through Daniel's iPad, viewing all the latest celebrity fashion stories. She was fascinated by how her idols dressed, especially her favourite, J. Lo. She imagined she was one of the hosts on the American TV show called *Fashion Police* where they discussed all the celebrity red-carpet events.

Another thing she enjoyed was that she could search for things from her home country and keep up to date with everything that was happening in Mexico. Her thoughts sometimes flitted to her brothers, especially Dani. She hated leaving him like that in such a vulnerable situation, but there was no going back. This was now her new life. With Daniel.

Daniel had bought her a nice mobile phone, the latest iPhone. He always called Rosa on his lunch break, and today was no different. They usually spoke for ten minutes. He always made her feel special and, most importantly, secure.

Rosa had just finished their call when she heard the intercom for the front door. She made her way to the monitor and saw Leah on the small screen, waving. Rosa pressed the entry button to let her in. She looked forward to her visits; they afforded her some company and a good girly catch up.

Leah breezed in, looking every inch a summer flower,

wearing big chrome shades, an off-the-shoulder, floral maxi dress and sunflower flip-flops.

'Hiya!' she screeched, her face flushed from the heat.

'Hola!' Rosa responded.

I love her dress, she has such style.

'It's baking out there. I dunno how much more of this heat I can bloody take!' she said, her bubbly personality shining as usual.

'Are you hungry? I can make you something to eat?' Rosa offered.

'No, I'm OK, thanks,' Leah responded. 'I did bring a little bottle of ice-cold wine, though.' Leah took the bottle out of her designer tote bag and marched into the kitchen. 'I'll get some glasses and we can sit out by the stream.'

Leah and Rosa sat at a wooden table just shaded by the overarching trees. Leah poured some wine as Rosa basked in the sunshine, watching the stream shimmering in the golden rays.

'Cheers!' Leah raised her glass towards Rosa. 'I love a cold glass of wine in the sun. Reminds me of being in Spain with my mum,' Leah reflected, swallowing the cool liquid.

Rosa smiled, not quite used to wine matinees.

'Wanted to ask you something, Rosa,' Leah continued.

Rosa turned her attention towards her, shielding her eyes.

Strange. What's she gonna ask me?

'Of course, what is it?' Rosa replied, whilst taking a tiny sip of her wine.

Leah put down her glass and removed her shades, staring directly at Rosa. 'Could you tell me a bit more about what happened with your brothers? I mean Daniel mentioned a few things . . .'

Rosa did not react, but she was shocked by Leah's directness.

What's with the questions? I like Leah but I'm not sure why she's digging.

Rosa took another sip. Leah leant forwards and touched her hand reassuringly.

'It's OK, babe, I'm not prying.'

Rosa took a deep breath. 'My brothers treated me bad, like a slave, since, well ... my parents were ...' She stopped, her mind searched for the right words. 'It's been tough. A lot of things happened in our life ... they changed a lot.' She didn't falter, keeping her emotions in check. 'This is so different for me. Daniel is different,' she mused, whilst gesturing at the garden.

Leah nodded in agreement, her eyes still searching Rosa's. 'He's different alright, and he loves ya to death. Just asking, you know. So, what're your plans?'

Rosa again became slightly agitated by the question, but she kept her cool. 'My plans? Maybe go to college to learn about fashion or cookery. I love cooking,' she responded and then lowered her voice. 'Maybe get married in the future, I don't know. Still getting used to all of this.'

'Sounds good, babe,' Leah championed, fanning herself with her hand. 'Fashion or cooking, yeah? Good options. So, tell me about Mexico—is it nice? I've seen pics online; was thinking of going to Cancun with some of the girls.'

Rosa got up, taking her wine glass with her, and walked over to the stream. She took a moment to gaze into the water. 'Mexico is beautiful. It's ... home.' There was a tinge of sorrow in her tone. She turned and came back to her seat.

Leah went to pour more wine into her glass.

'No, it's OK.' She put her hand over the top of the glass, stopping Leah. 'We grew up on beautiful land—trees, some goats, chickens.' Her eyes smiled at Leah. 'My father worked hard. He was a farmer, a good man. We were all happy . . . those men changed it all,' Rosa reflected, downing the rest of her wine. 'Cancun is lovely. Lots of gringos.'

Leah placed her shades back on her face. 'Bloody baking. Don't remember a summer like this ever.' She held the bottle to her forehead. 'So, marriage, huh? Don't think Daniel has ever thought of that yet.'

Rosa smiled.

Gosh, calm down, love. I'm not trying to marry Daniel tomorrow.

'Eventually, it's every girl's dream, no?' she countered.

'Sure, just curious.' Leah offered a fake smile, gulping the rest of her wine.

Late afternoon arrived, yet the temperature had not cooled. Leah left to fulfil a beauty appointment, and Rosa lay on the bed feeling drained from a mix of the heat and the wine. She knew Daniel would be home shortly, so she took the opportunity to have a quick siesta. Her mind was racing after her conversation with Leah.

Bet Jesus is still on the warpath.

He will kill me if he ever finds me. Dani, too.

I wonder if he recovered from his injuries.

Hope he knows what I did was for the best.

No regrets, right?

Daniel is such a sweetie.

I must repay him for what he has done—kept his word.

He's the diamond not me.

Love Leah but she's like the pigs, so many questions, she's over the top.

Rosa yawned then lifted herself from the bed.

Come on, Rosa, time to get ready. Daniel will be home soon.

Daniel chatted incessantly between mouthfuls of beef stew and potatoes. He was excitedly reeling off the news of his nomination for Car Showroom of the Year by the body of Elite Auto Traders. 'You know what this means?' he continued, chewing a large lump, filling the side of his mouth. His blue eyes lit with passion.

Rosa dissected her food precisely, fascinated by Daniel's enthusiasm.

'If I win, this puts me on the radar nationally. My showroom will be recognised as a market leader. He continued scraping up the last morsels of his food.

Rosa loved it when he was like this; it made her feel proud. She even found it amusing to see him so animated. His real cockney patter came to the fore, and his face flushed with energy.

'Sounds so good. I know you can win.' She tried to match his enthusiasm, raising her glass towards him.

'We need to go shopping, get some togs for the awards ceremony.'

'Togs?' Rosa quizzed.

'Clothes, babe.' Daniel laughed, wiping his mouth with a tissue. 'That was lovely, babe. I'm stuffed. Gonna have to get down to the gym to work this off.' Daniel reached over and took Rosa's hand, kissing the back of it delicately.

Rosa lay in Daniel's arms on the sofa. Both were relaxed and watching a movie, *Fast and Furious*. Of course, Daniel was a big fan.

Look at him, so engrossed.
He loves all this car stuff.
It's cute.
Hope he wins the award, he deserves it.

Daniel had this thing that he did: rubbing her neck softly any time they were close. Rosa never complained. In fact, it always turned her on. She pushed her body into him, making sure he felt her curves. Daniel responded by moving his hand further down her neck, his fingers stretching to the border of her cleavage.

Hmm, love when he touches me.
I could easily feel like this every day.

Rosa pushed herself further into him.

'Oi, cheeky. What about the movie?' Daniel laughed, distracted from the glow of the big screen.

'The movie can wait.' Rosa turned her face towards Daniel, pining for a kiss, and Daniel duly obliged.

The two became engrossed. Rosa had twisted her body to get more comfortable with the lingering clinch when the shrill call of the door intercom interrupted their moment. They continued to lock lips for a few more seconds until another high-pitched interjection jump-started Daniel into action. He groaned having to pull himself away from a pouting Rosa.

'God's sake, who the hell is that?' He reluctantly peeled himself away to attend to the door.

Rosa exhaled, frustratedly sitting up and fixing herself. 'Who is it?' she shouted.

'It's Leah, babe.'

Rosa rolled her eyes, pissed that her cosy Netflix-and-chill moment had been disturbed.

What does she want now?

Was looking forward to some . . .

Daniel returned, holding up a very drunk Leah.

'Budge up, babe, this one's had a few too many.' Leah's arm was slung around her brother's neck, her skin reddened from a day in the sun. 'Sorry, am I being a raspberry?' She slurred her words as she staggered into the room. 'That'll teach me to drink wine all day.'

Rosa stood up to help. She looked at Daniel, trying to contain her laughter, whilst putting her arm around Leah. 'Come on, Leah, sit here.' Rosa tried to grab her as Leah slumped onto the sofa.

'You must think I'm a right old pisshead,' Leah slurred again, falling back into the sofa.

'It's cool, Sis. We know you love a glass of the old vino.' Daniel sat down next to her, and Leah leant her head on his shoulder.

'I'll make some coffee.' Rosa winked at Daniel, leaving for the kitchen. As Rosa prepared the coffee, Daniel nursed his sister, whose heavy head was still leant on his shoulder.

Daniel turned up his nose. 'Cor, the whiff of you. How many have you had?'

Leah cackled with laughter. 'Too many. Don't know how I did Shauna's make-up.' She hiccupped, continuing to babble away. 'Did I break up a quiet night in?' She looked up at Daniel. The whites of her eyes were bloodshot, the same colour as her cheeks.

'Nah, it's cool, Sis.' Daniel was ever the gentleman.

'Do you love her?' Leah blurted out. 'Rosa.' She shuffled herself into a semi-upright position, leaning heavily on Daniel's thigh. The warm vapours of alcohol were still present. 'She wants to marry you.' She cackled again before holding her finger to her mouth. 'Sssh. Not sure if I trust her though, Dan. Her story is weird. All this stuff about being treated like a slave, dodgy brothers, fink she's a golddigger, Bro.' Leah rambled on, unable to control the volume of her voice.

Rosa had finished making the drinks and was about to enter the room. She could hear Leah's voice and caught bits of what she was saying. Rosa stopped short and waited outside, listening as Leah continued.

'Watch her, Dan, that's all I'm saying. Nice girl, very beautiful, don't get me wrong, but I don't trust her motives. Little Mexican girl, lost, evil brothers? Dunno about all that. I'm just saying be careful, Bro. I care about ya.' She finished her rant by kissing her brother sloppily on the cheek.

Rankled, Daniel held Leah's arms. 'Sis, you're drunk. Talking rubbish. Loudly, too. She'll be back in a minute.' Daniel became serious; a nerve had been touched.

Can't believe this.

Why is she saying all that to him?

Makes sense now why she was asking me all those questions.

What a bitch!

I would never use Daniel for his money, I love him.

Rosa pushed the door open and came back into the room. 'Here you go, Leah. I made one for you as well, Daniel.' Ever the hostess, she handed Leah her coffee.

'Tah, babes.' Leah took the mug with a weary smile as she looked at Rosa.

Daniel, with a mask of embarrassment, reached for his cup.

'Rosa, so gorgeous, *mwah.*' Leah blew a kiss towards her.

Rosa offered a half-smile then retreated back to the kitchen.

'Not having one, babe?' Daniel asked, more of a throwaway question just to deflect from his drunk sister.

'No, I'm taking a shower then getting ready for bed.' Her mood had now clearly shifted.

Rosa lay alone in the bed. She felt hurt but was more vexed at Leah's wild notions about her intentions.

I won't let her or anyone push me away from Daniel or this life.

I don't care about his money.

That's his, he earnt it.

Never about money, it's about him.

He came when no one else did, he could have walked away at any point but he didn't.

He wants me as much as I want him.

Papa always said, 'Loyalty above anything else.'

How dare she ...

Daniel entered the room almost tip-toeing, knowing he was walking on eggshells. 'Babe, you awake?' He spoke in a hushed voice, sitting on the bed beside her. 'God, bloody Leah. Told her to cut down on the wine.' He attempted to inject a little humour. 'She's passed out now. Sleeping like a baby,' he continued, stretching out his body next to Rosa, spooning her.

Rosa reciprocated, pulling his arms around her securely. Daniel kissed her tenderly on the back of her neck, sweeping her hair aside. Rosa shivered at his touch.

'We'll go shopping for togs tomorrow, babe.'

'No! I don't want anything, dresses, shoes, togs, whatever.' Rosa flipped herself around to face Daniel. 'I don't want to be a burden to you or anyone else.' Her tone was stern yet laced with raw emotion which took Daniel by surprise, especially when she turned her back to him.

'Hold up, what's all this about? Burden? Talk to me,' he demanded.

'Talk to your sister!'

'She's drunk!' Daniel snapped back; the first hint of anger surfaced. He continued attempting to turn her around to face him, but Rosa stubbornly resisted.

'Leave me to sleep. Tomorrow I will go.'

Daniel let go. He spun around and sat on the edge of the bed, pushing his hands through his normally immaculately-styled hair, which now looked like a bird's nest. He removed his watch, slamming it onto the bedside table. 'Where you gonna go? Back to them brothers?' He lowered his voice, trying to veil his fury.

His questions were met by silence. Rosa's breathing was the only inkling of her mood.

'Look, babes, Leah loves ya. She's just a bit, you know . . . overprotective.' Again there was no response from Rosa. Daniel took off his tee shirt then lay behind her. He hugged her closely, instigating a slight movement in Rosa. 'Babe, come on, please,' he continued. His charm offensive seemed to work as Rosa turned her body to face him, her eyes glassed over yet restraining the tears from spilling over.

A few minutes passed with no words. They just held each other close, though Rosa still fumed.

Still not happy with Leah.

She acted like a bitch today with her questions.
Then to be drunk and still carry on killing me to Daniel.
She's acting like a jealous sister.

Finally, she broke her silence. 'If you were poor, it wouldn't matter to me.' Her hot breath travelled onto Daniel's face. 'But get it straight, I'm no refugee or poor Mexican girl out for money.'

Daniel pulled her tighter. His blues eyes looked weary as their sparkle dulled. It was an insight into his internal conflict. 'Come 'ere.' He snuggled closer, nose to nose. He could smell Rosa's floral scent and it made his nostrils tingle like smelling salts. 'Diamond, that's why I love ya. I see everything in my future with you. Hopefully, one day, who knows? Marriage, kids . . .' Daniel whispered.

Rosa's breathing increased as she lapped up every word, now calm.

'Let's just call it a night; think we have both had enough for today.' Daniel diffused the tension as he stroked Rosa's face tenderly. 'It's all good, babe.' He kissed her on the forehead then lay down beside her, his facial expression one of relief.

Rosa

Chapter 10
Smashing pumpkins

Daniel mopped up the last of the sauce from his baked beans with a quarter piece of toast. He gulped down the rest of his coffee. 'Got to get the showroom spruced up today—got the competition auditors dropping in.' He sounded excited between swallows.

Rosa sat quietly sipping on her tea, whilst a hungover Leah slowly ate a toasted bacon sandwich.

'Urgh, feel like shit,' she mumbled, barely able to look up as her hair dangled over her face.

'Look like shit, too,' Daniel quipped, as usual, his cheery outlook bearing no reference to the previous night's discussions. 'Rosa, I'll come and get you this afternoon.' Daniel winked and nodded towards her.

Rosa remained cool, continuing to sip her tea.

Hope he realises I meant what I said last night.

Don't want his money or sympathy.

I'd rather survive alone than be somebody's burden.

Daniel picked up his phone and car keys. He mussed up Leah's hair as he went past.

'Ow, Dan, got a headache as it is,' she grumbled moodily.

He then walked around to Rosa, who was still sat with a long face. 'See you at around three, babe.' Daniel kissed her lips.

Rosa hardly responded. She just gave a curt smile. Her eyes were trained on Leah. 'Bye,' she said through pursed lips, barely audible.

Daniel kissed her again on the top of her head, then dashed out of the house into the sunshine.

Leah chucked the remains of her sandwich on her plate. She leant back, her cheeks bulging as she chewed, looking up at Rosa who was still ice-cold, staring into space. 'What's with the face this morning?' Leah asked, swallowing the remains of her food. 'Oh, babe, tell me I didn't say something stupid last night—' she covered her mouth with her hand '—I haven't had a mare, have I?' The realisation finally hit home.

Rosa remained unmoved, but her eyes held a burning gaze straight back at Leah. 'I love Daniel.' She delivered a dead-pan yet passionate reply. 'Not his money; it was never about his money.'

Leah stood up and walked over to Rosa, consuming her with a generous hug, squeezing her tightly. 'So sorry, babe, never meant to offend you. I know you've been through a lot.'

At first Rosa resisted, but she soon began to melt, starting with a huge sigh before wrapping her arms around Leah. 'It's OK,' she mumbled under the suffocation of Leah's enthusiastic embrace.

'Babe, I just wanted to be sure for Daniel, that's all.' She finally let go. Her usually unblemished face showed red patches working their way into her fake tan. She looked at Rosa, fixing her hair. 'State of me. I promise I'm never getting drunk again.' She laughed nervously. 'Sisters for life?' Leah held out her palm for a high five.

Rosa finally broke into a smile and slapped her palm against Leah's. 'Sisters for life,' she responded. But in her mind she knew she had to be careful around Leah, doubting whether she should ever confide in her again.

Rosa

Chapter 11
Franky says

Jesus sat alone on the step of the backyard. The sun was beaming onto his greasy head and the sound of the estate in summer was abundant—pounding bass lines reverberated through the jagged blocks, kids rode and ran up and down the passages shouting and laughing, a football bounced off of the concrete and dogs strained their howls.

Jesus sat in his customary white vest and a pair of blue cut-off jean shorts. His milk-bottle white, boney shins were exposed. He bounced a tennis ball back and forth against the yard wall repeatedly, catching it and tossing it back.

After a few minutes, Jesus stood. He continued bouncing the ball, still brooding and beginning to walk around in small circles, mumbling under his breath. The scrape of his back gate being pushed open alerted him. He paused, picking up a lump of rock from alongside the cracked pavement, anticipating whoever was there. He held his arm aloft, ready to strike his foe until he saw Dani gingerly limping into the yard.

'Fuck sake, man,' Jesus screamed at his crestfallen, injured brother. It was the type of welcome only Jesus could provide.

'Shit, Bro. Scared the crap out of me.' Dani staggered back on seeing his brother lurking, ready to hurl the lump of rock in his palm.

They sat on the ground, Dani in obvious pain, clutching his ribs.

'Twenty-four hours to get Franky's money back,' Dani stuttered, spitting blood from his swollen lips onto the ground; it dried on impact.

'How the fuck we supposed to do that?' Jesus responded, showing no empathy for his brother's painful ordeal. 'We're both dead.'

Dani looked at Jesus. His eyes were tired and bloodshot; his energy had been beaten out of him.

'How much?' Jesus hissed, still tossing the lump of rock around in his hand.

'Five grand for the coke plus another five for the problems I bring.'

Jesus smashed the rock against the wall, infuriated. He stood up. 'Ten grand? This is your fuck up, man.' Jesus lowered his voice as the sound of youths on bikes passed by their back gate.

'Rob a bank?' Dani muttered under his breath, with all the sincerity of a liar.

'Rob a bank? That's the best you can come up with?' Jesus finally stopped moving. He looked skywards, sweat dribbling down his neck, with the sun beaming into his eyes. 'Maybe that's it. We need to go on a spree.' He shielded his eyes and turned back to Dani, squinting. 'Twenty-four hours?' He began to bounce the ball again and walk around in a circle, leaving Dani, head down, spitting more blood onto the concrete.

.

Rosa

Chapter 12
Genie in a bottle

As always, Daniel was on time. In fact, he arrived back home just before three o'clock. Sat in a shiny, silver Mercedes Convertible, looking every part a successful man, he pressed a large navigation screen on the dashboard console. His phone ringtone blared until Rosa's voice came through the speakers in stereo.

'Hi, are you here?' she asked.

'Yes, babe, I'm outside,' Daniel replied, scrolling through his phone as he spoke.

'OK, be there in a sec.'

A few minutes later, Rosa appeared, looking radiant. Her long black hair was slicked into a ponytail, complemented by a bright pink short suit, courtesy of Leah, and a large pair of sunglasses. She stepped towards the car. Daniel, who was still scrolling through his phone, did a double-take when he caught sight of her.

'Oh, wow, look at you.' He started to honk the horn, tooting it excitedly, much to Rosa's embarrassment.

'Daniel, stop!' she shouted, giggling at the same time as she climbed into the car.

'You look stunning, babe. And it's about to get better as the belle of the ball needs a dress.'

Rosa leant over and gave him a long, smoochy kiss. 'I meant what I said. All of this is not what I'm here for,' she said, gesturing towards the car and apartment.

'OK, I get it. Can we go now?'

Rosa smiled, using her thumb to wipe the stain of her pink lip gloss from Daniel's lips. 'In the words of Rihanna, Daniel, "shut up and drive".' Rosa cracked up laughing at her own joke, leaving Daniel shaking his head as they sped off.

Rosa sat comfortably in the leather seat, enjoying the speed-generated breeze as they drove away from the city through beautiful country lanes flanked by lush yellow and green fields.

This is lovely, just what we needed to get away from all of the stuff from the other night.

She glanced over at Daniel through the darkened lenses of her sunglasses.

He's so sweet.

Look at him all excited about this award show.

I really hope he wins.

He deserves something and I know he would be so happy.

Can't wait to see him up there getting all of the praise.

I will stand proudly by his side.

Eventually, they reached a small village about forty-five minutes away from their home. It was quaint and lined with colourful flowers which glowed in the sunshine.

A small stream ran through the middle of the village, and a smattering of people—mainly the elderly and young families—meandered their way through.

'Where are we?' Rosa asked, enjoying her first taste of the real English countryside.

Daniel slowed down and parked next to a small bridge a few hundred yards past a row of boutique-style shops. 'We are in a little place called Rockcliffe. Mum and Dad used to bring us here when we were children.'

They exited the car and walked arm in arm back towards the shops.

'Friend of the family has an exclusive designer shop here. She once made a dress for Liz Hurley. Thought she might have a nice dress for you,' he explained calmly.

'Liz Hurley! English actress. Very beautiful,' Rosa gushed.

Daniel looked at her. 'Well done, babe. How'd you know that?'

Rosa smiled back at him. '*Heat* magazine.'

Once inside, they were greeted by a classy, middle-aged lady by the name of Gwen. She instantly recognised Daniel and greeted him like a son. 'Hello, young man. Look at you!' she said, giving him a motherly embrace.

'How are ya, Gwen?' Daniel responded.

'Really good, thanks. Can't take this heat, though.' She held him but looked past him at Rosa. 'And this beautiful young woman is?' Gwen shared a warm smile.

Daniel broke away, stepping back to introduce Rosa. 'This is Rosa.' He swept his arm away like a matador, allowing her to step forward shyly.

'Hello,' she said quietly.

'Hello, gorgeous.' Gwen stepped forwards and replicated the warm embrace she'd given to Daniel.

Rosa reciprocated, the sweet, floral smell of Gwen's perfume lingering as they separated.

'Gorgeous figure.' Gwen cast her eyes at Rosa. 'We'll have no problem finding something for you,' she continued, taking Rosa by the hand and walking towards the rails.

Daniel sat in a corner playing on his phone. Choosing dresses was not his forte, and the way Gwen had commandeered Rosa meant that it was better he relaxed whilst they selected outfits. Rosa picked several dresses to try on, every so often interrupting Daniel.

'What about this one?' Rosa held a little black number to her chest.

'Lovely, babe, try it on,' Daniel responded, not even looking away from his phone.

Rosa laughed, turning away and heading for the dressing room.

Moments later, Rosa appeared with Gwen behind her, fixing and smoothing the black dress which adorned her body. The dress fitted perfectly. It was an off-shoulder cut with a slit that exposed her olive-skinned leg. 'Daniel, I like this one.' She walked towards Daniel barefooted, catching his attention. He stood up.

A broad smile crept across his face. 'Yep, that's the one.' He walked towards her. 'Let's have a look then.' He took her hand and twirled her around.

He always makes me feel like the only girl in the world.
I love this dress, it's gorgeous.
Just want to make him proud on his big night.

'Gwen, looks like this is the one,' Daniel confirmed.

Rosa turned and hugged him. 'Thank you.' She planted a kiss on his cheek.

'OK, babe. Get changed while I sort things out with Gwen.'

Rosa went back to the changing room, leaving Daniel with Gwen.

'You've done well there, Daniel. She seems nice. Mum and Dad would be proud.' Gwen clasped his hand tightly.

'Yeah, I know. And she is.'

* * *

The big night had arrived—the National Automobile Award Show. It was being held at the glamourous Dorchester Hotel in London. Daniel was in high spirits but busy. His mobile phone was stuck in his hand on speaker as he raced back and forth between rooms, talking to his staff and the organisers of the show.

Rosa sat on the bed. She felt nervous for him and could see that even when he stopped to give her a kiss or ask if she was OK, he was preoccupied with the evening.

'Yes, mate, I'll be there on time, no worries. Lock up shop and bring the keys.' Daniel had just got out of the shower, wrapped in a towel with his phone still in hand, conducting things. His skin was rosy and his hair was wet and flopping over his face.

Rosa was waiting for Leah to arrive to do her make-up. They had less than an hour before they had to leave and she felt she had to intervene, so she got up and walked towards him.

Daniel was still barking down the phone but Rosa

gently took his hand and removed the phone, clicking it off midcall.

'Babe, what you doing?' Daniel half laughed. Rosa touched his face and kissed him gently.

'No more working; this is your big night. Enjoy it and relax.' She took his hand and led him to the bed. 'Come sit down with me.' She ushered him to the bed.

Gonna have to calm him down and I know exactly what to do.

Rosa began to unwrap her towelled robe, revealing her pert, wholesome breasts and just a tease of her shaved, dark pubic hair. Daniel laughed nervously.

'Babe? Leah will be here in a minute.'

Rosa ignored him, pulled his towel undone and took hold of his penis. Daniel let out a nervous moan as Rosa began to stroke him.

'Chill, we have time.' She spoke calmly, her confidence high as she stirred Daniel's dick from sleep mode to wide awake.

She moved in and began to kiss him open-mouthed on his lips. Daniel began to get excited, clearly approving the attention. Rosa continued to work her hand, massaging Daniel until he became fully aroused. She got on her knees and plunged her lips down onto his erect member.

Daniel rested back on the bed. He held Rosa's head as she worked her mouth up and down. 'Oh, babe, feels good,' he moaned, as she increased the intensity. Daniel gripped her hair and clawed the bed. 'I'm cumming,' he managed to get out.

Rosa pulled her mouth away just before Daniel exploded, jerking his body as his load shot into the air.

Rosa continued to squeeze him until he'd fully completed his orgasm.

'Bloody hell, that was . . . unexpected.' He looked at Rosa, who smiled back at him, wiping her mouth with her hand.

'You messed up my hair!' she giggled. 'Calm now?'

'Yes, I'm calm,' Daniel replied, catching his breath just as the intercom buzzed. 'Leah's here.' He jumped up off the bed. 'Go get cleaned up. I'll let her in.' Rosa fixed the robe around herself as Daniel planted a big kiss on her forehead. 'One in a million you are.' He dashed off to the bathroom.

An hour later and after a glam session with Leah, Rosa was ready for the award show. She looked radiant in the black dress with gold shoes. Her make-up was on point—rouge-red lipstick, just a faint blush of glitter foundation and gold eye shadow. Leah had even placed a small black diamante rose in her hair, which she had slicked back, flamenco style.

'Mate, you look amazeballs. So gorgeous. Gotta take a selfie for Insta.' Leah stepped back admiring her work, then held her phone high to snap a couple of pictures.

Daniel emerged looking fresh and sharp in a black suit, crisp white shirt and a black silk bow tie. 'Ready to make a move, babes? We've got less than forty-five minutes . . .' Daniel's voice trailed off as soon as he caught sight of Rosa.

'Aww, look at the pair of ya,' Leah commented. 'One more quick pic, Bro. Go on, get beside Rosa.'

They shuffled up next to each other and posed for their picture.

'Right, let's go!' a hurried Daniel instructed as he hugged Leah. 'Don't wait up!'

'OK. Well, good luck, bruv,' she shouted as they left.

On arrival at the Dorchester Hotel, Daniel squeezed Rosa's hand. 'This is it, babes. Looking forward to tonight.' His pearly-white teeth gleamed as he gave her that smile, the one that said, 'I am Daniel Rosewood and I am confident of winning the award.'

She knew him well enough now to realise that a man like Daniel just had that special something where life always dealt him a good hand.

Their car slowed to a halt and a smart, burgundy-uniformed valet opened the door. 'Good evening, sir. Madam.' The grey-haired custodian held out a white-gloved hand to help Rosa out of the car.

This is amazing, very posh.

I feel like a princess.

My God, I have never been somewhere like this before, this is so classy.

I've got bloody butterflies in my stomach, hope I don't stumble in these shoes and make myself look stupid.

Come on, hold it together, Rosa.

Try to be elegant, just hold on to him and put one foot in front of the other.

They stepped out together onto a plush red carpet.

'You OK, babe?' Daniel asked reassuringly.

Rosa nodded back.

It was an elegant entrance decked out with silver balloons and giant screens showing footage of luxurious super cars. Other guests filed in. It was a trail of smart suits and elegant dresses. Again, Daniel squeezed her hand as they made their way to the entrance crammed with photographers, film crews and hipster event organisers running around, ensuring people were in place.

Rosa's nerves intensified. She smiled bravely in the face of flashbulbs and men walking backwards with cameras pointing towards them.

Wow, this is like the Oscars.

I didn't think it would be so lavish.

This is the kind of thing I saw in my magazines and dreamt of, now it's actually happening.

I just need to stay cool.

My God, I need a drink.

They entered the hotel. There were more photographers taking official pictures against a backdrop with the National Automobile Awards logo. Rosa took it all in.

Amidst all the fuss and splendour, a female photographer approached her out of the press pack. 'Excuse me, babe. Hope you don't mind me saying, but you're stunning. My name's Mya—would love to get a couple of shots.' Her husky Sloane accent rose above the din.

Rosa looked at her. She, herself, was attractive. She wore a short, tight, red silk jumpsuit and had Farah Fawcett honey-blonde hair, beautiful green cat eyes and full lips coated with bright-red lipstick.

'Go ahead, babes, I'll get our table details.' Daniel winked and rubbed her hand. 'It's OK, be back in a sec. Knock 'em dead.' He smiled and walked away.

Rosa smiled shyly. She felt a hot flush rush through her body.

Is she serious?

Why me?
I guess they are gonna ask everyone.
This is weird, bit like that entertainment channel E!
But hey, why not?

Rosa took her position in front of the boarded logo backdrop. She felt awkward, not sure how to stand or pose.

Shit, I'm no model.
What shall I do?
Just stand and smile.
Why are all these people watching?
Hope I don't look stupid.

Mya raised her camera and began snapping, the shutter speed clicking a million times a second. 'Beautiful, babes, lovely. Just hold like that. Smile. Ahh, gorgeous.' Mya stooped down and held her head at different angles trying to get the best shots she could. 'All done, babes. Have a look. So, beautiful, what's your name?' Her breath smelt of cigarettes as she came close and held the camera screen up to show the pictures.

Rosa now felt hot under the lights and from all the eyes peering over at her. 'I am Rosa,' she replied coyly.

'Well, you should be a model, babe. Where you from?'

'Sinaloa, Mexico.'

Mya gave her a loose embrace. 'Sinaloa, yeah? You look wicked—can we swap numbers? I'd love to shoot you again.' Mya smized and handed her phone to Rosa. 'And your man's pretty hot, too. Good-looking couple.' She continued sizing Rosa up seductively, her top lip lined with beads of perspiration. Rosa tapped in her number and handed back the phone. 'I'll see you around tonight.' Mya squeezed her with a heartfelt hug.

Daniel returned just in time to rescue Rosa. 'Looked good, babes. Come on, I got our seats.'

The ballroom was grand, with large circular tables covered in white cloths, sparkling silver cutlery and bottles of champagne dunked in silver buckets positioned in the middle of each table. Daniel held Rosa's hand tightly, weaving their way through the room towards their seats, which were a few metres from the stage.

This is what I'm talking about, this is gorgeous.

Never been to anything like this before.

I feel like I'm in Hollywood.

So elegant, it's like my dreams have come true.

Sitting at their table were other business-type couples, mainly older ones. A silver-haired man sat with a younger woman, probably in her mid-twenties. She had a flaming head of hair and was pale-skinned with dark-red lipstick. The man, who was probably in his fifties, slick-looking with a silver-grey stubble beard, leant over to shake Daniel's hand.

'Bryn Fitzpatrick, Premium Automobiles. Daniel, I believe?' He gave Daniel's hand a firm shake. 'My wife Ella.' He glanced towards the young lady, who waved back.

'Nice to meet you, Bryn. Yes, Daniel Rosewood. I think we have spoken in the past. I remember the name vaguely.' Daniel turned towards Rosa. 'And this is my better half, Rosa.'

Bryn took Rosa's hand and kissed it softly. 'Rosa, the pleasure is ours,' he said with a slight Irish accent. Ella watched on, unimpressed by Bryn's overeager greeting.

Rosa smiled politely as his touch lingered.

'Up for anything tonight, Daniel?' he asked, turning his attention to cracking open a bottle of champagne and pouring it into four glasses.

'Yeah, Showroom of the Year.' Daniel took a glass and passed it to Rosa, then took one for himself.

'Me too,' Bryn replied. 'May the best man win.' He held up his glass for a toast, joined by Ella, who aimed a fake smile at Rosa. 'Cheers.' They all clinked glasses.

Not sure about him, he's a bit full of himself.

Urgh, a bit of a flirt, too.

Wonder why she's with him?

She can't be much older than me.

Him, though, makes my skin crawl, hope Daniel beats him.

The event was in full swing, and after a Michelin star, three-course meal, the compere began the award show. Rosa was well fed and watered as the drinks kept flowing. Daniel had been deep in conversation with Bryn, discussing cars and figures. She had never seen him in this work mode before but could see why he was so passionate about what he did.

Ella and Rosa spoke briefly. It was just superficial conversation, mainly about dresses and make-up, but Rosa got a sense that she was cool. People were receiving their awards and making boring speeches. Ella kept filling up Rosa's glass with white wine, much to her annoyance as she was trying to keep a clear head and not get drunk. She wanted to enjoy the evening and remember it with clarity.

Finally, the compere introduced the next award. It was Daniel's category: Showroom of the Year. Daniel and Bryn stopped their conversation and paid attention to the animated compere, who raised his voice when reading out the nominations. Daniel turned to Rosa. He gave her that gleaming smile as his name and showroom were read out. Rosa smiled proudly, clapping enthusiastically.

Oh my God, please win, come on.

I pray he says Daniel's name, he deserves this and I know he really wants to win, too.

Don't want this arrogant Bryn to have anything.

After a long pause, the compere made his announcement. 'And the winner is . . . Rosewood Automobiles!'

Rosa couldn't help herself, letting out a high-pitched yelp and hugging Daniel, who remained ice cool. He just smiled and planted a kiss her on lips, then shook hands with Bryn, whose facial expression was one of disappointment but grudging respect.

He mouthed at Daniel. 'Congratulations.'

Daniel stood on stage accepting his award. The audience clapped politely while Rosa whooped loudly. She was so proud and caught up that she almost forgot to take a picture on her phone. She held the screen up and snapped away.

Look at him, so cool, so smart.

I want to run up there and hug him but I'll let him have his moment.

Daniel returned to the table with a big grin on his face. He hugged and kissed Rosa. 'Weren't expecting that.' He winked at her before handing her the shiny silver award. 'We can stick that on the mantlepiece, babe.'

Rosa smiled back at him.

Mantlepiece?

I'm confused.

About an hour later and after numerous awards, Daniel looked at Rosa, who was beginning to flag from all the alcohol. 'Think we should call it a night, babe. What do you think?'

Rosa nodded. 'I'm ready.'

They made their excuses to Bryn and Ella, who were both disappointed to see them leave.

'Let's keep in touch, Daniel, and congrats again.' Bryn stood up and shook Daniel's hand again. He took Rosa's hand, but this time she took her hand away.

She smiled at Ella, who was looking a bit weary herself.

'Bye, Rosa. Lovely meeting you.' She took Rosa's phone and quickly tapped her number and name into her contacts. 'Call me. We can hang out, do lunch or drinks?'

Rosa nodded and smiled. 'Of course, that'll be nice.' She gave Ella a hug.

Daniel walked proudly, holding his award in one hand and gripping Rosa's hand in the other. Random people patted him on the back, shaking his hand. Rosa felt like a celebrity, and all the attention was on them, or maybe it was just that she felt tipsy. Out of the blue, they were again approached by Mya.

'Hey, can I get a pic of the winners?' Before they could answer, she began snapping away. 'Just one more ... great, thanks guys. Congratulations. Rosa, don't forget.' She smiled, then darted off back into the midst of the party.

'Let's go home, darling.' Daniel kissed her on the cheek as the valet brought his car back to the entrance.

Luckily Daniel had had only one glass to celebrate, so he was OK to drive. Rosa, on the other hand, was more than tipsy and ready to go home, but she'd had a great night, probably the best of her life. She was exhausted but high from the happiness of being with Daniel and seeing him achieve his great moment. Rosa slinked her body into the comfortable seat of the Mercedes and closed her eyes.

I am so happy.

Tonight Mama and Papa must be watching down on me, smiling.

They know their daughter is finally living the life she always wanted.

This is the best I've ever felt.

Finally I can relax and Daniel has been such a godsend.

He deserves everything.

Rosa

Chapter 13
What a bam bam

The clock was ticking for a fed-up Jesus and Dani. Jesus was angry and skulking around in the kitchen. The sink was piled with dirty dishes, and empty chicken shop takeaway boxes were strewn across the small table. Flies buzzed around the room in the heatwave.

Dressed, as usual, in his dirty white vest and cut-off jean shorts, Jesus kicked open the back door and stepped out into the yard. A sheepish, sweaty Dani, still hobbling from his injuries, followed him.

'Bro, we only have a few hours left before Franky wants his money.' Desperate Dani aired his concern.

Jesus ignored him, picking up his balding tennis ball. He turned to Dani with a thunderous scowl. 'First, you let Rosa leave, then you fuck up with Franky and now we owe him ten bags *and* you remind me of the time!' He threw the ball hard at Dani, smacking him in the eye.

'Ow! Fuck c'mon, man.' Dani recoiled at the impact of the ball as it stung his face.

Jesus moved towards him. 'I swear if you were not my blood, I would have killed you by now.'

Dani cowered as Jesus stepped closer to him, wagging his long, boney finger in his face. His fury and frustration signified his desperation; the small red veins in his eyeballs indicated his pain.

'OK, but we still have to try,' Dani pleaded. Jesus squeezed the tennis ball in his palm, stress coursing through his veins.

Dani suddenly limped towards the gate. He pulled it open and began to leave.

'Oi! Where you going?'

Dani looked back at Jesus, his eyebrows knitted tightly across his forehead in anger. 'We have to find the money from somewhere and it ain't standing here.' His voice trembled, breaking as he spoke.

Jesus tossed the ball to the floor and for once followed Dani's lead. They left the yard and went out into the sunshine.

As they walked through the estate, their differing shapes cast long shadows on the pavement.

'So, what's the plan, brother?' Jesus hissed. The sarcasm abounded in his question, which was ignored by Dani, who plodded on, shrugging.

It was like the blind leading the blind down a path of uncertainty, but one thing was certain: every step they took was another second closer to Franky's deadline.

A black, tinted-windowed Mercedes on the opposite side of the road slowed to a halt. Inside, Franky sat in the back seat, swiping rapidly on an iPad. A white tee shirt, the perfect canvas for his array of gold chains, and dark shades that fitted snugly onto his flattened nose made up his ensemble. His two accomplices sat in the front were the same men that had paid Jesus and Dani a visit—the one with the pirate's earring and gold tooth and his stocky, crisp-eating sidekick.

Franky coughed and hoiked up the phlegm in his throat. He pressed a button, making the window slide down, and spat out a big gob of spit. 'Dem fuckers have twelve hours,' he snorted and peered through the window at the two brothers, watching them like a predator watching its prey. 'Look at them. You think them two gonna bring my money?' he scoffed, shaking out a pile of white cocaine powder onto the screen of his iPad then snorting it up like a pig in a trough. He rubbed his nose vigorously.

'Shall we take them out now, boss?' the driver asked with an excited tone in his hoarse, cigarette-polluted voice. He raised a gun with a long silencer attached, poking it menacingly out of the window and aiming it towards Dani and Jesus.

Franky pondered for a few seconds. His sculpted body remained still as he peered out into the street. 'Nah, let's give them the time. If they flop, we'll kill 'em.' He pressed the button for the window to slide back up. A phone call interrupted them; the ringtone was the theme tune to *Mastermind*. 'Randy! Mate, how are ya?' Franky answered, motioning for the driver to move off.

The driver did as instructed and steered the car away. His partner pulled the gun back inside the car as they cruised past Jesus and Dani.

Franky continued his phone conversation whilst peering through the smoked glass window. 'Yeah, mate, party's still on. It's at mine now, bring your trunks.' He snorted with laughter, wiping the rest of the cocaine dust from the iPad screen and rubbing it onto his gums, then sucking the tips of his fingers.

Dani hobbled his way through the streets, closely followed by Jesus. They were on the prowl, and they kept their eyes peeled for something or someone of value so they could make a quick snatch or grab an old woman's jewellery or handbag.

They walked past a newspaper stand manned by an old man holding out the latest edition of the local paper. 'Free Herald!' he crowed at passers-by, thrusting a copy into anyone's hands.

He pushed one out towards Dani, who swatted it away onto the floor in front of Jesus. It landed open on a page with the headline 'Vroom, Vroom. Racy Stunner Shines at Automobile Awards' with a picture of Rosa and Daniel below it.

Jesus looked down, about to step over the paper, and stopped suddenly as if he had been hit by a bolt of lightning. He stooped down and picked up the newspaper. 'Holy fuck! Dani!' he squealed at his brother.

Dani turned around in a huff, hot and bothered. 'What?' he shouted back frustrated.

Jesus held the page up in his face. 'Look who I have just found.'

Dani stared at the page, snatching the paper out of his hands, his jaw dropping in disbelief. 'Fuckin' hell.' He looked at Jesus. 'We need to find this fucker fast.'

* * *

The evening sun began to dip into the horizon, leaving a deep-orange tinge painted across the skyline. Temperatures remained Mediterranean as Rosa and Daniel sat out by the stream enjoying a Magnum ice lolly and taking in the view. It had been a week since the award show and Daniel's chest was still puffed out with pride after his win. Rosa, too, felt great. It was probably the best she had felt since childhood.

'Remember Mya, that photographer at the awards?' Rosa asked Daniel as she licked the ice cream from the tip of the Magnum.

'Yeah, course. What about her?'

Rosa turned to Daniel, her eyes sparkling with excitement. 'Well, I called her to say thanks as she sent me some of the pics and she wants me for a photoshoot!'

Daniel turned to her, his face serious as he crunched down on the lolly. He considered her for a few seconds before shrugging casually. 'Course she does,' he responded, continuing to devour his lolly. Rosa waited with bated breath.

'So?'

Daniel smiled, giving himself time to swallow before answering. 'So, I think that's brilliant! When?'

Rosa breathed out a huge sigh of relief and broke into a big smile. She leant forwards, kissing Daniel on the lips. 'Thank you. It's tomorrow.' Rosa could hardly contain her excitement. She hugged Daniel tightly.

'Only thing is I have to go to the showroom tonight.' Daniel pulled away, and he could see the happiness drain from Rosa's face.

'What? No!'

Daniel playfully took a nibble from her lolly. 'Got a big audit coming up; just want to make sure all my paperwork is right.' He stroked her hair tenderly. 'Shouldn't be long, and I'll take you to the shoot tomorrow.'

Rosa put his hand to her face.

Hate when he has to work.

I was looking forward to a chilled evening but he's super dedicated and I admire that, so it is what it is.

Plus, how could I ever be mad at him.

Look at those beautiful blue eyes.

'OK, Mr Rosewood. Fair enough,' she responded, trying not to sound too disappointed. 'Don't be too long, though. I want you home with me later.' She kissed him on the lips, then playfully dabbed her lolly onto his nose, leaving a smidge of ice cream which she licked off seductively.

Jesus sat at the kitchen table staring down at the newspaper. He held the point of a sharp kitchen knife on Daniel's photo. He rubbed his chin and stroked his wispy beard, huffing, puffing and grunting every few seconds. He scored the blade around Daniel's face, his breathing becoming more intense.

Dani entered the kitchen, hyped up. 'I say we find this Rosewood Automobiles place and fuck him up.'

Jesus ignored Dani, continuing to stare down at the newspaper. He began to stab at it aggressively, perforating the picture multiple times until he made a final stab, leaving the knife rooted upright through the paper and into the wooden table. 'She looks so fucking happy.' Jesus finally raised his head to look up at Dani, his eyes sunken into his angled cheekbones. He stood up, pushing the chair back, and peered down at the newspaper picture. 'We find him and wipe that smile from her face.' He continued to seethe. 'Let's go.' Jesus brushed past Dani and strode out of the back door.

Dani, as usual, followed behind, slamming the door behind him and leaving the scored newspaper on the table.

* * *

Daniel, casually dressed in grey tracksuit bottoms and a blue Ralph Lauren Polo tee shirt, bounced out of the bathroom. His skin was reddened from the afternoon sun. He made his way over to Rosa, who was sat on the bed fiddling with various nail varnishes and make-up palettes. 'Babe, I'm off. Should be back in a couple of hours.' He bent down and planted a kiss on her lips. 'I would go for the red,' he quipped, pointing towards her gaggle of different-coloured bottles.

'Hmm, maybe. Don't be too long,' Rosa replied, pulling him towards her again for another kiss.

'Nah, won't be.' Daniel took his phone and keys from the dressing table and left Rosa to her own devices.

* * *

Daniel drove into the forecourt of his large showroom, which was protected by a large metal gate and fencing. He leant out of the window and aimed a remote-control fob at the gate. The sound of a beep indicated the unlocking of the tall grey gate. Daniel drove slowly towards the entrance. Unbeknown to him, out of the dark shadows emerged Jesus and Dani, who scampered in just before the gates closed. Daniel parked up while Jesus and Dani dipped low, hiding behind the sleek sports cars spread out along the concrete forecourt.

Dani breathed heavily, still wheezing from his rib injuries, which Jesus did not help by shoving him in the side.

'Shush, man.' He pointed towards Daniel, who was now making his way towards the door of the showroom, completely oblivious to the evil that lurked just a few yards away from him.

Daniel jangled the bunch of keys, selecting the correct one to unlock the door to the showroom.

Dani and Jesus crept closer, crouching along the tarmac. Jesus put his fingers to his lips, reminding Dani to stay quiet as they edged towards an unsuspecting Daniel.

Daniel paused as he opened the doors, turning briefly towards the parking lot. He glanced around into the night but noticed nothing out of the ordinary and made his way into the showroom.

Jesus signalled to Dani and they both ran towards Daniel. Jesus was like an antelope. In just a few steps, he was behind Daniel. He aimed a flying kick into Daniel's back, knocking him to the floor and sending him sprawling. His keys and phone smashed onto the tiles.

'Come on!' Jesus screamed at Dani, who belatedly caught up to his brother.

Daniel spun to see the silhouettes of Jesus and Dani standing in the doorway over him. 'Wait! Please, I don't keep any money here.' He slid back on his rear, scrambling away from the two figures who walked towards him.

'Shut the door,' Jesus ordered Dani, who carried out his task without question. 'Go get the keys and lock it.'

Dani scurried towards a stricken Daniel and picked the keys up. 'Which one is it?' He shoved the bunch of tangled keys into Daniel's face.

Daniel stretched out his hand, visibly shaking as he tried to select the right key. 'Please, mate, I honestly have nothing here.' He gave Dani the key, trying to get to his feet, only to be kicked back down by Jesus.

'He doesn't know who we are.' Jesus turned to Dani, who had now locked the door and joined his brother.

'Is this who she's with? Fucking posh boy prick.' Dani now felt a sense of power as he knelt down, staring directly into Daniel's face. 'We're Rosa's brothers.' He grinned.

The blood drained from Daniel's cheeks as he went into shock. 'Look, mate, I don't want any trouble.'

Jesus knelt down on the other side of him, his sweaty, boney face and wispy moustache close. 'Well, mi amigo, you are in a lot of trouble.' His Mexican accent was authentic as the rasp in his throat indicated devious intentions.

Bound and gagged, a battered Daniel sat trussed up in a chair. His face was fresh with lacerations and bruising.

Dani took the liberty to sit in every single car that was out on display, feeling like a kid at the fairground. He sat in the driver's seat of a gleaming Bugatti sports car, pretending to drive. 'Oh, shit, this car is so sick!' he enthused, gripping and turning the steering wheel and pressing all the buttons and gadgets.

Meanwhile, Jesus was all business, stalking around the office, digging through drawers and pulling out files. 'Where's the safe?' he quizzed, being deliberately destructive by kicking over boxes and sweeping his long arm across shelving which housed various pictures and car memorabilia.

Daniel shuffled, twisting and attempting to struggle free of the cables tied around his wrists. His speech was restricted to a muffle due to the black tape strapped across his mouth.

Jesus walked over to Daniel and ripped the tape away. 'Talk!' he ordered, loving the fact that he was in control.

Daniel's face was now mottled in a red blush. 'I don't keep money here,' he managed to splutter between gasping for air.

Dani leapt out of the Bugatti and limped his way over. 'What'd he say?' Daniel swivelled in the chair towards him.

'I said . . .'

A sharp, boney punch thumped across his face from Jesus, halting his plea and spinning Daniel around. Jesus grabbed the chair and pushed it so hard that it sped across the floor, smashing into one of the luxury cars. The impact flung Daniel to the ground.

Dani burst into a high-pitched, childlike laugh. 'Fuck, man, are you OK?' he asked insincerely.

Jesus pulled Daniel up from the floor still bound to the chair. 'Sit up, amigo.' He dragged him forwards, grabbing his blue Polo top, which now had spots of blood from a split lip.

He looked up wearily at the brothers who seemed to be revelling in their tyranny, especially Dani, who childishly smacked Daniel around the head just for fun.

Jesus crouched down, staring at Daniel eye to eye. 'So, here's the deal. We need 10k right now, tonight.'

Daniel's eyes widened. 'I don't have that,' he said, his voice cracking as he tried to speak.

'Look at dem cars, man.' Jesus took Daniel's head with both hands and spun it around.

'They must be worth thousands,' Dani interjected, trying his best to sound authoritative. 'He's got fucking loads of cash. Where is it?' His petulance came to the fore as he grabbed Daniel by the throat and choked him.

'I ... don't ... have ... money.' Daniel gasped for breath, kicking his legs feverishly while a grinning Dani enjoyed his role as the enforcer until he was pulled off by Jesus.

'Don't kill him yet. Need him alive.'

Dani reeled away, swinging his arms like an impetuous child. Daniel's head fell back. He gasped for air like a fish pulled from the depths of the ocean. 'Please. I'm telling ya I don't keep money here.'

Jesus walked behind him, grabbing him into a headlock and dragging the chair to the office, pinning him against a desk. 'So you and my sister Rosa. Tell me how that happened.' Jesus's voice was low and husky.

Poor Daniel had now lost all of his clean-cut appearance. He was bedraggled, bloodied and frayed. 'Just met one day.' Daniel sucked for air, trying to compose himself.

Jesus stepped back, took out his tobacco and rizla and began to roll a cigarette. 'Carry on. Where did you meet?'

Dani stayed in the background, sat on the bonnet of a sleek, black Porsche, watching on disgruntled.

'Launderette. Look, she's already told me about you,' he continued. 'She's done nothing wrong.'

Jesus sparked a flame from his lighter and took his time dragging on his rolled-up snout. 'I can tell that you like my sister. The question is: how much is she worth to you? I'd say at least ten thousand,' he sneered, smoke pluming from his sharp nostrils. He moved closer to a hesitant Daniel.

'I think he's lying.' Dani's voice echoed through the spacious showroom. 'I reckon there's money here—has to be.'

Daniel shook his head in defiance, the pressure intensifying within him.

'Search him, Dani. He must have a wallet.' Dani duly slid from the car and limped his way over to Daniel.

'It's in my car!' Daniel was broken and fearful of any further punishment.

'Keys, now!' The rasp of Jesus's voice cut straight through Daniel as Dani rifled through his tracksuit pockets, pulling out the car keys.

'Got 'em.' Dani held his arm up euphorically.

'Go get his wallet.' Jesus tugged on his cigarette as Dani scurried towards the door, unlocking it then hobbling out towards Daniel's car. Jesus watched him leave then turned his attention back to Daniel, flicking the butt of the roll-up at him. The dying embers of ash were sprinkled down Daniel's chest. 'She was raped. Did she tell you?' Jesus calmly walked around the chair, speaking casually yet knowing his words would be like a stab through Daniel's heart. 'Got pregnant. Had a miscarriage for some wasteman at school.'

Daniel tensed up as every word hit like a speeding juggernaut. He sucked in the air, trying to regulate his breathing, while Jesus continued his systematic destruction of Daniel's emotions.

'Rosa didn't tell you?' Jesus broke into a laugh for once, revealing his stained smoker's teeth. 'So she lied to you? She never told you the real reason I imposed rules.'

Daniel grimaced as Jesus continued his speech.

'No whores are allowed in my family.'

Dani returned with Daniel's wallet in hand and frowned when he heard the description of his sister. 'Here.' He handed his brother the wallet.

Jesus pulled out all of Daniel's credit cards and threw the empty wallet at Daniel. 'Pin numbers?'

Daniel's eyes bulged with fury as he processed the information Jesus had just dowsed him with. 'Don't know how you're related; she's cut from a different cloth.' Daniel's outburst was random yet not surprising. It was as if Jesus had flicked a switch in his brain, making him go from fear to fury. He spat out blood, disgusted with Jesus's crude reference.

Jesus marched towards him and grabbed his throat with his hand. He squeezed tightly, eyeballing Daniel nose to nose. 'Pin numbers now!' Jesus bared his teeth, inflicting more pain on his defenceless victim who was beginning to turn blue.

'I have no money for you!' he spluttered, barely able to string his words together.

Dani stepped into the office and yanked Jesus's hand away from Daniel's throat. 'You'll kill him, man!' He managed to pull his rabid brother away. 'We need him alive. He's got money, but he can't give it if he's dead.'

Jesus wiped his frothing mouth. 'Fuck! I swear if you don't show us where the money is, I'll finish you.' Jesus raked his hands through his greasy hair, pulling out his ponytail and freeing his hair to dangle over his sharp face. He took a deep breath before walking away irritated.

Dani looked at Daniel, who dribbled blood mixed with saliva down his chin and neck. Ensuring Jesus was out of earshot, he said, 'Give us the money, then we'll leave.' His tone edged on a remorseful whisper.

Daniel stared back at him, his eyes glassed over with tears and his body angled uncomfortably in the chair.

* * *

Rosa tossed and turned in the large bed. She seemed to be dreaming, her eyes flickering wildly before she forced herself awake. She turned onto her side, stretching out her arm and feeling for Daniel's body, but as she felt the other side of the bed, she realised that he was not there. She flicked on the bedside lamp and checked her phone. The time was 3:45 am.

Rosa sprang upright and rubbed her eyes. She checked the bed again and went back to her phone screen.

That's weird.

He should have been home by now.

Not even a text or a missed call.

Maybe he's sleeping downstairs.

Need to go pee then I'll check.

Rosa got up, walked into the bathroom and sat on the toilet, still yawning and sleepy. She spent her penny then flushed the loo. Washing her hands, she looked bleary-eyed into the mirror.

Can't sleep if he's not with me.

Flipping crazy dream as well about my brothers.

Those two will never leave me alone not even in my dreams.

She made her way back into the bedroom then downstairs to the front room, putting the lights on as she ventured down the steps. She opened the door but realised he was not home. She yawned and made her way back up to the bedroom. Her long black hair tumbled down her back.

He shouldn't have been this long, he said a couple of hours.

I know him, though.

Probably wants to make sure everything is spick and span.

But still thought he'd be back by now.

Rosa sat on the bed and something rankled her. Maybe it was the dream but more likely the gut feeling that something didn't seem right. She checked her phone again.

I'll call him, he's probably still sat in front of that computer after cleaning every single car in the showroom.

She tapped her phone and a picture of a smart-looking, smiling Daniel popped up onto the large screen with the word 'Calling' across it. Rosa put the speaker on and listened as the ringtone kicked in.

Daniel's half-smashed phone rattled on the floor. It lit up, showing a picture of a smiling Rosa with the name 'Diamond' across the shattered screen. It vibrated violently until Dani picked it up.

'Jesus, look!'

He brought the phone over to a fuming Jesus who was now sat on the roof of a sparkling silver Range Rover. His long lanky leg was hanging over the side as he smoked in his own world until Dani showed him the screen.

'It's fucking Rosa.' Dani's tone was hopeful as he saw his sister's face.

Jesus took the phone and answered the call, sucking deeply on the roll-up cigarette. 'Little Sister, what you doing up at this time?'

Dani found it exciting. He began to laugh and punch the air euphorically as if they had hit the jackpot. A tired and battered-looking Daniel could barely muster any movement and could only watch on.

Rosa froze on hearing Jesus's voice answering Daniel's phone. A minus-degree chill ran down her spine, and her heart inflated two-fold. She felt sick in the mouth, unable to even reply.

'Guess who we're with,' Jesus continued, revelling in his role as master tormentor.

Rosa could only hold the phone in her hand and listen to the familiar yet sinister voice.

What!

How has he got Daniel's ... oh shit.

'Where's Daniel?' she questioned, her voice shaking with trepidation. 'Where is he?' she screamed, the shock kicking in like a dose of morphine.

Jesus cackled down the phone. She could also hear Dani laughing and whooping it up in the background.

'If you've touched him, I swear ...' Rosa's anger boiled, mainly in fear of what to expect.

'Calm down, he ain't dead ... yet. Here, talk to him.'

Tears rolled down Rosa's cheeks as she listened.

Jesus clicked his fingers at Dani, motioning him to drag Daniel over. Dani duly obliged and hobbled at speed into the office, dragging the chair out from the office into the showroom.

Jesus jumped down from the car roof, pushing the phone into a weary Daniel's face. 'Talk,' he ordered.

Daniel, clearly injured, could hardly muster up any words. 'Hello, babe. You were bloody right about these two,' he said, sounding tired yet trying to inject a dose of humour to reassure her he was OK. Watching the two brothers, he spoke with almost a sense of relief. He knew Rosa would know he was still safe and alive, although his fate was less than certain.

'Daniel, just give them what they want . . .' Rosa pleaded.

Jesus took the phone away from his mouth and intervened. 'Such a disloyal bitch.' Jesus spat onto the ground. 'He needs to pay us ten thousand, then you can both die together. I will find you.'

A tearful Rosa sat on the edge of the bed, squirming and trying to control her emotions. 'Let him go and I will come home,' she desperately begged, her voice quivering as she took a sharp intake of breath. 'I'll come now—just let him go.' Rosa banged the side of her head with her fist. There was silence for what seemed to be an age until the phone went dead.

'Jesus! Daniel, please!' Rosa began to panic and fear the worst. She dialled back the number but to no avail; it went through to voicemail.

Shit!
OK, fuck.
Call the police.
No, no police.
Call Leah.

Rosa got up. She was delirious, walking around the bedroom and tearing her hair out. Her heart was pounding out her chest.

Fuck, fuck, fuck!

She tapped a number into the phone and placed it to her ear.

Pick up, please pick up.

Come on, Leah.

She crouched down onto her haunches, tears streaming down her cheeks. 'Leah, it's me. Daniel's in trouble. Come now, please!' A pause ensued before Rosa began to scream down the phone. 'I need you to come now!' She cut the phone off and threw it to the floor, falling back against the bed.

Leah pounded on the front door. She was dressed in her night clothes—a flimsy, silk pyjama short set with flip-flops and phone in hand. She shouted up at the window. 'Oi, Rosa, open the door!' She continued to pound away until Rosa opened the door.

She looked a mess, cheeks flushed, eyes glassed over with teetering tears.

Leah barged into the house. 'What the fuck's going on? Rosa, what's happened?' She bounded in, and seeing the state Rosa was in, she knew something serious was up. 'Tell me! What's going on?' Leah threw her keys and phone onto the table, grabbed Rosa by the arms and looked her in the eye.

Rosa bowed her head. She could hardly bring herself to talk, but eventually she had to. It was barely a whisper. 'Daniel . . . he's in really big trouble.'

Leah stared back at her, the expression on her face dramatically changed to shock as she braced herself for Rosa to share the news.

Daniel sat slumped in the chair, battered and bloodied, his eyes closed. He looked as if the life had been beaten out of him. Jesus skulked around, alone in his own world, trying to think of his next move. He barely had an intelligent brain cell and was stumped as to what to do next. Dani searched around in the office, digging through the files and desk drawers, creating havoc and smashing all the stuff from the shelves onto the floor, including Daniel's recent award.

Dani continued his deconstruction of the office until he had one metal cabinet left. 'What's in here then?' He pulled open the sliding doors and saw a black leather pouch on the bottom shelf. 'What's this?' He pulled it out. It was heavy and puffed out with something. Dani prized the zip lock open. 'Oh my days! Jesus!' he shouted excitedly. 'Come look what I found.' He stepped out across all the debris.

Jesus came over to see why he was so excited. Dani held the pouch open in front of Jesus. 'Look, he was lying all this time.'

Jesus took the pouch, taking out wads of pink fifty-pound notes. 'How much is in here?' He began to laugh with Dani, who shrugged, gleefully smiling like a drunken pirate who had just found a bounty of treasure.

'Fucking gringo made us do all this.' Dani slapped Daniel across the head.

Daniel hardly moved, remaining slumped and almost passed out in the chair. His voice was barely a whimper. 'I need that . . . it's . . . for the . . .'

Jesus walked over to him. He took one of the notes out of the bag and stuffed it into Daniel's mouth, making him gag. Saliva hung from his mouth and dribbled down onto his chest. 'Should have just gave us this in the first place, mi amigo,' Jesus hissed whilst flicking through the notes in the pouch. Daniel continued to choke and gag.

Dani grabbed Jesus. 'Let's go now, man. We got what we came for.' He pulled at Jesus who seemed reluctant to leave. He was intent on inflicting more pain.

Jesus flicked his lighter on and off, thinking about what to do next.

'Come on, let's go, bruv.' Dani suddenly had a sense of urgency. He became angsty but Jesus looked back at him. His face was tight.

'Nah, man, he has to perish or we're both going to jail.' He repeatedly flicked his lighter, the flame lighting up his sunken eyes.

Dani stared at him, afraid of what his brother was about to do. Daniel struggled with his last bit of strength to get free, but he was weak, injured and could barely breathe. Jesus smirked at Dani, then turned to Daniel and walked ominously towards him.

Leah gripped the steering wheel tightly. She drove at speed, her face wrought with panic. Rosa was sat beside her, a bag of nerves, upset and frazzled.

'Call the police and ambulance now!' Leah ordered, annoyed and scared and at the same time trying to concentrate on the road.

Rosa felt numb. She could hardly function, her mind awash with a thousand scenarios, but her main concern was for Daniel's safety.

'I said call the bloody police. Tell them to get there ASAP!' Leah screamed at Rosa, taking her eyes off the road for a few seconds, which caused her to swerve and bump her car tyre against the pavement. She lost control and skidded into the other side of the road. She braked hard to regain control, slamming the car to a halt. Luckily no other vehicles were on the road. Leah sucked in some deep breaths, trying to compose herself. 'Shit, I swear if anything . . .' She shot a look towards Rosa, who was struggling to contain her own feelings, gripping her phone, clearly shaken. 'Call them!' Leah screamed at her again.

'I am trying!' Rosa fiddled with the buttons then dropped the phone onto the floor.

'For fuck sake.' Leah stepped on the accelerator and sped through a red light, driving through the streets like a maniac.

As they neared the car showroom, they could see thick black smoke billowing up against the skyline, with flames blazing from the building below. The sound of sirens blared in the background. Leah accelerated a few more yards. She and Rosa stared in horror as they approached the showroom. Leah skidded to a halt in the middle of the road. Without turning the engine off, she pushed open the door, jumped out and ran towards the burning building in her pyjamas, losing a flip-flop in her haste.

Rosa could only sit and watch, frozen in her seat, her brown eyes bulging with fear. She was a mess and became hysterical.

Jesus, what have you done?

I can't believe this, it's not real, this can't be happening.

Please, God, what is happening?

Only the sound of the fire engine and the sirens of several police cars speeding past her shook her back to reality. Rosa opened the door and got out of the car. She walked like a zombie towards the showroom where Leah was hysterically screaming and pulling at the metal gates as the building blazed.

Rosa tried to choke back her tears but felt repulsed by the scene playing out in front of her. Leah was being dragged back by a couple of burly police officers, her arms flailing wildly. She sank to her knees, screaming for Daniel, as the fire took hold of the main building. Fire fighters broke through the gates. They were shouting orders at each other while dragging the heavy rubber hoses from the engine and frantically trying to get to the blaze.

Rosa stood petrified, unable to move. The reflection of the flames could be seen in her tearful eyes.

Leah broke loose from the grip of the police and turned to Rosa. 'This is you, it's your fault! You fixed this. I knew you were trouble. This is all because of you!' Leah was furious. She ran at Rosa, her face etched with pain and anguish.

Rosa flinched, anticipating the verbal and physical onslaught, but Leah was pulled away by the police.

'I'm gonna need you to calm down, miss,' one of the officers shouted aggressively.

The life had drained out of Rosa. She was in shock, just staring ahead, whilst Leah continued to wail and scuffle. Rosa was empty, her thoughts vacant, only jerked into life by the gruff voice of a burly officer.

'Move back, love. Come on, step back.'

She shook herself into action. Finally, the realisation struck and she walked forwards to comfort Leah. 'I'm sorry, Leah. I swear I had nothing to do with . . .'

Before she could finish her sentence, Leah screamed at her in a deep, demonic growl. 'Go away! I hate you. Look what you've done.'

Rosa, undeterred, stepped in and hugged Leah. She struggled to fight her off for a few seconds, eventually crumbling into Rosa's arms as they both stood watching the carnage unfold in front of them.

Forty-five minutes earlier

Dani was panicked. He could see the evil in Jesus's eyes as he circled a prone Daniel, flicking the flame from his lighter. 'Bro, come on, man. Fuck him.'

Jesus ignored Dani, disappearing into the ransacked office. He could be heard rummaging around and ripping up paper.

Dani looked down at Daniel. 'He's gonna burn you alive, bro.'

Daniel shuffled, trying his best to angle his way out of the chair.

Dani looked over his shoulder, checking Jesus's whereabouts, and quickly untied his victim's hands, whispering under his breath, 'I just want the money, bro. I ain't a killer. We'll leave you. Say it was just a burglary. Never saw our faces.' Daniel looked at him, his eyes wide with fright and confusion.

Dani heard Jesus coming back, so he slapped Daniel across the face, pretending to mock him. 'One for the road,' he cackled uncomfortably, spinning around to Jesus.

'Come on.' Jesus signalled towards the door and headed that way, quickly followed by Dani.

The smell of smoke began to take over the showroom, closely followed by small orange flames shooting from the office. The sound of the smoke alarm's high-pitched beep added to the drama as Jesus and Dani made their exit.

Even in excruciating pain, Daniel managed to squirm his body out of the chair. His body slammed against the hard floor, causing him to shriek in pain. He could see the flames rising, becoming more ferocious and out of control. He dragged himself across the floor and held onto one of the cars, trying to drag himself up to his feet.

Daniel could barely stand. His body was weak from the torture, but he knew he had to somehow get out before the blaze took hold. He paused for a few seconds to try and compose himself, fighting through the aches of his body. He clenched his teeth, grimacing as he inched away from the car. 'Arrghh, fuck.' The pain was too much, and he fell to the floor again, the agony intensifying. He began to crawl away from the flames, which were now spreading beyond the office and out into the main showroom area.

Daniel's legs were limp and slipping in a pool of his own blood which had formed on the floor. He willed himself on as the aggressive flames engulfed the shiny cars around him. Daniel knew his showroom and thought if he could make it to the fire exit, which was located about twenty yards to the back of the showroom, he would at least have a slim chance of escaping. Daniel hauled himself forwards, sliding his body along the ground, inching closer as the flames raged. He knew he had to use all his strength to save his life or perish and burn in his own prized supercar sanctuary.

Chapter 14
Back to black

The fire brigade had finally got the blaze under control. It was a sad sight to see—the smouldering building blackened and ruined and some of the cars on the forecourt scorched by the heat. Rosa and Leah sat opposite each other on the pavement, each covered in a red blanket.

Leah was inconsolable and shaking. Her head was in disbelief, unable to comprehend what she was seeing in front of her. 'He's gone, my brother's gone,' she sobbed, the tears streaming from her eyes.

Rosa put her arm around her. She was equally upset and couldn't bring herself to speak. She just wept quietly and bowed her head.

This is all my fault.

If he never met me, all this shit would never have happened.

My dumb fucking brothers.

I should have known eventually they would do something crazy.

My heart is so heavy, I've got him killed.
Everyone is going to say it's that Mexican girl's fault.
Why did he ever bring her home?
I'd rather die than Daniel, I'd have given my life instead
of them taking his.

Rosa's thoughts were interrupted by a couple of female uniformed officers.

'Sorry, ladies. We need to speak with you both, get a statement, if that's OK?' One of them crouched down, and Leah stared back at her.

'Where's Daniel? I want my brother. Find him, please can you find him?' Leah broke down hysterically. She could barely stand, let alone give a statement.

Rosa tried to hold it together but was struck by the enormity of the situation. She stayed rooted to the pavement, shaking her head and mumbling prayers under her breath.

'Come on, we can sit in the car.' The officer ushered them up and showed them to separate waiting police cars.

The two shadowy figures of Jesus and Dani slipped through a field of bracken and shrubbery. They were doing their best to avoid any suspicion and could still hear the faint sound of the sirens in the distance. Dani lagged in the wake of Jesus.

'Wait, man, slow down.' Dani was clearly struggling, holding his side. 'Let's stop for a minute. Shit, I need to catch my breath.'

Jesus turned around, his eyes visible as the early signs of dawn crept across the horizon. 'What's wrong with you?'

Dani held his torso and looked at his brother. 'Bruv, why'd you have to do that, man? We got the money.'

Jesus stomped over, aiming a kick out of frustration, which connected with Dani's thigh. 'Fuck him, flashy bastard.' Jesus spat on the ground in disgust. 'She betrayed us for him. They can both die, and so will we if we don't get this money to Franky.'

Dani winced from the pain. He stumbled, but for once, he held his stance and became aggressive, walking to face Jesus. 'We are not killers, man! That bullshit was wrong, Bro. No wonder Rosa . . .' Before he could finish his speech, Jesus whacked him across the face with the leather pouch. Dani staggered back, rocked by the force of the slap, but came back at him bucking like a wild bronco. He rushed Jesus, grabbing him with both hands around the waist and knocking him off balance.

They crashed into the bushes, rolling around. Dani tried to gain the upper hand, but for what Jesus lacked in size and strength, he more than made up for in deviousness, digging his two fingers into Dani's eyes.

'Agrrh.' Dani let out a howling scream, which echoed into the woods.

Jesus managed to climb on top of him, his skinny legs cut by the shrubs. He tried to get his hands around Dani's neck, but Dani bravely fought him off.

'Bro, you loco!' Dani shouted up at him while shoving and scratching his way out of the hold.

They continued to fight, not noticing the low beam of headlights creeping along the roadside. A black Range Rover was just visible through the early morning mist. The two continued to grapple, but the crunch of the tyres on the gravelled road suddenly caught their attention.

'Get off me, fucking hell,' Dani protested, pushing Jesus to the side. Both stopped their antics and immediately focused on the roadside.

'Duck down!' Jesus hushed Dani, putting his hand over his mouth. Both crouched down, static.

Footsteps crunched across the crisp greenery soaked in morning dew. A bright light from a torch shone like a wand across the wooded growth. Jesus stretched his long arm out to pick up the leather pouch, which had been discarded during the fight.

'Better come out before I start shooting.' A deep growl of a voice was projected towards them.

Jesus hesitated for a few seconds before getting a grip on the pouch, the torch light catching his hand.

'Who's that?' Dani whispered through Jesus's hand, which was still glued to his mouth.

'Ssh.' Jesus squatted, peeking through the bushes.

A shadowy figure moved quickly across the undergrowth military style, revealing himself behind them. It was Franky's cohort—the one with the pirate's earring. He stood above them, pointing an AK-47 rifle, wearing a tight black tee shirt covered by a heavy bulletproof vest and combat shorts with black boots. He inhaled a deep breath. 'Nothing beats the morning countryside air.' He smiled, still aiming the rifle at them.

Jesus and Dani were like two rabbits caught in the headlights. Both were scuffed, bruised and cut from their exertions.

'What's that there?' He aimed the muzzle at the pouch which Jesus had grabbed.

'We got the money!' Dani blurted out randomly, much to his brother's dismay.

'Chuck it here slowly,' their assailant ordered. Jesus aimed a dirty look at Dani before feebly tossing the pouch. Franky's cohort picked it up slowly, keeping his eyes on them the whole time. 'Now get up!' he barked. Both brothers acted on instruction and did exactly as told. Jesus scowled at Dani once again. 'Let's go! Walk to the car. We're going to a barbecue.' He prodded the rifle into Dani's back, shoving him forwards. They made their way to the roadside as the deep-orange sun began to rise through the mist.

Rosa sat in the back of a police car. She was accompanied by one of the female officers. She was a butch, hard-faced woman who looked beefy due to all her body armour and the utility belt. 'So your boyfriend owns that place?' she questioned, staring directly at a stunned Rosa, who nodded. 'What's his name?' The officer continued with her line of questioning, but Rosa seemed reluctant. She could not will herself to even speak; the culmination of the night's events rendered her numb.

This can't be happening.

What a nightmare.

Daniel's dead, he's really dead!

It's my fault.

I just can't.

... No, I'm gonna wake up from this.

I'm fucking freaking out here, this can't be real.

I was with him earlier today and now he's gone.

He's gone because of me, it all comes down to me ...

Rosa finally broke, the tears bursting out of her eyes like a busted dam. Her whole body shook as the inevitable breakdown arrived. The police officer offered a comforting hand, squeezing Rosa's hand tightly. 'His name's Daniel . . . Daniel Rosewood.' She looked at the officer and wiped her face, trying to control the waves of feelings she was experiencing. 'It's me who should be dead, not him. I've ruined everything.' Rosa was now a mess, her body shaking violently. She gagged, spewing bile onto her lap, unable to stop the huge wave of guilt that swept through her.

'Come, take this.' The female officer pulled some wet wipes from one of the utility belt compartments and rubbed Rosa's back, trying to help her calm down.

Leah was going nuts in the other police car. Her hurt quickly turned to anger, and she screamed at the officer, her face twisted in hate. 'Ask her. That bitch in the other car, ask her! It was her brothers. She set him up!' Leah continued to rant as the other female officer sat sternly, her face emotionless, watching Leah lose her shit. Leah's tears had dried, leaving translucent stains on her reddened face. She stared at the officer, her eyes wide, pausing from her rant.

'Leah, just take a moment,' the officer finally said, deadpan and calm. Her tone silenced Leah, who drew a breath and shook her head. 'Look at that.' She pointed through the car window to the burnt-out building; the level of destruction was now starkly visible in the sunrise.

A crackled message came through on the officer's radio.

'All units. Cordon needed. Paramedics as well. Body's been found round the back, all units code red.'

The officer looked at Leah. 'Stay here!' she ordered whilst opening the car door and leaving in haste.

Leah trembled with shock. She tried to react by getting out the car, but the doors had been locked by the exiting officer. Leah banged on the window. 'Oi, let me out! Is my brother alive or what? Fuck sake.' She continued to scream, kicking and banging on the window, watching outside as the paramedics and police converged around the building.

Rosa

Chapter 15
Wearing my Rolex

Loud techno music pumped from two large black speakers placed either side of a DJ. He was dressed in a bright-blue and pink Hawaiian shirt and white tennis-style shorts. The sun shone brightly and the heat was relentless. The DJ bopped alone, holding his hand up to his oversized white headphones as revellers danced and chatted excitedly.

Others jumped into the clear, blue pool, which was filled with bikini-clad girls playing on inflated lilos shaped like unicorns and pink flamingos. They screamed and splashed about with other guests—muscle-bound, tattooed men who tossed them like cabers over their shoulders into the water.

Franky, the host, bowled about on the lawn, checking everyone and everything was OK. He had white flip-flops, tight fluorescent-pink shorts and not much else but a beer in his hand. His tree trunk-like torso was reddened in the heat. He went over to the barbecue area where a tall black man with dreadlocks attended to the sizzling burgers, chicken pieces and other assorted items spaced out on the large charcoal-flamed grill.

Franky was clearly in his element, enjoying himself, dancing and laughing. His young boyfriend came over. His slight body was draped in a patterned silk geisha-type gown revealing his slender physique.

Franky grabbed him and pulled the gown back from his shoulders. 'Gimme a kiss, boy.' He pulled him in and engaged in a long tongue- and tonsil-devouring kiss, finally pulling himself away.

'Oi, oi, save the rest for later.'

He touched his face tenderly then smacked him on the bum. 'Go on, fuck off and enjoy yourself.' He dismissed his young partner, taking a burger from the barbecue. Franky was in a good mood, and the garden was filling up with more people.

Everyone was either snorting coke, popping pills, sucking on balloons or smoking a joint as they partied. It was a very hedonistic vibe.

Franky's phone was constantly buzzing. He walked around feeling pumped up, stopping only to stoop down to take a sniff from a mound of coke off the stomach of a gorgeous blonde wearing a gold bikini. Lying back on one of the many sun loungers, she smiled and stuck her tongue out playfully at him as he rubbed his nose vigorously.

'Randy. Yeah, where are you, mate? OK, coming.' He moved across the finely cut lawn towards the main house and saw his cohort standing on the decking with a dirty, bruised and cut-up Jesus and Dani. Franky clocked them and instantly looked annoyed. 'What the fuck, man? Take them to the basement.' He shooed them away.

Jesus and Dani watched the activities taking place in the garden but their expressions and demeanour were the extreme opposite of those of the revellers in front of them. The cohort grunted and dragged them away and into the house.

Franky continued to rant. 'Lock them up, then come and get a beer. We'll deal with them later.' He forced them back into the house, still chatting on his phone. 'Yep, Randy. Coming now.' He stomped his way back through his mansion.

Large, elaborate, brass-stemmed chandeliers hung from high ceilings. White marble floors and classy furniture made the interior look like a feature in *Harper's Bazaar*.

Finally Franky got to the front door. 'I'm here, mate. Hold on.' He cut the phone and opened the door.

Randy was a tall, well-built, bald, bearded black man. He was wearing dark shades and an open black shirt with a yellow sunflower print. He was flanked by at least five sexy, exotic-looking women, their skin resembling a colour palette from a L'Oréal make-up commercial. 'Mr Franky,' he said calmly, with a slight Dutch accent and the god-like presence of someone important.

Franky launched into a giant hug of his guest. 'Fucking hell, how long's it been?' Randy pulled back from the hug.

'Long enough,' he replied. Again, his silky voice was calm. He smiled, showing a glint of diamond-encrusted grills.

'Come in, man. All of you, come on in.' Franky ushered them all into the house and through to the garden.

The bass from the music outside reverberated through the walls of the dim underground basement where Jesus and Dani sat on the floor amongst old furniture and stacks of boxes. Jesus was vexed. He stared ahead with his hands tied behind his back.

Dani sat opposite him, looking tired and deflated from their overnight exertions, and he could barely string his words together. 'He's got the money. Why are we here?' he asked rhetorically, his face sweating and covered in mud, cuts and bruises.

'How the fuck do I know? This is all your fault. You and your dumb ideas.' His eyes bored into his brother and he spat towards Dani, the saliva landing on his arm.

'Fuck off, this is on you. I told you not to kill that guy, but nah, you had to set fire . . .'

Jesus wriggled frustratedly, his skeletal body jerking and jolting in his attempt to get to Dani. Instead, he aimed a weak kick in his direction. 'He had to die, and so will that slag of a sister of yours.'

Dani was incensed and tried to spit at his older brother, but he didn't have enough saliva. It just dribbled down his chin. 'Don't talk about her like that, she's our blood!' he exclaimed. For once, he stood up to Jesus.

Jesus observed him for a few seconds, his eyes filled with evil, but he bowed his head, unable to respond. Both sat stewing in their own bowl of guilt over their actions as the bass continued to thump through the walls.

The pool party was raucous and in full swing. There were between seventy and a hundred guests, all dressed in brightly coloured beachwear. Everyone was dancing and frolicking around the pool; screams and shrieks of laughter pierced the unrelenting music that pounded out of the speakers.

Randy sat like a king on the edge of a sun lounger, surrounded by his harem, who were all sat on yoga-style mats on the grass, now in their designer bikinis, sun hats and designer shades. They sipped drinks from red plastic cups, taking it all in. Randy chewed down carefully on a burger, surveying all the antics in front of him.

Franky dad-danced with his young boyfriend, his heavyweight, boxer-type torso jerking frantically to the techno music. His two cohorts looked out of place. Dressed in black vests and combat shorts with steel-capped boots, they watched on like hawks from a distance. A muscle-bound guest picked up a slim, limp, topless girl and carried her caveman style over his shoulders, then jumped into the pool to the cheers of others.

Franky broke away from his boyfriend and danced his way over towards Randy. He was sweating and coked up to the eyeballs. He dragged a sun lounger over to him and took a seat. 'Fucking brilliant. Think I'm gonna do a club night here now.' He wiped the sweat from his face.

Randy turned to him. 'Sounds like a plan.' His response was cold, with no real emotion. He turned to Franky, handing the plate with the burger on to one of his ladies. He lowered his shades. 'So let's get to business.' His diamond-encrusted teeth sparkled as he moved his lips.

Franky, still catching his breath, nodded in agreement. 'I got some good Pakistani H. I say let's partner up. You set up the European franchise.' He spoke rapidly, obviously hyped up.

Randy stared ahead. 'Hmm, do you think I need you to do that?' he responded coolly.

Franky wiped his face with his hands and shook his head wildly, trying to think straight. 'Mate, I got all that you need. The proper stuff.' He turned to Randy and they eyed each other, only to be interrupted by a gang of drunk revellers squirting water from super soaker guns directed at them and Randy's girls. 'Oi, piss off!' Franky yelled, half-laughing at them as they retreated and ran off across the lawn.

Randy was soaked, and he stood up and took off his shirt, revealing his thick, tattooed torso. His girls also looked annoyed, their flawless hair and faces wet.

'Shit, man. Fucking idiots. Sorry about that. It's cool, you'll dry off soon,' he pleaded with Randy, who shot a cutting look at Franky and wiped himself down with his shirt.

'It's OK, Franky.' He sat back down, putting his hand on Franky's shoulder. Franky signalled to his cohorts, and they came over like two faithful dogs to their master. 'Bring those two to my office. Be there in five minutes.' They nodded at the instruction and made their way towards the house. Franky turned his conversation back to Randy. 'Give me a few minutes. Got some other stuff to take care of. Have a drink, I'll be back.'

Dani and Jesus were dragged unceremoniously into a large room and dumped on the floor in front of a pink-skinned Franky, who sat behind a large desk with a bottle of tequila. He downed a shot, swallowing and coughing as the harsh alcohol grated against the back of his throat. 'Get on your knees,' he rasped.

Both did as instructed, staring up at Franky. His pirate-earringed cohort tossed the leather pouch onto the desk in front of Franky.

'Let's see what we got here.' He unzipped the pouch and took out the stacked fifty-pound notes, spreading them out across the table.

Dani glanced at Jesus.

Franky carefully counted each note, stopping only to pour another shot, which he downed, slamming the glass back onto the table and rubbing his nose before continuing his count. After around ten minutes, Franky stopped. He looked at all the notes stacked neatly in columns across the table. 'Seems like you're short.'

Jesus shook his head in defiance. 'No way, can't be. Count it again,' he ordered.

Franky looked down at him. 'You saying my count's off?' he snarled.

'It's all there, must be.' Jesus received a firm boot to his back from Franky's cohort that sent him face-down onto the floor.

'I'm telling you it's short. Four racks short.' Franky opened a drawer and took out a gun, tucking it into his tight shorts. He walked around the table with a look of disappointment and sighing heavily. Franky's flip-flops squished against the marble-tiled floor. He stood above them, his tight, fluorescent shorts blending with his reddened legs. 'Not good enough, boys. Looks like I'll have to . . .' He pulled the gun, waving it at both of them simultaneously. 'Gonna count down from ten before I blow your heads off.'

Dani crumbled, begging, his eyes welling up. 'Please, Franky. If you knew what we had to do . . .' Jesus shoved into Dani, giving him daggers.

The chimes of the doorbell echoed through the house, distracting Franky. 'Bloody hell, go see who's at the door. Probably more guests,' he instructed his cohort, who scuttled from the room on command. The doorbell continued to chime, sounding like wedding church bells, blending eerily with the thudding techno bassline. Franky, perturbed, turned his attention back to Jesus and Dani, who gazed up at him waiting for mercy.

Dani looked like a beaten man about to cry from the weight of his sins. 'Please, Franky. We did what we could,' he whimpered, his voice laden with exhaustion and drawing an evil look from Jesus.

'Please, Franky,' Franky mocked, taking the tequila bottle and pouring the contents over Dani's head. 'You Mexicans love tequila.' He chuckled to himself, only to be interrupted by a noisy commotion out in the hallway. 'Fuck sake!' Agitated by the interruption, Franky bowled towards the door, which burst open, and his cohort rushed back in.

'Fuck, Franky. It's the feds. There's loads of 'em.' He'd barely finished his sentence before being struck in the back by a taser gun, the electric volts stopping him in his tracks, his body jerking to the floor in front of Franky.

'Shit.' Franky ran around Jesus and Dani towards his desk. He pulled open the drawer and tried to scoop all of the money from the table into it before a wave of black SAS-styled police officers converged in the room.

'On the floor, get down now!' one of the officers shouted aggressively through a black gas mask.

Dani and Jesus, still on their knees as the police entered, could only watch as Franky did his best to conceal the money. He spun around, aiming the gun in their direction. 'Fuck off or I'll shoot the lot of ya!'

The police edged closer, three of them looking like guerilla bandits, their faces covered by masks. 'Put it down, Franky. Get on the floor.'

Franky stepped back and tried to pull open the patio doors. Three gunshots rang out melodically in time with the bassline. Franky fell back, his chest seeping blood through the gaping wounds, but his strength was superhuman—he still managed to lunge forward, aiming the gun.

'Put it down!' one of the officers shouted, but Franky, not one to follow instructions, pulled the trigger and unloaded shots.

The officers fired back, felling Franky like an elephant being hunted for its ivory. Jesus and Dani cowered, unable to move in the melee. They could only watch as Franky, strong as an ox even with several bullets lodged in his chest, used his last reserves of strength to try and stand before succumbing and collapsing to the floor.

Randy sat coolly watching the party in front of him until, from the corner of his eye, he saw hordes of police crash into the garden. They were shouting, but due to the loud boom of the techno music, their screams could not be heard. The other guests were too high and engrossed in the fun to notice until a line of officers swept across the lawn, grabbing anyone in sight. Randy didn't move. He looked at his girls and motioned to them to stay calm.

Panic set in as the other revellers realised what was happening. Some of them were so high that they began to jump and clap ecstatically on seeing the brutal way they were tackling the guests. Others jumped into the pool, thinking it was safer, while some continued to dance trance-like, looking up at the police helicopter which hovered over the house.

Chapter 16
There must be an angel

Leah sat alone in the waiting room, sipping from a white plastic cup. She shook and was hunched over, looking at her phone screen. Her bare feet were dirty. She crossed her leg over her knee, still wearing her silk pyjamas, and her body was half-wrapped in a red hospital blanket. She sniffed loudly, still tearful. A slight knock on the door interrupted her thoughts.

An Asian nurse in full uniform covered by a see-through plastic apron came into the room. 'Leah, is it?' she asked, prompting Leah to look up at her.

'Yes,' she answered, her voice barely audible and cracked from the pain of the last few hours.

'Can I sit?' The nurse pulled a chair next to Leah, who pushed her hair back, nodding. 'Your brother is still unconscious. Some superficial burns, mainly his hands, but he's stable.' She looked sympathetically at Leah, who put her plastic cup down and held her face, crying.

The nurse placed her hand on Leah's shoulder. 'I think he'll be OK. Do you want to see him?' She spoke softly, trying to have a hint of optimism in her tone.

Leah could only nod, choking back her tears. She was helped up by the nurse as she planted her bare feet firmly on the cold, lino floor.

'Take your time.' The nurse ushered her towards the door.

As she approached the ward, Leah could see that there were two uniformed police officers standing outside. She hesitated.

'It's OK, they are just here for protection,' the nurse reassured her, coaxing her forwards.

* * *

Rosa sat alone, confined in a small cell on a slim mattress placed on the floor next to a chrome toilet. The room was dark and bland, lit only by an irritating, flickering halogen bulb. Her knees were pulled up to her chest, and her head was bowed between her legs, her hair dangling and covering her face. She shivered even though she wore a grey sweatshirt and tracksuit bottoms. The sound of a key being turned in the lock made her look up.

She looked drawn and tired as a female police officer opened the large granite-coloured steel door. She stepped in holding a large bunch of keys. 'Rosa, you need to come with me.' Her voice was firm but compassionate.

Rosa took a deep breath, then managed to slowly raise her body from the floor. The officer came in and took her arm, leading her out of the cell and slamming the door behind them. Rosa was led into a small interview room.

There were two men dressed casually in jeans and tee shirts, police lanyards hung around their necks, standing talking to each other. As she entered the room, they looked over at her stony-faced and moved towards her. 'Take a seat.' One of the men, gruff-voiced, held out his hand encouraging her to sit on the seat opposite.

Rosa sat down as directed. She was confused, staring around the room.

'Hi, Rosa, I'm Detective Phil Dickinson. This is my colleague, Ben Grimes.' Both men sat down opposite her. They seemed cold and distant.

Rosa was instantly uncomfortable with their stance. She sat back in the chair, folding her arms in defiance.

'We need to ask you some questions about your brothers,' Phil Dickinson explained clicking on the black recorder, his gruff tone emphasizing the seriousness of the questions that were soon to be asked.

This is so unfair, why am I sitting here?

I've done nothing wrong, yet I'm being treated like a criminal.

I want to know what's happened with Daniel.

I'm tired, I'm drained, I stink.

Just want to be with him.

For a few seconds, she became emotional, fighting back tears. 'I don't know what happened. Daniel went to sort things out. I called and it was late, then . . . Jesus answered.' She wiped her nose with the sleeve of the sweatshirt.

'Jesus is your brother?' the detective asked.

'Yes. I haven't seen or heard from them in a while.' She chewed her fingernail which was still covered in red nail polish.

'So are you saying you were not a part of this?'

Rosa responded by slamming her hand down onto the table. 'No! I wasn't. I was waiting for him to come back home.' Her voice rose with a surge of passion. She was so vehement in her rebuttal that her face was twisted with a crazy expression. Her brown eyes stared wildly at the detectives, such was her offence. This stunned them into silence and they could only look at each other, searching in their minds.

The beep of the heart monitor every few seconds interrupted the silence. Daniel lay peacefully on the bed, eyes shut. His body was wrapped tightly under the blanket. His handsome face was covered in red marks and bruises, his hands and head were covered in bandages. Various pieces of medical equipment surrounded him, and his face was covered with an oxygen mask. Leah stood over the bed staring down at him, visibly upset and holding a ragged piece of tissue to her nose. She stretched out her other hand, touching his forehead. Her hand shook as she stroked him. It was hard for her to accept the sad state her brother was in, and she couldn't even imagine the ordeal he had gone through only a few hours earlier.

A knock on the door distracted her. She turned to see a doctor come into the room. He was older, had grey hair and was distinguished-looking, with gold-rimmed glasses which hung from his neck. 'Hi. You must be Leah Rosewood, correct?'

Leah nodded. She could barely muster the words to put a sentence together. 'Sorry, yes.'

The doctor stepped forwards. 'I'm the consultant, Dr Cohen. I have the results of our tests. Please take a seat.'

Leah wiped her face, stiffening up and bracing herself for whatever news was about to come her way. She slowly sat down as the doctor pulled a chair next to her.

'There is some bruising to the brain.'

Leah broke down.

'He has some superficial burns to the hands and internal bruising. We'll monitor.' He patted her shoulder to comfort her. 'He's going to be OK, but it will be a long recovery and he'll need a lot of care.'

Nodding, Leah took a sharp breath then began to wail, her hands covering her face.

* * *

Gosh, we're going around in circles.

They keep asking the same question.

How many times do I have to tell them I had nothing to do with it?

And I hate my brothers, I don't care anymore.

They are disgusting pigs; selfish, greedy bastards.

I don't know how they found Daniel, the showroom or anything and these stupid detectives are trying to link me to this.

They took my phone, everything.

Ridiculous, there's no way I would ever do this, never would hurt Daniel, he's my world.

Rosa was tired. All she wanted to do was get out of the station and find out what had happened to Daniel.

'So, how did you two meet?' Again, another inquisition

into her relationship with Daniel from Detective Phil Dickinson. He tapped his pen impatiently on the table.

'In a launderette.' Rosa's dry reply was an indication of her mood.

'Go on.' He continued to press ahead with his line of questioning until Rosa snapped.

'Look! He's my boyfriend! Why would I set him up to die and lose his business?' Her voice cracked with rage, fed up now with having to answer. Her emotions were all over the place, and she was at that point where she didn't care.

'Strange what people, even girlfriends, do for money,' Phil Dickinson said dryly, taking another stab at Rosa's armour.

Ben Grimes stepped in. His approach was more relaxed. He tried the old good cop bad cop routine to see whether he could break her down. 'How would you describe the state of your relationship?'

Rosa rolled her eyes and pushed back in her seat. 'We are fine, in love, he rescued me . . . I ran away from those two idiot brothers because I hate them!' Her voice broke, her true feelings laid bare. She stopped only to sip some water from the plastic cup. 'They are no longer my *familia*; my life is with Daniel now.'

Ben Grimes clicked the recorder off, the two detectives got up from their seats, picked up their notepads without a word and left the room, leaving Rosa alone. She just about held it all together, but inside was turmoil.

Fuck, man, why is this happening?
Why is no one telling me what's going on?
Is he dead?

Is he alive?

Have they got Jesus and Dani?

Am I being charged?

I mean seriously what the fuck!

They should be telling me stuff.

I'm his girlfriend I just need to know he's OK...

The female officer returned to the room. 'Come on, Rosa, you're out.'

Rosa turned to her, her eyes red with stress and tears. 'What?'

'You're being released for now. Come and get your things.' She opened the door, beckoning Rosa to leave.

Rosa looked at her confused but relieved. She dragged herself up from the chair, rubbing her eyes, before being led out of the room.

Leah's phone vibrated. She checked it and saw Rosa's name flashing on the screen. She rolled her eyes, sighing heavily, before answering. 'Hi, Rosa. What do you want?' She left the room where Daniel still lay unconscious and walked through the corridors of the hospital. 'Look, something you need to know, Daniel's alive. He's here—I'm at the hospital.'

Rosa's cry came through the phone.

'We're at St Michael's Intensive Care Unit.' Leah clicked off the call. She was exhausted and still angry, but she knew that she had to at least let Rosa know the truth.

Rosa arrived at the hospital and rushed frantically through the hospital ward, checking each room until she saw Leah standing in front of her a few yards away. She ran towards her, her heart racing. 'Oh God, Leah, I can't believe he's alive. Is he OK?' She tried to embrace Leah, who resisted her slightly, her overriding suspicion still affecting her judgement, plus the rancid smell of a police cell still lingered on Rosa's arms.

Leah looked her directly in the eye. 'He looks worse than he is, so brace yourself,' she warned, opening the door and ushering her into the room.

Rosa whispered prayers under her breath in Spanish and made a sign of the cross on her chest several times over. Her eyes on Daniel, she let out a pained, breathy scream. Leah watched on scornfully, standing at the end of the bed.

Rosa touched Daniel's bandaged hand, suppressing her tears. 'What did the doctors say?' she asked.

Leah stood, arms folded, looking down at the floor for a few seconds.

'What?'

'He'll need a lot of care, but he will make a full recovery,' she said dryly.

Rosa choked with relief. 'Thank God.' She bent over, placing a gentle kiss on his bruised cheek 'I'll take care of you,' she whispered.

Leah walked around the bed opposite Rosa. She rubbed her face. It had been a long night, but she still had pent-up energy to get off her chest. 'No, you won't.'

'Meaning?'

'Meaning I want you out. I'll take care of my brother.'

'Out?'

'Don't make this harder than it is. If it weren't for you and them bastard brothers of yours...' Leah raised her voice, unable to keep her emotions in check. 'I want you out!'

'Pardon? I ain't going nowhere—he needs me!' Rosa screamed back.

Her angry response invoked a heated exchange. They bickered back and forth, enraged and emotional, until a nurse came rushing into the room.

'Excuse me! What's going on here?' The middle-aged nurse provided a timely interruption to the warring ladies. 'This is an ICU, not a school playground, please!' Her firm words silenced them both.

Leah held her gaze of fury towards Rosa, who, in return, gave back a cold stare before turning away and looking down at Daniel. 'He needs me,' she repeated firmly, causing Leah to brush past the nurse and rush out of the room.

Rosa

Chapter 17
Seven seconds away

The police station resembled a war zone in the aftermath of Franky's barbecue even hours later. A frazzled-looking duty officer was still trying to process all of the arrested revellers, most of whom were still high, buzzing and bouncing off the walls. They were a long way from their cocktail of drugs comedown.

A few of them were still dancing, bobbing up and down in handcuffs and swimwear. Franky's young boyfriend, wrapped in his silk gown, was being comforted by a friend. He was distraught. Randy stood with his hands cuffed behind his back, staying cool. His female entourage sat squashed next to each other on the sidelines, their faces sour, looking a shade of the beauties they had been at the beginning of the day.

Jesus was locked up in a separate cell. He looked a state, dirty and bedraggled. He paced back and forth in the tiny room, cursing under his breath in Spanish. He put his head against the wall, headbutting it in frustration.

Dani was alone in an interview room, sat at a table across from Detective Phil Dickinson and Ben Grimes. They stared at him, giving him the silent treatment, which was excruciating for Dani, who shifted uncomfortably in his chair.

'What am I doing here?' Dani blurted out, unable to confine his angst.

Phil Dickinson turned to his partner, tapping a pen on his teeth. They both turned to face Dani; they could see he was on edge and ready to break. He wasn't built for this life, and they knew it; he was ready to spill the beans.

'Shall we start with the robbery, assault and arson at the showroom, Dani?' A deadpan question was delivered with only a sliver of empathy. 'See, we know you had dealings with Franky, so I'll give you a chance to explain yourself.' Phil Dickinson sucked the pen, then began to scribble on his notepad.

Dani was not hard to break down; he was already an emotional mess. 'Can I get some food? Chicken and chips,' he asked, which drew cackles from the two detectives.

'Listen, mate, you're not in a fucking restaurant. This is a nick, so start talking,' Ben Grimes instructed, slamming his palm on the surface of the table, causing Dani to flinch.

He ran his fingers through his cropped hair, thinking about all that he had endured.

'You know the man you assaulted survived? So when he recovers, he'll tell us anyway.' Phil Dickinson's deadpan tone laid it out for Dani.

'It wasn't supposed to go that far,' Dani finally croaked. He sipped some water from a plastic cup to quench his thirst. 'I fucked up. We just needed the money or Franky .

. .' He stopped as his thoughts returned to Franky taking bullets, a scene he would never forget.

'Money for Franky? Go on,' Ben Grimes goaded him, leaning forward with interest.

'Nah, I've said enough. I want a solicitor.' Dani folded his arms, sitting back defiantly. He was naïve, but he knew not to snitch to the pigs. Of course he wouldn't.

Phil Dickinson dropped his pen onto the pad. 'OK, smart arse, but a solicitor won't save you. You'll get a long stretch.' He got up and grabbed his notepad. Ben Grimes followed him, cutting a dirty look towards Dani before they left the room, leaving Dani to stew alone.

Jesus was altogether a different proposition. He sat with his bony arms folded, his stance rebellious, his lips pursed, while the same double act of Dickinson and Grimes sat across from him. He was still bloodied, dirty and smelling as if he had not washed in weeks.

'Come on, Jesus, may as well start talking. Dani and your sister Rosa have already dropped you in it.' Phil Dickinson now sounded fed up. He blew his nose into a handkerchief and pointed his finger at Jesus while rubbing his nose vigorously.

Jesus stroked his wispy goatee beard and gave a wry smile. He was a tougher nut to crack, hardened by his experiences. He was saying nothing.

'Were you responsible for the assault, arson and robbery of Daniel Rosewood—yes or no?' A frustrated Phil Dickinson banged his fist on the table, shaking the fragile cups of coffee.

Jesus smirked. 'No comment.' He was loving the control he held.

Phil Dickinson got up from the desk and reached over, grabbing Jesus's face. 'Now listen here, you little prick. I've just about had enough . . .'

Ben Grimes grabbed his shoulders, pulling him back. 'Let him go, Phil. Come on.'

The three tussled for a few seconds before Phil Dickinson eventually released Jesus, who broke into a heinous laugh. His reaction further agitated the flustered detective, who shoved Ben Grimes off him.

'Get off me,' he growled at his partner. Ben Grimes backed off and put his hands in the air.

Jesus continued to laugh childishly. 'That's assault. I'll make a complaint you know.' He pointed at Phil Dickinson, continuing to toy with him, much to his amusement.

Chapter 18
My love is your love

It had been three days since Rosa had been released. She had been living at the hospital, tending to Daniel every day. She had the same routine—she prayed next to him, wiped his face gently with a flannel rinsed in warm water and sat talking to him about all their memories and the plans she had for them together after he woke and had recovered. It was hard, especially as Leah was still breathing fire towards her, but she was determined to stick by his side, even in the face of Leah's fury.

Most days, Leah would come in around lunchtime. Even in this time of tragedy, she still preferred to go home at night and return the next day. She entered the room looking fresh in a short jean skirt, flip-flops and large shades. She brought a bag of food, water, toiletries and a change of clothes for Rosa, but their relationship was still fractious. Leah resented the fact Rosa was Daniel's chief carer but knew she couldn't stop her from staying.

They sat on opposite sides of Daniel's bed. Leah flicked through a magazine while Rosa cleaned her face with bacterial wipes, trying not to glance in Leah's direction.

I don't think I will ever forgive her for accusing me.

Look at him.

Why would I ever do this to him?

He's the love of my life.

I can't control what my brothers did, I don't even know how they found him.

No need for her to be a bitch to me.

It hurts, I thought we were friends, sisters even.

Rosa's thoughts were interrupted by the consultant, Dr Cohen, who came into the room looking professional, a stethoscope hanging from his neck. 'Good morning. How are you?'

Rosa nodded and Leah quietly murmured her response.

The consultant sensed an atmosphere and continued with his checks. 'Well, the good news is he is making good progress. In a couple of days, we can take him off the ventilator and sedation.' He turned to them both. 'He will need TLC, a lot of it,' he said, trying to ease the tension.

Rosa nodded in agreement, looking over at Leah. 'Thank you,' she said quietly, acknowledging Dr Cohen's positive statement.

Once Dr Cohen had left, Leah went back to her bitterness. She scowled at Rosa. 'I still want you out.' She pointed at Rosa, baring her teeth.

Rosa simply shook her head and carried on tending to Daniel, fixing his pillows and generally fussing. Leah came over to the bed. She took Daniel's hand and bent down, kissing his cheek. Rosa shook her head and smiled at her antics. She knew that Leah's fury still burned intensely, but she was adamant that she would not be parted from Daniel.

'Tell me, why would I set him up?' she asked Leah directly.

'Because girls like you—' she paused, remembering Daniel, then turned her back.

'Leah, I love him and you! Believe me, I wouldn't ever.' Rosa's plea fell on deaf ears and again, Leah chose not to answer.

Her face was hard as she returned to her chair. She picked up her magazine without a word and began flicking through the pages.

Rosa continued to fuss over Daniel, ignoring Leah and the hostile silence. Rosa's phone buzzed, the vibration disturbing the tense atmosphere that suffocated the room. Rosa picked it up and saw Mya's name on the screen. 'Hi, Mya. Give me a sec.' She could feel Leah's glare over the top of the pages as she left the room.

Rosa

Chapter 19
Love lockdown

Rosa stood brushing her teeth over a basin in the hospital toilets. It was not the best of facilities, but she was happy to be there just so she could be near Daniel. She washed out her mouth and splashed water onto her face. Staring into the tiny mirror, she saw a tired, sorrowful young woman who had the world on her shoulders. She had hardly slept, not that she could get much comfort from a hospital chair, but her dedication and guilt enabled her to tough it out. Not like Leah, who always left in the evening and came back glam and refreshed the next day. She was not the type of girl who could slum it, even for the sake of her brother.

Rosa dabbed her face dry with a harsh piece of toilet tissue. Her natural beauty had drained away from the stress and worry of the last few week's events. She was tired and her eyes were burning, but she held herself together. She began to pray, as she usually did in private, but this time, when she closed her eyes, she could see a strong image of her mother. She was smiling and telling her to be strong.

Mama, I miss you so much.

I am stronger now but I can't be loyal to those two after this.

I am alone.

Only Daniel has given to me without motive.

She continued to mumble her thoughts and talk to her imaginary mother. Maybe it was the overtiredness or some sort of spiritual intervention, but in that moment, Rosa felt the hands of her mother touching her face and the warmth of her hands cupping her cheeks.

I am strong, Mama, thank you . . .

Her moment of meditation was interrupted by heavy banging on the door. Rosa snapped out of her trance, quickly grabbing her toiletries. 'Just a minute,' she yelled, wiping her face before opening the door to find the on-duty nurse looking animated.

'He's awake and calling for you!'

Rosa was ushered out of the room and back to the ward.

Daniel was groggy. He was still adjusting to the lights, but once he saw Rosa, a flicker of happiness could be seen in his eyes. He tried to move, but his body was not quite ready to do what his brain commanded.

'Hello there.' Rosa's smile was wide across her face as she gazed down at him, touching his face tenderly. 'I've been waiting for you.' She giggled, choking back tears of happiness.

The nurse stood by watching for a few seconds. 'We need to give him time, but his vitals are good.' She rubbed Rosa's arm before leaving the room.

'I should call Leah.' She picked up her phone and called while still watching Daniel, who was like a newborn baby, his eyes adjusting to the light and surroundings. He groaned to signal his awareness. 'Leah, he's awake. Come now.' A short, curt message was all that was needed at that point.

Leah arrived, once again looking fresh but flushed from the heat that persisted outside. She sauntered in, a large tote bag slung over her shoulder and shades perched on her head. She barely acknowledged Rosa, walking straight over to Daniel and bending down to kiss him. 'Bruv, so glad to see you've come round. You had me shit scared.' She laid her head next to his and sobbed.

Daniel could hardly get away from being smothered by his sister. Just a few uncomfortable groans could be heard.

Rosa's happiness was confined. She covered her mouth with her hand, which shook as her joyful emotions danced underneath. She was so relieved. Just to see Daniel's blue eyes wide open again was the best thing she had seen in the last fraught few weeks. She took a seat, watching Leah fuss over her brother.

Thank you so much, God.

You answered my prayers now hopefully he can heal.

I don't care what happens to me, just glad he's going to be OK.

Leah angled a sly look in Rosa's direction. She gave her a paltry smile, a sort of appreciation seeing Rosa was the one who had been on twenty-four-hour watch. It was an underhand gesture of gratitude before she went back to playing Florence Nightingale.

It was late afternoon. Daniel was asleep, resting. The atmosphere was still toxic as the two women in his life sat across the bed in their own worlds. Rosa was exhausted; she could barely keep her eyes open.

Leah got up from her seat and walked over to her. 'Can I have a word outside?' Her voice was a low whisper, coaxing Rosa.

They left the room and walked down the corridor.

'Just wanted to say—' Leah began, only to be interrupted by Rosa.

'It's OK, I don't mind looking after him—'

Leah pulled her by the arm. 'What I wanted to say was,' she gave her a steely stare, 'Once Daniel is well enough to go home, you can go.' She spoke through gritted teeth. Her hand squeezed Rosa's arm until Rosa pulled it away and began to walk back to the room without a word. 'I mean it!' Leah screamed in her direction, her voice echoing down the corridor. She shook with fury, and her face was contorted with frustration. Leah knew she could not break Rosa, no matter how much she tried to push her away.

Rosa dug her heels in deeper; it was a battle of wills, but Leah would not give up.

She took out her mobile phone and began to scroll through her contacts. She pressed the button to make the call. She paced back and forth waiting. 'Hi, hello, Detective Dickinson? It's Leah, Leah Rosewood. Can we have a chat?'

Chapter 20
The lunatics have taken over the asylum

Being placed on remand, awaiting his day in court, was no fun for Dani, especially as he was being held in a separate prison to Jesus. He was like a little boy lost amongst a crowd full of demented souls.

Sat alone in his cell, Dani looked aimlessly around the room. Being younger than Jesus, he was detained in a young offender's facility. He had been there for a few weeks, ever since the madness of Franky's bloodbath barbeque and the aftermath. Still traumatised, he had been a vacant character trying to keep his head down and go unnoticed. Unfortunately for him, he was about to get a window into his future.

Every day at three o'clock, the inmates were let out into the yard for exercise and fresh air. Dani hated it. It was at the height of the afternoon heat. He felt exposed and vulnerable as the prying eyes from the rough bunch of inmates were cast in his direction. Most of the youths were in rival gangs, and unless you had an alliance with one of them, it left you open to intimidation. Dani was a lone sheep surrounded by a pack of hungry wolves.

Dani walked alone around the edge of the yard, isolated from the others. He did his best to stay invisible, but it was only a matter of time before he was hunted down by a group of five boys. They looked rough, rugged and built, with tattooed biceps. They were black, except for one. White, skin-headed, tall and lean, he leered over at Dani. Dani's heart was in his mouth. He knew the next few minutes would be uncomfortable, to say the least. He froze, then slowly backed away, but it was too late. His path was cut off and he had nowhere to go as they descended on him like hyenas around a dead carcass.

'Fuck you think you're going, likkle man?' the skinhead asked, his accent showing that he was born on the streets. An italic tattoo of the name 'Lainey' showed on his neck as he looked towards his gang. 'He don't know who I am.' They surrounded Dani, all smirking and posturing. 'Hold this, balls it.' The skinhead youth shoved a small scrunched-up plastic bag into his chest. He looked shifty with a sheen of sweat on his pasty face.

'What's your name?' One of the other boys pushed Dani in the head with his fingers.

Dani flinched, still holding on to the bag.

'Fucking hurry up, man. Balls the ting, innit.' The skinhead boy hit him in the chest again.

Dani panicked, his voice quivering with fear. 'Please, man, I can't,' he pleaded, but he was met with a heavy punch to the face, rocking him back as his knees buckled beneath him. 'Ow! Jeez, what the . . . I'm on remand, I can't.' He tried to stand but was surrounded by the herd all snorting and licking their lips like a pride ready to eat.

The skinhead punched Dani again in the stomach. 'I'm Lex. I'll come see you when I need it, El Chapo.' They all sniggered, then dispersed before the screws sniffed out anything untoward, leaving a sweaty and shaken Dani alone.

Dani quickly shoved the bag down the front of his thick prison tracksuit bottoms. He attempted to catch his breath, still winded from the blow delivered and sucking air into his sandpaper-dry mouth. The sound of the whistle and guards shouting like army officers signalled the end of recreation period. The inmates made their way back into the building. Dani took a few more breaths before stepping back towards the entrance.

The echoes of shouting and laughter from the wings made Dani shudder as he sat on the hard bunk. His dirty tee shirt was drenched with sweat patches under his arms, and his legs shook, doing repetitions of spasms. He wiped his forehead, spooked by his latest experience. He got up and paced up and down the small room, jittery and on edge. He peered out of the tiny window in the door to check that no guards were near.

'Fuck, man!' he uttered under his breath before shuffling back to his bunk. He stuffed his hands down his jogging bottoms and pulled out the plastic bag. It was filled with pills and small buds of weed wrapped in cling film. 'Ahh, shit.' He quickly stuffed the bag back down into his crotch just in time before a guard pushed open the door. Dani quickly straightened up and casually crossed his legs on the bed.

The brawny guard swung open the door. 'You got company. Come on, Leroy.' He stepped aside ushering in a new inmate—a lanky, basketball-player-type black boy with short dreads.

Leroy strode moodily into the room with his head bowed, holding his plastic bag of clothes.

'Five minutes, then muster.' The guard slammed the door shut, leaving them looking at each other.

'What's good?' Leroy's deep growl was an overture to Dani, who stared back like a rabbit caught in the headlights. Leroy chucked his bag onto the bunk above Dani. 'First time?' Leroy asked.

Dani nodded.

'My second time this year. Pussyhole judge.' He sat next to Dani, running his fingers through his tight, twisted locks. 'What you here for?' he asked, raising his head and looking at Dani, his dark skin glossed with a sheen of sweat.

Dani just stared into the distance for a few seconds. 'Few things, stupid things.'

Leroy nodded his head knowingly.

The recreation room was the hub where all the inmates gathered after dinner. It was a hive of activity. Music strained from a clapped-out cassette radio, some youths huddled around a worn-out pool table, others were raucous as they sat around a table playing cards. Dani sidled around the outskirts of the room by the bookshelves, trying not to be noticed. He browsed the dusty books, pretending to take an interest in a large encyclopedia. He pulled it from the shelf and turned the pages slowly, but he paid more attention to what was happening around him.

The gang led by Lex entered with an air of authority. He was obviously the big cheese in this place. His presence brought a different mood to the room; he was cocksure and confident with an edge. Even the guards turned away. Dani tried to ignore them, but unfortunately Lex homed in on him.

'Oi, El Chapo. Come over here, join us,' Lex shouted across the room, looking down at the other boys playing cards who all scattered at once in different directions, giving up their seats immediately.

Dani reluctantly joined them. He was still holding the large book in his hands. He was awkward, nervous and out of his depth but did as he was told.

'Need my shit, bro. Now is peak serving time.' Lex continued to play cards whilst addressing Dani, not even affording him a glance.

Dani squirmed and looked around, checking that no guards were watching. 'You want it now?' He sounded pathetic, his voice almost a whine. The gang all broke into laughter, making Dani feel worse. He gulped then tried his best to join in with the laughter, but it came out strained.

Lex threw his cards onto the table. 'Yeah, bruv, now!' he ordered. Dani dropped the book on the floor, dug into his crotch and pulled out the bag, quickly handing it to Lex. 'Now fuck off until I need you.'

His words cut through Dani, who picked up the book then scuttled away on command, bumping into Leroy on his way out and dropping the large book on the floor again.

Leroy picked it up and handed it back to him. 'Don't go back to the cell; they'll come after you,' he whispered from the side of his mouth while chewing on a plastic fork. He seemed calm, not bothered by Lex and his gang.

Dani hesitated, looking at Leroy, who signalled to come with him. Dani followed, latching on, hoping for some form of protection. Leroy led the way towards the pool table. He was greeted by a couple of boys who seemed familiar and happy to see him. Lex's gang were doling out the drugs to some of the other inmates who crowded around the table. It was not at all covert. Boys came lining up, handing over crumpled notes and coins and stuffing the pills straight into their mouths.

Leroy smacked the pool cue against the white ball, smashing the other balls in various directions. He walked slowly around the table, watching from the side of his eye as Lex and his motley crew continued their boisterous activities.

Dani stood close to the pool table near Leroy, trying to distance himself as much as possible. 'What's the deal with them lot?' he asked under his breath.

'We'll chat later.' Leroy continued to be coy. He seemed seasoned and took everything in his stride, the opposite of Dani, who was edgy and constantly uncomfortable.

A couple of guards strolled back into the recreational room. They could see what was blatantly going on but didn't get involved as they tried to usher the inmates back to their cells. They even laughed and joked with some of them who had clearly started to feel the effects of the drugs.

Lex got up from his seat in a jovial mood, stuffing the takings into his pocket. He turned around, searching for Dani, who stood next to Leroy at the pool table. 'Oi, Chapo.

Come 'ere.' Dani shuddered. He looked at Leroy, who ignored him. He'd hoped for backup, but Leroy continued to smash the pool balls around the table.

'Come on, Chapo. Ain't got all night.' Lex made his way towards a hesitant Dani, who still gripped the encyclopedia tight to his chest.

The blood drained from his face as Lex bounded over, but then Leroy stepped in front of Lex.

'Lexy Lex still causing trouble. Low him, innit.' Leroy's voice was a tired, deep growl that stopped Lex in his tracks.

Tension rose as the rest of the gang formed behind Lex. The guards watched on from a distance, sensing trouble brewing. 'Come on, move along, back to your cells!' one of the beefy guards yelled out.

The rest of the inmates began to jump around excitedly as the drugs kicked in. They were like happy chimps, hugging and leaping on the tables.

A steely-eyed Lex peered at Leroy, who remained calm and collected, holding on to the pool cue. 'Is that your man?' Lex questioned, pointing his tattooed fingers in Dani's direction.

The rest of his gang started to form a protective cordon around Lex, ready for action.

Leroy nonchalantly turned to Dani, then turned to face Lex. 'You know what? Man's a rookie, innit. You don't need him,' he spoke confidently, leaning back onto the pool table, cue in hand and staring back at Lex. This was psychological jousting. Who was going to blink first? Both stood their ground.

The guards rushed over, getting in between them. 'Come on, boys. Party's over.'

Lex sneered in Dani's direction as more guards rushed into the room, pulling the other inmates down from tables and chasing them around the room. They screamed and laughed loudly, high from the pills and causing a welcomed distraction from the tense standoff.

Most of the inmates were back in their cells, although the guards were still attempting to corral the rest of the singing stragglers back to theirs. It was chaos and eye-opening for Dani. He had never thought a detention centre would be so liberal. He always had in mind what Jesus had told him about his experience. This was way off from that. He sat on the lower bunk with the large book on his lap. He was nervous, tapping his fingers on the cover. Finally, Leroy returned to their cell.

'Yo, dude. What the fuck?' Dani jumped up to greet him, slinging the book onto the bunk.

Leroy sauntered in, twisting his short dreads with his right hand. 'You take the top bunk, I'm too tall . . .'

Dani stared at him in disbelief. 'Serious, man. What just happened out there?'

Leroy brushed past him, making his way to the chrome toilet bowl. He proceeded to urinate without a care in the world, much to Dani's disgust.

'Come on, man.' He sat back on the bunk, grimacing.

Leroy looked back at him. 'Better get used to it. Wait 'til I take a shit.' He laughed, continuing to pee in the bowl.

'So how come Lex didn't smash your face in?' Dani paced up and down the tiny room continuing to quiz Leroy, who was lying back bare-chested on the bunk, flicking through the encyclopedia.

'Some interesting stuff in here,' he commented, concentrating on the page.

'I'm fucked. Now Lex is gonna kill me.' Dani scraped his fingers across his shorn bonce.

Leroy slammed the book shut, fed up with Dani's histrionics. 'Sit down, Chapo.' Leroy's deep voice reverberated around the cell. Dani did as told and sat on the edge of the bunk. 'Lex is a don in this place. Untouchable. Knows the system, been in and out for years.' Leroy sat next to Dani, speaking casually. 'I've known Lex since we were nippers, grew up together . . .' Leroy paused reflectively, taking a deep sigh. 'I'm uncle to his kid, daughter.'

Dani looked at him confused. He wiped a gleam of sweat from his face. 'You're an uncle?'

'Yeah, he fucked my sister, so I'm Lainey's uncle. That's his kid's name.'

Dani rubbed his chin. 'That's why he didn't—'

Leroy interrupted. 'He tried to kill my sister. Wounded her coz she left him.' Leroy stopped, gathering his thoughts. The events were still raw in his mind. He took his time while Dani held his breath, waiting to hear what else he was about to say. Leroy leant back, stretching out along the bunk. His long legs made his feet hang over the end. 'I shot him.' He laughed. 'But he didn't die. Caught in the hand. Now he thinks he's immortal.' Leroy kissed his teeth and shook his head. 'Now we both in here.'

Dani was speechless, just absorbing all the information.

'Your turn. Why you here, Chapo?' Leroy rested back, relaxed, as Dani sat motionless.

'Shit. That's deep.'

The lights went out, plunging the cells into darkness. Voices from the guards and screams from the high inmates echoed through the corridors. Outside, a faint light from the slim window of the cell barely lit Dani's face.

He sighed deeply, rubbing his face from tiredness. 'Me and my brother got involved with this crazy gangster.' He started his confession, his speech slowing with every word.

Leroy shuffled his body into a comfortable position, sensing this would be a long drawl.

'And then my sister Rosa, she ran away with some dude. Rich guy—' Dani yawned. 'Anyway, we needed money . . . to pay Franky the gangster.'

Leroy sat up and pulled his long legs up to his chest. 'You robbed the rich guy, right?'

Dani nodded and sank back, relieved that he could finally talk. 'My brother, he's crazy. Set fire to his car showroom. I told him, but . . .' He stopped, recalling the night's events. It suddenly hit him and he became emotional.

Leroy put his hand on his shoulder. 'Don't worry about it. There's a reason why we're here, mate.' Leroy turned onto his side to rest, leaving Dani to gather himself before climbing up to his bunk where he lay on his back. He was teary-eyed, staring up at the ceiling, holding the book to his chest.

Time went by, and in the blink of an eye, dawn had broken. When Dani woke, Leroy was already up, bare-chested, performing some sit-ups on the cold floor. He rubbed his face and wiped his eyes before watching Leroy go through his rigorous exercise routine. 'Jeez, bro, it's early.' He leaned over. 'That was the best sleep I had in ages'

Leroy continued doing press-ups, displaying his long, sculpted torso. 'Really?' he asked without breaking a sweat.

Dani lay back, picking up the thick encyclopedia. 'Yeh, man. Don't think I ever slept before—always something going on.'

Leroy stood up and carried on limbering up and stretching.

Tension in the breakfast room was high. The guards seemed on edge, barking orders at the inmates and keeping a sharp eye on the room. Some of the inmates were still feeling the effects of the drugs and were in high spirits, messing around and shouting about their personal experiences. Dani entered alone. He hated this time, exposed to the other offenders just like shower time. He was nervous and hoped to blend into the background. He carried the big encyclopedia, which now accompanied him everywhere, just to appear busy and not get sucked into any of the action.

Dani collected his tray and stood patiently in line to get his slop of porridge and two slices of toast. The food was not great. It was extremely basic, but what other choice did he have? It's not like he could be eating a full fry-up made by Rosa. Moments later, Dani sat alone at the end of one of the communal tables. He finished his breakfast and flicked the pages of his book. He was quite interested in some of the information, so it was a great distraction. But distraction is what walked in next. Lex and his crew all stepped in with their usual menace. Dani caught them out the side of his eye, and his heart sank, as did his demeanour. Dani shrank down in his seat. Lex was too busy lapping up jokes with some of the other inmates to notice him at first but scanned the room and caught sight of him. He broke away from the pack and headed straight over towards him.

'Fuck sake,' Dani muttered under his breath, fearing the impending inquisition. He dragged his body upright and tried to look confident, but inside the porridge and toast he'd just consumed was turning like a tumble drier.

Lex, with his lean frame, was clothed in a white tee shirt and grey tracksuit bottoms. 'Morning, Chapo. I see you didn't wait for me to eat brekkie then?' He sat directly opposite, all sneer and smirk.

Dani shook his head. 'Nah, I just wanted to read my book.'

Lex glanced down at the encyclopedia. 'Yeah, is that right?' He took the book and slammed it shut, staring at Dani with his piercing blue eyes. 'No time for that today. You got work to do, Chapo.' His voice was stern; he obviously loved being in charge. It fed his ego; he was thriving on being top dog.

Dani gave him a look of defiance. 'I can't. I have court soon, don't wanna mess up . . .'

His plea was cut short when Lex stood up and leaned over him. 'I don't think you quite understand mi ah-fucking-migo. I ain't asking. I'm telling.' He stared down at Dani, whose defiance melted away like an ice cube in the heatwave outside.

He bowed his head in submission.

'I'll see you in the yard later. Oh, and don't bring your bodyguard.' Lex patted Dani's head, then headed back to his crew.

Dani tried to regain some composure but felt as if he had been sentenced already, condemned to a life of lunatics like Lex. Not forgetting what had happened to Franky and Daniel, he was probably safer in here, although that notion was laughable. He took a deep breath and got up to make his way back to his cell, taking his book with him. He was a lonely figure navigating his way through the rows of tables, past the rest of Lex's crew and the other inmates, who all watched as he clutched his book and walked swiftly out. On his return, he saw Leroy lying, eyes closed, on the bunk. 'Yo, man, where were you at breakfast?'

Leroy stretched out, opening his eyes and sleepily looking up at Dani. 'Thought I'd rest up after my workout. I'll grab some fruit. They always have something left over.' He was so calm that it infuriated an already stressed-out Dani.

He was only used to being around Jesus, who was constantly on the go. 'That fucking Lex, man, he's got me by the balls.' Dani sat on the end of the bunk, placing the book on his lap then putting his head in his hands.

'Bro, you're gonna have to handle that, otherwise it will get worse.' Leroy finally came to life. 'Stand up to him, otherwise you'll be his bitch.' He stood up, yawning. 'I'll be back, Chapo.' He put on his sliders and a tee shirt, then left the cell, leaving Dani to digest his words.

As Dani read the encyclopedia, he was actually fascinated by the pages on wildlife. He had never really taken the time to learn anything at school. He was too proud to learn and more interested in being Jesus's wingman than any sort of scholar. He was looking at a long stretch away, so what better time to get educated? He was engrossed until he was interrupted by one of the guards.

'Got a visit, mate. Chop, chop.'

Dani jumped up, chucked the book onto the top bunk and followed the guard out of the cell. He was wondering who his visitor was; he certainly wasn't expecting anybody.

The walk through the halls of the detention centre felt like the longest catwalk, but the audience was not a crowd of well-heeled designers, entertainers and models; they were hardened street criminals hawking his every step through a gauntlet of intimidation, shouts of abuse, pointing fingers and cigarettes flicked in his direction. Dani just wanted to disappear. He stepped quickly behind the guard, cowering.

Ushered into an office-type interview room, Dani was greeted by a short, tubby man with grey, ruffled hair. He was dressed in a scruffy shirt and waistcoat, sweating profusely from the outside heat. He seemed agitated or nervous, dropping his pen on the floor whilst trying to shake Dani's hand. 'Oops, sorry. Avi Lipschitz. I've been assigned as your solicitor, Mr Chavez.' He picked up the pen and shoved his hand into Dani's, shaking it firmly with a sweaty palm. 'Take a seat,' he invited Dani.

On the desk was a thick folder. Avi Lipschitz opened it and pulled out random sheets of paper. He looked up to the guard and signalled him to leave. 'I need some time with my client.' He put on his glasses, peering over the top of them. Dani was confused but he watched on as the strange solicitor scribbled some notes.

'Who assigned you?' Dani asked.

Avi stopped and looked up at Dani. He huffed and removed his glasses. 'Everyone is entitled to legal aid, even, ahem . . . criminals,' he said without reservation or empathy, just deadpan and factual. 'You are in a lot of trouble, and I haven't got long until your court case, so I suggest we get started.'

Dani raised his eyebrows. He was not prepared for all of the legal stuff, but at least he had the strange man to help him. He rested back in the chair, scratching his head. 'So what do you need from me?'

Avi Lipschitz stopped reading rapidly through the papers. He looked at Dani, took a tissue from his pocket and wiped his brow. 'Realistically, it's more about what you need from me.' He put the tissue back into his pocket and picked up a sheet of paper, browsing the words. 'You came to the UK on a CPP?'

Dani shrugged. 'What's that?'

'Crime protection program from Sinaloa, Mexico.' He put the sheet of paper down and picked up another one, reading it again. He had an unusual way of reading— scanning the pages by gliding his head from left to right, breathing heavily as he took in the information.

'I was young. I dunno. Just knew we were moved after my parents . . .' Dani paused as the painful childhood memory was raked up in his mind.

Avi Lipschitz nodded before interrupting. 'Thing is, with armed robbery, arson, assault and kidnap, plus the arrest at a well-known criminal's house—'

'We weren't armed,' Dani interjected. 'And I didn't do the fire. I told Jesus to leave it, but he—'

He stopped talking when the guard banged on the door and poked his head in. 'Ten more minutes,' he informed them, then closed the door.

Avi looked at Dani, this time with a more compassionate expression on his face. 'I'm not sure if you know this, but I'll tell you anyway—' he took a deep breath '—if you are found guilty, and that is a very realistic option, your sentence will be served in Mexico, as it's a violation of the CPP code.'

Dani's jaw dropped. 'Mexico!' he shouted, prompting the guard to burst through the door.

'Everything alright?'

Avi nodded towards him. 'Yes, I think I'm done for now.' He scrambled up the loose papers and put them back into the folder.

Dani was dumbstruck. He was still trying to digest the sirloin steak-sized piece of information.

Avi Lipschitz packed his belongings into a battered, black briefcase. He seemed overwhelmed himself and a bit out of his depth.

Dani grabbed his arm. 'Hey, I can't go back to Mexico, not to jail.' He clasped his arm tightly. 'I can't,' he repeated.

Avi Lipschitz pulled his arm away. 'I'll be back in a week. I need time to look at all of the evidence.' He picked up his briefcase and bolted out of the door, leaving Dani alone to contemplate the news.

Back on the landing, walking back to his cell, Dani saw Leroy leaning on the balcony overlooking the other cells and the rest of the wings.

'Bro, man's been missing.' He fist-pumped Dani as he arrived.

'Recreation time soon. We'll talk in the yard.' Dani headed straight into the cell, sat down and put his head into his hands. The wind had been taken out of his sails. He'd never thought of going back to Mexico again. Never in a million years.

Leroy entered and his tall body closed off the space as soon as he walked in the door. 'You good, fam? Look like you've seen a ghost.'

Dani shook his head. 'Nah, I'm not good. Let's just go to the yard.' He got up and rushed out of the cell.

The humidity was sticky and uncomfortable, and the heatwave showed no sign of ending. The only spot in the yard where there was a bit of shade was near the refuse shed, which, in the heat, was not the best place to sit due to the heaving stench of prison trash, plus the flies which irritatingly buzzed around the bins. But it was where Dani chose to pitch up, away from the main hub of inmates.

Dani sat with his back to the wall and his legs stretched out. The sweat dripped down his face and neck, leaving a puddle on the ground. He leant back and stared up at the sky, still trying to swallow all the information fed to him by Avi Lipschitz, which was going down like a cactus sandwich.

Leroy's long shadow appeared on the concrete. 'Shit, bro. Why you sitting here?' Leroy sauntered towards him, holding his nose. 'I brought your book.' He gave Dani the large encyclopedia. 'Keep reading, innit. Helps with distraction.' As much as it stank, Leroy sat beside Dani. 'Jeez, this heat is fucked.' A few beads of sweat had formed on his forehead. 'So . . .?' He turned his head towards Dani, who was still leaning back but with his eyes closed.

'I don't want to go jail in Mexico,' he said petulantly. He shook his head then looked at Leroy as if he had been hard done by.

'I feel you. I've seen *Banged Up Abroad*,' Leroy mused, twisting one of his short dreads. 'Never know, you might get off,' he said dryly.

Dani looked at him, unconvinced. 'Thanks, but I've got no chance.' He picked up the book and started to flick through some random pages. 'Got court in less than a month.' Dani glanced up at Leroy; he was about to say something but refrained.

'Think you should go to chapel, start praying.'

'Praying?'

Leroy stood up. 'Can't sit here, man, it stinks.' He walked away back into the burning sun as Dani watched on with a confused expression.

Dani returned to his cell. It was way too hot outside but not much cooler in the small cube of space which was deemed a room. He splashed his face with water from the tiny sink and wiped it. He rubbed his hands over his eyes, and by the time he had finished, the room was full of Lex and his gang. Dani jumped back, startled.

'Here he is. El Chapo, where you been?' Lex's band of brothers all gesticulated and sniggered on cue. Lex was bare-chested with his tee shirt slung over his shoulder, the Lainey tattoo scrawled across his neck and reddened. The other four of his crew stood behind him, one of them shutting the door then folding his arms.

Dani's heart was in his mouth; suddenly the small room had become smaller.

Lex edged forwards and took out a small plastic bag which was wrapped tightly into a small ball. 'Take it.' He shoved the bag towards Dani. 'Same again tonight; bring it to muster.' Lex moved closer, almost face to face. His breath smelt of old cigarette smoke. The sweat flowed down his skinned head.

'Look, Lex, I really can't,' Dani pleaded, his mouth getting drier with every word he spoke.

'OK, mate, cool.' Lex backed off with his hands in the air, one of them still holding the plastic bag. He turned his back to face his gang, signalling to his crew, who all moved forwards with menace.

Dani panicked. 'No, please, I beg...' The muscle-bound youths grabbed him round the neck; one of them punched him with a heavy blow to the stomach, winding him. His legs buckled underneath him. He coughed, gasping for breath, only to be pulled up again and hit twice as hard in the same area. He wheezed out a long choke before they picked him up again.

Lex came forwards, grabbed Dani's face and lifted it up so they were eye to eye. He stared at Dani, his face twisted with anger. 'I told you, Chapo, I don't think you know who I am.'

Dani tried to regain his composure, but he was dangling like a puppet on very loose strings.

'Do as you're told, Chapo.' Lex stuffed the bag into his mouth, making Dani choke again.

Choking and convulsing, his limp body was thrown to the ground.

Lex and his crew began to make their way out. 'See you at muster,' Lex spat at Dani before turning to leave but was met at the door by Leroy.

'What you man doing in my cell?' Leroy blocked their exit while seeing Dani writhing on the floor.

'Not your business, Leroy.' Lex stood face to face with him as his gang crowded the doorway.

'You lot come to my door, Lex, so it is my business!' An angry Leroy stood firm, pushing Lex back into the cell. 'So what, you bringing it to my door now?'

The rest of the gang, like a pack of wild dogs, started to lash out and throw punches at Leroy. They all rushed him. Leroy fought back but was overwhelmed by the numbers. A full-scale fight was in full swing. All of them, including

Lex, hammered down on Leroy, while Dani was still on the floor trying to breathe. He could see that Leroy was taking a beating, but he hadn't the strength to get up and help him.

Dani tried to cry out, but with the bag stuffed into his mouth, he was rendered helpless. He tried to grab the ankles of one of the gang, but the action was happening so fast it was a blur. Within seconds it was over. They all ran out, leaving Leroy slumped in a heap in the corner of the room. He was gurgling as if he could not swallow or breathe properly. Dani could see that he had been wounded as blood oozed from his side.

Dani managed to pull the bag from his mouth. He was trying to crawl over to Leroy but was weak himself. 'Help!' His faint attempts at a shout were reduced to a strained wheeze. 'Leroy!' He managed to crawl his way to his stricken cellmate, but as he got close and looked up at him, he could see the life drain away.

Leroy's eyes rolled back into his head, and only the sound of small, shallow breaths could be heard until his head tilted off at an obtuse angle.

'Guards, help!' Dani finally found his voice, which was a strained shriek. He put his hand onto Leroy, trying to cover the gaping wound where blood continued to spill out, running like a red river over Leroy's dark chocolate torso.

A couple of guards rushed into the cell to a scene of mayhem—two limp bodies on the floor, blood and a bag of drugs right next to them. One of the guards spoke into his radio, 'Code red. I repeat, code red!' Shortly after, the jarring sound of an alarm wailed throughout the halls of the prison.

One week later

Dani sat alone, staring directly ahead. In front of him was a solitary white coffin on a gold-coated stand. The scene was serene. A large white cross hung above on the bricked wall, and a few rows of empty pews were ahead of him. He had some bruises on his face and remained still. The sunlight shone through the stained glass windows, forming a rainbow on the coffin. 'So . . . this is the chapel?' he mumbled, looking at the coffin.

Two guards stood at the back of the room on either side of the door, a reminder that his freedom was still a distant reality. He looked sorrowful, staring blankly into the distance.

He broke into a laugh. 'You told me to pray; now I'm praying for you.' He wiped his eyes and shook his head. An image of his father appeared in front of him like a hologram. It was surreal, but he could see Hector clearly in his farmer's straw hat.

'Dani, I'm so disappointed in you. This is not how we brought you up. *Familia* is everything. Rosa has been treated disgracefully. As for Jesus—' Hector spat on the floor, the ultimate sign of shame.

'Papa, why are you here now? Where's Mama?' Dani spoke to an empty room, thinking he was seeing his father.

'Come home, Dani. Change your life.' The image of Hector continued to stare directly at him.

Dani got spooked. He stood up, his hands bound by the cold metal cuffs clipped around his wrists. 'You ain't real, you're dead!' he shouted. 'You're dead!' The guards began to move in. Hector's hologram dissipated in front of him. 'Leave me alone! You're dead!' he shouted whilst being dragged away by the guards. He continued to yell in the direction of the white coffin, 'Dead! Fucking dead!' He started crying as he was taken out of the chapel, leaving the sunlight shining down on the coffin.

Chapter 21
Do nothing

Daniel had made enough of a recovery to be discharged. Rosa was ecstatic, making final preparations at the hospital and packing up his clothes and belongings. It had been a long few months and Daniel, bless him, could not fully remember everything that had happened that night—not that he wanted to. He was withdrawn—not his normal, cheeky self—and in a state of numbness about it all. Leah and Rosa never really talked about the incident; it was like an unspoken secret. Instead, they just focused on getting him better.

Dr Cohen had warned them that it might be a slow and tedious recovery, with physio and counselling included, but at least he could convalesce in the comfort of his own home. Rosa had not left Daniel's side throughout his hospitalisation, and he was happy to have her there, not that he said much. But the way he held her hand gave Rosa enough confirmation that he knew she was there.

Leah hadn't helped the situation; she was still bitter and angry with Rosa. Their relationship had not thawed in the slightest, especially as the two detectives she'd called to shop Rosa, Phil Dickinson and Ben Grimes, had visited to eliminate Rosa from their investigation.

Rosa had told the truth, and her phone records proved she had not made any phone calls linked to Jesus or Dani. In fact, they confirmed that the only number she ever called from her phone was Daniel's, and the times matched her story about when she'd called him on the night of the robbery, only for Jesus to answer—much to Leah's embarrassment. She never even offered Rosa an apology. She was still sour and scratching around for anything to make Daniel see her point of view, but he didn't want to believe Rosa had been involved at all.

Rosa dabbed Daniel's hands with a wet cloth as he sat on the edge of the bed. He watched her moving from side to side. She looked pretty, her skin had that glow back and her big brown eyes finally had a spark of excitement. They twinkled when she looked at Daniel. 'Hey, why you staring at me? You see something you like?' she said playfully.

'Yes, I like very much,' Daniel replied. His speech was slower than his usual as a result of his head injury, but at least he seemed happy to be going home.

'First thing for you is a haircut and a shave!' Rosa joked. 'What is this?' She took a handful of his hair, which had grown to almost shoulder length.

'Maybe I'll be a hippy.' He grabbed Rosa by the waist. He was still as affectionate as always. Rosa bent down and kissed him on the forehead.

'Not if I get a pair of scissors.' She finished wiping his face and ran her fingers through his hair. 'Nope, it's got to go.' They both broke into laughter.

'OK, you win.' Daniel smiled.

Leah breezed into the room in her usual extravagant outfit—an oversized white sun hat, big shades, flowing hair and a lime- and lemon-coloured summer dress with flip-flops. 'Hello, bruv. Homecoming day!' She sounded excited for him, hugging him. 'Rosa,' she said, with a hint of authority, as if she was her boss. That was her way of greeting Rosa—not even a smile, a hug, nothing. Just a cold glance towards her, her pride dented.

One of the nurses entered the room pushing a wheelchair. 'Ready to go?' She smiled at Daniel.

'I don't need that. I can walk,' he replied. 'I drive cars faster than that!' he slurred slightly, breaking into laughter.

'Well, not today!' the nurse replied whilst positioning the wheelchair.

'It's only to get you to the car, bruv,' Leah chipped in. 'I'm parked at the entrance, so don't worry.' Leah grabbed the handles of the wheelchair, indicating to Rosa that she was taking the reins. 'Get all of his stuff. We'll see you downstairs,' she ordered, brushing Rosa aside, a point picked up on by the nurse, who winked at Rosa.

Silly cow.

She thinks she's so much better than me now.

Before this she was all nice like a sister.

I can't control what my idiot brothers did and they'll get theirs but she knows I am innocent and still she can't admit that she was wrong.

Dr Cohen arrived just as they were about to leave. 'Well, time to go, Daniel.'

Daniel extended his hand for a handshake.

Dr Cohen shook his hand then looked at both Rosa and Leah. 'You have these two great women to help you. I've no doubt you will soon be back to your best.'

Daniel nodded in agreement. 'Yes, thank you, Dr Cohen.' He smiled before Leah wheeled him out into the corridor.

Rosa picked up the bags and made her way out. She was stopped by Dr Cohen. 'Take good care of him,' he said, speaking calmly and rubbing Rosa's shoulder.

Rosa smiled back at him and left.

* * *

It feels weird being back here.

Doesn't feel the same after everything that's happened.

Rosa put away their things and looked around their bedroom. It was tidy, pretty much the same as that fateful night when she'd woken from her sleep to face a real-life nightmare. Daniel was downstairs in the living room with Leah. He was not strong enough yet to tackle the stairs, so he used that room as his base.

Rosa sat on their bed. She crossed her legs, tired but happy to be back home and out of that hospital. She scrolled through the pictures on her phone, many of her and Daniel. Her favourite one was a photograph taken at the Automobile Awards. That was her dream—standing next to her Prince Charming, glammed up and in love.

It is love, I really know it is.

I've never felt this way about anyone before and all this has just made it more real to me.

Still, it's not over.

Rosa lay back. The bed felt soft, far more comfortable than the chair she had slept in for the duration of Daniel's hospitalisation. She stared up at the picture on her phone screen. A tired smile crept across her face, her eyelids became heavy and she eventually dozed off, dropping the phone onto the bed.

Leah handed Daniel a cup of tea. He sat staring at the large-screen television that was on loud. Graham Norton's voice shrieked in the background.

'Thanks, Sis.' He took the cup and placed it on a table beside him.

Leah sat down next to him and ruffled his hair. 'I'll fix this for you tomorrow,' she said with a laugh and sipped her tea. She had done away with the sun hat and shades and was now looking slightly uncomfortable with her feet up on the sofa.

'Where's Rosa?' Daniel asked.

Leah put her cup down. 'Think she's sleeping. Listen, Daniel.' Her expression turned serious. She touched Daniel's hand. 'I've spoken to Mum and Dad. They think it's a good idea if she goes.'

Daniel pulled his hand away from Leah. He turned to her, his blue eyes slightly offended. 'What do you mean?' he responded with a puzzled look on his bearded face. 'No, she lives here with me. I don't care . . .'

Before he could finish his sentence, Leah interjected. She could see how upset Daniel was becoming, but she ploughed on with her agenda regardless. 'Dad thinks it for the best,' she tried to assure him, but Daniel reacted by pushing her hand away and shaking his head.

'That girl deserves a medal, not to be thrown out. Not having it, Leah.' His frustration began to rise. 'It's up to me; she's my girlfriend and it's my house.'

Leah sat back in a huff like a spoilt child who'd had her toys taken away. She blew out her cheeks. 'I'm just telling you, she needs to be gone by the time they get here.'

Daniel turned to her, biting his lip to suppress his offence. 'Get where?' he asked.

Leah took another sip of her tea, ignoring Daniel, which just annoyed him more. He grabbed her arm which caused her tea to spill onto her dress. 'Ow! That's bloody hot, Daniel.' Leah pulled her arm away and got up, the spillage seeping through her dress. She wiped her leg. 'Flipping hell, bruv, that hurt.' Leah put the cup down on the table and stood up, still fuming about the tea stain on her summer dress. 'They are flying in day after next, so she has to go!' Angry, she exited the room.

Daniel's cool persona had shattered; he was furious. 'When was this all agreed?' he blurted out, his voice raised.

Leah came back into the room and rubbed the sofa with a cloth. Her face was flushed. 'They wanted to see you, make sure you're OK.'

Daniel tried to get up from his seat but struggled for a few seconds before giving up. 'That's not fair. They should meet her too.'

Leah stopped. 'No! They want her gone, and I agree. I'll tell her tomorrow.'

Daniel sat back feeling defeated. His face was a picture of both fury and frustration. He picked up his tea and took a gulp, which scalded his throat as he swallowed. 'What did you tell them?' he demanded, his anger boiling.

Leah could hardly look him in the eye. 'Just told the truth.' She shrugged. 'They needed to know.' She sat back in her chair with her arms folded. 'It's for the best.' She was short and curt in her response, sounding confident that she had done the right thing, but Daniel was seething.

'Out of order, Leah.' His speech was still slower than normal, but the disappointment in his tone was very apparent.

Rosa opened her eyes. She felt as though she had slept for days. She checked the time on her phone. 7 am. The house was silent. It felt strange to be waking up in this bed alone; usually, she would have Daniel's warm body beside her. She yawned and stretched her body to the length of the bed before getting up. She ambled across the carpet for her usual peer through the window. Her favourite view from the house was the stream and gardens, the bright tinge from the sun already reflected in the rippling water. 'Hot, hot, hot,' she uttered under her breath, knowing another day of the cruel heatwave was upon them. She shuffled to the bathroom. It felt good to be in the comfort of her home.

It feels so good to be back today.

I just want to spend the day with Daniel, watch some films, eat some food and relax.

We can talk, play games and just be us again.

She had plans to cook a big breakfast for Daniel,

finally able to enjoy his company in comfort. She showered and dressed, humming a tune to herself. Wearing a white fitted crop top and cut-down shorts, she made her way to the living room to see Daniel.

Daniel lay stretched out on the sofa watching television. He had the remote in his hand, flicking over each channel randomly.

'Hey. Good morning, sleepyhead.' Rosa breezed in chirpily, making her way over to him. She nuzzled her face into his and hugged him tightly. 'How did you sleep?' She knelt in front of him, kissing him on the lips.

Daniel barely responded, his hair flopped over his face.

'Are you OK? Hungry?' she asked, sweeping his hair aside.

He found it difficult to look at her, knowing that Leah would soon burst her excitement bubble. 'Not hungry,' he replied.

She could tell he was off with her; this was not the loving, caring man she knew. 'Come on, sit up now. I'll help you into the shower,' Rosa fussed, helping him to sit upright. 'Is something wrong?' She sat beside him. 'Daniel?'

He was thinking deeply, internalizing his feelings. 'Help me to the shower,' he said, but sounded different. His tone was drab and dulled down by the thought of telling Rosa she could no longer stay with him, at least for a couple of weeks. He was already trying to process the best way to deal with the situation.

Rosa took his arms and helped him to stand. Daniel kept his head bowed, his hair messily covering his eyes. 'Daniel, are you OK? Feeling unwell?'

Daniel threw his arms around her and hugged her as tight as he could, flopping his body into hers.

'Hey, what's all this about?' Rosa held him, surprised by his sudden thrust of affection.

'Need to shower.'

'Come on, let's walk slowly.' Rosa guided him forward towards the bathroom. She retreated to the kitchen where she busied herself making some breakfast. She was disturbed by Daniel's behaviour.

What's got into him?

He doesn't seem right, he's never like this.

Just wish he would talk to me.

I thought he'd be happy to be home.

Yesterday he was fine but something is off and I'm going to find out because I can't feel good if he is upset about something.

Leah entered the kitchen, and instantly Rosa felt her bad energy as she helped herself to some coffee.

'Morning.' Rosa offered her a greeting.

'Morning,' Leah replied, still salty. She took her coffee and sat at the table. 'Is Daniel up?' Rosa carried on preparing the food.

'Yes, he's in the shower.' Her reply was terse. The tension between the two had not abated and was suffocating.

Leah continued to sip her coffee without as much as a verbal nod to Rosa.

'I'll go and check on Daniel.' Rosa put the food onto a plate and put it in the microwave, then made her way out of the kitchen, unable to keep up the pretence.

Daniel was sat on the sofa. His hair was wet and he was still half-dressed, looking frustrated in his boxer shorts, trying to figure out the material in his hands. 'I can't get my trousers on,' he half-joked, but the agitation was threaded through his voice.

Rosa chuckled to herself seeing him sitting with his hands twisted in the trouser legs. 'Come here, let me help.' She kissed him on the cheek and took the trousers from him, untying the knots he had created. 'Look, here we go. Come on, stand for me.' Rosa helped him to his feet and they laughed together as he stepped one foot into a leg and then the other.

'What am I like? Feel like a baby,' Daniel moaned as she pulled up his pants.

'It's OK, that's why I'm here' she reassured him.

Daniel shifted uncomfortably. 'Can we sit down?' He took Rosa's hands, guiding her to the sofa.

She knew he was about to say something she might not like, and she had an uneasy feeling in the pit of her stomach. Her heart beat faster as they sat down.

Daniel swept his hair aside out of his eyes. He finally looked at Rosa but his eyes were dull, not sparkling as they usually were when he looked at her. Rosa shuffled up next to him and squeezed his hand.

'Babe, what is it?' she asked.

Daniel swallowed hard, taking a breath before speaking. 'OK well . . .' He hesitated.

'Are you breaking up with me?' Rosa jumped in, unable to hold herself back. 'Please, just tell me,' she continued.

Daniel's chest sank, seeing her reaction. 'No, babe, listen,' he pleaded, fighting with his emotion. 'My parents are coming tomorrow.'

Rosa felt a slight wave of relief. 'OK, that's good, right?'

'Well, thing is. Because of what happened, you can't be here when they come.' He hung his head. It hurt him to say that, and he was still far from happy with himself at having to do this.

'What?' Rosa let go of his hand.

Daniel touched her face tenderly. 'I don't want you to go, and it'll only be for a couple of weeks.' He tried to let her down gently, but Rosa was incensed.

'You want me to go!' She raised her voice and moved away from Daniel.

'No, I don't, but . . .'

At this point, Leah came into the room, doing her best impression of a Kardashian, such was her over-the-top entrance. Rosa turned to her, then looked back at Daniel.

Oh, I get it now, Leah has got to him.

'Everything alright, Bruv?' Leah's entrance was like the cat that got the cream the way she sauntered in, seeing Daniel cringing in his seat.

Rosa knew she was the instigator of all this. 'So you want me to leave?' Rosa was enraged and folded her arms, staring at Daniel.

Before he could answer, Leah jumped in. 'Yeah, you can't be here. My family want nothing to do with ya.'

'This is all you, isn't it?' She pointed her finger at Leah, her face contorted with anger now. 'You're kicking me out, not him.' She turned back to Daniel who held his head in his hands at the two warring females who both held influence in his life.

'Can both of you just shut up!' he shouted, for once managing to spout out his sentence with feeling. A deafening silence fell in the room. 'Babe, I don't want you to go, but let me just sort it with my parents, then I'll call you,' he stuttered.

Rosa was flabbergasted by Daniel's comment. 'Really?' Her anger rose, especially towards Leah. 'Where am I meant to go?' Rosa stretched out her hand, pleading, towards Daniel.

'Look, I'll sort out an Airbnb.'

Rosa reached boiling point. 'This is *you*, I know it, all *you*.' Her voice rose to a scream. Leah just shrugged with a satisfied smirk on her face.

'Is this what you really want, Daniel?' She aimed her emotional outburst at him.

Daniel tried to get up from the sofa but was unsteady and didn't have the strength, which made him frustrated. 'No, babe. It's just, I'm stuck in the middle here.' He flopped back into his seat.

'Forget it. I'll go, but I won't be back.' She fought back the tears. 'I can't believe you.' She shot a sad look at Daniel, then turned and left the room, running up the stairs back to the bedroom.

Daniel rocked back and forth with his head in his hands. He started to groan in almost a pained wail.

Leah came to his aid. 'It's OK, Bruv. It's for the best,' she consoled him and tried to hug him, but Daniel pushed her away.

'No, leave me alone.' He continued to clasp his hands over his face.

Leah still hugged him. 'I'm your sister; I got your back.'

Her words caused Daniel to move his hands from his face. 'Is that so?' he spluttered, his eyes wide.

Rosa was heartbroken. Crying, she grabbed whatever clothes and belongings she could and stuffed them into a large sports duffle bag. She was in a spin and really had no sense of what she was doing.

That bitch, she's done that on purpose.

I feel betrayed by her and Daniel, how could he?

How could he believe her lies?

I never thought Daniel would ever turn on me, he needs me!

Oh my God, where am I going to go?

OK, Rosa, get yourself together.

Think, man, think!

OK let me just go.

No . . . hold up, call Mya.

Yes!

Call Mya.

Rosa flopped onto the bed. She dug around in her things and found her phone. She was in a state of panic as she scrolled through her phone. She sniffed and wipe her tears from her face. The phone rang at the other end.

Come on, Mya, pick up.

Please answer, come on . . .

Mya's husky voice came through the phone. 'Hi, babe, you alright?'

Rosa couldn't even speak, fighting to choke back her emotions.

'Babe, what's wrong?'

Rosa sniffed. 'I need you to come and get me.' Her voice shook as she spoke; she was barely audible.

'OK, I'm coming, babe. Where are you?' Mya's concern was clear and the urgency in her voice crackled through the phone. 'Send me the address—I'm on my way.' She hung up, leaving Rosa clutching the phone to her chest and sobbing.

Forty-five minutes had passed. Rosa sat impatiently on the bed. She looked broken, unable to make any sense of what had just taken place. Her phone began to buzz on the duvet. She picked it up and answered. 'Hi,' she whispered.

'I'm outside, babe.' Mya's voice was loud and clear.

Rosa stood up and looked at the bag on the bed. 'Be down in a minute,' she replied, before cutting the call. She picked up the bag then went down the stairs and headed to the living room.

Daniel and Leah turned towards her as she came into the room. She gave a cursory bitch look at Leah, then turned her attention to Daniel, who was clearly shattered from the day's events.

'Daniel, I'm going.' Rosa put on a brave face, not wanting to show any weakness in front of Leah. 'Call me if you want to talk.' She looked at him, waiting for a response. 'So you're not going to fight for me? Or ask me where I'm going?' Her accent reverted to her native tongue.

Daniel looked at Leah, hesitant before answering. 'Stay, we can talk some more.' Daniel didn't sound overly convinced with what he was saying.

Rosa took that as a signal. She turned on her heels and walked out of the door. 'Bye, Daniel.' She left quickly, leaving Leah and Daniel to themselves.

Stepping out into the hot, sticky sunshine, Rosa saw Mya parked in a candy-violet VW Beetle Convertible. She wore mirrored aviator glasses and a sleeveless, fitted, khaki short suit. Her hair was braided with cornrow plaits. Rosa quickly walked to the car, slung the bag into the back seat and got into the car.

'Alright, babes, what's gone on?' Mya gave Rosa a big hug.

Rosa fought back her tears, but the hug was what she needed. She couldn't help herself as the tears rolled down her cheeks. 'He told me to leave.'

Mya pushed her back, still holding her arms. 'Pardon?'

Rosa wiped her eyes. 'I didn't know what to do, so I called . . .'

Mya hugged her again, pulling her into her ample bust. 'Ahh, it's OK, babe. You can stay at mine.' Mya genuinely felt for her. She sat up and held Rosa's face. 'Have you eaten?' She touched Rosa's stomach.

'No.' Rosa shook her head.

'Right, it's brunch at mine then.' She kissed Rosa on the cheek. Mya pulled a box of cigarettes from her handbag. 'Want one?' Rosa shook her head. Mya lit up then started the engine. The song 'Love Don't Cost a Thing' by J. Lo blasted through the speakers. Mya immediately turned it down. 'Well, that was awkward.' She made a face to Rosa, who smiled at the irony.

'No, turn it up. I like that song,' she replied.

Mya turned up the volume. As they drove away, Rosa looked back at the door of the apartment, half-hoping that Daniel might still appear. Mya rubbed her leg and gave a smile of assurance. Rosa offered half a smile back, knowing that the reality was that she was driving away from her future and the only man who had ever treated her properly and made her feel loved. She was gutted, and it would take a while before she could ever forgive him. It hurt, it really did.

Rosa

Chapter 22
Set fire to the rain

They arrived at Mya's place. A row of converted warehouse buildings with large glass windows looked like they would feature in an episode of *Grand Designs*. They were situated right by the River Thames, about a mile from the Docklands. Mya pulled in next to a large brown door with the silver number '6', approached by a gravel pathway lined with exotic plants.

'Home, babe.' She switched the engine off. They both sat for a few seconds as the sun glinted off the large windows of the apartment. 'Look, babe, stay as long as you need to.' Mya's sincerity came across—she was real—and Rosa felt cool with her.

'OK, thank you.' Rosa smiled and rubbed her hand.

They got out of the car, Rosa took her bag from the back seat and they headed inside.

Mya's apartment was beautiful. It was a large, spacious, modern conversion with an open-plan kitchen.

White-patterned cast-iron beams held up the high-roofed structure, and it was sparsely furnished with a white leather couch and a glass table decorated with various magazines and pictures. The rest of the space doubled as a photography studio. A couple of rows of framed pictures hung on the far wall in front of a camera and lighting set-up.

Rosa looked around as Mya breezed in, throwing her keys onto the countertop.

'Sit down, babe, I'll make us some lunch.' She walked to the fridge, her fit, yoga body shapely and snug in her khaki short suit.

Rosa looked out at the view through the large glass window. The River Thames was just beyond a tree-lined communal park. She stared ahead, still numb.

Can't believe what's happened this morning.

I was expecting to spend the day with him and now I don't even know if I'll see him again.

She pinched the top of her nose, trying to suppress another outpouring.

'Come on, we can sit on the balcony. You can tell me what happened.' Mya led the way, and Rosa put her bag down and followed her.

Rosa sat alone at a round glass outdoor table shaded by a large cream umbrella. The view was the only beautiful thing in her life right now. The shimmer of the sun on the surface of the old, murky river and surrounding greenery was a calm distraction.

Mya came out holding a bowl of pasta with various salad vegetables, chopped and sprinkled with cheese and walnuts. 'Hope you like it; it's all vegan.' She placed the bowl down then disappeared back into the apartment. She came back holding a bottle of wine and two glasses. 'Here, babe, take them. I'll get the plates.' She went off again.

Rosa took the bottle and glasses and placed them on the table. Mya finally sat and shared the food with Rosa. She had laid out quite a spread, with bread rolls and olives to complement the wine, which she poured into Rosa's glass.

Mya poured herself one then held up her glass. 'Here's to fucking life and everything it throws at us!' She clinked her glass against Rosa's then downed a healthy mouthful. 'Let's eat,' she encouraged Rosa, who picked up an olive, popping it into her mouth.

The heat was stifling; just a slight breeze cut through the desert-like dryness.

'Thanks, that was nice.' Rosa sipped a mouthful of wine.

Mya rested back, stretching out her legs. 'Babe, you don't have to talk about it, but I'm here to listen.' She lifted her shades onto her head, revealing her green cat eyes. She seemed very chilled and comfortable in her skin.

Rosa checked her phone, then gave a big sigh. 'Thought he would've at least texted me.' She put her phone on the table. The horrible feeling that she had in the pit of her stomach did not seem to budge; she felt empty although she had just eaten.

Mya lit another cigarette and looked out to the river. 'Men, strange humans,' she said wistfully, blowing out a plume of blue smoke which danced into the air.

'It was her.' Rosa's voice was laced with bitterness. She drank some more of the wine, and every mouthful gave her more courage to speak. 'Know what? He offered me an Airbnb—can you believe that?' Her voice trembled with disappointment as she chucked some more wine down her throat.

Mya sat up, stubbing the cigarette out in a pottery ashtray. She reached over and touched Rosa's hand. 'He probably don't understand, babe. I mean his head must be all over the place. Give it time.' Again, Mya's calm vibe made Rosa feel assured.

She's right, maybe he just feels confused and he still ain't recovered properly.

She has put shit into his head, Leah.

She tossed the rest of her wine into her mouth.

Just hope he calls, I miss him.

Rosa helped Mya clean up after lunch. She stood at the sink washing the dirty dishes. Although she still felt disappointed by the day's events, a couple of glasses of wine and a good feed had made her feel a bit better.

Mya had been great and smiled at her as she disposed of the leftovers. 'I have a class in a bit. Why don't you come?' Mya asked, her hoarse smoker's voice smothered with a healthy dose of empathy. 'Yoga, it'll be good for you,' she continued.

Rosa thought for a few seconds as she rinsed the plates. 'If you don't mind, I'll stay here. I just need to have some time to myself.' She smiled at Mya, grateful that she was being accommodating, but she really didn't feel like doing anything. The wine made her woozy and her energy had been sapped out of her.

'It's cool, babe, but I'm dragging you with me next time,' Mya joked.

Rosa smiled. Mya had a great knack for making her feel special, even though she hardly knew her, but what was important was that at a time when it mattered most, she was that friend in need.

Rosa lay curled up on the sofa, checking her phone every few seconds. Mya had left for her yoga class, leaving Rosa to wallow. It was still a surreal feeling, especially after the events of the last few months. Rosa slid her body upright. She picked up a couple of photographs from the table. They were of a young model—a nice girl, all cheekbones and teeth. Rosa put them back. She got up and walked towards the camera set-up and framed pictures on the wall. She looked through the lens of the camera for a few seconds, then moved away, walking past the pictures. She stared at each of them. They were all female models on various magazines—*Grazia, ES, Health & Beauty*—an impressive array of elegant shots.

They are all so beautiful, Mya is really good.

Rosa stepped out onto the balcony. The sun had just dipped behind the trees; it was a fraction less hot than earlier but still a warm, sticky evening. She stared out, taking it all in and sighing, her heart heavy. She was still trying to work out how she'd got here.

Mya returned wearing her light-blue and orange lycra gym wear that hugged her curves. She threw down her backpack, her skin flushed. 'Honey, I'm home,' she shouted, energy still fresh.

Rosa came out rubbing her wet hair with a towel. She had changed into baggy pyjama bottoms and a fitted tee shirt. 'Hi, hope you don't mind but I had a shower.'

Mya stepped into the room. 'No, that's cool, babe. I need one too!' she joked. 'How ya feeling?'

Rosa sat on the sofa. 'I'm OK.' She smiled at Mya. 'How was class?'

Mya came and sat beside her. 'Yeah, was great. Next time you're deffo coming!' She nudged Rosa. 'It might help take your mind off things.'

Rosa nodded. 'OK.' She laughed.

Mya leaned forwards, taking her trainers off. 'Cor, smell my feet! Gonna hit the shower.' She jumped up. 'Thought we could do Uber Eats for dinner. Pizza? Vegan, of course,' she said as she walked down the length of her spacious room heading for the bathroom. 'Oh, and you can take the spare room. I'll clear some of my stuff away.' She disappeared into the bathroom, leaving Rosa with the towel wrapped around her head like a turban.

She sat back, picking up her phone again.

Still nothing.

No call, text, nothing.

He don't even want to check if I'm OK, does he even care?

She threw her phone onto a cushion next to her and sat back angry, shaking her head in disbelief.

Rosa helped Mya move a large case full of photography equipment. They slid it across to the back of the room.

'Been meaning to do all this for ages, babe,' said Mya, out of breath. Perspiration dribbled down her neck towards the grey, half-cut tee shirt she now wore with some cut-down matching shorts. A single bed was squeezed against the wall. Mya clambered over a few more boxes. 'There, should have enough space now.'

Rosa helped shift the last of the boxes full of wires and devices. 'It's OK, this is how my flat was when I lived with my brothers.' She laughed. At least she still had a morsel of humour, even in her latest predicament. Rosa managed to lift her large sports bag onto the bed, unzipping it to take out some of her clothes. She pulled out a couple of dresses.

'Oh, that's nice.' Mya took one of the dresses—the red number she'd worn to the dinner at Geraldo's. Mya held it up against her body and pretended to waltz elegantly in the confined space like on *Strictly*. Rosa watched on, trying not to laugh, until Mya broke out into a pretty bad robot, her short body jerking into a few awkward angles and her facial expressions contorted.

Rosa could not hold it anymore and she cracked up.

Mya joined her, laughing hard. 'What else you got?' Mya started pulling her things out of the bag and checking all of her shoes and dresses.

Rosa pulled out a black velvet box and stared at it as Mya continued checking out her garments. She opened the box and the diamond necklace and earrings glistened.

Mya stopped. 'What's that?' Inquisitive, she ogled the gleaming pieces.

Rosa handed her the box. 'A gift from Daniel.' Her laughter dried up, as did Mya's.

'This is so beautiful, can I?' Mya asked. Rosa nodded as she took the necklace from the box. 'Wow, gorgeous.' She placed it around Rosa's neck. The cool silver gave her a shiver down her spine. 'Oh, babe, so nice.' Mya marvelled at Rosa's innocent beauty, transfixed by the gleam of the diamonds against her skin. Her gaze lingered on Rosa's brown eyes.

Rosa felt slightly uncomfortable and giggled shyly.

'I've got a great idea.' Mya broke her gaze, and her husky tone went up a couple of octaves. 'But we need more wine!'

* * *

The sound of Kylie Minogue blasted from the small Alexa device. The neon-blue LED circular glow added to the ambience. Rosa was dancing around barefoot with the red dress on and the diamond necklace clipped around her neck. Mya held a half-empty bottle of wine and poured more into Rosa's glass. They both sang along to the song 'Can't Get You Out Of My Head' karaoke style, holding each other like a couple of drunk sailors.

Mya's energy was crazy. She showed off her full repertoire of shimmying dance moves, using the bottle as an imaginary microphone. A drunken Rosa sipped her wine and danced around off-balance. She had moves, her Mexican rhythm evident as she wound her body sexily around. 'Nah, nah, nah . . .' they sang along loudly to the tune, laughing and giggling. This was the most Rosa had ever let loose. All her feelings and inhibitions had vanished with the wine.

Mya gulped a mouthful from the bottle. 'Hmm, wait. I have a little something else.' She let go of Rosa's hand and skipped into her kitchen. 'Nah, nah, nah, can't get you outta my head' she sang as she opened one of the drawers and pulled out a joint. Mya boogied her way back over to Rosa, waving the joint in front of her. 'Yeah, babe.' She put the joint into her mouth; it hung from her lips as she grabbed Rosa's hips and danced closely.

Rosa laughed, her mind giddy. She took the joint from Mya's mouth and put it between her lips, smiling while Mya flicked her lighter on. She held it to the joint and Rosa sucked in. She took it down then started coughing as the smoke hit the back of her throat. She gulped more wine, spluttering, 'Oh my days.' She wiped her mouth, still wheezing and coughing.

Mya took it from her and puffed hard on it, blowing out a thick plume of smoke. She placed it back into Rosa's mouth seductively.

Rosa took another pull, this time inhaling without the coughing. She took it down and blew the rest of the smoke out just as the music subsided. 'Ahh, man. Alexa, play "Jenny From The Block" by J. Lo,' a now euphoric Rosa shouted. 'This is my favourite!' she shouted as the din of the heavy beat kicked in.

Mya turned her back, pushing her tight, round booty into Rosa's crotch and twerking wildly on her. Rosa carried on dancing and enjoying herself. She touched her necklace, and as she closed her eyes, the intoxication hit home. Mya turned around to face her, moving in close and placing the joint back into her mouth. She held it as Rosa sucked on it. It felt good—all her stress and worries about Daniel and Leah had evaporated.

Rosa felt free—dancing, drunk—it was just the release she needed. Mya continued to dance up close, her face almost nose to nose with Rosa. Her cat eyes stared deep into Rosa's. Although the song was up-tempo, they rocked slowly, swaying side to side. The headiness hit them both.

Mya played with Rosa's hair, running her fingers through playfully. 'Never seen someone so beautiful,' she whispered, her lips close to Rosa's ears and her hot, smoky breath leaving her ear moist.

Rosa could only respond with a shy giggle.

Mya took the joint from her lips. 'Stunning,' she slurred. She pushed herself against Rosa, her firm breasts squashing against hers. They continued to sway slowly. Mya's eyes locked into Rosa's and she moved her head forward, pouting her lips and kissing Rosa. It was a slow, lingering, full on one.

'Oh, I need to sit down.' Rosa drew away and plonked herself down onto the sofa. 'I feel high.' Rosa sprawled out and the red dress rode up, revealing her legs.

Mya sat down beside her, still chugging away on the joint before placing it into an ashtray on the table. The song finished, introducing a few seconds of silence. 'Babe, you alright?' Mya asked, watching a clearly drunk Rosa lying motionless.

She forced out a 'Hmm' then dragged herself upright. Her hair fell in her face. She laughed, trying to regain some kind of composure as Mya watched on.

'I've got an idea.' Mya leapt up and stumbled towards her camera set-up. She switched on the bright lights, positioning the reflector umbrellas.

Rosa watched on, her head still spinning. 'What you doing?'

'Come over, sit here.' Mya beckoned Rosa.

She stood up. Unsteadily, she navigated her way through the room to Mya.

'Sit here.' Mya set a chair in front of the lights and the tripod on which the camera was perched. She helped Rosa to sit on the chair, covering her eyes as the bright bulbs beamed at her. She was woozy, her head bowed. Mya seemed to be able to function whilst high and drunk. She moved the camera tripod at an angle.

'You're taking my picture?' Rosa asked, shielding her eyes.

Mya removed the lens cap from her camera. She looked at the digital screen and could see Rosa sat perfectly in position. 'Look up, babe,' she ordered. Rosa looked up, squinting into the lights, her body hunched.

'Noo! I look wrecked,' she protested.

Mya came over and lifted Rosa's head with her hands. 'Babe, we just messing.' She fussed around, fixing Rosa's hair and dress.

Rosa giggled. 'No, I feel awful.' She tried to push Mya away, but her arms were limp.

'Trust me, babe, you're stunning.' Mya's husky voice slurred as she placed her hands on Rosa's bare shoulders. 'Just a few test shots.' She stumbled back over to the camera. 'OK, look at me,' she directed Rosa, getting her shot prepared, staring at the small screen.

Rosa tried to compose herself but burst out laughing. 'I can't.' She tried again to hold in her laughter.

Mya began snapping away, the shutter clicking at speed. Rosa tried to look sexy; she was playful, swishing her hair and touching her necklace.

'Gorgeous, babe, honestly,' Mya encouraged, still clicking frame after frame.

Rosa laughed again, shrugging. 'How should I pose?' Again, she was giggling, tilting her head back and pouting her lips for fun.

'One more. Five, four, three, two, one!' Mya screamed, whooping wildly at Rosa. 'Look, I got some good ones.

They look great.' Mya flicked through all of the frames, showing Rosa as they sat on the sofa.

Rosa wasn't really taking it all in as she was still in a haze. She leant her head on Mya's shoulder, watching as she clicked from frame to frame.

'Not bad for a bit of fun. I reckon I could do something with these.' She was excited as she looked through the selection of shots.

Rosa closed her eyes, drained by the events of the day. Mya continued until she stopped on one shot of Rosa that caught the lens perfectly. Her smile was genuine, her eyes looked bright and the necklace against her olive-skinned cleavage gleamed perfectly in contrast to the vibrant, red dress. Mya zoomed in; she studied the photo then looked at Rosa who was now drawing some deep breaths and falling asleep. Mya kissed her on the forehead. Rosa stirred. A small smile formed on her face as she continued to sleep. Mya stared at the picture, zooming up close to Rosa's face.

Rosa opened her eyes. She was blinded by the sun rays that shone brightly through the tall arched windows. She could barely raise her head as the throb of a headache kicked in. She managed to drag herself into an upright position. Mya's body was curled up against her, fast asleep. Rosa rubbed her eyes, adjusting to the light. Her throat was dry and she felt awful. She rubbed her head and managed to get up without disturbing Mya and made her way into the kitchen, twisting her creased dress which was wrapped around her midriff. Rosa poured herself a large glass of orange juice and drank almost half in one gulp. She stepped gingerly into the front room. Mya was still out cold, hugging a cushion beneath her head. Rosa smiled then went to the balcony. As she stepped out, the oven-like air hit her. She sat at the table, placing the glass of juice down.

Oh, my head, I feel awful.

If this is what a hangover feels like, I never want another one.

She touched the necklace. It was the only thing that linked her to Daniel. The sentimental value was greatly appreciated at that moment.

A few minutes later, a groggy-looking Mya shuffled her way out to join her. 'Babe, what a fucking night.' She kissed Rosa on the cheek then sat down, taking the glass and drinking the remains of Rosa's orange juice. 'Oh, so nice.' She wiped her mouth. 'Hot again.' She shielded her eyes from the bright sun.

'I haven't danced like that for ages.' Rosa laughed, feeling slightly embarrassed at her antics. 'But thank you, I needed to have some fun.'

Mya stretched out, yawning. 'I reckon we should go for a picnic.'

Rosa looked back at her confused. 'A picnic?'

'Yeah, let's go to one of the big parks—sandwiches, fresh fruit and ice cream!'

Rosa's energy went up a level at the mention of ice cream. 'No wine.' Rosa shook her head and they both laughed.

'No wine!' Mya repeated.

The park was filled with people enjoying the heady temperatures, sunbathers, roller skaters and children running in the grass. Mya and Rosa found a spot in the shade of a large tree. They were perched on a mound overlooking a pond with ducks and elegant white swans indulging in the bread being thrown at them by kids and parents. Mya placed down a small chiller box. She looked funky in a straw summer hat, a tangerine summer dress and flip flops.

Rosa was casual in white shorts and a red vest top, with her hair slicked back into a ponytail. She unfurled a mini blanket. 'This is so nice,' she enthused whilst carefully placing it down on the grass. She sat eating her sandwich with a borrowed pair of sunglasses over her eyes.

Mya sat beside her in a yoga pose under her large hat, and they watched the world go by.

'I've never seen London like this,' Rosa mused between chews, appreciating the views. 'Only when Daniel took me out.' She paused on reflection and swallowed the last of her food.

'London in the summertime is wicked,' Mya's husky voice confirmed. Rosa turned to her, lifting her shades.

'Mya, I just wanted to say thank you. I have no money to give you, but I promise—'

Mya stopped her mid-sentence. 'Babe, don't, it's cool.' She put her arm around Rosa, giving her a reassuring hug.

'Hate how my brothers always seem to control my life. I thought I was finally free, meeting Daniel. Have you ever been in love?' she asked Mya, who sat passively listening.

'Oh, babe, don't go there.' She broke into a husky laugh, rubbing Rosa's back.

'I don't understand how they found Daniel, his showroom, it don't make sense...'

Mya looked at her. 'So, what happened? I mean you told me some, but . . .'

Rosa turned to her and took off her shades.

I trust Mya, she has really helped me out and I need to speak to someone just to make some sense of all of this.

* * *

'Fucking hell, babe, that's deep.' Mya lit a cigarette, shaking her head under her floppy sun hat.

Rosa lay on her back looking up into the green leaves hanging from the branches of the tree that protected her from the laser-like rays of sunlight. 'Yes, that's what happened, but please keep it between us,' she asked a still shocked Mya.

'Course, babe. Your brothers sound nuts and that Leah, what a bitch.' She continued to puff on her cigarette, swatting away a rogue wasp buzzing around the half-eaten food. Mya stubbed out her cigarette then cleared away the rubbish into a bag, clearing some space to lie next to Rosa. She shuffled up on the blanket, taking off her hat and resting it on her stomach. She took Rosa's hand and snuggled up to her. 'You got me now, babe. I'll look after you.' She kissed her on the cheek then played with Rosa's hair. She was always kissing and touching Rosa, but she never thought anything of it. She just took it as Mya being caring, like a big sister, but Mya seemed to have deeper feelings. 'I reckon you could model; you can earn good money,' she suggested.

Rosa turned to look at Mya. 'Me? No, I'm no model!' She burst out laughing.

A chilled Mya gazed admiringly at Rosa's smooth skin; she touched her face. 'The camera loves you, babe, honestly. I know some people—'

'No, thanks, but right now I just need to figure things out.' Rosa smiled politely back at Mya, taking her hand and moving it away from her face. She placed her shades back on and rested.

It had now been a few weeks since she had been at Mya's place. Rosa loved the vibe in the house; it was like hanging with a best friend. Mya had made her feel more than welcome, and she made sure in return she helped out by keeping the place clean and cooking meals for Mya. She had attended some yoga classes as promised and actually enjoyed it. Mya was cool but often busy; she worked a lot with different photoshoots and various people often came to the apartment. She could see how connected she was within the industry, which was something that impressed her.

During that time, she still had not heard from Daniel. It was as if he had erased her out of his life. She checked her phone often but nothing, not even a text. She had left him several messages, over a hundred, plus voicemails, but no response. Rosa's heart was broken. As much as she tried to move on, she could not believe that their relationship didn't mean anything.

So disappointed about Daniel, he doesn't care about me.

I know Leah and his parents must have convinced him to stay away from me.

He's just thrown me away like a piece of trash.

Who am I anyway?

Just poor little Rosa from Mexico, I was never good enough to be his.

All of the gifts, his words, everything was just a lie and when it came down to it, he didn't even fight for me.

Does he care if I'm dead or alive?

I looked after him, why would he just forget about me?

Rosa sat in her favourite spot in the small communal park below Mya's apartment. She'd often come out whenever Mya had clients; it was her little place of peace. She liked to people watch, mostly the other residents and their families enjoying the everlasting heatwave. She scrolled through her phone, checking the texts, swiping through the selfies of her and Daniel in better times. It was painful for her to look at them, especially the images of Daniel.

Can't believe that's the same man, he's like a stranger.

Feels like I never really knew him.

She found it hard to move on from the day he'd told her to leave. The image of him sitting there, unable to look at her in Leah's presence, made her feel sad and empty every time she thought about it.

What can I do?

I can't stay here forever, I need to find a job.

Mya can't let me stay forever, I thought it would just be a few days, two at the most.

It's been weeks and it don't look like he's going to call me so I need to move on.

Her racing thoughts were interrupted by Mya.

'Rosa! Babe, guess what?' Mya bounced enthusiastically towards her, almost skipping with excitement. As usual, she looked sexy in a shiny, gold bikini top and a see-through, patterned sarong which complemented her shapely curves. Her hair was braided into cornrows.

Rosa looked up. She could not help but smile at Mya's energetic prancing. 'What?' Rosa shouted back at her, feeling excited but not knowing what she was excited about.

Mya bounded over exuberantly, waving her phone in her hand. She ran the last few yards to a very intrigued Rosa, who stood up watching as she approached.

'What's happened, are you OK?' She barely got her words out before being engulfed by a big hug. 'Hey, what's going on?' She laughed whilst hugging Mya.

'OK, now don't be mad at me.' Mya's smoky voice cracked as she caught her breath. She took a step back, her feline eyes gleaming at Rosa, with a mischievous smile on her face. 'So, *Heat* magazine—'

'*Heat* magazine?' she repeated. Mya fanned her hands in excitement.

'Yes! *Heat* magazine has bought your story. I spoke to a friend and showed him the picture I took . . .'

Rosa's expression quickly changed from happy to confused in seconds. 'My story? What picture?'

Mya continued, barely able to get her words out. 'They're paying five thousand. I thought that would be a nice little start-up for you . . .'

Rosa stepped away. 'You told them my story?' she responded, trying to process the information just fed to her.

Mya smiled. 'Yeah, babe, they loved it.'

Rosa walked away.

What has she done?

I don't want my story out there, that's not going to help me with Daniel or anyone.

I don't want to be the poor little victim.

She turned back to Mya. 'Why did you do that?' Her face began to redden and not just from the heat.

'I wanted to help, babe. This is a good way to get you on your feet.' Mya's energy subsided with each word; she could see Rosa's annoyance building.

'Get on my feet?' she repeated, her blood boiling. 'You should have asked me first. Daniel will see this and think . . .'

Mya took a step towards her and held up her phone. 'Five thousand pound, babe. Look, it's all here.'

Rosa pushed her hand away. 'I don't want money. My life is not for sale.' She shoved her way past Mya and walked back towards the apartment.

'Rosa!' Mya hurried after her. 'I don't understand—thought you'd be happy.'

Rosa paced up and down the kitchen. She was upset, holding her head in her hands and visibly shaking as she tried to control her feelings.

Mya came rushing in after her and stopped Rosa in her tracks. 'Hey, tell me, what's the problem?'

'So the pictures we took drunk, you gave to a magazine and told them about my life. Why?' she screamed, unable to hold in her anger.

Mya stepped back, shocked at Rosa's reaction. 'Whoa! Let's just calm down here, babe. I think you're being a bit . . .' This was the last thing she'd expected, especially in her own home. She became defensive, offended by Rosa's tone.

'Ungrateful?' Rosa finished her sentence, still in disbelief.

Mya suddenly felt disrespected. She came back at Rosa, her expression switching to incredulous. 'Er, yes. I did this to help you get on your feet, maybe help with a deposit for a place of your own.'

Rosa spun away. She couldn't believe what was happening. She stepped back and forth, zigzagging across the kitchen before turning back to Mya who, by now, had a full-on resting bitch face ready to repel anything that came at her.

'So, you don't want me here?' Rosa's red mist had descended; her thoughts had become irrational and unreasonable. 'Everyone is going to see my personal life, with some stupid picture wearing a diamond necklace, and think what?' Her voice trembled in anger and disappointment. She stared at Mya, on the brink of exploding. All of the pain, hurt and feelings that had built up over the last few months became a tsunami about to crash over Mya.

Mya could see that Rosa was irate. It also made her upset, and she fought back the tears. 'Babe, I only wanted to help. You know I would never do anything to hurt you, never.' She walked towards Rosa, arms outstretched going in for a hug, but Rosa pushed her away.

'You betrayed me. I trusted you.' Rosa ran off towards her room, leaving Mya stood there trying to compute what had just occurred. Rosa stuffed her clothes into the same large sports bag she had arrived with. She was fuming, not thinking straight and angry that Mya, the one person she'd trusted, had sold her out.

I'm not staying here, what gives her the right to take my personal life and sell it to some tacky magazine without even asking me?

What's everyone gonna think?

They will say, 'The poor little Mexican girl from Sinaloa whose brothers torched her boyfriend's business sits there in a diamond necklace crying about how hard her life has been!'

I don't want to be judged and I don't want five thousand dirty pounds.

I thought Mya would be loyal but no, she's just like Leah.

If she thought this would help, she should have asked first.

Mya opened the door. 'What are you doing?' She stepped in, seeing Rosa clearing all her stuff, and tried to stop her. 'I didn't tell you to go. Please, just stop.' Mya grabbed her hands. She was tearful and shaken. 'Can we just talk?' Mya sat on the bed, dragging Rosa down with her. A loud clap of thunder was heard outside, followed by a deep rumble. 'Think it's finally going to rain.' Mya smiled, wiping away her tears, attempting to inject a dose of humour.

'I can't stay here,' Rosa whimpered, her head bowed, unable to face Mya. 'I trusted you but . . .' She stopped short, taking a deep breath.

'No, babe. Look, I'll try and get it stopped, but it might be too late. I honestly think you've taken this all wrong.' Mya caressed Rosa's face tenderly. 'Just think about it.' She continued sweeping away Rosa's hair.

Rosa calmly removed her hand. 'I'm sorry, Mya, I must go.' She stood up and grabbed her bag.

Mya clung to her arm. 'You don't have to leave, babe,' she pleaded, but Rosa's pride had been dented enough.

She refused Mya's plea, let go of her and walked

out. Mya followed her out of the room. 'You're making a mistake, Rosa, come on . . .'

Rosa turned and looked back, her eyes still brimming with tears of rage. 'Thank you for being there when I needed.' She held her gaze for a few seconds before turning away and walking out of the door.

'Wait! You're overreacting. Can we just talk?' Mya yelled. The front door slammed in sync with another clap of thunder, which shook the room. Mya stood alone, baffled and helpless.

Rosa walked aimlessly, still dressed in a tee shirt, shorts and flip flops. She had no internal sat nav; she just walked along the banks of the old river. The air was humid, but the smell of rain hung ominously in the air like the dark clouds which eclipsed the bright-orange sun. She was trying not to cry, her natural stubbornness not allowing her to show her real emotions, but she knew she was alone. Now she had nobody.

Rosa walked across a bridge, and the backdrop was spectacular. The riverside buildings shimmered on the surface of the water under the dark, charcoal skies. Again there was a loud clap of thunder, this time accompanied by a bolt of lightning cutting across the sky. Huge drops of rain began to splatter onto the ground in front of her. It was the first time any rain had fallen in months, giving relief from the relentless sun and sticky heat. Rosa continued to walk, the rain now a downpour. Finally, her tears broke like a dam. She trudged across the bridge into the street, soaked to the skin. Her tears merged with the raindrops that ran down her face.

Chapter 23
Me, myself and I

For hours, Rosa walked the streets. It was a scary place to be, with all sorts of weird stares and people approaching her, mainly homeless beggars and youths trying to chat her up. Luckily the downpour had ceased and the evening sun replaced the dark clouds, which had parted and drifted away into the distance. She was tired, and every step she took felt painful, like walking across broken glass. With no other option, she decided to go home to the council flat from which she had fled, knowing Jesus and Dani were locked up.

Rosa had made her way back to the street that led to the estate. It was late now, and her body ached, especially her legs and feet. She was sweaty and hungry, her energy had diminished and the bag she carried felt heavier every step she took. She walked past the convenience store that she'd often run to. Looking in the window, she saw the store owner.

He looked back at her, recognised her face, smiled and waved.

Rosa barely mustered a smile and trudged on. She dropped the bag to the floor as she stood at the entrance to the council estate. She stared at the dark tower blocks which dwarfed her small frame.

Oh, Lord, back to this.

Feels like déjà vu but a nightmare.

Whatever happens, this is what I have to do, just have to make the most of it.

She took a deep breath, picked up the bag and continued along the walkway, which was full of the same boisterous youths she thought she had left far behind in her life. Now she had to run that gauntlet again, but she knew what to expect.

As she drew closer, the sound of heavy drill music pumped from a car parked on the kerbside. The youths noticed her and started to make various noises, whistling, barking and cackling.

Here we go, back to this crap.

Just keep walking, ignore them.

I swear the way I feel they just need to leave me alone.

She approached them and they parted, letting her walk past. Rosa kept her head down, noticing the smell of weed, smoke and alcohol. She looked a mess and could feel all of their eyes on her.

'Oi, pretty ting, let me help you,' one of the boys called.

Rosa rolled her eyes and continued to walk, very conscious of the fact she was wearing next to nothing. Her skin crawled knowing that she had at least eight pairs of eyes ogling her.

'Come on, sexy, low me a blow job or suttin,' came another crude voice, followed by raucous laughter.

She swallowed, kept her head straight and walked; a welcome back, indeed. Breathing heavily, Rosa finally made it to the back gate. She took another deep breath, then pushed the gate open. She felt anxious not knowing what to expect. It pained her to be back but her pride was the driver for the decision to leave Mya's place. She stepped into the backyard, the gate scraping along the concrete.

OK, made it, let's see what state those two left this place in.

Sucks to be back but I just have to make the most of it, this is my home now.

She opened the back door and, as usual, it was unlocked. She was hit by the rancid smell of festering refuse as flies buzzed around the tiny kitchen. She stepped in tentatively, holding her nose as the pungent stink overwhelmed her. She was greeted by a sink full of dirty dishes, half-eaten boxes of takeaway food, overflowing rubbish and stifling heat. Her heart sank as reality smacked her squarely in the face. She looked around and saw the newspaper on the table with the knife still stabbed into the picture of her and Daniel at the award show.

Rosa left the door open, trying to get as much air in as possible. Bravely she walked through to the living room, dropping her bag in the hallway. It was pretty much the same—messy with boxes of old phones and devices scattered around the dark, dank-smelling room. Rosa sighed heavily as she looked around.

Home sweet home, eh.

Jeez, will have to sort all this tomorrow.

I'm too tired to start cleaning now.

She carried on her inspection of the flat and saw a pile of letters stacked by the front door. She picked them up and flicked through them. They were mainly junk mail and takeaway menus, but a brown envelope addressed to her caught her eye. She ripped open the envelope and read.

From the Crown Prosecution Service . . .

Dear Miss Chavez, You are required to attend Southwark Magistrates Court to provide a witness account for case number 0000234761 Plaintiff D Rosewood versus Jesus and Dani Chavez on the date of . . .

Shit, am I a witness against my brothers?

I'm confused, how am I a witness?

This can't be right.

She continued to read.

You are required by law to attend on the said date. Failure in doing so may result in legal action against you under section . . .

Shit, this is next week!

I don't have time to think now, too much to deal with . . .

Rosa scrunched up the other envelopes and made her way back to the kitchen. She chucked them into the rubbish, except the court letter. She felt saddened. How could she choose between Daniel and her brothers? It weighed heavily on her mind as she began to clear away the rubbish from the table.

Returning to her bedroom felt strange. It was as if she'd been on a short vacation and now had to come back to reality. She sat on her bed, which seemed smaller than she remembered, and checked her phone.

Eight missed calls from Mya and three messages.

Most were Mya apologising for upsetting her but also asking Rosa to reply and let her know she was safe. Rosa began to tap on her phone keyboard. The least she could do was to let Mya know she was safe. She sent the message then threw her phone aside. Instantly, a message pinged back. It was Mya. Rosa read the message then again tossed her phone on the bed.

I love Mya but I'm too angry and exhausted to think about anything now.

She lay down on her pillow and closed her eyes. It had been an ordeal and there was more to come, especially now with the court case.

Morning came around quickly, and the sun pierced through the gaps between the bedroom curtains. Rosa shifted, tossing and turning, until eventually she opened her eyes. She squinted for a few seconds, adjusting to the bright light. Staring around at her tiny room, it felt as though she had dreamt all of the last few months. She struggled up, still sleepy. She checked her phone: still no messages or calls from Daniel but a couple from Mya. She opened the messages.

Glad to hear you're safe, I tried to stop the magazine but couldn't.

Sorry, babe.

Still got your money if you need it, hope to speak soon, Mya.

Rosa gave a big sigh and flopped back onto the pillow. She scrolled through her phone, checking the latest social media, specifically Daniel's account. There were no new updates. The last few pictures posted were the ones of them both at the award show and dinner. Just seeing them took her back. It wasn't a dream; she had actually had a relationship with this man. He was real, and what they had been through was real, too. It hurt to know the man she loved had simply abandoned her, with no concern for how she felt.

She went onto Leah's page and saw two pictures of Daniel with his family at a dinner table. He was the only one not smiling, sat next to his dad. He looked himself again—his hair had been cut and he was smartly dressed. Rosa zoomed in on his face. He looked solemn, while Leah and her parents cheesed hard.

Look at her, happy now she got what she wanted as if nothing ever happened.

Daniel looks sad.

I'll send him another message, hopefully he'll get in touch.

After dragging herself out of bed, Rosa was on a mission to clean up the house. She had got dressed, just a casual tee shirt and cut-off jeans, with her hair pulled back into a ponytail.

She was in the kitchen, wearing rubber gloves, scrubbing every area down with disinfectant. The back door was open, letting the sun beam in from the clear blue skies as the temperature began to rise once again. The radio played in the background.

It took her hours to clear all of the trash from both the kitchen and living room. She didn't care about any repercussions from her brothers because in some sense she was free now, but whether her brothers would be was down to her. She took out the boxes of brick-a-brack and old devices, leaving them next to the large communal dustbins. Sweat trickled down her face as she scrubbed hard to remove the bloodstains from the chair where Dani had last sat after his battering.

Rosa drew back the curtains and opened the windows to let the sun and some much-needed air into the living room. She looked around, and in all her time there, she had never seen the room so clean and clear. It was actually a nice little space. She sat down on the sofa to take a breather. She removed the rubber gloves to wipe the sweat from her brow.

I can actually do something with this place, a few plants and flowers, new rug, some pictures and maybe a TV.

Only one problem: I have no money, but at least I have something to work towards.

She smiled, resting back for a few minutes. She took a break from her hard morning's graft, satisfied with her achievement. She still had to tackle the boys' room and the bathroom, but for now, she sat back, content with her work. Once again she checked her phone, which was stuffed into her front pocket. No messages or a reply from Daniel. She shrugged and pushed the phone back into her pocket. She dragged herself back up, picked up the gloves and went to her brothers' room.

Eww, this place is so disgusting.

Rosa heaved a couple of times, gagging from the awful, musty stench as she tip-toed through to the window.

They live like pigs, look at the state of the room.

Rosa unlocked the window and fought with the jammed frame until she eventually managed to shove it open. She had tied a bandana over her nose, masking her from the full toxicity of the smell. She pulled the curtains aside, letting in the light, which only revealed the tip which her brothers called a bedroom. Plates with dried food covered in blue, mouldy fur, empty cans of fizzy drinks, dirty clothes, curdled bottles of milk and old trainers were scattered everywhere. Rosa gagged again, barely able to hold back the vomit from spewing out of her mouth.

Yuck, this is so nasty, stinks of piss as well.

What have these two been doing in here all this time?

Rosa gingerly picked up all the rubbish and threw it into a large black bin liner. It was a filthy, dusty cesspit but she persevered, determined to rid the flat of everything that reminded her of Jesus and Dani. For over an hour she bagged so much trash that it took her three trips to the communal bins. She sprayed air freshener throughout the house each time she traipsed up and down the stairs. Eventually, she managed to clear the room down to the bare bones of the basic furniture—a shabby wardrobe and two tatty single beds which had seen better days. Rosa put the last of their clothes, pillows and bedsheets into black bags.

Oh, man, this is awful but I've done most of it now.

A tired yet satisfied Rosa sank down to the floor, her back against the wardrobe. She took the bandana from her face and wiped her forehead. A gentle breeze swept into the room as she drank a bottle of water.

That was hard work, thank God I don't have to do that again.

I'll get the council to come and collect the old furniture.

As she rested back, she noticed an old trainer box wedged underneath Jesus's bed. She scrambled onto her knees, reached underneath and pulled the box out. Rosa placed the box on her lap; it was a fair weight and dusty. Intrigued, Rosa opened it.

What's this?

Rosa took out four tightly rolled stacks of twenty-pound notes, each held together by a rubber band. She held the money in her hand.

What the hell?

She took the rubber band off one of the rolls and counted the notes. Two hundred and eighty pounds. Her heart began to beat faster. She removed the band from another roll and counted.

One, two, three, four, five.

Shit, that's three hundred pounds in that one.

By the time she had counted out all the rolls, there were notes spread all around her on the floor.

Bloody hell, a thousand and sixty pounds!

Shit, what was Jesus doing to have all this money?

This must be a sign, a gift from God or something.

Shit, I can't believe this.

Excitedly, Rosa pulled out the rest of the papers that were stuffed into the box. She recognised the handwriting on the papers as Jesus's—childlike, untidy, misspelt words and scratched-out lines. Rosa read one of them; they were letters to her father, ramblings from her older brother.

I hate you, Papa.

It's all your fault, you killed Mama for greed . . . I hate you more than those bandits, you deserved to die but not Mama . . .

Rosa stopped, taking a deep breath before continuing.

London is a dump.

Because of you, we are here suffering . . . why did you bring those devils to our home?

Fuck you, bastard . . .

Rosa was overwhelmed. The pain he was going through was clear; his anger made sense now. These letters showed how deeply affected Jesus had been by everything that had happened the night his mother was killed and where all his moods stemmed from. It was hard for her to continue, but she felt compelled. Speechless, she read a final letter.

My papa, the devil who burned our family . . . they should have took you and left Mama.

I miss Mama, Rosa misses Mama, and Dani is young.

He didn't deserve this life.

Fuck London, fuck Sinaloa, fuck the world.

I hope you burn in hell . . .

Tears streamed down Rosa's face. She scrunched up the letter, agonising over what she had just read. Surrounded by the money scattered around her, she felt numb and empty. She looked around the room. The sun dipped behind the tower blocks obscuring the view, although it still managed to shine a shard of light across her chest.

Chapter 24
Who do you think you are?

The burnt-out remains of Rosewood Automobiles, blackened by the dark smoke stains that were embedded in the bricks, stood out starkly against the blue sky.

Daniel stood in front of the building, leaning on a black cane. He took his shades off and surveyed the damage. The forecourt which once held expensive, shiny supercars was now empty. Stained concrete and the rust-coloured windows charred by the flames resembled a medieval haunted house. He shuffled towards the gates, which were shackled by a thick chrome chain and padlock.

Leah joined him, her white linen jumpsuit a clean contrast to the derelict building. Her hair tumbled immaculately over her bare shoulders, and her eyes were covered by large, opal-framed shades. 'How'd ya feel?' Her question needed no answer.

Daniel's grim expression screamed sadness. His pearly-white smile was absent as he turned to Leah, his lips pursed. 'Gutted, Sis. But I'll build again.' His speech had much improved. He was more decisive, trying to inject a dose of optimism into the bleak situation. He looked healthy apart from the cane, dressed in white shorts, a red polo tee shirt and flip-flops.

'The insurance will pay out and we'll go again.' Leah placed her arm around Daniel. 'Let's go home.' Leah ushered him towards the car.

On the drive back, Daniel peered out of the window watching the world go by. The welcome breeze swept through his hair. This experience had changed him—he seemed forlorn, looking out into the distance. His usual spark of cockney charm had been doused. Leah was the opposite, chatting away and rambling on about online clothes sales and beauty products.

Daniel turned to her. 'I want it back now.' He cut her in mid-flow.

Leah touched his leg. 'Want what back?' Her voice wavered.

'My phone ... can I have it?'

Leah cleared her throat. 'I just kept it, Bruv, to let you recover in peace.'

Daniel continued to stare out of the window, frustrated. 'I'm not a child, Leah.' He stamped his cane on the floor of the car.

Leah pushed her shades onto her forehead and looked across at him, her face flushed. 'OK, I'll give it back.' Leah huffed and covered her eyes with the large shades, annoyed.

Daniel glanced over at her as he rested back in the chair and quietly stewed.

* * *

Daniel sat in the kitchen staring at a tall glass of water, deep in thought.

Leah came in and slid his phone onto the table. 'I didn't think you needed any distractions.'

Daniel grabbed the phone and tapped in his password. The phone came to life with the ping of a string of texts.

'Just looking out for your best interest,' Leah continued, her tone sincere, as Daniel eagerly opened each message. He frantically read one after the other.

'I've missed all these messages from Rosa.' He showed Leah the phone screen. 'My best interest, huh?' He gave her a scornful look.

'You heard what Mum and Dad said; she's not the one for you.' Leah was still determined to sway Daniel's opinion.

Daniel struggled to stand, grabbing the edge of the table for support. 'It's not about what anyone thinks. I love her, accept it!'

Leah held her hands up in surrender. 'OK, it's fine, Dan. Have it your way; I'm out of it.' Leah made to walk away, then turned to Daniel. 'I'll support you in court to put her brothers away, but after that . . .' She dusted her hands off, indicating she was done with it. She was the little sister always having the last word.

He picked up the glass of water, took a large gulp and swallowed slowly.

Daniel sat on his large bed, his back against the headrest. He kept reading the messages from Rosa. The screen light glared into his face. He tossed the phone onto the bed, ran his fingers through his hair, then picked the phone up again. He tapped the screen, then put the phone to his ear. He waited for a few seconds until the person answered. 'Hi, it's me.' He let out a nervous laugh. 'Yes, Daniel.' He laughed again.

'What do you want, Daniel?'

Daniel sat up as a sudden burst of energy coursed through him. Finally, he was able to talk to Rosa and tell her exactly what had happened, but the tone in her voice did not guarantee that he would get that chance.

Chapter 25
Loyalty

Rosa walked into a semi-crowded bar. She looked gorgeous in a figure-hugging white jumpsuit. Gold, strapped wedges gave her height, her hair flowed down and was swept to one side and her natural good looks had returned. She looked well and had obviously invested some of her brother's hidden cash on a new wardrobe. Eyes from the gawping groups of men followed her.

'Hey, Rosa, over here.' An excited voice stood out amongst the mumble of conversations and the light, jazzy background music. Ella stood tall, her red hair an instant beacon. She waved excitedly, looking equally classy. Her slim body was fitted in a blingy, emerald-green, shoulder strap dress, and her pale skin was slightly rosy from the days of constant sunshine. Rosa made her way over, and Ella greeted her with a warm hug. 'You look stunning, girl. Come on, I've got a booth.' She took Rosa's hand and led her to a discreet cubbyhole with black velvet seats away from the main bar. They placed their bags on the table. Ella touched Rosa's hand. 'I'm so glad you called. I couldn't remember if I gave you my number that night. I was so drunk.' Ella laughed, her mood in stark contrast to the night they first met when she'd spent most of the evening looking glum next to her husband Bryn.

'Well, a lot has happened since I last saw you.' Rosa smiled, her lips shimmering with translucent lip gloss.

'Same here,' Ella replied.

A hunky, Mediterranean-looking waiter sharply dressed in a white shirt and black trousers approached their booth. 'Drinks ladies?'

Ella scanned him up and down. She looked over at Rosa and winked, and they both broke into a fit of giggles. The waiter smiled warmly, his eyes checking the two of them out.

'A bottle of Prosecco, please.' Ella drawled her request, trying to sound seductive. Rosa tried not to laugh, smiling broadly at the cool waiter.

'Of course.' He turned away and walked off towards the bar.

Ella watched him like a hungry hawk focused on its prey. 'Not bad. Bit young but not bad.' She rubbed her chin.

Rosa laughed. 'Excuse me, you are married,' she joked.

Ella rolled her eyes. 'Don't remind me.' She swept her hair away from her face. Her slim, long fingers were manicured with sunset-orange nail polish to match her hair. 'Things between me and Bryn—' she paused while pouring more Prosecco into her glass, the effects already making her reflective '—have not been good for a while.' She sipped her drink. 'He's no fun anymore. It's either work or the golf club, no Ella time,' she mused.

Rosa took a small sip of her Prosecco; her face still twisted at the taste of it. 'How long have you been married?' she asked.

Ella burst out laughing. 'Too long.' Her laugh was forced, papering over the intrinsic pain she was feeling. 'I hate the man. He's a controlling narcissist up his own arse; think I was just his bit of young fluff.' Her voice trailed off, a hint of regret threaded through her tone as she spoke.

I knew he was a weirdo when I met him, slimy man.

Rosa's remembered his lingering handshake.

'I'm only there for the money and lifestyle.' She took another mouthful of her drink, swallowing slowly. 'Always left to my own devices, anyway. Shopping, spa days, hey! We should do a spa day.' She suddenly perked up. Rosa looked a bit confused.

'Spa day?'

Ella laughed. 'Yeah, sauna, steam, massages—'

'Oh, like beauty treatments?'

Ella put her glass down. 'Yes, pamper day.'

'Yes!' Rosa replied with excitement. She high-fived Ella. 'I need one.' Her excitement was short-lived once the thought of the last few months hit home.

'So, how's that handsome boyfriend of yours?' Ella asked, swishing the last bit of her drink around in the tall flute.

Rosa's eyes dimmed with sadness. 'We're not together at the moment. It's a long story.' The hint of her accent leaked into her words.

Ella sat up, surprised. 'Really? Well, you better start at the beginning, then.' She took the bottle out of the ice bucket, topped up Rosa's glass, then poured herself another.

The young waiter came back to remove the empty glasses. 'Anything else, ladies?' he asked with a cheeky smile on his face.

Ella placed a black Amex credit card into his hand. 'Just charge it to that, please.' Again her eyes flirted with him. He took the card and walked away. 'See, it's so easy. These men all think they're God's gift.'

Rosa shook her head and laughed. 'Thank you, Ella, I needed this.'

Ella made her way around to sit next to Rosa. She hugged her. 'Same here. I'll come with you to court to support you, and after court, spa day, right?' She held Rosa. 'And take that money from Mya. Fuck it, it's *Heat* magazine.' They laughed and high-fived again as the waiter returned.

Rosa excused herself from the table and went to the restroom to freshen up. Each door had a diamond-patterned mirror on the outside. She stepped out of the plush cubicle, looked at her reflection, fixed her jumpsuit, then walked over to the sink to wash her hands.

A small, old African attendant sat looking tired on a stool next to a row of paper towels and bottles of perfume. Rosa smiled at her, then stared into the mirror, twisting the chrome, waterfall-styled tap.

Rosa's olive skin glowed. She felt a little tipsy; Prosecco never helped her head. Her brown eyes sparkled in the reflection but concealed the worry she felt as the court case loomed.

Tonight has been fun, Ella is so sweet but she needs to leave that disgusting gringo.

It's nice to have someone to talk to and she's cool.

The last few weeks have been difficult.

Now Daniel has called and the first time I'll see him is at the court, plus facing my brothers.

Just want this all to be over.

The little African restroom attendant handed her a paper towel. 'Beautiful woman, *mwah.*' She kissed her fingers towards Rosa, indicating perfection.

Rosa dried her hands, throwing the paper towel into the black basket bin. 'Gracias,' she replied, checking her face and touching up her lip gloss.

Come on, girl.

Get your act together, let's enjoy tonight then worry about the rest of the week later.

She chose a bottle of fragrance from the rows of bottles lined up and squirted the spray onto her wrists. She left some money for the sweet, little African lady then left.

Rosa sat holding a bowl of cereal in her living room, which now looked like a comfortable space. She had spent some of the money on a centrepiece—a large, white rug which now covered most of the stained carpet in the middle of the room, along with a clear white table topped with a vase of pink lilies. A large, printed throw covered the old sofa, and a large, rectangular picture of a paradise island hung on the wall. Rosa slowly slurped the remains of the cereal, still in her nightwear. The sun shone brightly into the room. Today was the day, her day in court.

Feel nervous about today, it's gonna be weird seeing Daniel again after so long.

He's been sending me cute messages.

Says he misses me, told me Leah hid his phone so he never got any of my calls or texts.

She's such a hater, snake in the grass, not looking forward to seeing her.

Have to face Jesus and Dani.

Shit, they will hate me forever.

Hopefully God will protect them, especially Dani.

Rosa placed her bowl on the table and checked the time on her phone.

OK, an hour to get ready.

Ella, bless her, she's coming to drive me.

Mya texted to say she'll be there, too.

Still haven't forgiven her but she's supporting me . . . we'll talk after.

Rosa stood up and took the empty bowl to the kitchen, which had also had a bit of a makeover. It was now a much cleaner and brighter space. Being independent seemed to suit her. The peace of mind she had relaxing in her own home without her overbearing brothers breathing down her neck was a relief. At times she felt lonely, but she was gradually growing into her own person. The only thing she had on her mind was the court case; the thought of having to stand in front of all those people filled her with dread.

Rosa lay soaking in the bath, one leg dangling over the side of the tub, surrounded by red candles illuminating the tiny space. She wiped her face, which was wet with sweat, then rested her head back and dunked her hair into the water.

Whatever happens today will be what's meant to happen.

All I can do is hope that them two don't cause a scene.

Daniel's going to expect me to stand by him, it's all a mess.

She submerged her body beneath the water, hoping it would cleanse her fears for the coming hours.

The shrill of her mobile ringtone rang loudly through the house. Rosa was finally dressed in a plain-fitted white shirt and black trousers, her hair pulled into a ponytail. She rushed into her bedroom and picked up the phone from her bed. 'Hey, Ella. Yes, come around the back. I'll meet you at the gate.' She popped her feet into her shoes and fidgeted, putting a pair of earrings into her ears. She was nervous and agitated. She grabbed the last of her things before rushing down the stairs to greet Ella.

The sound of heels clopping against the concrete of the backyard signalled Ella's entrance. 'Hi, Rosa. I'm here.' Ella looked smart in a tartan-print skirt and a black, short-sleeved blouse.

Rosa came out to greet her looking rushed and flustered. 'Hey.' She blew out her cheeks. 'Come in. You found it, then.' She gave Ella a hug in the backyard.

'Yeah, bit ghetto round here. Is it safe?' Ella looked spooked in the draining afternoon heat.

'It's OK' Rosa replied while locking the door.

'You ready?' Ella held her, staring directly into her eyes.

Rosa nodded, trying to compose herself. 'Yes, let's go.' The two linked arms and walked out through the gate.

Upon their arrival, a small huddle of people, including the press, loitered outside the entrance of the court. Rosa walked alongside Ella, hand in hand.

'Here, put these on.' Ella handed her a pair of sunglasses as the photographers began to descend.

Cameras all trained their lenses on them. Rosa put on the shades and squeezed Ella's hand.

'Just be calm and say nothing,' Ella reassured her as the frenzy began, with a series of camera shutters whirring into action.

Several reporters rushed towards them, sticking microphones into Rosa's face. 'Rosa Chavez, in your story you claim you knew nothing about the robbery.' Another reporter shoved the *Heat* magazine cover into their faces. It was the first time Rosa had seen herself on the cover with the headline 'Mexican Beauty Rosa Chavez: My Life, Love and Brothers'.

Rosa frowned; it shocked her to see her face on the cover, the same picture Mya took when she was drunk. Although it looked good, never in her wildest dreams had she thought she would grace the front cover of one of her favourite magazines in this situation. It was surreal to see herself looking glamorous in a shiny diamond necklace and now to be thrust into this frenzy of madness.

'No comment,' Ella spoke firmly on Rosa's behalf. 'Always wanted to do that,' she whispered in her ear as they made their way up the steps into the reception area of the court.

Stepping into the cool of the air-conditioned building was a welcome relief, both from the relentless heat and the pack of press hounds. It was quite frightening, worse than being hassled by the youths on her estate. Rosa sucked in a lungful of air. 'Wow, was not expecting that.'

Ella smiled and ushered her towards the court clerk—a broad-framed, serious-faced woman in her mid-fifties with the intimidating stance of a headmistress. Rosa handed her the letter. She checked the details then instructed her, 'Please wait in room number two. You will be called.' Her lips pursed without even a complementary smile.

Rosa and Ella turned to make their way towards the waiting room. They took a few steps then were confronted by Daniel and Leah, who walked slowly towards them. Rosa's heart skipped a beat on seeing Daniel, especially as he was walking with the aid of a cane. She stopped, watching them as they came closer.

Ella sensed Rosa's hesitation and put her arm around her waist. 'Come on, it'll be alright.' Her words of encouragement failed to register.

Oh my God, this is what I was scared of.

Shit, he looks serious.

My legs have gone to jelly, just be normal, smile, say hi and keep walking.

Rosa tried to compose herself as they approached. She could tell by Leah's face that this was not going to be a civil reunion. She looked as though she had smelt something rotten; her face screwed up at the sight of Rosa.

'Hi.' Rosa broke the ice coyly, almost ashamed to look Daniel in the face. It felt awkward; she was not sure whether to hug him, shake his hand or keep on walking.

Finally, Daniel took the lead. He leaned in and gave her a kiss on the cheek. The electricity of feelings she had for him reignited through her body. 'Hello, babe. Long time,' Daniel replied. His usual confidence seemed to have returned.

Leah barely mustered a smile or even afforded Rosa or Ella a proper greeting. Instead, she pulled a copy of the *Heat* magazine from her garish, hot-pink, Michael Kors tote bag. 'Playing the victim again, huh?' The rage in Leah's voice exhibited her deep-seated gripe. She still saw Rosa as a thorn, a pain point in her life.

Rosa ignored her and looked up at Daniel. 'It's not what you think; I can explain,' she said softly.

Her plea did not impress Leah, who brushed past her, giving Ella the evils for good measure as she stomped away. Her heels clinked through the corridor.

Daniel rubbed his forehead. His hands trembled. 'Look, I just want this all over with, get it off my back,' he said through gritted teeth.

Rosa nodded in agreement. 'Me too.' Her face expressed sadness, knowing Daniel would have to relive his traumatic ordeal, and in the next few hours, her paradoxical choice would change the future of everyone's life.

'You know what you've got to do—tell the truth! They deserve everything they get.' He held her hand firmly, his blue eyes dulled and displaying his angst.

She looked up at his tightened face. Rosa felt his clammy hands, and it tugged at her heart strings. It was hard to contain her mixed feelings. She knew from that moment what she had to do.

Daniel let go of her hand and made his way towards Leah.

'Shit, that was way intense.' Ella took Rosa's hand, unimpressed. 'Come on.'

They walked towards the waiting room. Rosa glanced back, looking for Daniel, but he had already entered the court with Leah.

Rosa sat alone in the waiting room, nervous and conflicted. She chewed her nails, something she had not done since childhood. Her knees trembled uncontrollably.

Ella joined her, handing over a bottle of water. 'Here you go.' She rubbed her back. 'I don't envy you, but I admire your strength.' She sat down beside Rosa, pulled out a tiny make-up mirror and checked her face, fixing her flame-coloured locks.

The court usher, a tall, suited man, entered the room and checked his clipboard. 'Miss Chavez?' He looked towards them, nodding ominously.

Rosa's heart leapt now that her moment had arrived.

God, be with me this is going to be tough.

Ella hugged her. 'Be OK, darling,' she encouraged as Rosa stood up, taking a deep breath.

She fixed her blouse and followed the usher without apprehension or even turning to Ella. Her thoughts were now focused.

The old courtroom was small. The dark, oak furnishings were dull compared to the red and gold coat of arms stuck to the front of the judge's desk. It was packed with people. Every seat was taken in the gallery, and eager hacks waited as if it was a theatre show. Rosa looked around, slightly overawed. She saw Jesus, his hair pulled into his normal, greasy ponytail. His sharp face broke into a sinister smirk upon her entrance. He folded his arms, resting back and nudging Dani, who was a shadow of himself. He was pale, gaunt, slimmer and his usual cropped hair was overgrown.

Rosa's legs hesitated before her step up onto the stand. Shaky, she tried to stay composed. She looked around the room and saw Daniel sitting with his solicitor, looking tense. She glanced up at the gallery to a couple of rows of different faces. She saw Leah peering down at her, fanning her face with the same copy of *Heat* magazine that she'd brandished in Rosa's face earlier. Ella took her seat, and she also spotted Mya, who made a heart-shaped greeting with her hands. Rosa smiled.

Flipping hell, this is worse than I expected.

Look at those two, poor Dani he looks awful.

Jesus, urgh, still makes my blood boil.

Look at him thinking it's a joke...

'Miss Chavez, please read this oath out before the court.' A clerk handed her a laminated sheet.

Rosa read out the oath, her voice meek.

The judge entered wearing an old red cloak. His wig did not cover the strands of grey hair partially covering his forehead. Stern faced, he started the proceedings.

He instructed Avi Lipschitz to approach for questioning; his black suit was tatty and dusty. He scraped together some sheets of paper and bumbled his way from the desk to face Rosa. 'So, Miss Chavez. You are seemingly the only real witness, yet you saw nothing. A phone call, I believe.' He looked down at one of the papers and scanned along the page. 'A phone call, is that correct?' He walked up close to the stand.

Rosa noticed Jesus laughing in the background; his petulance was a momentary distraction.

'Correct or not?' Again, Avi jabbed her with his question.

Rosa stared down at him, his grey, ruffled hair resembled the judge's wig. 'Yes, that's correct.' Rosa looked across to Daniel, who sat upright with his hands on the desk.

'So you could not see whether your brother, Dani Chavez, was actually there?' Avi pointed his chubby finger towards Rosa. Her heart raced.

'I know he was there.' Her words flew out; she didn't know what else to say as she looked directly at Dani.

He returned a look of sadness, relief and shame. Avi stepped back, clasping his papers. 'How could you be so sure?' He was now trying to play up to the jury, wagging his finger as he strode back forth.

Rosa took a deep breath. She was torn.

Jesus leapt up. 'She's a whore! A disloyal bitch,' his voice rasped, layered with his Mexican accent.

Gasps echoed all around the room. A security guard sprang into action, rushing over to suppress Jesus's animated barrage towards his sister. Rosa gasped, horrified by his behaviour.

The judge banged his gavel. 'Restrain him!' His sergeant-like voice boomed through the room. 'Court adjourned. Twenty-minute recess while we get some order.' He got up from his seat and disappeared into his chambers while Jesus was being wrestled and bundled out.

Rosa left the stand and was ushered back into the waiting room. Up in the gallery, Leah had a satisfied smile on her face looking down at Daniel, who was steaming and talking to his solicitor. The jury all rose and filed out of the courtroom. Rosa paced up and down the waiting room, trying to stay composed. She filled her water bottle from the water machine and put the bottle to her mouth, gulping down the cold liquid.

This is crazy.

Jesus, what the fuck?

I'm a whore?

Bastard, that's not fair how could he say that in front of all those people!

Rosa was furious and embarrassed by her brother's outburst. She crushed the bottle in her hand and threw it into the grey, metal dustbin.

A knock on the door interrupted her. The court usher poked his head around the door. 'We're ready to go again. I'll give you a minute.' He realised Rosa's state and allowed her the time to calm down and compose herself.

Right, let's do this, I want this over.

Rosa made her way towards the door.

Back in the courtroom, the atmosphere seemed to have intensified. The earlier fracas had created an almost theatre-like setting, worthy of a bucket of popcorn. Jesus sat in his seat, handcuffed, next to a burly security guard. Dani was the same. The judge once again started the proceedings, instructing Daniel's solicitor to approach Rosa for questioning.

He was young, in his early forties, slick and sharp-suited, with a green, double Windsor tie. 'Miss Chavez, is it true that at the time of the incident, you and Mr Rosewood were in a relationship?' His voice was much more sincere, calm but professional.

Rosa's eyes diverted towards Daniel. 'Yes,' she responded, affirmed by a nod of her head.

'Tell me what happened that night.' He turned to the jury, sweeping his arms out to Rosa like a conductor.

Rosa cleared her throat. 'Daniel went to the showroom—'

'What time?'

Rosa tried to remember. 'Maybe around eight-thirty in the evening. He had an audit and wanted to make sure everything was in place.'

Daniel gave a furrowed look up at the gallery towards Leah.

Rosa continued, and the jury listened intently, hanging on her every word. 'I fell asleep. When I woke, I noticed he hadn't returned.'

The sharp solicitor folded his arms again, milking the moment. 'And what time was that?'

Avi Lipschitz watched on, blindly scribbling down random notes.

'It was late, maybe three thirty am,' Rosa answered, feeling a little more comfortable with his line of questioning.

'So when you woke and noticed he was not home, what did you do?' He went back to the desk and picked up a folder.

'I called him.'

Jesus pointed his bony fingers at Rosa, whispering across to Dani in Mexican. Dani told him to shush, putting his fingers to his lips, agitated.

'OK, so you called him, and did he answer?'

Rosa swallowed, staring at Daniel, who tensed his frame, reliving those chronicled moments. She was about to speak but hesitated, glancing up towards the gallery. All the faces looked serious. Everyone was on the edge of their seats. Journalists scribbled feverishly in their notepads.

Ella winked at Rosa, a well-needed sign of encouragement. Leah peered down, resting her hand on her chin. Rosa turned back to face her brothers.

Jesus was making 'slit your throat' signs with his hand before bursting out into a pathetic laugh. 'That's your hombre, huh? That's *familia* now, right? Disloyal bitch,' he rasped again, unable to help himself, which drew murmurs of disapproval from the gallery and the jury, who scowled, offended.

'Quiet, or you'll be in contempt as well,' said the judge.

A hush went around the room. Avi Lipschitz threw his pen down onto his papers and rested back with his arms folded, defeated.

Daniel's solicitor waited until the furore subsided. 'Did Daniel Rosewood . . . your boyfriend . . . answer?'

Rosa looked directly back at the solicitor. 'No, Jesus my brother did.' She choked out a whimpered cry, which came unexpectedly. 'Daniel didn't.' She trembled and put her hand to her mouth to hold back her emotions.

'And Dani?'

'I could hear him laughing in the background. I knew it was him.'

Daniel's solicitor opened his folder. 'Phone records indicate that you only called Daniel's number. No other numbers at all prior to that night; therefore, no indication of involvement in this robbery.'

'No.' Rosa looked directly at Daniel. He sat back, relieved, and nodded his head in acceptance. Rosa trained her eyes up at Leah, a gaze of vindication.

'What did Mr Chavez say to you?' He carried on his questioning relentlessly now that he had the attention of the judge and jury.

Rosa sucked in another deep breath, her hands cupped in front of her. She now stood defiant, her doubts evaporated by Jesus's behaviour. She knew, at that moment, he would never change, but Dani maybe had a chance. But it was too late. She had grown too much to ever go back to her old life.

I have to do the right thing.

I'll be hated forever but Mama would want me to do the right thing.

'He insulted me, then threatened to harm Daniel if he didn't give them money. I was scared for Daniel. I told him just do what they asked. I could tell he was injured.'

The solicitor glided over to the jury. 'So the two suspects, Dani and Jesus Chavez, were both on the premises at the time of the robbery. There could be no one else responsible for the arson, kidnap, assault and robbery at Rosewood Automobiles. No further questions, Your Honour.' He walked back over to his seat, giving Daniel a satisfied pat on the back.

'Mr Lipshcitz, any further questions?' the judge asked.

Avi tapped his pen against his notepad pensively, looked over towards Dani and shrugged with a face of disappointment. 'No, Your Honour.' At a loss, he conceded.

'Miss Chavez, you can leave now, thank you.' The judge's tone was sympathetic as he waved her out of the room.

Rosa turned and stepped down from the stand. A drone of mutterings erupted from the gallery.

'Rosa!' Dani yelled out.

Rosa turned around. 'It's OK.'

His empty eyes glassed over, accepting his fate. Jesus shuffled in his seat, scowling and vexed. He gave Rosa an evil glare before she left swiftly, happy to get out of the room.

Rosa crouched down in the corridor with her back against the wall. Her energy was drained. She covered her face with her hands and gave big sigh, unable to hold back the wave of relief and emotion. Her body shook, the bottled feelings she'd held inside for so long finally uncorked.

Ella and Mya came rushing to her aid. 'Ah, babe, you alright?' Mya crouched down and hugged her. Ella did the same from the other side, all three of them huddled for a few seconds.

Ella looked at Mya. 'Guess you're Mya?'

Mya smiled. 'Yes.'

Ella introduced herself.

'Ella, come on, let's get her up.'

'Can we go?' She breathed deeply, blowing out her cheeks and unsteadily rising to her feet.

'You did well, babe.' Mya's husky voice was comforting.

They were about to leave when Daniel appeared from the court, limping into the corridor, cane in hand. 'Rosa, wait!'

The three of them turned around to see Daniel trying to walk at speed towards them.

'Just give me a minute,' he continued, until he arrived in front of her.

Ella and Mya stood protectively around Rosa.

'It's OK, honestly I'm OK,' she assured them.

Mya and Ella backed away, still watching on.

Daniel touched her face tenderly. 'What you just did in there was brave, thank you,' he said, softly rubbing her cheek, much to the displeasure of her two friends. 'They've given us a break, then I'm on the stand to tell them my side.'

Rosa collected herself, moving Daniel's hand from her face. Her eyes were reddened, sorrowful but defiant. 'Do what you have to do.' Her voice cracked with emotion, her mind all over the place, and she could barely think straight.

Daniel turned to look at Ella and Mya, who watched on, unimpressed. He turned his attention back to Rosa. 'Can I call you later? Once this is all over.'

Rosa sniffled. She cupped Daniel's face with her hand. 'I'm sorry, but I need time.' Her tone was decisive, leaving Daniel shell-shocked.

'Please, we need to sort things out,' Daniel stammered, his speech momentarily impaired.

'Just focus on today.' Rosa took a deep breath then walked away, leaving Daniel standing alone. She linked arms with Ella and Mya and braced herself as they walked to the court entrance.

The sun beamed down on the patrons basking in the courtyard of a city pub. It was busy, full of workers taking advantage of a long liquid lunch. Rosa sat with Ella and Mya around a circular wooden table. She still wore the shades given to her by Ella, masking her eyes from the bright sunshine. She sipped slowly on a glass of lemonade with ice, while Mya and Ella checked out the interview in *Heat* magazine.

'Babe, it's not that bad. Makes you sound like a brave, smart woman.' Mya tried to justify her reasons for her actions.

'Yeah, it's not that bad,' Ella chipped in, tying her red hair up into a bun.

Rosa removed the shades from her face. 'It's not the point.' She still seemed down in the mouth, affected by the events of the day. She shot a look at Mya, whose face was evenly tanned, her freckles dotted on her high cheekbones. 'It's done now.' She shrugged. 'I still think you betrayed me, but I get you were trying to help.' She reached out her hand and grabbed Mya's.

'Honestly, babe, that's all it was.' Mya reciprocated and rubbed Rosa's hand.

'She still wants paying, though,' Ella chimed in again, while sipping on a large glass of red wine.

'Of course. I still have the money for you,' Mya reassured her.

Rosa's phone received a message, the high-pitch alert interrupting the conversation. Rosa checked her phone. 'It's Daniel.' She read the message. One word. 'Guilty.' Without a word, Rosa showed it to Ella and Mya.

'Oh, babe, it's over.' Mya once again squeezed her hand.

Rosa's face became flushed as she soaked in the information. It dawned on her that she was now free. The burden of her brothers had been lifted. A weary smile sneaked across her face, yet her overall feeling was one of sadness for Dani. She knew he was under the spell of Jesus. Her baby brother had been for a long while. Rosa looked at Ella and Mya. 'My *familia* now, you're both stuck with me.' She managed a small giggle.

Ella stood up and thrust her glass into the air. 'Yay! Sisters before misters!' she shouted, causing the afternoon drinkers to turn their attention to their table.

Rosa put her head in her hands. 'Loco, sister.' She forced a laugh.

Oh lord, these two crazy girls.

Her phone received another text. It was Daniel again. 'Speak later?' it read. Rosa watched Ella and Mya trying to outpose each other and take selfies. She switched her phone off and picked up the magazine, perusing the cover.

She took off her shades and held the magazine next to her face. 'Hey, it's me!' she joked. Mya turned her phone screen to Rosa and snapped a few pictures.

Rosa

Chapter 26
Fool's paradise

A small fire blazed in the corner of the backyard; the smoke billowed into the air. The black smoke created a blemish on the blue-skied canvas. Rosa stood watching and holding a small can of lighter fluid in one hand and a small pot of water in the other. The box full of Jesus's letters turned to ash as the seconds passed.

That's the last of their crap, good riddance.

She sighed before tossing the pot of water onto the fire. The court case was thankfully a distant memory now and an experience she would never forget, but time had passed and Rosa was ready to continue with her life. Of course, it was hard for her, alone and isolated, but she did what she could. The money from the magazine story had helped her. Mya was right, it was a good start-up.

Rosa finally had a bank account and she was good with her money. She spent some of it on a television and a new bed, with some small furnishings to make the flat more comfortable. She saved the rest and prioritised buying food.

Daniel was regularly in touch by text. He was apologetic, especially about the way she had been treated by Leah, but Rosa, although she missed him, felt content just to keep in touch and refuse his many requests to meet up. She did not feel ready to embrace him back into her life. She needed time to heal after all of the drama, but she still had Ella and Mya to keep her sane and lift her up when she felt down. This was a different Rosa, more independent. Confident, but still deeply hurt.

Rosa spent most of her time cooking and trying out different recipes. She had booked herself into part-time culinary classes at a local college. It was only a couple of hours a week, but it was her one time of solace that took her away from reality. She also began those yoga classes, dragged along by Mya twice a week. She really had no choice and felt it was a good way of building back the bridges with her after the whole *Heat* magazine scenario.

Rosa went out of the backyard; the evening heat had slightly decreased, assisted by a nice cool breeze. She walked through the estate wearing a grey vest, black shorts and flip-flops. Her hair flowed over her shoulders. As usual, the gangs were out in force. The gauntlet always had to be run. The same boys smoking weed and playing loud music blocked her path with their bikes and deliriously barking dogs.

'Sexy peng ting,' one of them hollered at her as they stepped aside, allowing her to walk through the centre of their circle. 'I know your bros are banged up, so what you saying?' A dark-skinned, bearded, bald-headed youth, with red eyes and dripping with sweat, walked beside her. The afternoon odour of his stale aftershave wafted into her nostrils.

'I'm saying leave me alone.' Rosa looked up at him, her brown eyes indicating her lack of interest in anything that came out of his mouth.

He stared back at her with a look of confusion. 'We from the same ends, man, no need to be so boujee, bitch.' Her rejection hit a nerve. Rosa continued to walk. The youth kissed his teeth and went back to his friends with his tail between his legs and spouting off some obscenities in her direction.

Rosa walked along the parade, heading to the grocery shop. People milled about, wilting from the heat. It felt weird not to be under any duress or scared because Jesus was in a bad mood. She could breathe, take her time and actually take in her surroundings.

Making dinner for Ella and Mya tomorrow so need to get some supplies.

Mexican black bean and rice burritos with salsa salad and guacamole.

Mya loves it strictly vegan, of course.

It's nice that the girls support me and come to my place, I don't know what I'd do without them.

I do miss Daniel but he hurt me so I just need my time alone.

Rosa entered the store. The same shopkeeper sat behind the counter reading a foreign newspaper. He peered over the pages and, on seeing Rosa, he smiled and greeted her warmly. 'Hi, how are you, Miss Chavez?' He was familiar now, friendly every time he saw her.

Rosa smiled back. 'Need some stuff for dinner,' she replied, as she browsed the shelves and picked up a basket.

'I have favour to ask,' he said, putting the newspaper down on the counter. 'Wait there.' He got up from his stool and rushed into the back of the shop shouting, 'Aleema! Aleema!'

Rosa waited, wondering what he was doing.

The shopkeeper came back with a young girl no more than ten years old. 'My daughter Aleema.' He pulled the shy child behind him; the little Eastern-European girl with dark hair and big eyes looked at Rosa and shyly smiled. The shopkeeper pulled a copy of the *Heat* magazine with Rosa's face on the cover from under the counter. 'Please sign for Aleema. I told her about you.' He shoved the magazine towards Rosa.

Oh, wow, didn't expect this.

I'm not famous or anything.

She looked back at the child, smiling. 'OK, Aleema, I'll do it for you.'

The shopkeeper ruffled the young girl's hair as Rosa took a pen from the counter and scrawled her name across the cover.

'Here you go, Aleema.' The young girl's face lit up with glee as Rosa handed her the magazine. 'I don't look like that all the time, as you can see,' she joked, much to the happiness of the shopkeeper.

'You need phone?' He thrust his phone at her.

'No, I have one now.' Rosa laughed.

'OK.' He clasped his hands together as if he was praying. 'Thank you. Aleema, go now.' He ushered his daughter back. She smiled at Rosa in awe as she clutched the magazine and retreated to the back of the shop.

Rosa relaxed in front of her television watching a documentary about young girls in a tough prison. She slowly ate a bowl of ice cream, fascinated by the plight of women the same age as her. Her phone began to ring, interrupting her focus. She picked it up to see an incoming FaceTime call from Daniel. Her heart leapt. She stared at the screen for a few seconds, taking the spoon out of her mouth, before answering. 'Hi, Daniel.'

His handsome face appeared on the screen. He looked well and his bright, white smile returned when he saw her face. 'Hello, babe. What you doing?'

Rosa tried to fix her hair. 'Nothing, just watching TV,' she replied.

Aww, look at him, still very handsome.

Daniel smiled at her for a few seconds. 'I really miss you. I want to see you.' She could tell he meant it.

It's so hard for me, and such a gamble.

I mean what if he decided to give up on me and meet someone else?

Maybe I should give him a chance, it wasn't all his fault.

'I miss you too,' she replied, reassuring him that her feelings were still there.

'So let's go to dinner next week?' Daniel asked enthusiastically, giving her that winning smile. It always melted her.

Rosa took a deep breath. 'OK, but no dinner. Come to the launderette; we can talk there,' she blurted out, not really thinking.

Daniel's expression was one of both shock and surprise. 'The launderette?' He laughed. 'OK, launderette it is then.' He nodded. 'You look beautiful by the way, my diamond.' His charm was never lost on Rosa, who rolled her eyes, feeling flattered, and a rush of flutters floated through her body. He knew how to tug on her heartstrings. 'OK, we'll speak.' Daniel blew her a kiss.

Rosa returned the gesture. 'Bye, thanks for calling.' She cut the phone and sighed deeply, still conflicted about how they could find a way forward. Her heart wanted him, she missed his company and their closeness, but it was difficult for her to erase the stain of the episode with Leah and how he never fought for her at the time she really needed him.

High-pitched laughter broke out in Rosa's tiny kitchen. The girls had arrived and were making sure the night was already one of crazy antics and jokes. Ella's flame hair was slicked back into a ponytail showing her clear, porcelain face, which was covered by a pair of Ray-Ban shades. Her long legs protruded from denim hot pants as she tried her hand at twerking to the R&B songs which played from Rosa's radio.

Mya cracked up, nearly choking on her red wine, which she held up high in the air, the other hand free to slap Ella on her rear. Her honey-blonde hair flowed gorgeously down her back. She was casual in a red, flowing, pleated dress and silver sandals. 'Go on, Rosa, show her how it's done!' Mya screamed between belly laughs.

Rosa was too busy tending to the food. She looked sexy making an effort as the host, her jet-black hair in ringlets complementing her little black dress and gold hooped earrings. She turned and gave Mya a saucy lap dance for a few seconds before they all fell about laughing again. 'OK, who's hungry?' Rosa turned, placing a bowl of salsa salad on the table.

It was cramped but intimate as Ella and Mya sat at the table. Rosa smiled. It felt so good to be able to have a girls' night in her own home. She had whipped up a feast and was proud of her efforts. They all sat crammed at the table eating the vegan burritos.

'Oh my gosh, babe, this is delish.' Mya chomped, barely able to get her words out.

'Hmm, agreed. Those classes are paying off then?' Ella chimed in.

'Thanks,' Rosa replied, scooping some salad onto her plate. 'So, Daniel FaceTimed last night.' She was tentative when speaking about him, knowing what Mya and Ella thought about his behaviour towards her previously. 'We're going to meet next week.' Rosa rushed her words out, getting it off her chest.

Ella and Mya stared at each other mid-mouthful, pausing before they both cracked a smile. 'That's good, right?' Ella asked her.

Rosa shrugged. 'I think so; we'll see.' She placed a slice of tomato into her mouth.

'Well if it don't work out, there's always me.' Mya winked at her playfully and seductively licked her finger.

Rosa started laughing. 'You need to behave!' she reprimanded Mya, who pretended to cry at her response.

Once they had eaten, they sat in the living room. Ella was drunk and jabbering non-stop about how boring sex was with Bryn, much to the fascination of both Rosa and

Mya. 'I just think, "Please bloody get it over with, same position all the time, boring!"'

Mya looked at Rosa and touched her face. 'That's why I like exploring, babe.' Her husky voice sounded tired as the night wore on. 'There's more excitement in the unknown.' Again she flirted with Rosa, who kissed her hand playfully.

'I'm taken,' she responded, letting her know her mind was still very much with Daniel.

The morning after, Rosa was awakened by heavy banging on her front door. She was tired and groggy. At first she thought she was dreaming until she heard the sound again, four loud bangs. She jumped up, her head heavy after the late night. The girls had left earlier and caught an Uber home, but Rosa still felt as if she had only slept for a few seconds before the early interruption.

Alright, I'm coming.

Bloody hell, what is so urgent at this time?

She was bleary-eyed as she stepped carefully down the stairs in her nightwear. At the front, through the frosted glass, she could make out the figures of a man and a woman.

Rosa opened the door partially, peering around to see two official-looking individuals. 'Hello,' Rosa croaked dryly.

'Miss Chavez?' the man asked. He was a tall, black official with thick-rimmed spectacles and a slim, grey handlebar moustache.

'Yes,' Rosa answered, her head still fuzzy.

'My name is Calvin Prince and this is Caroline Watts.'

His companion, holding an ID badge, poked her head around to peer in. She was short, white, plain-faced and podgy. 'Hiya, Rosa, we're from the CPP.'

Rosa rubbed her face and opened the door fully. 'Ok,' she replied, bemused.

'Can we come in and have a chat?' Caroline Watts's chirpy voice jerked Rosa into life.

'Sure.' She let them in and guided them to the living room, which still displayed the remnants of the night before—empty wine bottles and half-filled glasses next to an ashtray with the butts of Mya's cigarettes. 'Sorry about the mess.' She yawned and pointed the two towards the sofa. 'Do you mind if I just get dressed?'

They shook their heads in sync. 'No, you go ahead. We'll wait here,' Caroline Watts replied, slightly impatiently.

Their eyes wandered around the room before they took a seat on the sofa. Calvin Prince removed a folder from his briefcase and took a pen from his shirt pocket. He opened the folder and scribbled some notes.

Rosa returned after a few minutes, phone in hand and dressed in tracksuit bottoms and a tee shirt with the word 'Glamorous' emblazoned across the front. She was still tired but curious as to why she had suddenly received attention from the CPP.

'How have you been?' Calvin Prince opened the dialogue as he fixed his glasses. He tried his best to sound warm and accommodating.

'I'm fine, thank you.' Rosa yawned again as she replied. *What's this about?*

They have never come here before and I didn't receive any letter to warn me of their visit.

Rosa looked at the empty wine bottles and lipstick-stained glasses and suddenly became very conscious of the state of the place.

Caroline Watts took a deep breath; this seemed to be her cue to butt in. 'We're aware that you're living here alone now after your brothers ...' She paused, leaning over and taking a sheet of paper from Calvin Prince's folder. 'Jesus and Dani.' She read their names off and turned her attention back to Rosa. 'The thing is, being convicted of a serious crime is a violation of the Crime Protection Program.' She took a breath, allowing Calvin Prince to interject.

'Basically, we can no longer house them under this program.'

Rosa shrugged, nonplussed. She tied her hair into a ponytail. 'OK, I don't mind, they're out of my life now.' She sat back comfortably in the chair.

Caroline Watts looked at Calvin Prince, who cleared his throat, knowing that there was more information pending. 'OK, I need to be clear with you. Your brothers will both be deported as a consequence of their crimes.' He adjusted his glasses.

Rosa stared at him in confusion. 'Deported? To where?' She suddenly sat up, the cogs in her mind whirling into action.

'Back to Mexico,' Caroline Watts affirmed starkly; her chubby cheeks filled with a rush of blood as she spoke.

Rosa began to laugh, more out of shock than amusement. 'They will go to jail in Mexico?' she asked, finding the news almost unbelievable.

'Yes, I'm afraid so.' Caroline Watts nodded confidently.

Rosa took a moment to digest the information.

Those two will never survive in a Mexican jail, especially Dani.

Another uncontrollable laugh inadvertently came out. 'Right, OK. Well, thanks for coming to tell me, but I don't care,' she replied, shrugging again and checking her phone.

Caroline Watts sat forwards on the edge of the sofa. 'We understand your position. We've read the court case. It must have been a hard time . . .'

Rosa nodded, still trying to take in the news. She got up from the chair, walked over to the window and drew back the curtains, allowing the bright sunshine into the room. She cracked a window open and turned to the two of them. 'OK, what else?' she asked abruptly, sensing there was more to come and seeing their body language was slightly uncomfortable.

'Please, take a seat.' Calvin Prince's tone was more sympathetic.

Rosa became more uneasy as the minutes went by.

'Miss Chavez, may I call you Rosa?' Calvin Prince asked politely, as a flushed-looking Caroline Watts took a bottle of water from her handbag, flipped open the top, then sucked noisily from the plastic nozzle. 'Rosa . . . this flat is provided by us on the basis that you stay within the remits of the law. Because of the violation by your brothers—' he paused, taking a breath '—the policy states that we may withdraw our protection, including providing you with accommodation.' He got his words out, circled some paragraphs on the sheet of paper and handed it to Rosa.

Rosa read the words on the paper, but they may as well have been written in hieroglyphics as nothing made sense to her. 'I don't understand.' She handed it back to Calvin

Prince and frowned. The mood had changed; her gut was telling her something was off, and by the way Calvin Prince looked at Caroline Watts, she knew they were not here to give her good news.

'What we're saying is we'll have to remove you from the program due to the violation,' Caroline Watts stated flatly.

Hold up, wait!

Are they kicking me out?

I've not done anything.

Rosa's mind now raced with a million different scenarios. She could not compute the news she was receiving. 'Are you saying I have to leave here?' Her voice shook with emotion.

'You have twenty-eight days to vacate.' Calvin Prince flicked through a section of his folder.

'We can still support you, help you to apply for housing ...' Caroline Watts mentioned hastily before sucking down some more of her water.

Calvin Prince handed the forms to Rosa. 'It's all there.' His expression revealed a shade of embarrassment as he looked at Rosa.

'This is bullshit!' Rosa's mood suddenly changed. 'How could you do this? I didn't violate anything. I've done nothing wrong!' She tossed the papers onto the floor. 'This is not fair!' She crossed her arms defiantly. 'Where am I supposed to go?'

Caroline Watts offered a paltry smile while Calvin Prince closed his folder and wiped a glisten of sweat from his forehead. 'I know it's come as a bit of a shock.' Caroline Watts tried her best to be empathetic, but that just riled up Rosa even more.

Rosa stood up, then paced back and forth in front of them. 'You never came here, ever. I was raped at fifteen—where were you!' she screamed. By now the news had hit her hard. She was fuming and not in control. 'And when those two treated me like a slave . . . where was my protection, huh?' She continued her animated rant. 'You put me in this dump of an estate and forgot about me until my brother . . .' Her phone began to ring, interrupting her flow. She looked at it and saw Mya's name flashing. She answered and put the phone on speaker. 'Mya,' Rosa spoke.

'Hi, babe. OMG, I was so fucked last night—it was wicked!' Mya's voice resonated loudly through the phone.

Rosa stopped Mya mid-flow. 'Have to call you back.' She cut the call. Still angry, she tried to compose herself. 'I'm still being punished because of them two . . . it's not fair.' Her voice was strained.

Caroline Watts and Calvin Prince sat unimpressed by Rosa's emotional performance. They glanced at each other as if to confirm their decision and nodded in tandem before getting up. 'We are sorry. As we said, you can appeal.' Calvin Prince tucked the folder under his arm and picked up his briefcase.

Caroline Watts followed suit, clutching her handbag from the floor. 'We'll see ourselves out,' she said in a subdued voice.

Rosa was left alone, trying to take everything in.
What just happened?
How is this possible?
I just started to feel good about my life.
I've fixed up this place and now they want me to leave

because of those two stupid brothers of mine, for their dumbass crimes.

Surely they can't do this to me, this is crap . . .

Rosa sat on her new double bed with a towel wrapped around her, tucked in just above her bust. Her wet hair dangled over her shoulders. She was still in a state of shock, feeling as though she had been hit by a high-speed train, the way her head was spinning. She stared into space. The news she had received less than an hour ago still had not sunk in. She looked around the room, stopping at the neat pile of magazines. She picked up the *Heat* magazine with her smiling face staring back at her. She stared at herself. She hated that image. It reminded her of a time where she was going through her toughest moment, the opposite of what she portrayed. She tossed it onto the floor and put her head in her hands, running her fingers through her wet hair.

A week had passed since the CPP's visit. Rosa performed some yoga stretches in the middle of her living room. The classes she attended with Mya were the only solace she could redeem from what had been a rough week. The yoga helped her to diffuse the tension. Luckily she had Ella and Mya, who had both offered her a place to stay, but Rosa's pride would not allow her to take them up on their offer. She did not want to spend any time living under the same roof as the creepy Bryn, and after the stuff with Mya the last time, she thought it was better for now not to go back. It would be hard, and with little money, she was running out of choices, but she was determined to find a solution.

Today she was meeting Daniel, who had been texting her cute messages leading up to their rendezvous, saying how much he was looking forward to seeing her and trying to persuade her to come to dinner instead of meeting at the laundrette. But Rosa knew it was better this way. She wanted to see him in a realistic environment, rather than be swallowed by his romantic overtures. She lay on her back, her eyes closed and the image of her mother came into her mind.

Mama, I know you're watching over me, thank you.

She could hear her mother's voice. She was annoyed and disappointed by the deeds of her sons.

God will deal with those two, they are the Devil's spore but you, Rosa, make your choices and life will reward you.

Be strong, my angel, you have come so far.

Rosa opened her eyes; she sat up out of her trance-like state.

Right, OK.

Come on, let's get it together, I've got an hour before I meet Daniel.

I'm actually looking forward to seeing him but it's weird.

I feel nervous, since the case things have been different.

Rosa slipped into a pair of jeans and pulled on a blingy-red hoodie. The long heatwave had finally succumbed to grey clouds and cooler winds. It was a welcome change after months of dry, stifling heat. Rosa checked her face in the mirror. She looked tired, her fresh-faced beauty replaced by worry. Having less than three weeks to pack her belongings and leave her home was a daunting prospect. She applied some lipstick, rose red to match her hoodie, and a quick spray of fragrance, nothing else. She decided to downplay her looks. She knew Daniel, and for her, there was no reason to make an impression.

The turn of the weather did nothing to quell the huddle of youths in the gangway. The same heady stench of weed and alcohol lurked in the air as the reddened eyes of the estate's youths once again turned to Rosa. She walked quickly, her head bowed, blocking out the usual catcalls and the noises which emanated from the tower blocks which housed all the other desperate souls.

The cool wind was refreshing to Rosa and the people on the parade. It was still busy; the late afternoon school run increased the bustle. Rosa checked her phone and found a message from Daniel.

Stuck in traffic, be there soon.

Rosa put the phone back into her pocket. She walked past the convenience store and saw the shopkeeper's daughter Aleema waving at her through the window. She stopped and looked at her, then pulled a funny face. Aleema covered her mouth laughing, then did the same back to Rosa, who smiled and waved before continuing towards the laundrette. Her thoughts of what might transpire over the next hour returned.

When she entered, it was empty; there was only the old attendant in the back office chatting on the phone. She glanced over to Rosa but didn't acknowledge her and continued her chat. Rosa took a seat on the wooden bench, the same one she had sat on all those months ago. A lot had happened since that day when Daniel had walked in and commanded her attention.

The old lady finally came out of the room. She glared at Rosa. 'You washing?' she asked in her croaky voice as she walked towards Rosa. 'I know you.' She came and sat beside Rosa, her musty odour mixed with tobacco attacking Rosa's nostrils. 'Glad it's cooler; can't take the bloody heat,' she muttered.

Rosa nodded in agreement, shuffling a couple of inches away from her.

She regarded Rosa; her cataract-ladened eyes looked tired. 'It's not a waiting room if you ain't washing,' she grumbled.

Rosa looked back at her. 'I'm just meeting some . . .'

Daniel appeared at the door. He looked a bit flushed, as if he had been running, but he looked well. He had no cane and he looked handsome and smart, wearing skinny jeans and a red hoodie and holding a bouquet of red roses. 'Hello babe . . . snap!'

His voice made Rosa's heart leap. It felt strange to see him again standing there in the doorway. It gave her flashbacks as he pointed to her red hoodie, smiling.

The old attendant recognised Daniel, too. 'Oi, you two. No, not again.' She got up from her seat, wagging her crinkly finger at Daniel.

Rosa giggled to herself, amused at the way she was telling Daniel off. 'I promise we'll behave,' she assured the old attendant, who walked away back to her office, mumbling under her breath. 'You look well,' Rosa said. She stood up to greet him. It was awkward; she wasn't sure whether to hug him or be stand-offish, but as usual, Daniel confidently strode towards her.

'Here, I bought these for you.' He handed her the bouquet, his eyes sparkling on seeing her. He gave her a tight hug, but it felt weird.

Rosa took the flowers. 'Thanks,' she replied coyly; it was hard not to feel excited. When she felt him the old feelings came flooding back, but she knew she had to keep her cool.

'So, here we are again.' Daniel looked around at the old laundrette. He seemed healed, and the old confidence was back, along with his pearly-white smile. 'Why here?' he asked.

Rosa backed away and sat down on the bench. 'Just easier to talk,' she replied, her voice deadpan.

Daniel took a seat next to her, his sweet musk a more welcoming smell than the old attendant's musty mix. 'I feel like we were the two caught in the middle of all of this,' Daniel mused. His breath was fresh and minty. He tried to touch her hand, but Rosa pulled away. 'Babe, what's up?' Daniel turned to her, looking into her eyes.

Rosa tried to hold back; she didn't really know how to feel. 'Daniel, you hurt me.' Her words jolted Daniel, cutting the cosy reunion short. 'Really hurt me. I believed in us.' Her heart was heavy, and her voice cracked with emotion. Rosa cleared her throat, trying to maintain her composure.

'Babe, I got hurt, too. Physically, mentally, do you know I had to do counselling? I still have nightmares!' His outburst caught her off guard.

'I know, I was there . . . in the hospital, remember?' Rosa's voice rose, increasing the intense blame game.

'Look, maybe this was a bad idea.' She stood up and made to leave.

Daniel grabbed her hand. 'No, come on, let's start again.' He tugged her back, beckoning her to sit down. 'I want to get past this. That's why I've been messaging you. I want to make up properly.' He didn't let go of her hand; instead, he lifted it and kissed it tenderly. 'Please, let's start again. I've missed you,' he pleaded, his tone calmer than before.

Rosa sat down. 'Sorry, just have a lot going on.' She rested back against the wall.

'I'm here, talk to me.' Daniel tried his best to coerce her out of her strop.

'I'm so sorry for what my brothers did to you—they make me sick.' Rosa had melted somewhat and rested her head on Daniel's shoulder.

Daniel rubbed her thigh. 'Well, sorry to say, I have no sympathy,' he replied, firm in his opinion.

Rosa sighed heavily, nodding her head in agreement. 'What about the showroom?'

Daniel stared ahead at the empty machines. 'Well, the insurance came through. I'll start again.' He grew thoughtful. She could tell it hurt him; that was his passion, but she knew he would be successful again.

The old attendant shuffled past pushing a broom across the floor. She ignored them and continued to sweep the floor.

'I have to leave my flat. The CPP want me out.'

Daniel sat up, looking at her shocked. 'Ahh, babe, you serious?' He touched her face and stroked her cheek. She loved when he touched her; it was hard for her to contain her feelings for him.

'Yes, I am. I have three weeks.'

Daniel broke into a smile. 'Come and live with me, problem sorted.' The passion in his voice was abundant. He was actually excited.

'What about that cow Leah?' Rosa sat up, her demeanour changed at the mention of her name.

'She's gone; we haven't spoken since the trial.' Daniel jumped up and stood in front of Rosa. He grinned at her, standing tall, the handsome man who'd reeled her in like a big catch from the depths of her ocean of despair. 'It's sort of the reason I wanted to take you to dinner instead of meeting here.' He looked around at the laundrette; the basic setting was not exactly a dimly lit restaurant with shiny cutlery. Daniel began to dig into his pocket; his tight jeans made the task that much harder.

The old attendant watched them, leaning unsteadily on the broomstick.

'What are you doing?'

Daniel dropped down on one knee. 'Wanted to do this over candles and champagne but . . .' He swiped his hair to the side, fixing himself.

'Daniel!' Rosa watched him kneeling in front of her. It evoked a moment of memories. Her love for him had never left.

'Rosa, my little diamond.' Daniel held a small black velvet box which he opened, revealing a large, shiny diamond ring. Rosa stared down at it for a few seconds. She looked back at Daniel and covered her mouth, astonished. 'Rosa Chavez, a diamond for my diamond, will you do me the honour—'

Rosa squealed. It was an uncontrollable, natural and unfiltered reaction.

'Of being my wife.' Daniel finished his sentence.

Rosa's body tensed up as she tried to contain a rush of adrenaline and emotion.

Is this for real!

Is he really asking me to marry him?

No, this can't be happening, this is so . . .

'Well, come on, love what's the answer?' the old attendant croaked. Her face cracked a smile for once.

'Daniel, we can't, can we?' Rosa gushed.

'Why not?' He smiled back at her, his blue eyes a lighthouse of hope. 'Well . . .?'

Rosa paused. 'Yes! Of course.' Her love for him overrode any feelings or thoughts of their hardest moments. She was overwhelmed.

Daniel stood up. 'Thanks, my knee was flipping killing me,' he joked.

Rosa stood up and threw her arms around his neck; he put his arms around her waist, holding her close. Rosa knew he was the one she wanted; her knight had rescued her again from another possible disaster. She kissed him on the lips and a sense of relief and hope washed over her. She pulled back. 'But, I'm a changed woman. I can't rely on you for everything . . . I know what I want.'

Daniel could not help beaming at her. 'Yeah, you're the boss.'

Rosa held the bouquet, staring at her ring. Daniel held her and they sat close on the bench. 'So beautiful, thank you.' She could not stop staring at the oversized, gleaming diamond. 'So, what next?' Rosa asked, her voice still hushed in disbelief.

'Come back to mine. The place has missed you.' Daniel stroked her hair.

'OK.' Her short reply was sure. That's exactly where she wanted to be—next to Daniel.

* * *

Rosa walked into an office building with modern marble floors and bronze handrails on the stairs leading up to a mirrored reception desk. She was dressed smartly in black heels and a fitted black dress with a leather biker's jacket. She went slowly up the steps then made her way to the reception desk.

The receptionist was blonde, in her late fifties, with a fake tan and painted make-up doing its best to cover her crow's feet. 'Hi, can I help?' she asked cheerily.

'I'm here to drop off my keys,' Rosa replied. She searched in her handbag and pulled out a set of keys.

'Ah, right, what's the address?'

'23 Crofton Court.' She put the keys onto the desk while the receptionist stared at her computer screen.

'Miss Chavez?' she asked.

'Yes.' Rosa watched as the receptionist flicked through a pile of envelopes stacked in front of her.

'Ahh, here it is.' She handed Rosa the envelope. 'Sign here, please.' She handed her a clipboard, and Rosa signed. 'OK, well that's it! All done, good luck.' The receptionist offered her a fake sunshine smile.

Rosa returned the fake smile before turning away. She opened the envelope, which contained her passport and some other papers.

That's it, I'm free now.
Got my life back, time to look forward to my future.
She walked down the stairs confidently and made her way out.

* * *

Rosa sat alone in a restaurant. She applied some lip gloss while browsing the menu. A waitress brought over a bottle of water. 'Thank you,' Rosa acknowledged, smiling.

'Will you be wanting to order?' A European accent was detected.

'Not yet, I'm waiting for my friend. Oh, she's here.' Rosa looked past her, seeing Ella walking in.

'Hey, Rosa, sorry I'm late. Had to wait for Bryn for a lift.' She rolled her eyes.

Rosa stood up to greet her, and they hugged. 'I'll let you off. You look nice.' Rosa stepped back admiring Ella's bohemian jacket, orange and black to match her silky, flame hair.

'So let's have a look then.' Ella sat down excitedly, grinning mischievously.

Rosa thrust her hand out, showcasing her ring.

'Shit, that's some ring.' She took Rosa's hand, admiring the thick-cut diamond set on a silver band. 'OMG, Rosa, you're getting married, ahh!' she screamed, unable to control her happiness.

'It's crazy, I still can't believe it!'

Ella high-fived her. 'Good on you, girl. I'm happy, but you're sure, right?' She looked at Rosa, who nodded.

'Yeah, I am,' Rosa replied.

'Sure as you'll ever be, right?'

Rosa put her hands over her face and screamed into her hands.

'Lucky bitch,' Ella hissed, pretending to be jealous. 'Did you tell Mya?'

'Yes, she's away for a shoot, but I sent her a message.'

'She'll be gutted. I know she's got the hots for you.' She burst into laughter.

Rosa shook her head. 'What!'

'You know it's true, babe.' Ella mimicked Mya's voice, causing Rosa to crack up.

'Shut up, you're being silly. Let's eat.' Rosa picked up the menu, still shaking her head and chuckling at Ella's random remark.

Rosa washed her face in the sink. She stood up, looking into the mirror, dressed in her bra and knickers. Daniel came into the bathroom and stood behind her, putting his hands on her waist.

It does feel good to be back and in his company.

He's been nice, he hasn't changed which is a relief.

The nightmares are scary, though.

I can see how the robbery affected him but it feels right for me to be here.

This is my home now, we're gonna make it work.

'You OK, babe?' Daniel looked at her in the mirror.

Rosa smiled back, dabbing her face with cotton wool. 'Yes, I'm fine. Ready for bed.' He craned his neck around, kissed her on the cheek and rubbed her shoulders.

'Don't be long. I'll warm up the bed for you.' He smiled, giving her a pat on her bum before leaving the room.

Rosa

Epilogue
No ordinary love
Tijuana, Mexico

Dani ran frantically through a crowded, dank corridor. He bundled his way past a group of men dressed in vests and shorts, sporting crew cuts and with bodies covered in tattoos. He looked scared. His face was gaunt and slim, a stark contrast from his previously chubby cheeks.

He skidded around a corner and bumped into a thick-set, older man with a thick moustache, dirty vest and a bull-horned, cowboy-buckled belt. He was known around the prison as Capo. 'In a rush, amigo?' He stood glaring at Dani and chewing a plastic spoon.

Dani backed off, fear in his eyes. He turned to run but was surrounded by a gang of five young men with their arms folded, not allowing Dani any space to move. 'Please, Capo. I never done anything, I swear.' He turned, dropped to his knees in front of Capo and desperately grabbed onto his leg. 'I beg, please let me go.' Dani clung tightly but felt a blow to the back of his head, knocking him to the ground.

He lay on the dusty concrete doubled up in pain before he was dragged up.

Capo grabbed his neck, grinning and showing his yellow, nicotine-stained teeth. Dani struggled for breath as frothy saliva dribbled out the side of his mouth.

'I told you, steal from me and I will kill you.' He squeezed tighter.

Dani began to choke and gasp for breath as his eyes rolled into their sockets.

'Capo, guards,' one of the gang members warned, not that it stopped his vice-like grip.

'I'll see you tonight.' Capo's nostrils flared. He let go, leaving Dani to drop like a sack of spuds. The men all dispersed a few seconds before the guards came around to see Dani's motionless body on the floor.

Jesus sat in the yard with a group of men playing cards on a rickety, plastic table. In contrast to his brother, he was relaxed, sucking on a cigarette, with his hair pulled tightly into a ponytail. His bony body was buried under a large white tee shirt.

Another convict—fat, stocky and sweaty—came over and leaned down. He whispered into Jesus's ear then walked away back into the yard.

Jesus slammed down his cards and got up from the table, much to the annoyance of the other men. They shouted a few obscenities at him, but Jesus ignored them and walked away towards the main building which housed the majority of the prisoners. He shoved his way past fellow inmates in the crowded tunnels until he reached the cells. It was a hellish maze that smelt of musty men, weed, smoke and stale food. Jesus looked around frantically, his bony body barely able to handle the bump and jostle from the other sneering, muscle-toned inmates.

Jesus finally reached cell fifty-two, a small, dingy, concrete box that housed ten plus men. He walked in, sweat dripping from his face and leaving a dark wet patch on his tee shirt. He went in, eyes searching, until he saw Dani cowering in the corner, shaking, with his head bowed. Jesus kicked him hard in the leg. 'What the fuck have you done now?' he rasped, crouching down to Dani's eye line. 'Look at me!' he shouted, grabbing Dani's face.

'I didn't do it. Tell Capo, I swear . . .'

Jesus stood up holding his head. 'Capo? Shit, tell me you didn't piss off Capo?' Jesus walked away in disbelief before coming back at Dani and slapping him across the head. 'What did you do?' His anger ramped up, knowing that whatever Dani did or didn't do, he was going to pay either way. 'Get up, you prick.' Jesus tried to drag Dani up, but he resisted, shielding himself from the rain of blows he was sure would follow. 'Fuck, I can't believe you. It's your fault we're in here.' Jesus lashed out again and slapped him several times in the head.

Dani squealed in pain. 'Stop! Please stop!' He broke down into a wail of tears. 'Don't wanna be here no more. Kill me, I beg you.' Dani's pathetic pleas fell on deaf ears.

Jesus offered no sympathy for his sibling; instead, he spat at Dani in disgust. 'You deserve whatever you get.' He stomped away, furious, as other inmates watched on.

Dani was left in a heap on the squalid floor, weeping and jabbering to himself. 'Kill me, Jesus. Just kill me.' He looked up, his dirty face reddened from the slaps administered by his brother, only to see the other cellmates staring at him.

The hollow, ghoulish eyes of lost souls watched on, void of any sort of empathy to his plight.

Morning broke and the sun barely shone through the slits of windows which offered only a glimpse of daylight. Most of the other inmates were up, shouting loudly for the guards. A mob had gathered outside the tiny cell, and they crowded around, trying to get a glimpse. Something had happened, and by the furore it had created, it was something serious. The guards came in mob-handed and tried to squeeze through the crowd into the cell. They aggressively pulled people out of the way, the urgency etched on their faces. Finally, they broke through and shouted at the other inmates to stand back.

The gaunt figure of Dani hung from one of the bars on the window, his chest bare, blood dripping from his mouth and a ripped blanket tied around his neck. His eyes were still wide open as if expressing the shock he felt in the moments before he took his last breath. A sorry end to his young, troubled life in the dingy, derelict ruins of the prison.

Jesus was queued up, waiting to get a spoonful of the slop that they called breakfast. He casually smoked a cigarette, surrounded by the usual hordes of hungry, sweaty men. His greasy hair dangled over his face, covering his squinted eyes. He was completely unaware of Dani's fate.

Capo barged his way through the crowds. The other inmates parted ways upon recognition, bowing their eyes to the floor as he passed. Capo approached Jesus, who tried to stand aside, but Capo stopped, standing only a few inches away from him. 'Your coward of a brother.' His morning breath of stale cigarettes warmed on Jesus's face. Capo slid his index finger across his throat, indicating that Dani had perished.

Jesus dropped his cigarette. 'He's dead?' he asked rhetorically. He knew what Capo meant, and his response was just a confirmation statement.

Capo brushed his thick moustache with his hand. 'Now you inherit his debt.' He sneered at Jesus as drops of sweat drizzled down his forehead.

'No! Capo, wait.' Jesus pulled Capo's thick arm back. A cardinal sin. He was not thinking clearly. He let go, immediately realising his mistake. 'Sorry, Capo, please forgive me.' He held up his hands in surrender.

Capo turned and landed a bare-knuckled, fighter-style punch that exploded onto Jesus's nose, causing a flood of blood to gush out. Jesus staggered back and his knees buckled underneath him.

'The debt has now doubled,' Capo stated, his tone menacing. 'Don't let me have to find you.' He fixed his trousers, pulling them by his cowboy belt buckle, then disappeared through the crowds, leaving Jesus a bloody mess on the floor.

Rosa

El Paraiso Beach Resort
Cancun, Mexico

The sun pierced through the leafy palm trees on the perimeter of the five-star hotel. A large jelly bean-shaped pool glistened as the strong rays of light reflected off the surface.

Rosa lay stretched out on a sun lounger. Her skin was glowing, she wore a red bikini with gold fasteners and a large pair of sunglasses covered her eyes.

Daniel swam to the edge of the pool. He surfaced, slowly climbing up the chrome-handled steps. His taut, lean physique looked toned. 'Oi, lazy bones, come for a swim.' He walked to Rosa's lounger and climbed onto it next to her.

'Hey, you're all wet!' Rosa squirmed away from him, laughing.

Daniel picked her up playfully. 'Now's your turn.'

'Daniel, no!' Her voice squealed with delight.

Daniel ran to the edge of the pool and threw her in as she screamed wildly. Daniel laughed heartily, tickled by his own antics.

Rosa swam to the surface, turned around onto her back and gazed up to the sun. 'I'll get you back for that.' She smiled, kicking her feet to propel her in the water.

Ella and Mya walked towards them across the decking, holding cocktails in their hands. Both looked stunning in their respective swimwear. Mya's fit figure was complemented by a see-through sarong.

'The bridesmaids are back!' Ella shouted, announcing their return gleefully. Her red hair flowed from underneath a large straw sun hat, her pale skin slathered in sun cream.

Daniel clapped as he saw them. 'Ahh, well done, ladies. I'm parched.' He smiled, taking one of the cocktails from Ella.

'Sip slowly, Daniel. Don't want you hungover for the big day.' She lifted her sunglasses and raised her eyebrows at him. They all sat on their sun loungers except for Rosa, who continued to float on her back in the pool.

'So nice of you to pay for us to come out here; it's beautiful.' Mya chinked glasses with Daniel and looked around, admiring the splendour of the hotel grounds.

'It's fine. I know she'd want you guys out here, too,' he said, resting back onto his lounger. 'Plus you're the bridesmaids, so a no brainer, really.' He took another sip of his cocktail. His wet hair was now slicked back as he watched Rosa finally get out of the pool. 'Enjoy that?' He beckoned her over to him.

She looked gorgeous as she stepped onto the decking dripping wet, her sun-kissed figure caressed by her bikini.

Mya afforded herself a cheeky ogle. She lowered her shades as Rosa collapsed onto Daniel's lounger.

Ella slapped Mya on her thigh, noticing her sly glimpse. 'Oi, help me with this umbrella. That sun is frying me here.' Ella stood up to drag the large sun umbrella over her lounger. 'Come on,' she insisted.

'How ya feeling, babe?' Daniel kissed her on the cheek as they lay taking in the views.

'I feel great for the first time in my life,' Rosa replied, snuggling up and resting her head onto his chest. 'Thank you.' She kissed him on the neck. 'I can't wait until I'm Mrs Chavez-Rosewood.' She giggled on saying the name.

Daniel lifted his head. 'Oh, is that what it is then, Chavez-Rosewood?'

'If you don't mind, I still want my family name. For my mum,' she responded, looking up to him. Her brown puppy eyes rendered Daniel helpless.

'Chavez-Rosewood it is.' As always, he did what he had to do to make her happy.

The afternoon had progressed, still hot and sticky. Daniel and Rosa frolicked in the pool, floating on a giant, luminous orange lilo. Mya was chilled on her lounger, reading a magazine, and Ella lay silently wrapped in her beach towel with her hat covering her face.

A hotel waiter came over to collect the empty cocktail glasses. 'More drinks?' he asked.

Mya, who didn't even look up at him, just offered her hand as a sign of surrender.

Rosa finally exited the pool and walked over to Mya dripping wet. She playfully splashed some excess water over her before sitting between her legs. 'So, ladies, what you wearing for dinner tonight?' Her tone was full of excitement as she wrung the water from her hair.

Ella turned over slowly. She looked groggy, her skin was reddened and her cheeks were particularly flushed. 'I don't feel well; it's too hot. Might go back to my room for a bit.' Her voice was weak as she rose slowly.

'Too many cocktails, methinks,' Mya commented as Ella barely managed to sit up.

'No, might have sunstroke, just need a lie-down.' She gradually rose to her feet before wearily walking away barefooted across the decking.

'Ella, wait! I'll come with you.' Mya put her magazine down and quickly gathered her things. She kissed Rosa on the cheek. 'I'll see you at dinner, babe.'

Daniel stood in front of a long mirror bare-chested, spraying aftershave onto his chin. The hotel suite was large and classy; tall, floor-to-ceiling windows offered a panoramic view of the beach through see-through net curtains. A large, circular bed covered with mustard-coloured pillows was the centrepiece, with a flat-screen television mounted onto the tiled feature wall.

Rosa came out of the walk-in bathroom wearing a fluffy hotel robe.

'Babe, we're going to be late.' Daniel turned to her while slipping on a crisp, white shirt.

'Won't take me long; just got to dry my hair,' Rosa replied. She took her time, sat down at the dressing table and rubbed various creams and lotions on her legs.

Daniel fastened the buttons on the cuffs of his shirt. The hotel phone rang loudly in the room, interrupting their conversation.

Rosa answered while brushing through her wet hair. 'Hi, Mya, are you ready? . . . What! Ahh, no . . . OK.' She replaced the handset. 'Ella's not coming; she's not well.' She looked up at Daniel. 'I'll go and see her before dinner.'

Daniel slipped on a pair of tight black trousers and walked back to the mirror. 'What a lemon. Too much drink. She's ruined the surprise.' He continued checking himself out in his reflection.

'What surprise?'

'Well, I needed a best man so . . .' He paused and spun back to Rosa with a devious look on his face. 'Bryn's here. He's my best man. We're meeting for a quick drink before dinner.'

Rosa stood up bolt upright. 'Pardon?' She walked towards Daniel, her robe slightly open revealing her lacy, black underwear. 'Why did you invite him?'

Daniel placed his hands on her shoulders and kissed her on the forehead. 'I told you, he's my best man. Ella will be happy he's here.' He smiled. 'Plus we got some business to talk about, so why not?'

Rosa backed away and shook her head. 'You never said.' She carried on getting ready, disappointed by Daniel's revelation.

Ella is going to freak out I know it.

She is going to want to kill Daniel for bringing him here.

He should have asked me first if I want that awful man at my wedding, he makes my skin crawl.

Poor Ella, she's gonna feel worse when I tell her.

Rosa and Mya stepped out into the hotel corridor arm in arm. Both looked elegant in their evening gowns. Rosa was in an all-black, fitted, satin dress, her jet-black hair slicked up into a high ponytail with a red rose slotted into the side. Her skin glowed as her fresh tan accentuated her olive skin. Mya strutted in a pair of cream high heels, slick, fitted black pants and a leopard print, off-the-shoulder blouse. Her golden hair was full and curly. They walked to Ella's room. Rosa knocked on the door and waited patiently for what seemed like ages.

Mya impatiently pounded on the door. 'Ella, it's us,' she yelled, until eventually the door slowly opened.

Ella poked her head out, her face ashen and her skin red from the afternoon heat. She let them in and crawled back onto the bed.

'Babe, you look awful,' said Mya, never one to be diplomatic. Her smoky voice was as insensitive as her comment.

They stood over the bed looking down at Ella, who was curled up, holding a plastic bottle of water.

'Do you want us to call the hotel doctor?' Rosa asked.

'No, I just need to sleep.' Ella barely managed to speak as she sucked down the rest of the water from the bottle.

Mya nudged Rosa. 'Tell her,' she whispered.

'Ella . . . have to tell you something.' Rosa spoke softly, knowing the news would probably send Ella over the edge. 'Bryn's here.' She squeezed her words out through pursed lips.

'Oh, you are kidding,' Ella groaned, her voice a drawl. She managed to drag herself into an upright position, her hair flopping over her face. She burped, then began to cough.

Mya ran to the mini bar and took out another bottle of water. 'Here, babe.' She unscrewed the top and fed her some water, which made her cough more.

Rosa watched on as Ella spluttered. 'Sorry, it's Daniel's idea. He wants a best man!' Rosa rubbed Ella's back as she delivered the news.

Ella flopped back onto the bed. 'Unbelievable!' she groaned, covering her mouth. She looked shell-shocked. She was feeling rough already, but this just compounded her day. 'Great. Listen, you guys. Go enjoy dinner. I know how to handle Bryn,' she said, shooing them out and trying her best to remain optimistic.

Rosa looked down at her. 'Get some rest. I'm going to need you both for the big day.' She hugged Ella and took Mya's hand. They walked out, leaving Ella to wallow in the large bed alone.

Rosa and Mya checked their appearance in the mirror in the lift.

'Poor girl, but it's all about you; this is your wedding, babe, and it will be wicked.' Mya winked at her before the lift doors opened out into the main banqueting room.

It was an intimate setting adorned with large chandeliers. Round tables set with lily-white table cloths and silver cutlery were spread around the room. There was an open kitchen where the chefs busily prepared a variety of food and flames shot up randomly from the hot stoves. An outside cocktail bar area was lit by multicoloured lanterns.

'Wow.' Rosa was blown away by its extravagance. She squeezed Mya's hand excitedly. 'Now this is what I'm talking about!'

They stepped out confidently. The eyes in the room followed them as they stepped elegantly across the carpeted floor. Rosa spotted Daniel at the bar, standing next to the ingratiating Bryn Fitzpatrick.

Hold your tongue, don't embarrass Daniel.

It will be hard but just smile and be friendly as much as you can.

After all, he is still Ella's husband.

Rosa and Mya joined Daniel and Bryn, who was slickly dressed in black trousers and a grey, silk, paisley-patterned shirt which complemented his silver-fox appearance. His face lit up like a naughty school kid on seeing the two beauties arrive.

'Took your time,' Daniel said, giving Rosa a kiss on the cheek. 'You remember Bryn, babe?' He stepped aside, introducing Bryn, who stepped forwards.

'Yes, how are you?' she responded.

Bryn leaned in, took her hand and kissed it tenderly. 'Congratulations. Looking forward to the big day as much as my man here?' He winked at her then looked at Daniel.

'Yes, I am.' She smiled politely.

Creep.

'And this is Mya.' Daniel, ever the gentleman, introduced her.

'Yes, I remember seeing you at the awards. Sharp with that camera, you were.' Bryn's Irish accent was subtle in his smooth tone.

'Ahh! Yes, that was me.' Mya produced a forced smile. 'Have you checked on Ella? She's not feeling too good.' Her tone was caustic while taking out a cigarette from her purse.

'Ay, no flies on you, is there?' Bryn tried to laugh off her comment. 'Playing the drama queen, I suspect. She'll be alright.' He returned fire coldly, distracted by a couple of American blondes on spring break walking into the bar area.

'Right, I think our table's ready,' Daniel interjected, relieving the awkward undertone that was brewing.

Bryn laughed raucously, dabbing the side of his mouth with a napkin. 'So, he's running around the fairway with just a sock on his cock. Freezing it was!' He wheezed out another laugh, his squeal up a pitch. 'Sock on his cock ...'

Daniel laughed with him half-heartedly as Bryn revelled in his own humour. Mya rolled her eyes, sipping some wine from a large glass. Rosa shot Daniel a terse look as she sliced her food fiercely.

'Never play golf then, Daniel?' Bryn continued to dominate the table conversation.

'Not really,' Daniel replied, swishing around the last of his wine.

'Need to get you on the course.' Bryn talked on. 'After the honeymoon. I promise, love.' He winked at Rosa, self-assured and arrogant.

My God, this man won't shut up, he loves himself.

Why Daniel asked him to be the best man I'll never know.

No wonder Ella is happy when he's away on the golf course.

The meal had finished, and it was early evening. Rosa kicked Daniel's foot under the table as an indication that she was ready to go back to their room. Mya was bored out of her skull listening to another Bryn anecdote about the Irish boy who conquered the world—of course, it was his own biopic. She placated his ego, hoping for a moment when she could escape his constant drivel about how successful he was.

'I'm ready for bed.' Rosa yawned. 'Need to get my beauty sleep for tomorrow.' 'What about you Mya?' She placed her hand on Mya's hand, her large diamond engagement ring sparkling under the lights.

'Yes, oh boy, I am so ready, babe.' Mya's already husky voice cracked with tiredness.

Bryn rubbed his grey stubble and smiled. 'It's been a pleasure, ladies. See you on the aisle.' He raised his wine glass to Rosa and Mya. 'Nightcap, Daniel?' Bryn beckoned over a waiter, much to Rosa's annoyance.

She wanted to spend some intimate time with her soon-to-be husband.

Daniel shrugged sheepishly. 'Won't be long, babe.' He hugged her warmly.

'No more alcohol! I want you fresh for tomorrow,' Rosa demanded as she rose from the table with Mya.

'Goodnight, ladies.' Bryn waved them away and glanced over at the two American blondes who were heading out to the bar, winking at them as their eyes caught his.

Mya stood on the balcony of her room enjoying a cigarette. The air was still warm and other hotel guests were enjoying a late drink by the pool bar. Mellow background music played, entertaining the guests as the night lights turned the pool water aqua. Mya held her camera in her other hand. Every now and again she snapped a shot of the exotic surroundings under the stars. She looked down and saw Bryn, Daniel and the two blondes walk out onto the patio. She watched on curiously, continuing to puff her fag.

Daniel, Bryn and the women sat on a couple of loungers across from where the main guests had congregated. She could see that Bryn was holding a bucket of champagne and was leading the conversation, breaking out into laughter every few seconds.

Mya stubbed her cigarette out in an ashtray. She could tell by the sound of their high-pitched squeals of laughter that the two women were taken in by his Irish charm.

Bryn, ever the showman, was no doubt recycling his golfing stories. His animated enactments were clear. Daniel sat passively watching on until one of the women sat on his lap and put her arms around his neck. She began whispering in his ear.

'Holy shit,' Mya muttered, raising the camera slowly to her eyeline. She snapped away, taking a few pictures.

It was then that the other woman followed suit and sat on Bryn's lap. She could see him allowing her to share the bottle of champagne by putting the bottle to her mouth and breaking into laughter each time they took a shot of the drink.

'This is why I hate men.' Mya sighed, aiming her camera and zooming in on both of them. 'Shit, dude. Daniel, what are you doing?' Mya retreated to her room and picked up her phone. She walked back out to the balcony and looked down.

By now Daniel was sat on his own, and the woman who had been on his lap took up a seat beside him.

Mya was just about to call Rosa, but she saw Daniel get up. He gestured to Bryn that he was calling it a night, made his excuses and left the group. Mya put her phone down and watched him walk back into the hotel. She flicked through the shots on the small screen of her camera and studied the one of the blonde on Daniel's lap. 'Damn, boys will be boys.'

* * *

The morning of the wedding had arrived. The group minus Ella were all sat al fresco eating breakfast. Rosa had a face like thunder, obviously annoyed at Daniel for staying out late.

I told him no more alcohol.

He came in late and could barely get up this morning.

I don't want to marry a man who acts like that.

Daniel gulped down a large glass of orange juice. He looked tired and slightly hungover from the previous night's events. He was quiet and dared not speak to Rosa, knowing he was in the doghouse, at least for now.

Bryn, on the other hand, was full of life—shades on, grey hair slicked back, wearing a tight, white Hugo Boss tee shirt. He hadn't a care in the world, chattering away as he cleaned off a full fried breakfast.

Mya sat quietly, dressed in her yoga gym wear. She wore a large pair of shades and picked at a bowl of fruit covered in yoghurt.

'Here she is,' Bryn announced, seeing Ella appear from the hotel, trudging towards the breakfast table.

She looked better than the day before but still displayed the effects of her illness. Her hair was tied into a bun, and her skin was reddened from the sun. She looked moody as she took a seat at the table.

'Get some breakfast—you look like a withering twig,'

Bryn ordered, flinging his arm around her, causing her to flinch and remove his arm promptly.

'Hey, Ella, how you feeling?' Rosa asked.

'Better thanks,' she replied solemnly; her usual effervescence seemed drained out of her.

Rosa gave her a strange look.

That ain't Ella, she's usually up for it—bubbly—today she's off.

I'll chat to her later, I need my bridesmaids today.

'Fancy some yoga to calm your nerves?' Mya whispered into Rosa's ear, knowing Rosa was upset with Daniel and with the events of last night still nagging her.

Rosa, who still had a sulk on, nodded silently.

'Ella, fancy some yoga? Bridesmaids only,' Mya stipulated, ensuring Bryn heard her loud and clear.

'Yoga, honey? That's new. Never done a jot of exercise back home.' Bryn wheezed a laugh at Ella. 'She's alright, we're going for a little stroll afterwards, aren't we?' He rubbed the back of Ella's neck.

She shied away then got up from the table. 'Rosa, I'll meet you in the bridal suite at two.' Sour-faced, she got up from the table, tagged by Bryn.

'Daniel, I'll come to yours to get ready. Catch ya later, ladies.' He waved at Mya and Rosa, but they both blanked him. Their morning mood was not one of tolerance for Bryn Fitzpatrick.

The mid-morning Cancun heat was already sweltering and sticky. Rosa and Mya were in the last stages of their yoga stretches.

'Two, three, breathe,' Mya instructed, as they both relaxed, sweating from their exertions. 'Nice. Has that helped calm your nerves?' Mya drank thirstily from a bottle of water, perspiration covering her face.

Rosa lay back on the yoga mat and shielded her eyes from the sun, equally sweaty and catching her breath. 'He really pissed me off.' The hurt in her voice was still clear. 'Today's our wedding day and he's hungover.' She sulked, not impressed that Daniel had let his gentleman persona slip for once.

Mya raked her hair back and blew out a big sigh. 'Babe . . .' She agonised for a few seconds, biting her lip. 'Look, there's something I have to tell you.'

Rosa sat up. 'What?' Her senses pricked up.

Mya squirted some more of her water down her throat.

'What?' Rosa asked again impatiently.

Mya hesitated, tying up her golden locks to eat up a few more seconds of thinking time. 'Right, OK. I'm not saying anything happened, but . . .' Mya reached for her sports bag and took out her camera.

'What is it?' Rosa stared at her, puzzled, as Mya flicked through the shots on her camera screen. She handed the camera to Rosa.

'I think it was more Bryn, but . . . I think you should see.'

Rosa couldn't believe what she was looking at. 'Wait . . . when was this?' She continued to examine the photograph.

'Last night. I saw them from my balcony.' Mya knew how disappointed Rosa would be. 'As a friend, I thought you should know.' Mya rubbed Rosa's shoulder, attempting to reassure her, but Rosa gave her back the camera and instantly got up and walked away. 'Rosa, wait!' Mya called out to her, but it was too late; the damage was already done. With only a few hours left until the wedding ceremony, Mya knew she had just thrown a big spanner in the works. She placed the camera back into her bag. 'I thought you should know, I got your back,' she said to herself. Her words were hollow, not having any impact on Rosa, who had already stormed away and marched back towards the hotel.

Ella's bare feet made an imprint in the white sand, only to be washed away by the frothy ripple of waves that swept up onto the beach.

Bryn walked ahead of her, strolling bare-chested, holding his tee shirt in his hand. 'So glad I came; needed a change of scenery.' He raised his arms in the air as if to embrace the sun rays streaming down on him.

Ella, arms folded and head down under her large sun hat, stared at the sand. Her white summer dress was soaked at the bottom from the splashes of the waves. 'I'm not glad,' she mumbled to herself despondently, trailing behind him.

A couple of bikini-clad girls exited from the sea. Bryn blatantly stopped and watched them, allowing them to walk past him. 'Ladies,' he greeted them, grinning. They giggled and made their way across the beach.

Ella stopped and sat down on the sand, looking out to sea. Bryn turned back and came to sit beside her.

'Why you got to be like that?' Ella asked, her voice trembling as she tried to restrain her emotions.

'Be like what?' Bryn responded bluntly, sitting beside her. Leaning back onto his elbows, he raised his sunglasses onto his head and stared out to the sea.

'It's hurtful; it's like I don't exist,' Ella blurted out, fed up with his antics and roving eye.

'Chill out, Ella. I hate dramas.' Bryn's tone was cold, cutting and unsympathetic. He snorted and spat onto the sand.

Ella began to weep and held her hand over her mouth. Tears rolled down her flushed cheeks. 'What am I to you?' she cried, searching for an answer, any type of reconciliation or comfort from her man.

Bryn picked up a handful of sand, letting it run through his fingers. He pondered for a few seconds. 'Frankly . . . a pain in the arse.' He dusted the sand from his palms then got to his feet. 'Come on or we'll be late.' He slung his tee shirt over his shoulder and walked back towards the hotel.

The waves washed over her feet as she sat alone with her head buried into her knees.

Rosa was furious, throwing her clothes at Daniel, who was crouched down onto his haunches, cowering, with his head in his hands. 'Babe, please, calm down!'

Rosa carried on chucking various clothing items at him. 'I'm not marrying you!' She paced back and forth in her flip-flops, grabbing her things from the wardrobe, sniffing, trying to hold back her tears.

'Stop, please! Don't shout—it's triggering my flashbacks.' Daniel curled his body into the corner, shaking with fear on the floor.

Rosa stopped in her tracks when she realised how her tantrum was affecting him.

'Please just calm down,' he begged, removing his hands from his face. He fell back, the weight of relief rendering him useless. His PTSD rattled him in any type of confrontation.

Rosa sat down on the bed in the middle of a pile of clothes.

'Can I explain?' he pleaded with her, struggling up from his position. 'Bryn asked them to join us. They were drunk. I left as soon as I could.' Daniel managed to stagger over to the bed and sat down next to Rosa. He tried to take her hand, but Rosa pulled it away.

'I won't be with a man that's unfaithful,' Rosa sobbed. 'We're meant to be getting married in hours.'

Daniel shook his head. 'Babe, you know I would never . . .' He tried to console her by putting his arm around her, which at first she resisted, but eventually she allowed him to sit closer and hold her. She could feel him shaking. 'Sorry, I know what it looked like, and Mya . . .' He paused, collecting himself.

Rosa turned to him. 'She was only being a friend.' Her mood softened as each moment passed. 'I'm sorry, too. Didn't mean to scare you.' She squeezed his hand.

They sat silently amongst a pile of clothes on the bed, just holding each other. The shambolic scene a few moments ago had left them both in more of a mess than the clothes they sat on.

'I really want you to be my wife,' Daniel reaffirmed. He sounded apologetic, desperate, even, just to hear something from Rosa to take the edge off the tension. 'I have no one else now, just you. Not Leah or my parents,' he continued, trying for her to see his point of view.

'Me too,' Rosa spoke softly. 'No family . . . just you.' She wiped away a rogue tear. 'Just want the man I marry to be loyal.' She lifted Daniel's head, her brown eyes yielding a hint of optimism.

Daniel nodded, his blue eyes gazing deep into hers. 'I want this, I want us.' He leaned forwards and planted a kiss on her lips. 'Are we gonna do this?' he asked, as a smile appeared on his face.

Rosa began to laugh and squeezed Daniel's cheeks. 'Yes, but get rid of Bryn as soon as we are man and wife.' A surge of new energy washed over her. 'Right, get out. I need to start getting ready.' She pushed him away, but Daniel leaned in for another kiss. 'No! Not until we are married. Then you get all of this.' Rosa smiled, pointing towards her body. She pulled Daniel up and shoved him towards the door. 'I'll see you soon!' Her excitement had returned as she sent him out, closing the door behind him. Rosa took a big, deep breath and scratched her head as she looked at the mess in the room. 'Right, now I have to find my dress.'

A large, horizontal mirror lined with bright bulbs sat on the top of an ivory dressing table reflected the three individual facial expressions of the bride and bridesmaids all sat next to each other, lost in their thoughts. Ella sat getting her hair styled, still with a strop on and stewing after her beach encounter with Bryn. Her eyes were sad and searching as she sipped on a glass of Buck's Fizz. Mya was reflective, in deep thought about her actions earlier, while a make-up artist worked contours onto her cheeks, and Rosa sat in the middle, quiet but with a nervous smile on her face, knowing the time soon approached when she would be marrying the man who had changed her life, as her hair was twirled into ringlets.

'Hey, ladies! Come on, what's with the moods?' Rosa burst into life, trying to inject a dose of excitement into the room. 'Come on, let's get some tunes on. This is my last hour of freedom!' She put her arms around her two besties and pulled them into her. Up-tempo Latin music played through her phone.

'He's such an arsehole,' Ella moaned to Mya, downing the remainder of her drink. She was now dressed in her lilac silk, off-the-shoulder bridesmaid's dress. Her red hair flowed down over her sunburnt shoulders.

Mya shimmied her body to the music, busting a few erratic dance moves, now feeling vibrant. Her dress matched Ella's, her tresses flicked and curled lusciously and her skin was tanned. 'Oh, forget him, he's punching above his weight anyway.' She continued to dance and wiggle her derrière. She pulled Ella towards her and twirled her around. They both burst into laughter, sharing a moment and twirling each other around.

Rosa stepped out of the dressing room looking absolutely stunning. It stopped Mya and Ella dead in their tracks.

'Yes! Oh my gosh. So gorgeous, babe.' Mya's voice croaked with emotion.

The music died down, enhancing Rosa's entrance. Mya was right, she looked divine. She wore a pure white, A-line, asymmetrical, silk dress with a chiffon-ruffled skirt. Diamonds were woven into the bodice, and her tanned, olive-skinned shoulders were the perfect foil to the white material. Her hair was ringleted like a maiden from a period drama; a diamond, flower-shaped tiara was placed over her forehead and her ear lobes were pierced with the dainty diamond earrings Daniel had bought her.

'Come here.' Ella began to tear up, taking Rosa by the hand. 'An absolute doll.' She admired her while Mya grabbed her camera and took pictures.

'Do I look OK?' Rosa asked. Her body was shaking as she tried not to let the nerves get the best of her. 'I don't want to cry, it will ruin my make-up.' She laughed. The dress was short enough to show off her silver high heels.

'Daniel is a lucky young man.' Ella gave Rosa an air hug, conscious of not getting any make-up on her dress.

I feel so strange.

The butterflies are having fun in my stomach, this is like a dream.

Wish Mama was here to hold my hand.

I could never do this without these two crazy girls.

I need to calm down, this is really happening.

Who would have thought little Rosa from Sinaloa would be here in Mexico getting married to a handsome, kind, Englishman?

It's amazing after everything.

'Pinch me, girls! Is this about to happen?'

Mya stepped back and continued to capture the moments. 'Yes, bitch, you're about to get spliced.' She burst out laughing.

'Thank you, girls. So glad you're here.' Rosa fanned herself with her hands, attempting to control her flutters.

A nervous Daniel stood on the sand under a decorated wicker arch which was placed on the beach a few yards from the sea. He was barefooted, dressed in a white shirt, a lilac waistcoat and navy-blue trousers. Through his Ray-Ban shades, he stared ahead, the sun beaming down on his red face. He took a handkerchief and wiped the sweat from his forehead. His trance-like posture was interrupted by Bryn, who joined him and placed his hand heavily on Daniel's shoulder.

'There's still time to back out.' He laughed. His sharp Acqua Di Parma infusion drifted into Daniel's nostrils.

Daniel smiled. 'Funny. No, I'm marrying this girl even if I get sunburn waiting for her,' he replied, shaking Bryn's hand.

'Good luck, Rosewood, she's a beaut.' Bryn's outfit matched Daniel's.

They were joined by the registrar—a short, fat, Mexican man dressed all in white with a large-brimmed Panama hat. 'Hello, my name is Raul. You must be Daniel.' He shook Bryn's hand.

'No, not me. That's him.' Bryn laughed, pointing to Daniel.

'So sorry.' The registrar switched his attention to Daniel and reached out his hand. 'Mr Daniel, congratulations.' He bowed his head.

'Thank you.' Daniel nodded.

There were no guests, just three seats positioned in front of the arch, a reminder of what both Daniel and Rosa had forfeited to get to this point. Obviously, Leah and his parents were not in favour of his relationship after the fire and robbery, and as for Rosa, her brothers' fates had been decided by their irresponsible and selfish acts, so they had only each other.

A four-piece mariachi band walked out, all dressed in traditional Mexican wear, and began to play and walk down the red-carpeted path towards the beach, signifying the entrance of the bride. Other guests from the hotel watched on from the balcony and outside bar. Mya came out first, camera in hand, trying her best to stay elegant in her dress, snapping the setting and the band as she walked out towards Daniel.

Daniel took his shades off and handed them to Bryn. He took a deep breath, the anticipation heightened. He fixed his shirt and lilac cravat. He looked smart, he always did, but he wanted to make sure he looked his best on his big day. A big smile spread across his face, knowing his diamond was about to be stood in front of him.

Mya arrived and gave him a courtesy kiss on the cheek. 'Good luck,' she whispered in her husky voice. She looked at Bryn, smiled politely and nodded to the registrar before stepping aside near her seat and adjusting her lens to take more pictures.

The band approached slowly, playing an up-tempo tune.

Rosa slowly made her way out with Ella, their arms locked together. Rosa held a posy of white roses sprinkled with diamante pieces. She looked stunning; her dress fitted her flawlessly, rippling in the slight breeze.

Ella held two posies of flowers as they made their way down the aisle.

'Ella, wait.' Rosa stopped.

'What's wrong?'

'Need to take these damn shoes off.'

Ella looked down at her feet, confused. 'What, now?'

'Yes, I want to feel the sand on my feet,' Rosa replied, bending down and undoing the straps.

'OK then.' Ella shrugged, watching Rosa take her shoes off.

She removed them and left them where she stood. 'That's better. OK, I'm ready.' She composed herself then continued towards Daniel.

Ella smiled at Daniel as she gave him Rosa's hand. She kissed him on the cheek. 'Good luck, love you.' She turned to Rosa and blew her a kiss. Bryn grinned at her, but Ella's face hardened, disgusted by his attempt to play the nice guy. She turned to Mya and handed her the posy as they took their seats.

Bryn smirked, rubbed his forehead and sat next to her.

Rosa dreamily stared into Daniel's eyes, which sparkled in the sunshine. He looked happy but nervous. She was hoping that their earlier confrontation had been forgotten in this special moment. He broke into a smile and mouthed, 'You look beautiful.'

Rosa's heart leapt. She wanted to hug him and smother him in kisses but knew that moment would come shortly. She smiled back at him shyly, looking radiant under the late afternoon sun.

The cheerful registrar began the ceremony. His Mexican accent made it slightly harder to understand what he was wittering on about, but it didn't matter.

Rosa and Daniel were in their own bubble, adoringly gazing into each other's eyes.

This really does feel like a dream.

I swear I'm gonna wake up and be back in that flat with Jesus and Dani squabbling over petty shit.

Her mind fleetingly wandered back to when she felt anonymous and at her worst.

'OK, now we have the exchange of the rings.' The jovial registrar offered the open Bible to them.

Ella handed the small black velvet box to Rosa as Bryn stood up and dug in his trouser pocket. He pulled out a red velvet box, which he handed to Daniel. They opened the boxes and took the rings out—both silver—placed them on the pages of the Bible and handed the boxes back to Bryn and Ella.

'Daniel Rosewood, do you take Rosa Chavez to be your wife? To love her, cherish her and look after her forever!' The voice of the registrar was energetic. He looked at Daniel, who had a moment, pausing briefly to gather his emotions before answering.

'Yes . . . I mean, course I do!' he blurted out, causing Bryn to laugh out loud and shake his head in disbelief.

Mya continued to play the role of wedding photographer as she snapped the moment Daniel slid the ring onto Rosa's finger, placing it next to her engagement ring. Rosa felt chills run down her spine as the ring went on.

Oh my God, this is crazy.

She tried not to, but she couldn't help tearing up a little bit.

'Now, Rosa Chavez.' The registrar rolled her name with exaggeration. 'Do you take Daniel Rosewood to be your husband? To love him, cherish him and look after him forever!' Again, he injected his joviality into the proceedings.

Rosa slipped the silver band onto Daniel's finger. Her hand trembled, and she let out a nervous laugh before answering. 'Yes, I do!' she replied, her pent up anxiety dissipated the moment the ring was on.

'I have the pleasure and honour of pronouncing you man and wife. You may now . . .'

Before the registrar could finish his sentence, Daniel pulled Rosa towards him and planted a big, deep, sloppy kiss on her lips. Cheers and whoops went up from Ella, Mya and Bryn, who clapped wildly, and also from the audience who watched on from the hotel balcony.

'OK, you've kissed the bride.' The registrar shrugged. He took off his hat and bowed as they continued their lip-locking session. The mariachi band sparked into action and played another up-tempo song.

'I love you,' Daniel gushed as Rosa wiped her lipstick from his mouth.

'Love you too,' she replied, before they were swamped by Ella and Mya hugging them.

'Ahh, that was so nice. Congrats.' Ella's happiness was genuine for Rosa.

'Congrats, mate.' Bryn shook Daniel's hand.

'Right, let's get some lovely pics by the sea.' Mya whisked them away.

Daniel, always the gentleman, thanked the registrar and clapped the band. 'Thank you all. Cheers, Bryn, appreciate it,' he shouted over as he was being dragged away by an eager Mya.

Inside the cool, air-conditioned sanctuary of the hotel, a small, intimate, private room was decorated with silver and white balloons. One circular table covered in a white tablecloth was set for five. Plates and silver cutlery were set around a glass bowl of flowers. Ella, Mya and Bryn sat patiently waiting. A young DJ stood alone in a shiny gold shirt behind the decks of his one-man disco, which was lit up by multicoloured, flashing fairy lights. A row of waiters and waitresses stood steadfastly against the wall.

'I'm dying for a cigarette.' Mya fanned herself, her exertions as photographer and bridesmaid taking their toll.

'I'll come,' Ella offered as she looked over at Bryn and gave him a dirty look, letting him know he was still on the naughty step.

Bryn picked up one of the shiny, silver knives and checked his teeth, ignoring her.

'Ladies and gentleman, the bride and groom are ready to enter!' the DJ bellowed through the microphone. 'Please stand and show your appreciation.' His accent sounded more American than Mexican.

The doors were opened. Rosa and Daniel made their entrance, striding in hand-in-hand with big smiles on their faces. Mya, camera in hand and agile in her tight dress, bent down and took pictures at an angle as the two made their way to the table. Rosa danced the last few yards and waved her posy in the air. Ella and Bryn stood and clapped as they entered. Bryn put his fingers to his mouth, producing a sharp whistle like a sheepherder calling a sheepdog.

Ella huffed and rolled her eyes. 'Annoying,' she muttered under her breath.

'Hey!' Rosa came to the table and hugged them once again before they all took a seat.

Mya stood outside on the decking by the pool, sucking down on her Benson and Hedges as if her life depended on it.

Ella stood next to her, finally able to handle the slightly cooler temperature. 'So glad for them it all worked out,' she said, as she watched a few hotel guests around the pool bar.

'Yeah, she deserves happiness. Daniel's alright.' Mya smoked the last of her cigarette.

Ella turned to her. 'Thought you might be jealous.'

Mya blew out a plume of smoke. 'What?' she replied, stamping out the butt with her silver shoes.

'Come on, I can see that you fancy her,' Ella said bluntly, flicking her red mane into shape.

'She's a sweetie and hot but taken,' Mya responded, a slight tone of disappointment threading her husky voice. 'Anyway, we're friends; I'll have that.' Mya looked at Ella. Her catlike, green eyes shone like jewels in the night sky.

'Keep your hands off her.' Ella wagged her finger at her jokingly and put her arm around Mya. They both laughed as they made their way back inside.

The sound of Ed Sheeran's song 'Thinking Out Loud' signalled the first dance. Rosa held Daniel tightly and leaned her head on his shoulder as they danced slowly. Daniel had no rhythm; he was stiff but managed to get his limited steps right.

'I can't believe it, Mrs Rosewood,' he whispered into her ear.

She pulled him closer, kissing him softly on the lips. 'By the way, it's Chavez-Rosewood, remember?' She smiled at him.

'Yeah, whatever,' he agreed. He was just happy to have his wife in his arms.

Their three guests watched on. Mya was doing her duty taking pictures of their most intimate moment.

'Come on.' Rosa waved them over to join them.

Bryn stood up and held out his hand to Ella, offering a truce. Ella sucked up her ego and took his hand reluctantly. She hadn't danced with him since their own wedding years ago. She was a shy nineteen-year-old then, naïve and in love with the thought of a better life, but today she knew she was only a pretty trophy to her chosen life partner. Still, she took to the dance floor knowing she was only putting up with his grubby hand around her waist for the sake of Rosa's happiness.

'Smile, it's a wedding, for God's sake.' Bryn, ever the uncouth narcissist, always wanted the upper hand.

Ella resisted, but Bryn pulled her closer to him. The smell of whiskey on his breath was off-putting as they danced next to Rosa and Daniel.

Daniel sat at the table with Bryn, watching the three girls get down on the dancefloor. The DJ was now spinning some Latina reggaeton tunes.

'So that idea of an online showroom, I like it,' Bryn slurred, as the effects of several glasses of whiskey kicked in. His shirt collar was open and his cravat dangled low on his chest.

'Yeah, customers can view then order, they pay online and we deliver,' Daniel responded eagerly, still fresh and sipping slowly from a flute of champagne. 'Need your clientele, only elite customers,' he continued. 'Rich daddies buying their kids their first Ferrari.'

Bryn broke into a smile. 'Let's do it.' He stretched his hand out to shake Daniel's hand.

Daniel reciprocated. 'Cheers.' He smiled back at Bryn.

Ella, Mya and Rosa held hands and danced around in circles, laughing and joking. They were tipsy and enjoying themselves. Rosa looked over at Daniel; he raised his glass to her and she smiled back. She looked the happiest she had ever been. It was her night to remember and she was going to enjoy every last minute.

The next morning, Rosa and Daniel sat alone on the beach, holding each other and basking in the glory of their wedding day. The sunrise caused an orange glow across the horizon and the sea was calm.

Daniel had organised a continental breakfast of croissants, fruits and juices, which were laid out on a small tray. Daniel fed her a strawberry. 'How's it feel?' he asked, as Rosa took a bite from the bright-red fruit.

'Hmm, what?'

'To be my wife,' he continued, biting on the last bit of the strawberry.

'I'm still high. I'll never forget this.' She sighed. 'It was perfect, thank you.' Daniel hugged her tightly. 'And you?' She gazed up into his eyes.

'What do you think, you lemon!' He laughed and kissed her forehead. 'I've finally got my diamond. Just promise me we don't end up like Ella and Bryn.' He held her chin and lifted her face, staring into her eyes.

Rosa burst out laughing. 'No way!' she replied, cupping her jewelled hand around his face.

'Good, phew!' Daniel pulled her in for another kiss, with which she duly obliged—a lingering soft one.

They sat curled up in each other's arms, watching the sun grow in the distance, tinting the calm waves of the sea as its orange reflection illuminated their silhouettes.

Rosa

About the Author

Originally from Tottenham, North London, I began my career as a child actor starring in a BAFTA award-winning children's drama at the age of fifteen. I then turned my writing skills to music and featured as a rapper in the successful UK hip hop band *The Sindecut,* who were signed to Virgin Records in 1990, completing a UK and European tour with Soul to Soul.

After almost twenty-five years in the music industry, I followed my passion for writing by attending a creative writing course at Enfield College in North London.

Within three years, I'd written my first book entitled *This Functional Family*, which was published by Book Guild Publishing in 2011. The book received positive reviews and enabled me to join an esteemed list of UK black authors.

I kept my momentum by writing and directing independent music videos, which also led to writing and directing my first independent short film entitled *The Ride* in 2013.

In 2015 I self-published my second book through Authorhouse entitled *The Life and Times of Stanley Spank,* my first novel, which received positive reviews on Amazon Books.

In 2016 I completed an MA in writing for screen and stage at Regents University, London.

In February 2017 I saw my first short play called *The Weather Girl* produced and performed at the Harlow Playhouse as part of the new writer's festival *Write Here, Write Now*. In July that year, I also directed a short play called *Home* as part of the Six Degrees of Separation showcase at the Courtyard Theatre.

I have recently been working on writing film and television drama and have worked with script editor and recognised television producer Yvonne Grace from 2018 to the present day, completing three drama series and a feature film. I have currently completed two new book manuscripts, firstly a children's book entitled *The Adventures of Winston Trotter and Friends* and this novel, *Rosa*.

My passion for writing has afforded me many opportunities, but I still feel I have a lot more to offer and achieve. I am now ready for the next platform and would love to see my creations on television.

Contact details:
- 📧 Email – lyndon_haynes@yahoo.co.uk
- 📷 Instagram – Mr_lyndonh
- 🐦 Twitter – LyndonHaynes
- 💼 Linked In – Lyndon Haynes
- 📘 Facebook – Lyndon Haynes

Printed in Great Britain
by Amazon